AN HONEST THIEF
AND OTHER STORIES

THE WORKS OF
FYODOR DOSTOEVSKY
Translated from the Russian by
CONSTANCE GARNETT

The Brothers Karamazov
The Idiot
The Possessed
Crime and Punishment
The House of the Dead
The Insulted and Injured
A Raw Youth
The Eternal Husband and other stories
The Gambler and other stories
White Nights and other stories
An Honest Thief and other stories
The Friend of the Family and another story

FYODOR DOSTOEVSKY

•

AN
HONEST
THIEF

AND OTHER STORIES

*Translated from
the Russian by*
CONSTANCE GARNETT

HEINEMANN : LONDON

William Heinemann Ltd
15 Queen St, Mayfair, London W1X 8BE

LONDON   MELBOURNE   TORONTO
JOHANNESBURG   AUCKLAND

FIRST PUBLISHED	1919
REPRINTED	1923
NEW IMPRESSION	1950
REPRINTED (RESET)	1957
REPRINTED	1962, 1971
REPRINTED	1976

434 20405 6

PRINTED IN GREAT BRITAIN BY
REDWOOD BURN LIMITED, TROWBRIDGE AND ESHER

CONTENTS

	Page
AN HONEST THIEF	1
UNCLE'S DREAM	21
A NOVEL IN NINE LETTERS	179
AN UNPLEASANT PREDICAMENT	194
ANOTHER MAN'S WIFE	258
THE HEAVENLY CHRISTMAS TREE	308
THE PEASANT MAREY	313
THE CROCODILE	320
BOBOK	362
THE DREAM OF A RIDICULOUS MAN	382

An Honest Thief

ONE morning, just as I was about to set off to my office, Agrafena, my cook, washerwoman and housekeeper, came in to me and, to my surprise, entered into conversation.

She had always been such a silent, simple creature that, except her daily inquiry about dinner, she had not uttered a word for the last six years. I, at least, had heard nothing else from her.

"Here I have come in to have a word with you, sir," she began abruptly; "you really ought to let the little room."

"Which little room?"

"Why, the one next the kitchen, to be sure."

"What for?"

"What for? Why because folks do take in lodgers, to be sure."

"But who would take it?"

"Who would take it? Why, a lodger would take it, to be sure."

"But, my good woman, one could not put a bedstead in it; there wouldn't be room to move! Who could live in it?"

"Who wants to live there! As long as he has a place to sleep in. Why, he would live in the window."

"In what window?"

"In what window! As though you didn't know! The one in the passage, to be sure. He would sit there, sewing or doing anything else. Maybe he would sit on a chair, too. He's got a chair; and he has a table, too; he's got everything."

"Who is 'he' then?"

1

"Oh, a good man, a man of experience. I will cook for him. And I'll ask him three roubles a month for his board and lodging."

After prolonged efforts I succeeded at last in learning from Agrafena that an elderly man had somehow managed to persuade her to admit him into the kitchen as a lodger and boarder. Any notion Agrafena took into her head had to be carried out; if not, I knew she would give me no peace. When anything was not to her liking, she at once began to brood, and sank into a deep dejection that would last for a fortnight or three weeks. During that period my dinners were spoiled, my linen was mislaid, my floors went unscrubbed; in short, I had a great deal to put up with. I had observed long ago that this inarticulate woman was incapable of conceiving a project, of originating an idea of her own. But if anything like a notion or a project was by some means put into her feeble brain, to prevent its being carried out meant, for a time, her moral assassination. And so, as I cared more for my peace of mind than for anything else, I consented forthwith.

"Has he a passport anyway, or something of the sort?"

"To be sure, he has. He is a good man, a man of experience; three roubles he's promised to pay."

The very next day the new lodger made his appearance in my modest bachelor quarters; but I was not put out by this, indeed I was inwardly pleased. I lead as a rule a very lonely hermit's existence. I have scarcely any friends; I hardly ever go anywhere. As I had spent ten years never coming out of my shell, I had, of course, grown used to solitude. But another ten or fifteen years or more of the same solitary existence, with the same Agrafena, in the same bachelor quarters, was in truth a somewhat cheerless prospect. And therefore a new inmate, if well-behaved, was a heaven-sent blessing.

Agrafena had spoken truly; my lodger was certainly a man of experience. From his passport it appeared that he was an

2

old soldier, a fact which I should have known indeed from his face. An old soldier is easily recognised. Astafy Ivanovitch was a favourable specimen of his class. We got on very well together. What was best of all, Astafy Ivanovitch would sometimes tell a story, describing some incident in his own life. In the perpetual boredom of my existence such a story-teller was a veritable treasure. One day he told me one of these stories. It made an impression on me. The following event was what led to it.

It was left alone in the flat; both Astafy and Agrafena were out on business of their own. All of a sudden I heard from the inner room somebody—I fancied a stranger—come in; I went out; there actually was a stranger in the passage, a short fellow wearing no overcoat in spite of the cold autumn weather.

"What do you want?"

"Does a clerk called Alexandrov live here?"

"Nobody of that name here, brother. Good-bye."

"Why, the dvornik told me it was here," said my visitor, cautiously retiring towards the door.

"Be off, be off, brother, get along."

Next day after dinner, while Astafy Ivanovitch was fitting on a coat which he was altering for me, again someone came into the passage. I half opened the door.

Before my very eyes my yesterday's visitor, with perfect composure, took my wadded greatcoat from the peg and, stuffing it under his arm, darted out of the flat. Agrafena stood all the time staring at him, agape with astonishment and doing nothing for the protection of my property. Astafy Ivanovitch flew in pursuit of the thief and ten minutes later came back out of breath and empty-handed. He had vanished completely.

"Well, there's a piece of luck, Astafy Ivanovitch!"

"It's a good job your cloak is left! Or he would have put you in a plight, the thief!"

But the whole incident had so impressed Astafy Ivanovitch

3

that I forgot the theft as I looked at him. He could not get over it. Every minute or two he would drop the work upon which he was engaged, and would describe over again how it had all happened, how he had been standing, how the great-coat had been taken down before his very eyes, not a yard away, and how it had come to pass that he could not catch the thief. Then he would sit down to his work again, then leave it once more, and at last I saw him go down to the dvornik to tell him all about it, and to upbraid him for letting such a thing happen in his domain. Then he came back and began scolding Agrafena. Then he sat down to his work again, and long afterwards he was still muttering to himself how it had all happened, how he stood there and I was here, how before our eyes, not a yard away, the thief took the coat off the peg, and so on. In short, though Astafy Ivanovitch understood his business, he was a terrible slow-coach and busy-body.

"He's made fools of us, Astafy Ivanovitch," I said to him in the evening, as I gave him a glass of tea. I wanted to while away the time by recalling the story of the lost greatcoat, the frequent repetition of which, together with the great earnestness of the speaker, was beginning to become very amusing.

"Fools, indeed, sir! Even though it is no business of mine, I am put out. It makes me angry though it is not my coat that was lost. To my thinking there is no vermin in the world worse than a thief. Another takes what you can spare, but a thief steals the work of your hands, the sweat of your brow, your time . . . Ugh, it's nasty! One can't speak of it! It's too vexing. How is it you don't feel the loss of your property, sir?"

"Yes, you are right, Astafy Ivanovitch, better if the thing had been burnt; it's annoying to let the thief have it, it's disagreeable."

"Disagreeable! I should think so! Yet, to be sure, there are thieves and thieves. And I have happened, sir, to come across an honest thief."

4

"An honest thief? But how can a thief be honest, Astafy Ivanovitch?"

"There you are right indeed, sir. How can a thief be honest? There are none such. I only meant to say that he was an honest man, sure enough, and yet he stole. I was simply sorry for him."

"Why, how was that, Astafy Ivanovitch?"

"It was about two years ago, sir. I had been nearly a year out of a place, and just before I lost my place I made the acquaintance of a poor lost creature. We got acquainted in a public-house. He was a drunkard, a vagrant, a beggar, he had been in a situation of some sort, but from his drinking habits he had lost his work. Such a ne'er-do-weel! God only knows what he had on! Often you wouldn't be sure if he'd a shirt under his coat; everything he could lay his hands upon he would drink away. But he was not one to quarrel; he was a quiet fellow. A soft, good-natured chap. And he'd never ask, he was ashamed; but you could see for yourself the poor fellow wanted a drink, and you would stand it him. And so we got friendly, that's to say, he stuck to me. . . . It was all one to me. And what a man he was, to be sure! Like a little dog he would follow me; wherever I went there he would be; and all that after our first meeting, and he as thin as a thread-paper! At first it was 'let me stay the night'; well, I let him stay.

"I looked at his passport, too; the man was all right.

"Well, the next day it was the same story, and then the third day he came again and sat all day in the window and stayed the night. Well, thinks I, he is sticking to me; give him food and drink and shelter at night, too—here am I, a poor man, and a hanger-on to keep as well! And before he came to me, he used to go in the same way to a government clerk's; he attached himself to him; they were always drinking together; but he, through trouble of some sort, drank himself into the

5

grave. My man was called Emelyan Ilyitch. I pondered and pondered what I was to do with him. To drive him away I was ashamed. I was sorry for him; such a pitiful, godforsaken creature I never did set eyes on. And not a word said either; he does not ask, but just sits there and looks into your eyes like a dog. To think what drinking will bring a man down to!

"I keep asking myself how am I to say to him: 'You must be moving, Emelyanoushka, there's nothing for you here, you've come to the wrong place; I shall soon not have a bite for myself, how am I to keep you too?'

"I sat and wondered what he'd do when I said that to him. And I seemed to see how he'd stare at me, if he were to hear me say that, how long he would sit and not understand a word of it. And when it did get home to him at last, how he would get up from the window, would take up his bundle—I can see it now, the red-check handkerchief full of holes, with God knows what wrapped up in it, which he had always with him, and then how he would set his shabby old coat to rights, so that it would look decent and keep him warm, so that no holes would be seen—he was a man of delicate feelings! And how he'd open the door and go out with tears in his eyes. Well, there's no letting a man go to ruin like that. . . . One's sorry for him.

"And then again, I think, how am I off myself? Wait a bit, Emelyanoushka, says I to myself, you've not long to feast with me: I shall soon be going away and then you will not find me.

"Well, sir, our family made a move; and Alexandr Filimono- vitch, my master (now deceased, God rest his soul) said, 'I am thoroughly satisfied with you, Astafy Ivanovitch; when we come back from the country we will take you on again.' I had been butler with them; a nice gentleman he was, but he died that same year. Well, after seeing him off, I took my belongings, what little money I had, and I thought I'd have a rest for a time, so I went to an old woman I knew, and I took a corner in her room. There was only one corner free in it.

6

She had been a nurse, so now she had a pension and a room of her own. Well, now good-bye, Emelyanoushka, thinks I, you won't find me now, my boy.

"And what do you think, sir? I had gone out to see a man I knew, and when I came back in the evening, the first thing I saw was Emelyanoushka! There he was, sitting on my box and his check bundle beside him; he was sitting in his ragged old coat, waiting for me. And to while away the time he had borrowed a church book from the old lady, and was holding it wrong side upwards. He'd scented me out! My heart sank. Well, thinks I, there's no help for it—why didn't I turn him out. So I asked him straight off: 'Have you brought your passport, Emelyanoushka?'

"I sat down on the spot, sir, and began to ponder: will a vagabond like that be very much trouble to me? And on thinking it over it seemed he would not be much trouble. He must be fed, I thought. Well, a bit of bread in the morning, and to make it go down better I'll buy him an onion. At midday I should have to give him another bit of bread and an onion; and in the evening, onion again with kvass, with some more bread if he wanted it. And if some cabbage soup were to come our way, then we should both have had our fill. I am no great eater myself, and a drinking man, as we all know, never eats; all he wants is herb-brandy or green vodka. He'll ruin me with his drinking, I thought, but then another idea came into my head, sir, and took great hold on me. So much so that if Emelyanoushka had gone away I should have felt that I had nothing to live for, I do believe. . . . I determined on the spot to be a father and guardian to him. I'll keep him from ruin, I thought, I'll wean him from the glass! You wait a bit, thought I; very well, Emelyanoushka, you may stay, only you must behave yourself; you must obey orders.

"Well, thinks I to myself, I'll begin by training him to work of some sort, but not all at once; let him enjoy himself a little

7

first, and I'll look round and find something you are fit for,
Emelyanoushka. For every sort of work a man needs a special
ability, you know, sir. And I began to watch him on the quiet;
I soon saw Emelyanoushka was a desperate character. I
began, sir, with a word of advice: I said this and that to him.
'Emelyanoushka,' said I, 'you ought to take a thought and
mend your ways. Have done with drinking! Just look what rags
you go about in: that old coat of yours, if I may make bold
to say so, is fit for nothing but a sieve. A pretty state of things!
It's time to draw the line, sure enough.' Emelyanoushka sat
and listened to me with his head hanging down. Would you
believe it, sir? It had come to such a pass with him, he'd lost his
tongue through drink and could not speak a word of sense.
Talk to him of cucumbers and he'd answer back about beans!
He would listen and listen to me and then heave such a sigh.
'What are you sighing for, Emelyan Ilyitch?' I asked him.

" 'Oh, nothing; don't you mind me, Astafy Ivanovitch.
Do you know there were two women fighting in the street
today, Astafy Ivanovitch? One upset the other woman's
basket of cranberries by accident.'

" 'Well, what of that?'

" 'And the second one upset the other's cranberries on
purpose and trampled them under foot, too.'

" 'Well, and what of it, Emelyan Ilyitch?'

" 'Why, nothing, Astafy Ivanovitch, I just mentioned it.'

" ' "Nothing, I just mentioned it!" Emelyanoushka, my
boy, I thought, you've squandered and drunk away your
brains!'

" 'And do you know, a gentleman dropped a money-note on
the pavement in Gorohovy Street, no, it was Sadovy Street.
And a peasant saw it and said, "That's my luck"; and at the
same time another man saw it and said, "No, it's my bit of
luck. I saw it before you did." '

" 'Well, Emelyan Ilyitch!'

8

" 'And the fellows had a fight over it, Astafy Ivanovitch. But a policeman came up, took away the note, gave it back to the gentleman and threatened to take up both the men.'

" 'Well, but what of that? What is there edifying about it, Emelyanoushka?'

" 'Why, nothing to be sure. Folks laughed, Astafy Ivanovitch.'

"Ach, Emelyanoushka! What do the folks matter? You've sold your soul for a brass farthing! But do you know what I have to tell you, Emelyan Ilyitch?'

" 'What, Astafy Ivanovitch?'

" 'Take a job of some sort, that's what you must do. For the hundredth time I say to you, set to work, have some mercy on yourself!'

" 'What could I set to, Astafy Ivanovitch? I don't know what job I could set to, and there is no one who will take me on, Astafy Ivanovitch.'

" 'That's how you came to be turned off, Emelyanoushka, you drinking man!'

" 'And do you know Vlass, the waiter, was sent for to the office today, Astafy Ivanovitch?'

" 'Why did they send for him, Emelyanoushka?' I asked.

" 'I could not say why, Astafy Ivanovitch. I suppose they wanted him there, and that's why they sent for him.'

"A-ach, thought I, we are in a bad way, poor Emelyanoushka! The Lord is chastising us for our sins. Well, sir, what is one to do with such a man?

"But a cunning fellow he was, and no mistake. He'd listen and listen to me, but at last I suppose he got sick of it. As soon as he sees I am beginning to get angry, he'd pick up his old coat and out he'd slip and leave no trace. He'd wander about all day and come back at night drunk. Where he got the money from, the Lord only knows; I had no hand in that.

" 'No,' said I, 'Emelyn Ilyitch, you'll come to a bad end.

9

Give over drinking, mind what I say now, give it up! Next time you come home in liquor, you can spend the night on the stairs. I won't let you in!'

"After hearing that threat, Emelyanoushka sat at home that day and the next; but on the third he slipped off again. I waited and waited; he didn't come back. Well, at last I don't mine owning, I was in a fright, and I felt for the man too. What have I done to him? I thought. I've scared him away. Where's the poor fellow gone to now? He'll get lost maybe. Lord have mercy upon us!

"Night came on, he did not come. In the morning I went out into the porch; I looked, and if he hadn't gone to sleep in the porch! There he was with his head on the step, and chilled to the marrow of his bones.

"'What next, Emelyanoushka, God have mercy on you! Where will you get to next!'

"'Why, you were—sort of—angry with me, Astafy Ivanovitch, the other day, you were vexed and promised to put me to sleep in the porch, so I didn't—sort of—venture to come in, Astafy Ivanovitch, and so I lay down here. . . .'

"I did feel angry and sorry too.

"'Surely you might undertake some other duty, Emelyanoushka, instead of lying here guarding the steps,' I said.

"'Why, what other duty, Astafy Ivanovitch?'

"'You lost soul'—I was in such a rage, I called him that— ' if you could but learn tailoring work! Look at your old rag of a coat! It's not enough to have it in tatters, here you are sweeping the steps with it! You might take a needle and boggle up your rags, as decency demands. Ah, you drunken man!'

"What do you think, sir? He actually did take a needle. Of course I said it in jest, but he was so scared he set to work. He took off his coat and began threading the needle. I watched him; as you may well guess, his eyes were all red and bleary, and his hands were all of a shake. He kept shoving and shoving

10

the thread and could not get it through the eye of the needle; he kept screwing his eyes up and wetting the thread and twisting it in his fingers—it was no good! He gave it up and looked at me.

"'Well,' said I, 'this is a nice way to treat me! If there had been folks by to see, I don't know what I should have done! Why, you simple fellow, I said it you in joke, as a reproach. Give over your nonsense, God bless you! Sit quiet and don't put me to shame, don't sleep on my stairs and make a laughing-stock of me.'

"'Why, what am I to do, Astafy Ivanvitch? I know very well I am a drunkard and good for nothing! I can do nothing but vex you, my bene—bene—factor. . . .'

"And at that his blue lips began all of a sudden to quiver, and a tear ran down his white cheek and trembled on his stubbly chin, and then poor Emelyanoushka burst into a regular flood of tears. Mercy on us! I felt as though a knife were thrust into my heart! The sensitive creature! I'd never have expected it. Who could have guessed it? No, Emelyanoushka, thought I, I shall give you up altogether. You can go your way like the rubbish you are.

"Well, sir, why make a long story of it? And the whole affair is so trifling, it's not worth wasting words upon. Why, you, for instance, sir, would not have given a thought to it, but I would have given a great deal—if I had a great deal to give—that it never should have happened at all.

"I had a pair of riding breeches by me, sir, deuce take them, fine, first-rate riding breeches they were too, blue with a check on it. They'd been ordered by a gentleman from the country, but he would not have them after all; said they were not full enough, so they were left on my hands. It struck me they were worth something. At the second-hand dealer's I ought to get five silver roubles for them, or if not I could turn them into two pairs of trousers for Petersburg gentlemen and have a piece over for a waistcoat for myself. Of course for poor people like

11

us everything comes in. And it happened just then that Emelyanoushka was having a sad time of it. There he sat day after day: he did not drink, not a drop passed his lips, but he sat and moped like an owl. It was sad to see him—he just sat and brooded. Well, thought I, either you've not a copper to spend, my lad, or else you're turning over a new leaf of yourself, you've given it up, you've listened to reason. Well, sir, that's how it was with us; and just then came a holiday. I went to vespers; when I came home I found Emelyanoushka sitting in the window, drunk and rocking to and fro.

"Ah! so that's what you've been up to, my lad! And I went to get something out of my chest. And when I looked in, the breeches were not there. . . . I rummaged here and there; they'd vanished. When I'd ransacked everywhere and saw they were not there, something seemed to stab me to the heart. I ran first to the old dame and began accusing her; of Emelyanoushka I'd not the faintest suspicion, though there was cause for it in his sitting there drunk.

" 'No,' said the old body, 'God be with you, my fine gentleman, what good are riding breeches to me? Am I going to wear such things? Why, a skirt I had I lost the other day through a fellow of your sort . . . I know nothing; I can tell you nothing about it,' she said.

" 'Who has been here, who has been in?' I asked.

" 'Why, nobody has been, my good sir,' says she; 'I've been here all the while; Emelyan Ilyitch went out and came back again; there he sits, ask him.'

" 'Emelyanoushka,' said I, 'have you taken those new riding breeches for anything; you remember the pair I made for that gentleman from the country?'

" 'No, Astafy Ivanovitch,' said he; 'I've not—sort of—touched them.'

"I was in a state! I hunted high and low for them—they

12

were nowhere to be found. And Emelyanoushka sits there rocking himself to and fro. I was squatting on my heels facing him and bending over the chest, and all at once I stole a glance at him. . . Alack, I thought; my heart suddenly grew hot within me and I felt myself flushing up too. And suddenly Emelyanoushka looked at me.

" 'No, Astafy Ivanovitch,' said he, 'those riding breeches of yours, maybe, you are thinking, maybe, I took them, but I never touched them.'

" 'But what can have become of them, Emelyan Ilyitch?'

" 'No, Astafy Ivanovitch,' said he, 'I've never seen them.'

" 'Why, Emelyan Ilyitch, I suppose, they've run off of themselves, eh?'

" 'Maybe they have, Astafy Ivanovitch.'

"When I heard him say that, I got up at once, went up to him, lighted the lamp and sat down to work to my sewing. I was altering a waistcoat for a clerk who lived below us. And wasn't there a burning pain and ache in my breast! I shouldn't have minded so much if I had put all the clothes I had in the fire. Emelyanoushka seemed to have an inkling of what a rage I was in. When a man is guilty, you know, sir, he scents trouble far off, like the birds of the air before a storm.

" ' Do you know what, Astafy Ivanovitch,' Emelyanoushka began, and his poor old voice was shaking as he said the words, 'Antip Prohoritch, the apothecary, married the coachman's wife this morning, who died the other day——'

"I did give him a look, sir, a nasty look it was; Emelyanoushka understood it too. I saw him get up, go to the bed, and begin to rummage there for something. I waited—he was busy there a long time and kept muttering all the while, 'No, not there, where can the blessed things have got to!' I waited to see what he'd do; I saw him creep under the bed on all fours. I couldn't bear it any longer. 'What are you crawling about under the bed for, Emelyan Ilyitch?' said I.

13

" 'Looking for the breeches, Astafy Ivanovitch. Maybe they've dropped down there somewhere.'

" 'Why should you try to help a poor simple man like me,' said I, 'crawling on your knees for nothing, sir'—I called him that in my vexation.

" 'Oh, never mind, Astafy Ivanovitch, I'll just look. They'll turn up, maybe, somewhere.'

" 'H'm,' said I, 'look here, Emelyan Ilyitch!'

" 'What is it, Astafy Ivanovitch?' said he.

" 'Haven't you simply stolen them from me like a thief and a robber, in return for the bread and salt you've eaten here?' said I.

"I felt so angry, sir, at seeing him fooling about on his knees before me.

" 'No, Astafy Ivanovitch.'

"And he stayed lying as he was on his face under the bed. A long time he lay there and then at last crept out. I looked at him and the man was as white as a sheet. He stood up, and and sat down near me in the window and sat so for some ten minutes.

" 'No, Astafy Ivanovitch,' he said, and all at once he stood up and came towards me, and I can see him now; he looked dreadful. 'No, Astafy Ivanovitch,' said he, 'I never—sort of—touched your breeches.'

"He was all of a shake, poking himself in the chest with a trembling finger, and his poor old voice shook so that I was frightened, sir, and sat as though I was rooted to the window-seat.

" 'Well, Emelyan Ilyitch,' said I, 'as you will, forgive me if I, in my foolishness, have accused you unjustly. As for the breeches, let them go hang; we can live without them. We've still our hands, thank God; we need not go thieving or begging from some other poor man; we'll earn our bread.'

"Emelyanoushka heard me out and went on standing there

14

before me. I looked up, and he had sat down. And there he sat all the evening without stirring. At last I lay down to sleep. Emelyanoushka went on sitting in the same place. When I looked out in the morning, he was lying curled up in his old coat on the bare floor; he felt too crushed even to come to bed. Well, sir, I felt no more liking for the fellow from that day, in fact for the first few days I hated him. I felt as one may say as though my own son had robbed me, and done me a deadly hurt. Ach, thought I, Emelyanoushka, Emelyanoushka! And Emelyanoushka, sir, went on drinking for a whole fortnight without stopping. He was drunk all the time, and regularly besotted. He went out in the morning and came back late at night, and for a whole fortnight I didn't get a word out of him. It was as though grief was gnawing at his heart, or as though he wanted to do for himself completely. At last he stopped: he must have come to the end of all he'd got, and then he sat in the window again. I remember he sat there without speaking for three days and three nights; all of a sudden I saw that he was crying. He was just sitting there, sir, and crying like anything; a perfect stream, as though he didn't know how his tears were flowing. And it's a sad thing, sir, to see a grown-up man and an old man, too, crying from woe and grief.

" 'What's the matter, Emelyanoushka?' said I.

"He began to tremble so that he shook all over. I spoke to him for the first time since that evening.

" 'Nothing, Astafy Ivanovitch.'

" 'God be with you, Emelyanoushka, what's lost is lost. Why are you moping about like this?' I felt sorry for him.

" 'Oh, nothing, Astafy Ivanovitch, it's no matter. I want to find some work to do, Astafy Ivanovitch.'

" 'And what sort of work, pray, Emelyanoushka?

" 'Why, any sort; perhaps I could find a situation such as I used to have. I've been already to ask Fedosay Ivanitch. I don't like to be a burden on you, Astafy Ivanovitch. If I can

15

find a situation, Astafy Ivanovitch, then I'll pay it you all back, and make you a return for all your hospitality.'

" 'Enough, Emelyanoushka, enough; let bygones be by-gones—and no more to be said about it. Let us go on as we used to do before.'

" 'No, Astafy Ivanovitch, you, maybe, think—but I never touched your riding breeches.'

" 'Well, have it your own way; God be with you, Emel-yanoushka.'

" 'No, Astafy Ivanovitch, I can't go on living with you, that's clear. You must excuse me, Astafy Ivanovitch.'

" 'Why, God bless you, Emelyan Ilyitch, who's offending you and driving you out of the place—am I doing it?'

" 'No, it's not the proper thing for me to live with you like this, Astafy Ivanovitch. I'd better be going.'

"He was so hurt, it seemed, he stuck to his point. I looked at him, and sure enough, up he got and pulled his old coat over his shoulders.

" 'But where are you going, Emelyan Ilyitch? Listen to reason: what are you about? Where are you off to?'

" 'No, good-bye, Astafy Ivanovitch, don't keep me now'— and he was blubbering again—'I'd better be going. You're not the same now.'

" 'Not the same as what? I am the same. But you'll be lost by yourself like a poor helpless babe, Emelyan Ilyitch.'

" 'No, Astafy Ivanovitch, when you go out now, you lock up your chest and it makes me cry to see it, Astafy Ivanovitch. You'd better let me go, Astafy Ivanovitch, and forgive me all the trouble I've given you while I've been living with you.'

"Well, sir, the man went away. I waited for a day; I expected he'd be back in the evening—no. Next day no sign of him, nor the third day either. I began to get frightened; I was so worried, I couldn't drink, I couldn't eat, I couldn't sleep. The fellow had quite disarmed me. On the fourth day

16

I went out to look for him; I peeped into all the taverns, to inquire for him—but no, Emelyanoushka was lost. 'Have you managed to keep yourself alive, Emelyanoushka?' I wondered. 'Perhaps he is lying dead under some hedge, poor drunkard, like a sodden log.' I went home more dead than alive. Next day I went out to look for him again. And I kept cursing myself that I'd been such a fool as to let the man go off by himself. On the fifth day it was a holiday—in the early morning I heard the door creak. I looked up and there was my Emelyanoushka coming in. His face was blue and his hair was covered with dirt as though he'd been sleeping in the street; he was as thin as a match. He took off his old coat, sat down on the chest and looked at me. I was delighted to see him, but I felt more upset about him than ever. For you see, sir, if I'd been overtaken in some sin, as true as I am here, sir, I'd have died like a dog before I'd have come back. But Emelyanoushka did come back. And a sad thing it was, sure enough, to see a man sunk so low. I began to look after him, to talk kindly to him, to comfort him.

" 'Well, Emelyanoushka,' said I, 'I am glad you've come back. Had you been away much longer I should have gone to look for you in the taverns again today. Are you hungry?'

" 'No, Astafy Ivanovitch.'

" 'Come now, aren't you really? Here, brother, is some cabbage soup left over from yesterday; there was meat in it; it is good stuff. And here is some bread and onion. Come, eat it, it'll do you no harm.'

"I made him eat it, and I saw at once that the man had not tasted food for maybe three days—he was as hungry as a wolf. So it was hunger that had driven him to me. My heart was melted looking at the poor dear. 'Let me run to the tavern,' thought I, 'I'll get something to ease his heart, and then we'll make an end of it. I've no more anger in my heart against you, Emelyanoushka!' I brought him some vodka. 'Here, Emelyan

Ilyitch, let us have a drink for the holiday. Like a drink? And it will do you good.' He then held out his hand, held it out greedily; he was just taking it and then he stopped himself. But a minute after I saw him take it, and lift it to his mouth, spilling it on his sleeve. But though he got it to his lips he set it down on the table again.

" 'What is it, Emelyanoushka?'

" 'Nothing, Astafy Ivanovitch, I—sort of——'

" 'Won't you drink it?'

" 'Well, Astafy Ivanovitch, I'm not—sort of—going to drink any more, Astafy Ivanovitch.'

" 'Do you mean you've given it up altogether, Emelyanoushka, or are you only not going to drink today?'

"He did not answer. A minute later I saw him rest his head on his hand.

" 'What's the matter, Emelyanoushka, are you ill?'

" 'Why, yes, Astafy Ivanovitch, I don't feel well.'

"I took him and laid him down on the bed. I saw that he really was ill: his head was burning hot and he was shivering with fever. I sat by him all day; towards night he was worse. I mixed him some oil and onion and kvass and bread broken up.

" 'Come, eat some of this,' said I, 'and perhaps you'll be better.' He shook his head. 'No,' said he, 'I won't have any dinner today, Astafy Ivanovitch.'

"I made some tea for him, I quite flustered our old woman— he was no better. Well, thinks I, it's a bad look-out! The third morning I went for a medical gentleman. There was one I knew living close by, Kostopravov by name. I'd make his acquaintance when I was in service with the Bosomyagins; he'd attended me. The doctor came and looked at him. 'He's in a bad way,' said he, 'it was no use sending for me. But if you like I can give him a powder.' Well, I didn't give him a powder, I thought that's just the doctor's little game; and then the fifth day came.

"He lay, sir, dying before my eyes. I sat in the window with my work in my hands. The old woman was heating the stove. We were all silent. My heart was simply breaking over him, the good-for-nothing fellow; I felt as if it were a son of my own I was losing. I knew that Emelyanoushka was looking at me. I'd seen the man all the day long making up his mind to say something and not daring to.

"At last I looked up at him; I saw such misery in the poor fellow's eyes. He had kept them fixed on me but, when he saw that I was looking at him, he looked down at once.

" 'Astafy Ivanovitch.'

" 'What is it, Emelyanoushka?'

" 'If you were to take my old coat to a second-hand dealer's, how much do you think they'd give you for it, Astafy Ivanovitch?'

" 'There's no knowing how much they'd give. Maybe they would give me a rouble for it, Emelyan Ilyitch.'

"But if I had taken it they wouldn't have given a farthing for it, but would have laughed in my face for bringing such a trumpery thing. I simply said that to comfort the poor fellow, knowing the simpleton he was.

" 'But I was thinking, Astafy Ivanovitch, they might give you three roubles for it; it's made of cloth, Astafy Ivanovitch. How could they only give one rouble for a cloth coat?'

" 'I don't know, Emelyan Ilyitch,' said I, 'if you are thinking of taking it you should certainly ask three roubles to begin with.'

"Emelyanoushka was silent for a time, and then he addressed me again—

" 'Astafy Ivanovitch.'

" 'What is it, Emelyanoushka?' I asked.

" 'Sell my coat when I die, and don't bury me in it. I can lie as well without it; and it's a thing of some value—it might come in useful.'

19

"I can't tell you how it made my heart ache to hear him. I saw that the death agony was coming on him. We were silent again for a bit. So an hour passed by. I looked at him again: he was still staring at me, and when he met my eyes he looked down again.

" 'Do you want some water to drink, Emelyan Ilyitch?' I asked.

" 'Give me some, God bless you, Astafy Ivanovitch.'

"I gave him a drink.

" 'Thank you, Astafy Ivanovitch,' said he.

" 'Is there anything else you would like, Emelyanoushka?'

" 'No, Astafy Ivanovitch, there's nothing I want, but I— sort of——'

" 'What?'

" 'I only——'

" 'What is it, Emelyanoushka?'

" 'Those riding breeches——it was——sort of——I who took them——Astafy Ivanovitch.'

" 'Well, God forgive you, Emelyanoushka,' said I, 'you poor, sorrowful creature. Depart in peace.'

"And I was choking myself, sir, and the tears were in my eyes. I turned aside for a moment.

" 'Astafy Ivanovitch——'

"I saw Emelyanoushka wanted to tell me something; he was trying to sit up, trying to speak, and mumbling something. He flushed red all over suddenly, looked at me . . . then I saw him turn white again, whiter and whiter, and he seemed to sink away all in a minute. His head fell back, he drew one breath and gave up his soul to God."

Uncle's Dream

From the Annals of Mordasov

CHAPTER I

MARYA ALEXANDROVNA MOSKALEV is the leading lady in Mordasov, and of that there can be no possible question. She behaves as though she were independent of everyone and everyone else were dependent on her. It is true that scarcely anyone likes her and, indeed, very many people sincerely hate her; but on the other hand everyone is afraid of her, and that is just what she wants. Such a desire betokens a high degree of diplomacy. How is it, for instance, that Marya Alexandrovna, who is desperately fond of gossip, and cannot sleep all night if she has not heard something new the day before, how is it that with all that she knows how to deport herself so that it would never occur to anyone looking at her that this majestic lady was the greatest gossip in the world, or at any rate in Mordasov. One would suppose, on the contrary, that gossip would die away in her presence, that backbiters would blush and tremble like schoolboys confronting their teacher, and that the conversation would not deal with any but the loftiest subjects. She knows about some of the Mordasov people facts so scandalous and so important that if she were to tell them on a suitable occasion and to make them public, as she so well knows how to do, there would be a regular earthquake of Lisbon in Mordasov. And at the same time she is very reserved over these secrets and will only tell them in extreme cases, and then only to her most intimate female friends. She confines herself to frightening people, with hints at what she knows, and likes better to keep a man or a lady in continual apprehension than

21

to deal them a final blow. That is intelligence, that is diplomacy! Marya Alexandrovna was always distinguished among us by her irreproachable *comme il faut*, upon which we all model ourselves. As regards *comme il faut* she is without a rival in Mordasov. She can, for instance, kill, tear to pieces, annihilate a rival with a single word, a performance we have witnessed; and at the same time she will have the air of not observing that she has uttered that word. And we all know that this ability is characteristic of the very highest society. In fact, at all such tricks she is a match for Pinetti. Her connections are immense. Many persons who have visited Mordasov have been delighted with her hospitality, and have even kept up a correspondence with her after their departure. Someone even wrote her a poem, and Marya Alexandrovna showed it to us all with pride. One literary visitor dedicated to her his novel, which he read aloud to her in the evenings, and this made an extremely agreeable impression. A learned German, who came from Carlsruhe expressly to study some kind of worm with horns, which is found in our province, and who wrote four quarto volumes on the creature in question, was so enchanted by Marya Alexandrovna's hospitality and politeness that to this day he keeps up with her a correspondence of the most respectful and highly moral tone, from Carlsruhe. Marya Alexandrovna has even been compared in one respect with Napoleon. This comparison was of course made in jest by her enemies, more by way of sarcasm than truth. But while fully admitting the oddity of the comparison I make bold to ask one innocent question: why was Napoleon's head turned at last when he was too greatly exalted? The champions of the old dynasty used to ascribe this to the fact that Napoleon was not only not of royal blood, but was not even a *gentilhomme* of good family, and so was naturally alarmed at last by his own exalted state and was conscious of his real position. In spite of the obvious cleverness of this surmise, which recalls the

22

most brilliant period of the old French court, I venture to add in my turn: how was it that Marya Alexandrovna's head was never under any circumstances turned, how was it that she always remained the leading lady in Mordasov? There were occasions when everybody asked: "How will Marya Alexandrovna act now in such difficult circumstances?" But the circumstances arrived and passed and—all went well! Everything remained satisfactory, as before; even better than before. Everyone remembers, for instance, how her husband, Afanasy Matveyitch, was deprived of his post owing to his incompetence and feeble-mindedness, which excited the wrath of an inspector from the capital. Everyone thought that Marya Alexandrovna would be depressed, would be humbled, would entreat and petition, would, in short, be crestfallen. Nothing of the sort: Marya Alexandrovna grasped that nothing could be gained by petitioning, and played her cards so well that she lost nothing of her influence in society, and her house is still looked upon as the house of most consequence in Mordasov. Anna Nikolaevna Antipov, the Public Prosecutor's wife, a sworn foe of Marya Alexandrovna's, though externally her friend, was already trumpeting her victory; but when we saw that Marya Alexandrovna could not be easily put to confusion, we realised that she had sent her roots far more deeply down than we had supposed.

By the way, since we have mentioned him we will say a few words about Afanasy Matveyitch, Marya Alexandrovna's husband. In the first place he was a man of very presentable exterior, and indeed of very correct principles, only on critical occasions he somehow lost his head, and looked like a sheep facing a new gate. He was extraordinarily dignified, especially in his white tie at nameday dinners, but his dignified air and presentability only lasted till the minute when he began to speak. Then there was nothing for it, if I may say so, but cotton wool in one's ears. He certainly was not worthy to belong to Marya Alexandrovna; that was the universal opinion, he had only kept his position through the genius of his wife; in my private judgment he ought long ago to have been in the kitchen garden scaring sparrows. There and only there he might have been of real unquestionable service to his fellow-countrymen. And so Marya Alexandrovna acted admirably in sending Afanasy Matveyitch to their country place, two and a half miles from Mordasov, where she had a hundred and twenty serfs—in parenthesis I may say, the whole property, the whole fortune upon which she so worthily maintained the dignity of her household. Everybody knew that she had kept Afanasy Matveyitch about her solely because he was in the government service and in receipt of a salary and . . . of other sums. As soon as he ceased to receive a salary and other sums, she immediately removed him to a distance on account of his incompetence and absolute uselessness. And everyone commended Marya Alexandrovna's clear-sighted-ness and decision of character. In the country Afanasy Mat-veyitch is in clover. I went to see him and spent a whole hour with him fairly pleasantly. He tries on his white cravats, cleans his boots with his own hands, not from necessity but simply for love of the art, because he likes his boots to shine; he drinks tea three times a day, is exceedingly fond of going to the bath-house, and—is contented. Do you remember the horrid scandal that was concocted among us a year and a half ago concerning Zinaida Afanasyevna, the only daughter of Marya Alexandrovna and Afanasy Matveyitch? Zinaida Afanasyevna is unquestionably beautiful, and is extremely well educated, yet she is three-and-twenty and is still unmarried. Among the reasons people give for Zina's being unmarried, one of the chief is considered to be the sinister rumour of some strange intimacy a year and a half ago with a wretched district school-master—a rumour which has persisted to this day. Even now there is talk of some love-letter written by Zina and said to have been passed from hand to hand in Mordasov; but I should like to know if anyone has seen that letter. If it has passed from hand to hand what has become of it? Everyone has heard about it, but nobody has seen it. I, at any rate, have never come across anyone who has seen this letter with his own eyes. If you drop a hint about it to Marya Alexandrovna she simply fails to understand you. Now let us assume that there really was something, and Zina did write the love-letter (I fancy, indeed, that it must have been so), how skilful it all was on Marya Alexandrovna's part! How adroitly was this awkward, scandalous affair suppressed and stifled! Not a trace, not a hint! Marya Alexandrovna takes no notice now of this ignoble slander, and at the same time, God knows how she may have worked to save the honour of her only daughter from the slightest slur. And as for Zina's not being married, that's very natural: there are no eligible young men here. The only fitting match for Zina would be a reigning prince. Have you ever seen a beauty like her? It is true that she is proud— too proud. They say that Mozglyakov is paying her his addresses, but it is hardly likely to come to a marriage. What is Mozglyakov? It is true that he is young, not bad looking, a dandy, has a hundred and fifty serfs not mortgaged, and comes from Petersburg. But in the first place, you know he is not quite sound in the upper storey. He is feather-headed, a chatterbox, and has some very new-fangled ideas. And after all what is an estate of a hundred and fifty serfs, especially with new-fangled ideas! That marriage won't come off.

All that the kind reader has read so far was written by me five months ago entirely from excess of feeling. I may as well confess betimes I have rather a partiality for Marya Alexandrovna. I wanted to write something like a eulogy on that magnificent lady, and to put it in the shape of a playful letter to a friend, on the model of the letters which used, at one time, in the old golden days that, thank God, will never return, to be published in the *Northern Bee* and other periodicals. But as I have no friend, and have, moreover, a certain innate literary timidity, my work has remained in my table drawer as my first literary effort and a memento of peaceful recreation in hours of leisure and comfort.

Five months have passed, and all at once a wonderful event has occurred in Mordasov: early one morning Prince K. arrived in the town and stopped at Marya Alexandrovna's house. The consequences of this arrival have been innumerable. The prince spent only three days in Mordasov, but those three days have left behind them momentous memories that will never be effaced. I will say more: Prince K. produced, in a certain sense, a revolution in our town. The story of that revolution is, of course, one of the most significant pages in the annals of Mordasov. That page I have made up my mind at last, after some hesitation, to put into literary shape and lay before the criticism of the honoured public. My story will contain the full and remarkable history of the exaltation, glory and solemn downfall of Marya Alexandrovna and all her family: a worthy and alluring theme for an author. First of all, of course, I must explain what there was wonderful in Prince K.'s arriving in our town and staying at Marya Alexandrovna's —and to do that I must, of course, say a few words about Prince K. himself. And that I will do. Besides, the biography of that personage is absolutely essential for all the further development of our story. And so I will begin.

CHAPTER II

I WILL begin by saying that Prince K. was not so extraordinarily aged, but yet he was so decrepit, so worn out, that as one looked at him the thought instinctively occurred to one that in another minute he might drop to pieces. Extremely queer stories of the most fantastic kind were repeated in Mordasov about this prince. People even said that the old man was off his head. Everyone thought it very strange that the owner of an estate of four thousand serfs, a man of distinguished family, who might, if he had chosen, have had a great influence in the province, should live in solitude on his magnificent estate, a complete hermit. Many had known Prince K. when he was staying in Mordasov six or seven years before, and they declared that in those days he could not endure solitude and had not the faintest resemblance to a hermit.

All that I could ascertain about him, on good authority, however, was this:

In his young days, which were, however, long ago, the prince had made a brilliant début, he had led a gay life, flirted, had made several tours abroad, sang songs, made puns, and had at no period been distinguished by the brilliance of his intellectual gifts. Of course he had squandered all his fortune, and found himself in his old age without a farthing. Someone advised him to visit his estate, which was beginning to be sold by auction. He set off and arrived in Mordasov, where he stayed six months. He liked provincial life extremely. During those six months he dissipated all he had left, to the last halfpenny, spending his whole time in gambling and getting up various intrigues with the ladies of the province. He was, moreover, extremely good-natured, though of course not without certain princely airs, which were, however, regarded in Mordasov as characteristic of the highest society, and so, instead of annoying people, they positively impressed them favourably. The ladies especially were in perpetual ecstasy over their charming visitor. A number of curious reminiscences of him were preserved. People said among other things that the prince spent more than half the day over his toilet, and was, it appeared, entirely made up of different little bits. No one knew when and where he had managed to become so dilapi-

27

dated. He wore a wig, moustaches, whiskers, and even a little 'imperial'—all, every hair of it, false, and of a magnificent black colour; he rouged and powdered every day. It was said that he had little springs to smooth away the wrinkles on his face, and these springs were in some peculiar way concealed in his hair. It was asserted, too, that he wore corsets, because he had lost a rib jumping somewhat clumsily out of a window on one of his amorous adventures in Italy. He limped with the left leg; it was maintained that the leg in question was an artificial one, and that the real one had been broken in the course of another similar adventure in Paris, and that he had been provided with a new cork leg of a special pattern. But what will not people say? It certainly was true that his right eye was a glass one, though it was a most skilful imitation. His teeth, too, were false. He spent whole days washing in various patent waters, scenting and pomading himself. It was recalled, however, that even then the prince was perceptibly beginning to grow feeble, and that he had become insufferably garrulous. It seemed as though his career were drawing to its close. Everyone knew that he had not a farthing. And all of a sudden, quite unexpectedly, one of his nearest relations, a very aged lady who had lived for many years in Paris and from whom he could have had no expectations, died, just a month after the funeral of her legal heir. The prince found himself quite unexpectedly the heir to her fortune. A magnificent estate of four thousand serfs, about forty miles from Mordasov, all came to him. He at once prepared to go to Petersburg to settle his affairs. Our ladies got up a magnificent subscription dinner in his honour. It is recalled that the prince was enchantingly gay at this farewell banquet, he made puns, made everyone laugh, told the most extraordinary anecdotes, vowed that he would return as quickly as possible to Duhanovo (his new property), and promised that on his return there would be a continual round of fêtes, picnics, balls, and fireworks. For a

28

whole year after his departure the ladies talked of this promise, and awaited their charming old friend with immense impatience. While awaiting his return they even made up parties to Duhanovo, where there was an old-world manor-house and garden, with acacias lopped into the shape of lions, with artificial mounds, with lakes, upon which boats sailed up and down, with wooden images of Turks playing a pipe for figureheads, with arbours, with pavilions, with pleasure grounds, and other attractions.

At last the prince returned, but to the general surprise and disappointment he did not even call at Mordasov on his way, but settled at Duhanovo and lived like a hermit. Strange rumours began to circulate, and altogether from that period the prince's history became obscure and fantastic. To begin with, it was asserted that he had not been altogether successful in Petersburg, that some of his relations and future heirs tried to take advantage of the prince's mental feebleness in order to get him put under some sort of supervision, fearing that he would squander everything again. What was more, some people declared that they had tried to put him in a lunatic asylum, but that one of his relations, a gentleman of consequence, had taken his part, explaining frankly to the others that the poor prince, half dead and half a dummy already, would probably soon die altogether, and then the property would come to them without the help of a lunatic asylum. I repeat again: what will not people say? especially in our town, Mordasov. All this, so it was said, scared the prince terribly, so much so that he became a transformed character and turned into a hermit. Some of the Mordasov gentry went from curiosity to call upon him, but were either not received or met with a very strange reception. The prince did not even recognise his old acquaintances. It was asserted that he did not want to recognise them. The Governor, too, paid him a visit.

He returned with the news, that in his opinion the prince

29

really was a little off his head, and ever afterwards he made a wry face at any allusion to his visit to Duhanovo. The ladies were loud in their indignation. At last a fact of prime importance was discovered, namely, that the prince was entirely in the power of one Stepanida Matveyevna, a woman no one knew anything about, who had come with him from Petersburg, was stout and elderly, and went about in cotton dresses with the keys in her hands; that the prince obeyed her in everything like a child and did not dare to take a step without her permission, that she even washed him with her own hands, that she spoilt him, dandled him and comforted him like a child, and that finally she kept away from him all visitors, and especially the relations, who had been gradually beginning to visit Duhanovo to see how things were going. People in Mordasov discussed this incomprehensible relationship a great deal, especially the ladies. It was added that Stepanida Matveyevna had unchecked and independent control of the prince's whole estate; that she dismissed the stewards, the bailiffs and the servants, and collected the revenues; but that she ruled it well, so that the peasants blessed their fate. As regards the prince himself, it was learned that his days were spent almost entirely on his toilet, in trying on wigs and dress coats; that he spent the rest of his time with Stepanida Matveyevna, that he played his game of cards with her, tried his fortune with the cards, only now and then going for a ride on a quiet English mare, on which occasions Stepanida Matveyevna invariably accompanied him in a closed chaise in case of mishap, for the prince rode on horseback chiefly for effect, and could hardly keep in the saddle. He was sometimes seen also on foot, wearing an overcoat and wide-brimmed straw hat; with a lady's pink neckerchief round his neck, with an eyeglass in his eye and a wicker basket for mushrooms, cornflowers and other wild flowers; Stepanida Matveyevna always accompanied him, while behind them walked two tall footmen, and the carriage

30

followed to be ready in case of need. When he was met by a peasant, who stepped aside, took off his hat, bowed low and said: "Good-day, prince, your Excellency, our sunshine," the prince promptly turned his lorgnette upon him, nodded graciously and said to him affably: "*Bonjour, mon ami, bonjour!*" Many such rumours were current in Mordasov; they could not forget the prince: he was such a near neighbour! What was the general amazement when one fine day there was a report that the prince, the eccentric hermit, had arrived in Mordasov in person and was staying at Marya Alexandrovna's! All was bustle and excitement. Everyone was eager for an explanation, all asked one another what it meant? Some prepared to call on Marya Alexandrovna. The prince's arrival struck everyone as a wonder. The ladies sent one another notes, prepared to call on one another, sent their maids and their husbands to make inquiries. It seemed particularly strange and hard to understand why the prince should stay at Marya Alexandrovna's rather than at anyone else's. Anna Nikolaevna Antipov was particularly annoyed, because the prince was a very distant relation of hers. But to solve all these questions it is absolutely necessary to call on Marya Alexandrovna herself, and we cordially invite the kind reader to do so. It is true that it is only ten o'clock in the morning, but I don't think she will refuse to receive an intimate friend. Us, at any rate, she will certainly admit.

CHAPTER III

TEN o'clock in the morning. We are in Marya Alexandrovna's house in the main street, in the very room which the lady of the house on solemn occasions calls her *salon*. Marya Alexandrovna has also a boudoir. In this *salon* there are well-painted floors, and rather nice wall-papers that were ordered expressly

31

for the walls. In the rather clumsy furniture red is the pre-
dominating colour. There is an open fireplace, over the
mantelpiece a mirror, before the looking-glass a bronze clock,
with a cupid on it in very bad taste. In the space between the
windows there are two looking-glasses from which they have
already removed the covers. On little tables in front of the
looking-glass there are two more clocks. Against the wall at
the further end is a magnificent piano, which was procured
for Zina. Zina is musical. Round the glowing fire arm-chairs
are set, as far as possible in picturesque confusion; among
them a little table. At the other end of the room another
table covered with a cloth of dazzling whiteness; on it a silver
samovar is boiling and a pretty tea-service is set out. The
samovar and the tea are presided over by Nastasya Petrovna
Zyablov, a lady who lives with Marya Alexandrovna in the
capacity of a distant relation. Two words about this lady. She
is a widow, she is over thirty, a brunette, with a fresh complexion, and with lively dark-brown eyes. Altogether she is
good-looking. She is of a gay disposition and much given to
laughter, rather sly, of course, a scandalmonger, and very
capable of managing any little affair of her own. She has two
children, they are somewhere at school. She would very
much like to get married again. She is rather independent in
her behaviour. Her husband was an officer in the army. Marya
Alexandrovna herself is sitting by the fire, in the very best of
spirits, and in a becoming light green dress. She is highly
delighted at the arrival of the prince, who is at this moment
upstairs, engaged in his toilet. She is so delighted that she
does not even think it necessary to conceal her joy. Before her
stands a young man, telling her something with animation. It
is evident from his eyes that he is anxious to please his listeners.
He is five-and-twenty. His manners would not be bad, but
he frequently flies into raptures, and he has, besides, pre-
tensions to wit and humour. He is very well dressed, fair,

and rather nice looking. But we have spoken of him already; he is Mr. Mozglyakov, of whom great things are expected. Marya Alexandrovna privately thinks that he is rather empty-headed, but gives him a warm welcome. He is a suitor for the hand of her daughter Zina, with whom, in his own words, he is madly in love. He turns every moment to Zina, trying to extract a smile from her lips by his wit and gaiety. But she is perceptibly cold and careless in her manner to him. At this instant, she is standing apart, at the piano, and turning over a calendar with her fingers. She is one of those women who excite general enthusiasm and wonder whenever they appear in society. She is incredibly beautiful; tall, a brunette, with exquisite, almost black eyes, a graceful figure and a superb bust. Her shoulders and arms are antique, her foot is fascinating, she has the step of a queen. She is a little pale today; but her full, crimson, exquisitely chiselled lips, between which gleam even, little teeth like threaded pearls, will haunt your dreams for the next three days if once you glance at them. Her expression is grave and severe. Monsieur Mozglyakov seems to fear her intent gaze, at least he winces when he ventures to glance at her. Her movements are disdainfully careless. She is dressed in simple white muslin, which suits her exquisitely, but then everything suits her. On her finger is a ring woven of hair, and from the colour, not her mamma's. Mozglyakov has never dared to ask her whose hair it is. That morning Zina is particularly silent and over-melancholy, as though preoccupied. Marya Alexandrovna, on the other hand, is ready to talk without stopping, though she, too, glances at her daughter from time to time with a peculiar, suspicious look; she does so, however, stealthily, as though she, too, were afraid of her.

"I am so delighted, so delighted, Pavel Alexandrovitch!" she prattles, "that I am ready to cry aloud my joy out of the window to every passer-by. To say nothing of the charming surprise you have given Zina and me by returning a fortnight earlier than you promised; that goes without saying! I am awfully glad that you have brought the dear prince with you. You know how fond I am of the fascinating old darling! But no, no! You won't understand me. You young people can't understand my enthusiasm, however much I might assure you of it! You don't know what he was to me in the past, six years ago. Do you remember, Zina? I forgot, though, you were staying with your aunt at that time. . . . You would not believe it, Pavel Alexandrovitch, I was his mentor, sister, mother! He did what I told him like a child! There was something naïve, tender and ennobling in our relations; something even, as it were, Arcadian. . . . I really don't know what to call it! That is why he thinks of my house alone with gratitude, *ce pauvre prince!* Do you know, Pavel Alexandrovitch, you may perhaps have saved him by bringing him to me! I have thought of him with a pang at my heart these last six years. You wouldn't believe it, he positively haunted my dreams. They say that monstrous woman has bewitched him, ruined him. But at last you have torn him out of her clutches! Yes, we must take advantage of the opportunity and save him altogether! But tell me once more how did you succeed in doing it? Describe your whole meeting as fully as possible. Just now I was in such excitement that I only attended to the central fact, though all the little details, so to speak, make up the real flavour of it! I am awfully fond of trifling details, even on most important occasions what I notice first is the small points . . . and . . . while he is still engaged in his toilet. . . ."

"But it is all just what I have told you already, Marya Alexandrovna," Mozglyakov responds with readiness, perfectly willing to tell his story for the tenth time, it is a pleasure to him. "I was travelling all night, of course I did not sleep all night, you can imagine what haste I was in," he adds, turning to Zina; "in short, I swore, I shouted, I demanded horses. I even made a row at the posting stations over getting horses; if it were printed it would make quite a poem in the latest fashion! But that is off the point! At six o'clock in the morning I reached the last station, Igishevo. I was all of a shiver, but I did not want to warm myself; I called for horses! I frightened the overseer's wife, who had a baby at the breast, I think I must have upset her milk. . . . The sunrise was enchanting. The hoar frost, you know, all crimson and silver! I took no notice of anything; in short, I was in desperate haste! I took the horses by storm; I snatched them from a collegiate councillor, and almost challenged him to a duel. I was told that a quarter of an hour before some prince had set off from the station travelling with his own horses; he had spent the night there. I scarcely listened. I got into my sledge, flew off, as though I were let off the chain. There is something like it in Fet, in some elegy of his. Just six miles from the town, at the cross-road leading to the Svyetozersky Monastery, I saw that something surprising had happened. A huge travelling coach was lying on its side, a coachman and two footmen were standing beside it in perplexity, and heartrending shrieks and wails were coming from the carriage, that lay on its side. I was thinking of driving by: 'Let it lie on its side; it is no business of mine.' But I was overcome by a feeling of humanity, which, as Heine expresses it, pokes its nose into everything. I stopped. I, my Semyon and the driver—another true Russian heart—hastened to their assistance, and so the six of us together hoisted up the coach at last and set it on its legs, though indeed it had none, for it was on runners. Some peasants on their way to the town with wood helped too. I gave them a trifle. I thought, no doubt this is the same prince! I looked. My goodness! It was he, Prince Gavrila! 'What a meeting!' I cried out to him. 'Prince! Uncle!' Of course he scarcely recognised me at first sight; however, he almost knew me . . . at a second look. I must confess, however, that he hardly understands who I am now, and I believe he takes me for someone else and not a relation. I saw him seven years ago in Petersburg; but of course I was a boy then. I remembered him; he impressed me—but how should he remember me! I introduced myself; he was enchanted, embraced me, and at the same time he was trembling all over with fright and crying—he really was crying, I saw that with my own eyes! One thing and another—I persuaded him at last to get into my sledge and to come for at least one day to Mordasov, to rest and recover. He agreed without any ado. . . . He told me he was going to the Svyetozersky Monastery to visit the monk Misail, whom he honours and reveres; that Stepanida Matveyevna—and which of us relations has not heard of Stepanida Matveyevna? she drove me off with a broom from Duhanovo last year—that this Stepanida Matveyevna had even received a letter telling her that someone of her folks in Moscow was at the last gasp; her father, or her daughter, I don't remember which exactly, and I am not interested to know, possibly father and daughter both together, with, maybe, the addition of. a nephew, a potman in some public-house. . . . In short, she was so upset that she made up her mind to part from her prince for ten days, and flew off to adorn the capital with her presence. The prince stayed quiet for one day, for another, tried on his wigs, pomaded, and painted himself; he tried to tell his fortune with the cards (maybe with beans too), but could not put up with it without Stepanida Matveyevna. He ordered his horses and set off to the Svyetozersky Monastery. Someone of his household, fearing the absent Stepanida Matveyevna, ventured to protest, but the prince persisted. He set off yesterday, after dinner, stayed the night at Igishevo. He left the station at daybreak, and just at the turning that leads to Father Misail's, went flying with his carriage almost into a ravine. I rescued him, persuaded him to visit our common and deeply respected friend, Marya Alexandrovna; he said that you were the most fascinating lady he had ever known—and here we are, and at this moment the prince is upstairs adjusting his toilet with the assistance of his valet, whom he has not forgotten to bring with him, and whom he never will, under any circumstances, forget to take with him, for he would sooner die than consent to appear before ladies without certain preliminary preparations, or rather, adjustments. . . . That's the whole story! *Eine allerliebste Geschichte!*"

"But what a humorist he is, Zina!" cries Marya Alexandrovna, after hearing his story. "How charmingly he tells it. But listen, *Paul*, one question: explain to me exactly what relation you are to the prince! You call him uncle?"

"Upon my word, Marya Alexandrovna, I do not know how or in what way I am related to him; it's seven times removed, I believe, maybe even seventy times seven. It's not a bit my fault; it's all Aunt Aglaya Mihalovna. Aunt Aglaya Mihalovna does nothing but count over the relations on her fingers, though; it was she forced me to go to see him last summer at Duhanovo. She should have gone herself! I simply call him uncle, he answers to that name. That's all our relationship for today, anyway . . ."

"All the same, I repeat that it must have been a prompting from on High that led you to bring him straight to me! I tremble to think what would have happened to him, poor darling, if he had got into anyone else's hands instead of mine. They would have pounced upon him, torn him to pieces, devoured him! They would have fallen upon him as though he were a gold mine—I dare say they would have robbed him! You cannot imagine what low, greedy, artful people there are here, Pavel Alexandrovitch! . . ."

"Upon my soul, to whom should he have been taken if not to you? What are you saying, Marya Alexandrovna?" puts in the widow, Nastasya Petrovna, as she pours out the tea. "You don't suppose he might have been taken to Anna Nikolaevna's?"

"But why is he so long coming? It's really strange," says Marya Alexandrovna, getting up from her seat impatiently.

"Uncle, do you mean? Why, I expect he will be another five hours up there dressing! Besides, as he had quite lost his memory, he has perhaps forgotten that he is on a visit to you. You know he is a most extraordinary person, Marya Alexandrovna!"

"Oh, come, come! What nonsense."

"Not nonsense at all, Marya Alexandrovna! He is half a made-up dummy, not a man! You saw him six years ago, but it is only an hour since I have seen him. He is half a corpse. He is only a reminiscence of a man; they have forgotten to bury him, you know! His eyes are artificial, his legs are made of cork, he is all worked by springs, he even talks by machinery."

"My goodness, what a giddy fellow you are, to listen to you!" exclaims Marya Alexandrova, assuming a stern air. "Aren't you ashamed, a young man, and a relation, to talk like that about that venerable old man? To say nothing of his boundless kindliness"—and her voice takes a touching note—"remember that he is a relic, a scion, so to speak, of our aristocracy. My friend, *mon ami!* I understand that you are led into this frivolity by those modern ideas of which you are always talking. But, my goodness! I share those new ideas myself. I realise that what is at the root of your views is generous and creditable. I realise that there is, indeed, something lofty in those new ideas; but all that does not prevent my seeing the direct, so to speak, practical side of things. I have seen something of the world, I have seen more than you have, and, last of all, I am a mother, and you are still young. He is an old man, and so in our eyes he is absurd! What is more, last time you said that you would certainly emancipate your serfs, and that you must do something for the public weal, and all that comes from poring so much over your

38

Shakespeare or somebody! Believe me, Pavel Alexandrovitch, your Shakespeare has had his day, and if he were to rise again he would not with all his cleverness understand anything about our life. If there is anything chivalrous and sublime in our contemporary society it is to be found only in the highest rank. A prince in a sack is still a prince; a prince in a hovel is as good as a prince in a palace! Here Natalya Dmitryevna's husband has built himself something like a palace—and yet he is Natalya Dmitryevna's husband and no more! And if Natalya Dmitryevna were to stick on fifty crinolines she would still remain the same Natalya Dmitryevna, and would add nothing to herself by it. You, too, represent the highest rank to some extent because you are descended from it. I consider myself not far removed from it, and it's an ill bird that fouls its own nest! But you will find out all this of yourself, *mon cher Paul*, better than I can tell you, and will forget your Shakespeare. I predict it. I am persuaded that you are not in earnest even now, but are talking like that because it is chic. But I have been chattering too long. You stay here, *mon cher Paul*, I will go upstairs and find out about the prince. Perhaps he wants something, and with my stupid servants . . ."

And Marya Alexandrovna goes hurriedly out of the room at the thought of her stupid servants.

"Marya Alexandrovna seems very much pleased that that dressed-up creature, Anna Nikolaevna, has not got hold of the prince. And you know she keeps declaring that she is related to him. She must be bursting with spite now!" remarked Nastasya Petrovna; but observing that she received no answer and glancing at Zina and Pavel Alexandrovitch, she grasped the situation at once and went out of the room as though on some errand. But to reward herself for her discretion she stopped just outside and listened at the door.

Pavel Alexandrovitch turned at once to Zina. He was in great agitation, his voice was quivering.

39

"Zinaida Afanasyevna, you are not angry with me?" he asked, with a timid and imploring air.

"With you! What for?" said Zina, raising her wonderful eyes and looking at him with a faint flush.

"For coming back so soon, Zinaida Afanasyevna! I could not resist it, I could not wait another fortnight. . . . I positively dreamed of you. I flew back to hear my fate. . . . But you frown, you are angry! Surely you will not refuse to let me hear something decisive?"

Zinaida certainly did frown.

"I expected you would talk of that," she answered, dropping her eyes again, in a firm and severe voice, in which there was a note of vexation. "And as that expectation was very dainful to me, the sooner it is over the better. Again you insist, that is, beg for an answer. Very well, I will repeat it to you again, for my answer is still the same as before; wait! I tell you again—I have not made up my mind yet, and cannot promise to be your wife. That is not exacted by force, Pavel Alexandrovitch. But to comfort you, I will add I do not definitely refuse you. Note, too, in giving you hope now of a favourable decision, I do this entirely out of consideration for your impatience and anxiety. I repeat that I wish to remain perfectly free in my decision, and if I tell you in the end that I do not consent, you must not blame me for having given you hope. And so realise that!"

"And so what does that amount to?" cried Mozglyakov in a plaintive voice. "Is that hope? Can I extract any hope at all from your words, Zinaida Afanasyevna?"

"Remember all I have told you and extract what you choose. It is for you to decide, but I will add nothing more. I do not refuse you yet, but only tell you, wait. I tell you again I reserve a perfect right to refuse you if I think fit. There is another thing I must tell you, Pavel Alexandrovitch; if you have returned before the time fixed for my answer in order to work upon me in indirect ways, relying on outside support, on the influence of mamma, for instance, you have made a great mistake in your calculations. Then I shall refuse you straight out. Do you hear? And now—that's enough, and please, until the right time, do not utter one word more on this subject."

All this speech was pronounced dryly, firmly, and without hesitation, as though it had been studied beforehand. Monsieur Paul felt that he had been made a fool of. At that moment Marya Alexandrovna returned. And almost immediately after her Madame Zyablov.

"He will be down directly, I fancy, Zina! Nastasya Petrovna, be quick, make some fresh tea!" Marya Alexandrovna was positively a little excited.

"Anna Nikolaevna has already sent to inquire. Her Anyutka has come flying to the kitchen to ask questions. I bet she's cross now!" Nastasya Petrovna announced, rushing up to the samovar.

"What is that to me!" Marya Alexandrovna said over her shoulder to Madame Zyablov. "As though I were interested to know what your Anna Nikolaevna is thinking. You may be sure I shan't send anyone to her kitchen. And I wonder, I really wonder why you persist in regarding me as an enemy to poor Anna Nikolaevna, and not you only, but everybody in the town. I appeal to you, Pavel Alexandrovitch! You know us both. Come, what reason have I to be her enemy? Over precedence? But I don't care in the least about precedence. Let her be first, let her. I am ready to be the first to go and congratulate her on being first. And, after all, it's quite unfair. I will take her part—I am bound to take her part! She is maligned. Why do you all attack her? She is young and fond of fine clothes—is that a reason, pray? To my thinking fine clothes are better than something else—like Natalya Dmitryevna, who is fond—of what one really can't talk about. Is it because Anna Nikolaevna is always gadding about and can't

41

stay at home? But my goodness! She has had no education, and of course she finds it tedious to open a book or occupy herself with anything for two minutes together. She flirts and makes eyes out of window at anyone who passes in the street. But why do people assure her she is so pretty when she has nothing but a white face? She is ridiculous at dances, I admit. But why assure her she dances the polka so splendidly? She wears impossible hats and head-dresses; but is it her fault that God has given her no taste, but has made her so easily taken in? Assure her that it looks nice to pin a bit of coloured paper in her hair, and she would stick it in her hair. She is a scandal-monger—but that's the way here: there is no one in the town who does not talk scandal. Sushilov, with his whiskers, is always there, morning, noon, and almost night. But, dear me! No wonder, when her husband plays cards till five in the morning. Besides, there are so many bad examples here! Moreover, it *may be* only scandal. In short, I shall always stand up for her, always. But, good gracious, here is the prince! It is he, it is he! I should know him among a thousand! At last I see you, *mon prince!*" cried Marya Alexandrovna, and she flew to meet the prince as he entered.

CHAPTER IV

AT the first casual glance you would not have taken the prince for an old man at all, it was only on a closer and more attentive inspection that you discerned that he was a sort of corpse worked by mechanism. All the resources of art were utilised to disguise this mummy as a young man. A marvellous wig, whiskers, moustaches, and a little imperial, all of a superb black, covered half his face. His face was whitened and rouged with extraordinary skill, and there was not a trace of wrinkles upon it. What had become of them? There is no knowing. He was dressed in the height of fashion, as though he had stepped out of a fashion plate. He had on a visiting jacket or something of the sort, upon my word I don't know what exactly, but it was something extremely fashionable and up-to-date, created especially for morning calls. His gloves, his cravat, his waistcoat, his linen, and so on, were all of dazzling freshness and artistic taste. The prince limped a little, but limped so elegantly that it seemed as though it were prescribed by fashion. He had an eyeglass in his eye, the very eye that was itself of glass. The prince was saturated with scent. In talking he drawled certain words in a peculiar way, perhaps from the weakness of old age, perhaps because all his teeth were false, perhaps for the sake of greater dignity. Certain syllables he pronounced with extraordinary sweetness, with a special stress on certain vowels. *Yes* with him was turned into *ye-ess*. In all his manners there was a certain carelessness, acquired in the course of his life as a dandy. But if anything of his old fashionable life was still preserved, it was preserved as it were unconsciously in the form of some vague reminiscence, in the form of some outlived buried past, which, alas! no cosmetics, corsets, perfumers or barbers could bring to life again. And so we shall do well to begin by confessing that if the man had not lost his wits he had long ago lost his memory, and was now constantly muddled, repeating himself, and even babbling at random. One needed a special knack to talk to him. But Marya Alexandrovna could rely upon herself, and at the sight of the prince she flew into unutterable ecstasy.

"But you have not changed, not changed in the least!" she exclaimed, seizing her visitor by both hands and making him sit down in a comfortable arm-chair. "Sit down, prince, sit down! It's six years, six whole years since we have met, and not a single letter, not one line all that time! Oh, how badly you have treated me, prince! How angry I have been with you, *mon cher prince!* But—tea, tea! Oh, my goodness, Nastasya Petrovna, tea!"

"Thank you, tha-ank you, I am sor-ry," the prince lisped (we forgot to say that he lisped a little, but that, too, he did as though it were the fashion). "I am so-or-ry! And only fancy, last year I qui-ite meant to come here," he added, looking round the room through his lorgnette. "But they scared me: you had cho-le-ra here, I was told. . . ."

"No, prince, we haven't had cholera here," said Marya Alexandrovna.

"There was the cattle plague here, uncle!" Mozglyakov put in, anxious to distinguish himself. Mary Alexandrovna looked him up and down with a stern expression.

"To be sure, cattle pla-ague or something of the sort. . . . So I stayed at home. But how is your husband, my dear Anna Nikolaevna? Still at his pro-se-cuting duties?"

"N-no, prince," said Marya Alexandrovna, a little disconcerted; "my husband is not prosecutor . . ."

"I'll bet uncle has got mixed up and takes you for Anna Nikolaevna Antipov!" cried the sharp-witted Mozglyakov, but he pulled himself up at once, observing that Marya Alexandrovna seemed to be wincing apart from these explanations.

"Oh, yes, yes, Anna Nikolaevna, and . . . and . . . (I keep forgetting!) Oh, yes, Antipov, An-ti-pov it is," the prince acquiesced.

"N-no, prince, you are very much mistaken," said Marya Alexandrovna, with a bitter smile. "I am not Anna Nikolaevna, and I must say I didn't at all expect that you wouldn't know me. You have surprised me, prince. I am your old friend Marya Alexandrova Moskalev. Do you remember, prince, Marya Alexandrovna ? . . ."

"Marya A-lex-and-rovna, only fancy! And I actually supposed that you were (what's her name)—oh, yes, Anna Vassilyevna. . . . *C'est délicieux!* So I have come to the wrong place. And I thought, my dear fellow, that you were taking me to Anna Matveyevna. *C'est charmant!* It often happens like that with me, though. . . . I often go to the wrong place! I am satisfied, always satisfied, whatever happens. So you are not Nastasya Vassilyevna? That's interesting. . . ."

"Marya Alexandrovna, prince, Marya Alexandrovna! Oh, how badly you have treated me! To forget your best, best friend!"

"Oh, yes, my be-est friend . . . *pardon, pardon!*" the prince lisped, gazing at Zina.

"That is my daughter, Zina. You don't know her, prince, she was away when you were here last, in the year 18—, do you remember?"

"Is that your daughter? *Charmante, charmante!*" muttered the prince, eyeing Zina with avidity through his lorgnette. "*Mais quelle beauté!*" he murmured, evidently struck by her.

"Tea, prince," said Marya Alexandrovna, calling the prince's attention to the page standing before him with the tray in his hands. The prince took the cup and looked attentively at the boy, who had pink and chubby cheeks.

"A-ah, is this your boy?" he said. "What a pret-ty boy! A-and I am sure he behaves ni-icely. . . ."

"But, prince," Marya Alexandrovna interposed hurriedly, "I have heard of your terrible adventure! I must confess I was frightened out of my wits. . . . Weren't you hurt? Make sure! It is not a thing to neglect."

"He upset me! He upset me! The coachman upset me!" the prince exclaimed, with extraordinary animation. "I thought the end of the world was coming or something of the sort, and so I must own I was so frightened that—holy saints forgive me! —I didn't know whether I was on my head or my feet! I hadn't expected it, I hadn't expected it! I did not ex-pect it at all. And it's all the fault of my coachman, Fe-o-fil. I rely upon you now entirely, my dear fellow: do what is necessary and investigate the matter thoroughly. I am per-suaded that it was an at-tempt on my life."

"All right, uncle; all right," answered Pavel Alexandrovitch. "I will investigate it thoroughly. Only listen, uncle! Forgive him this once, won't you? What do you say?"

"I won't forgive him on any account. I am persuaded that he was trying to ta-ake my life. He, together with Lavrenty, whom I left at home. Only fancy, he has got hold of some new ideas, you know! There is a sort of scepticism in him . . . in short, he is a communist in the fullest sense of the word! I am positively afraid to meet him."

"Ah, what you say is so true, prince!" exclaimed Marya Alexandrovna. "You wouldn't believe what I suffer from these good-for-nothing servants myself! Imagine, I have two new servants, and I must say they are so stupid that I am simply struggling with them from morning till night. You wouldn't believe how stupid they are, prince!"

"Oh, yes; oh, yes. But I must say, I really prefer to have a footman rather stupid," observed the prince, who like all old men was delighted when people listened to his chatter with obsequious attention; "it somehow suits a footman, and really is a vir-tue in him if he is simple-hearted and stupid. Only in certain cases, of course. It makes him more im-pos-ing, it gives a solem-nity to his countenance; it gives him a greater air of good breeding, and what I insist on most is a servant's good bre-ed-ing. Here I have my Te-ren-ty. You remember my Te-ren-ty, my dear fellow, don't you? As soon as I looked at him I predicted that he was destined to be a hall-porter! Stupid—phe-nom-en-ally. He stares like a sheep looking at water. But what imposing dignity ! What solemnity! Such a pale pink double chin! You know, with a white cravat in full get-up, it does produce an effect. I took the greatest fancy to him. Sometimes I look at him and feel quite fascinated; he might be writing a dissertation—such a solemn air! In fact he is a regular German philosopher Kant, or perhaps more truly, a fat, overfed turkey-cock. Perfectly *comme il faut* for a man-servant."

Marya Alexandrovna laughed with enthusiasm, and even clapped her hands. Pavel Alexandrovitch seconded her with all his heart; he was extremely entertained by his "uncle". Nastasya Petrovna laughed too—even Zina gave a smile.

"But what humour, what gaiety, what wit you have, prince!" exclaimed Marya Alexandrovna. "What a precious gift for noting the most subtle, the most amusing point! . . . And to vanish from society, to shut yourself up for five whole years! With such a talent! But you might write, prince! You might be another Von Vizin, another Griboyedov, another Gogol! . . . ."

"Oh, yes; oh, yes!" said the prince, highly delighted; "I might, and do you know I used to be remarkably witty in old days. I actually wrote a vau-de-ville for the stage. There were several ex-qui-site lines in it! It was never acted, though. . . ."

"Ah, how charming it would be to read it, and, do you know, Zina, it would be *à propos* now! They are getting up theatricals here—for a patriotic object, prince—for the benefit of the wounded. . . . Your vaudeville would be the thing!"

"Of course! I am ready to write it again, indeed . . . though I have completely forgotten it. But I remember there were two or three puns, such that . . ." (and the prince kissed his finger-tips) "and altogether when I was abro-ad I made a re-gu-lar fu-rore. I remember Lord Byron. We were on friendly terms. He danced the Cracoviana enchantingly at the Vienna Congress."

"Lord Byron, uncle! Upon my word, uncle, what do you mean?"

"Oh, yes, Lord Byron. Though perhaps it wasn't Lord Byron, but someone else. Quite so; not Lord Byron, but a Pole, I remember perfectly now. And that Pole was ve-ry ori-gi-nal,

47

he gave himself out for a count, and it afterwards turned out that he was some sort of head cook, but he did dance the Cracoviana most en-chant-ing-ly, and at last he broke his leg. I wrote some verses on that occasion too:

> "Our dear little Pole
> To dance was his rôle."

And what came then, I can't remember.

> " 'When he broke his limb
> No more capers for him.' "

"Oh, that must be how it went, uncle," exclaimed Mozglyakov, entering more and more into the spirit of the thing.

"I think that is what it was, my dear fellow," answered the old man, "or something like it. But perhaps it wasn't it, but anyway, the verses turned out very successfully. . . . The fact is I've forgotten some things that have happened. It comes from being so busy."

"But tell us, prince, what have you been doing all this time in your solitude?" Marya Alexandrovna inquired with interest. "I have so often thought of you, *mon cher prince*, that I must confess I am burning now with impatience to have a full account of it all."

"What have I been doing? Well, altogether, you know, I have a great de-al to do. Sometimes—one rests; and sometimes, you know, I go for walks and imagine all sorts of things. . . ."

"You must have a very powerful imagination, uncle!"

"Extremely powerful, my dear boy. I sometimes imagine such things that I won-der at myself afterwards. When I was in Kaduev . . . *À propos!* I believe you used to be deputy governor at Kaduev?"

48

"I! uncle? Upon my soul, what do you mean?" exclaimed Pavel Alexandrovitch.

"Fancy, my dear fellow, and I have been taking you all the while for the deputy governor, and I was wondering to myself how is it that all of a sudden you had got quite a different face. . . . He had such a dig-ni-fied face—intelligent, you know. He was an exceptionally intelligent man, and he was always com-pos-ing verses, on all sorts of occasions. He was a bit like the king of diamonds in profile. . . ."

"No, prince," Marya Alexandrovna interposed, "I vow you will ruin yourself by living like that! To shut yourself up in solitude for five years, to see no one, to hear nothing! But you are a doomed man, prince. Ask anyone among those who are devoted to you, and everyone will tell you that you are a doomed man!"

"Really!" exclaimed the prince.

"I assure you it is so; I am speaking to you as a friend, as a sister. I am speaking to you because you are dear to me, because the memory of the past is sacred to me! What have I to gain by pretending? No, you must reform your life fundamentally, or you will fall sick, you will waste away, you will die. . . ."

"Oh, dear me! Am I really going to die so soon?" exclaimed the prince, panic-stricken. "And do you know, you have guessed right! I am frightfully troubled by hæmorrhoids, especially at certain times. . . . And when I have attacks of it I generally have the most re-mark-able symptoms (I will tell you all about them). . . . To begin with . . ."

"Uncle, you will tell about that another time," Pavel Alexandrovitch interposed, "but now . . . isn't it time for us to start?"

"Oh, yes! Another time if you like. Possibly it is not so very interesting to listen to now I come to think of it. . . . At the same time it is a very curious complaint. It has several stages. . . . Remind me, my dear boy, I will describe this evening in de-tail one thing that happened. . . ."

"But listen, prince, you ought to try a cure abroad," Marya Alexandrovna intervened again.

"Abroad? Oh, yes; oh, yes! I certainly shall go abroad. I remember when I was abroad in the 'twenties, it was won-der-fully gay. I almost got married to a French *vicomtesse*. I was tremendously in love with her at the time, and wanted to devote my life to her. I did not marry her, though; some-body else did. And such a strange thing happened, I was absent only two hours and the other man won the day, a German baron, he was; he was put into a madhouse for a time afterwards."

"But *cher prince*, what I meant was, that you must think seriously about your health. There are such doctors abroad . . . and besides, a change of life does so much! You really must abandon your Duhanovo, if only for a time."

"Ce-er-tain-ly! I have made up my mind to do so long ago, and, do you know, I mean to try hy-drop-athy."

"Hydropathy?"

"Hydropathy. I have tried hy-drop-athy once already. I was at the waters then. There was a Moscow lady there, I have forgotten her surname, only she was a very poetical lady, about seventy; she had a daughter, too, about fifty, a widow with cataract in her eye. She, too, almost talked in verse. After-wards she had a very unfortunate mishap: she killed one of her serf girls in a rage and was tried for it. And, do you know, they took it into their heads to make me try the water cure. I must say I had nothing the matter with me; but they kept in-sisting: 'Try the cure, try the cure!' Simply from delicacy I began to drink the waters; I thought I really should be better for it; I drank and drank and drank and drank. I drank up a perfect waterfall, and, do you know, hydropathy is really a very good thing and did me a very great deal of good, so that if I had not fallen ill, I assure you I should have been perfectly well. . . ."

"That is a very just conclusion, uncle. Tell me, uncle, have you studied logic?"

"Upon my word, what questions you ask," Marya Alexandrovna observed sternly, much scandalised.

"I did study it, my dear boy, but very long ago. I studied philosophy, too, in Germany. I went through a whole course, but even at the time I couldn't remember it. But . . . I must own . . . you have so frightened me about this illness that I feel quite upset. I'll come back directly though. . . ."

"But where are you going, prince?" cried Marya Alexandrovna in amazement.

"I will be back directly, directly . . . I simply want to note down a new idea. . . . *Au revoir* . . . ."

"What a specimen!" cried Pavel Alexandrovitch, and he went off into a fit of laughter.

Marya Alexandrovna lost patience.

"I don't understand, I don't understand in the least what you are laughing at," she began with heat. "To laugh at a venerable old man, at a relation, to take advantage of his angelic kindness and to turn every word he utters into ridicule! I blushed for you, Pavel Alexandrovitch! Tell me, please, what do you find absurd in him? I saw nothing to laugh at in him."

"When he does not know people, when he sometimes talks nonsense?"

"But that is the effect of the awful life he is leading, of his horrible imprisonment for the last five years under the eye of that fiendish woman. One ought to pity him and not to laugh at him. He did not even know me, you were a witness of that yourself. That was, so to speak, a flagrant example! He absolutely must be saved! I suggested to him to go abroad simply in the hope that he might get rid of that . . . market woman!"

51

"Do you know what? We ought to find him a wife, Marya Alexandrovna," cried Pavel Alexandrovitch.

"Again! You are incorrigible, Monsieur Mozglyakov!"

"No, Marya Alexandrovna, no! This time I am speaking seriously! Why shouldn't we marry him? It's an idea. *C'est une idée comme une autre.* What harm could it do him, kindly tell me that? On the contrary, he is in such a position that only such a step could save him! He is still legally able to marry. To begin with, he would be rescued from that trollop (excuse the expression). Secondly and chiefly—imagine that he picks out a girl or, better still a widow—sweet, kind, sensible, tender and, above all, poor, who will look after him like a daughter and realise that he has been a benefactor to her in giving her the title of his wife. And what could be better for him than a noble and upright creature who would belong to him and would be continually at his side, instead of that . . . female. Of course she ought to be pretty, for even to this day uncle loves a pretty face. Did you notice how he kept looking at Zinaida Afanas-yevna?"

"But where will you find such a bride?" asked Nastasya Petrovna, listening attentively.

"Ah, there it is: why, you, for instance, if you were willing! Allow me to ask: aren't you perfectly suitable as a match for the prince? In the first place you are pretty, secondly you are a widow, thirdly you are a lady, fourthly poor (for you really are not very well off), fifthly you are a very sensible woman and consequently will love him, keep him in cotton wool, send that person about her business, take him abroad, will feed him on semolina pudding and sweetmeats, all that up to the time when he leaves this transitory world, which will happen within a year and possibly within two or three months. Then you will be a princess, a wealthy widow, and as a reward for your pluck you can marry a *marquis* or a general! *C'est joli,* isn't it?"

"Why, my gracious! I believe I should fall in love with

him, poor dear gentleman, out of mere gratitude if only he made me an offer!" exclaimed Madame Zyablov, and her dark expressive eyes gleamed. "But that's—all nonsense."

"Nonsense? If you like, it needn't be nonsense! Ask me nicely and then you may cut off my finger if you are not engaged to him today! Why, there is nothing easier than to persuade or tempt uncle into anything! He always says, 'Oh, yes; oh, yes!' You have heard him yourself. We will marry him so that he will hardly notice it. We will deceive him and marry him, perhaps: why, it is for his benefit, mercy upon us! . . . You might dress up in your best to be ready for anything, Nastasya Petrovna."

Monsieur Mozglyakov's enthusiasm knew no bounds. Sensible though she might be, Madame Zyablov's mouth watered.

"I know I look a perfect slut today without you telling me," she replied. "I have grown shockingly careless, I have no ambition. That's how it is I go about such a grub. Why, do I really look like a cook?"

All this time Marya Alexandrovna was sitting with a strange look on her face. I am not mistaken if I say that she heard Pavel Alexandrovitch's strange proposition with a sort of dismay, as though disconcerted by it. . . .

At last she recovered herself.

"All this is very nice, no doubt, but it is all nonsense and absurdity, and what is more—quite out of place," she interruped Mozglyakov sharply.

"But why, my dear Marya Alexandrovna, why is it nonsense and out of place?"

"For many reasons, and first of all because you are in my house and the prince is my guest, and I allow no one to show a lack of respect for my house. I look upon your words as nothing but a jest, Pavel Alexandrovitch. But, thank goodness, here is the prince!"

"Here I am," cried the prince, walking into the room. "It's

wonderful, *cher ami*, how many different ideas I've had today. And at other times, perhaps you wouldn't believe it, I seem to have none at all. Nothing all day."

"That's probably from your tumble today, uncle. It has upset your nerves, and that is how it is . . ."

"I put it down to that myself, my dear fellow, and think that the accident has been really ben-i-fi-cial. So that I have made up my mind to forgive my Feo-fil. Do you know what, I believe he was not trying to take my life after all, what do you think? Besides, he has been punished only lately by having his beard shaved off."

"His beard shaved off, uncle! Why, he has a beard as big as the German Empire."

"Oh, yes, as big as the German Empire. You are generally very correct in your con-clu-sions, my dear boy. But it is a false one. And only fancy how it happened; I was sent a price list. The superbest beards for coachmen and gentlemen newly imported from abroad, also whiskers, imperials, moustaches, and so on, and all of the best qual-i-ty and at the most moderate prices. I thought I would send for a beard just to see what it was like. So I wrote for a coachman's beard, it really was a beard worth seeing! But it turned out that Feofil had a beard of his own almost twice as big. Of course we were puzzled what to do: to shave his off, or to send back the one they had sent us and let him wear his natural one? I thought and thought about it, and came to the conclusion that it was better for him to have the artificial one."

"Probably because art is better than nature, uncle!"

"That was just it. And what distress it caused him when his beard was shaved off! As though he had parted with his whole career together with his beard. But isn't it time for us to start, my dear boy?"

"I am ready, uncle."

"But I hope, prince, that you are only going to the

Governor's," Marya Alexandrovna exclaimed in excitement. "You are mine now, prince, and belong to my family for the whole day. I am not going to tell you anything about the society here, of course. Perhaps you want to go to Anna Niko- laevna's, and I have not the right to disillusion you; besides, I am fully persuaded that time will tell its own story. But re- member that I am your hostess, sister, nurse for the whole of today, and I must own that I tremble for you, prince! You don't know these people, you don't know them."

"Rely on me, Marya Alexandrovna. Everything shall be as I promised you," said Mozglyakov.

"Oh, you feather-head! Rely on you! I expect you to dinner, prince. We dine early. And how I regret that on this occasion my husband is in the country. How delighted he would have been to see you. He has such a respect for you, he has such a genuine affection for you."

"Your husband? So you have a husband, too?" the prince queried.

"Oh, my goodness, how forgetful you are, prince! Why, you have utterly, utterly forgotten all the past! My husband, Afanasy Matveyitch, surely you have not forgotten him? He is in the country now, but you have seen him a thousand times in old days. Do you remember, prince, Afanasy Matveyitch?"

"Afanasy Matveyitch! In the country, only fancy! *Mais c'est délicieux!* So you have a husband too? What a strange thing, though? That's exactly like some vaudeville: 'The hus- band's on the stair, but the wife has gone to . . .' Excuse me, I have forgotten! Only the wife had gone off somewhere also, to Tula or to Yaroslav, anyway it's very funny."

" 'The husband is on the stair, but the wife has gone to Tver,' uncle, "Mozglyakov prompted him.

"Oh, yes! Oh, yes! Thank you, my dear boy, Tver it was. *Charmant, charmant.* So that it rhymes also. You always drop into rhyme, my dear boy. I didn't remember whether it

55

was to Yaroslav or to Kostroma, but only that his wife had gone off somewhere too. *Charmant, charmant!* I have a little forgotten what I was beginning to speak about, though. . . . Ah, yes, so we are starting, my dear fellow. *Au revoir, Madame. Adieu, ma charmante demoiselle,*" added the prince, turning to Zina and kissing his finger-tips.

"To dinner, to dinner, prince! Don't forget to make haste back," Marya Alexandrovna called after him.

CHAPTER V

"YOU might just glance into the kitchen, Nastasya Petrovna," she said, after seeing the prince out. "I have a presentiment that that monster Nikita will be sure to spoil the dinner! I am convinced that he is drunk by now. . . ."

Nastasya Petrovna obeyed. As she went out she looked suspiciously at Marya Alexandrovna and observed in her signs of exceptional agitation. Instead of going to look after the monster Nikita, Nastasya Petrovna went into the bigger drawing-room, from there through the corridor to her own room, from there into a little dark apartment, something like a lumber-room, where there were trunks standing, garments of some sort hanging, and the dirty linen of the whole family stored in bags. She went on tiptoe to the closed door, held her breath, stooped down, looked through the keyhole and listened. This door was one of the three doors of the very room in which Marya Alexandrovna and Zina had remained, and was always kept shut and locked.

Marya Alexandrovna considered Nastasya Petrovna a sly but exceedingly frivolous woman. No doubt the idea did at times occur to her that Nastasya Petrovna had no scruples and was given to eavesdropping. But at the present moment Marya Alexandrovna was so much engrossed and excited that she quite forgot to take certain precautions. She sat down in an easy chair and looked significantly at Zina. Zina was conscious of that gaze fixed upon her, and a feeling of uneasy depression began to weigh upon her heart.

"Zina!"

Zina slowly turned her pale face towards her, and lifted her dreamy black eyes.

"Zina, I intend to speak to you about an extremely important matter."

Zina turned completely round to her mother, folded her hands, and stood waiting. There was a look in her face of vexation and sarcasm, which she tried, however, to conceal.

"I want to ask you, Zina, what you thought today of *that* Mozglyakov?"

"You have known what I think of him for ever so long," answered Zina reluctantly.

"Yes, *mon enfant;* but it seems to me that he is becoming too persistent with his . . . attentions."

"He says he is in love with me, and his persistency is excusable."

"Strange; you used not to be so . . . ready to excuse him. On the contrary, you invariably attacked him whenever I spoke of him."

"It is strange, too, that you always defended him and were so set on my marrying him, and now you attack him."

"That is almost so. I don't deny it, Zina; I did desire to see you married to Mozglyakov. It was painful for me to see your continual depression, your unhappiness, which I am quite capable of understanding (whatever you may think of me) and which poisons my sleep at night. I felt sure at last that nothing but a complete change of life could save you! And that change must be—marriage. We are not well off and cannot, for instance, go abroad. The asses here are surprised that you are three-and-twenty and not yet married, and concoct a regular

57

legend to explain it. But is it likely I should make a match for you with a local councillor, or with Ivan Ivanitch, our attorney here? Is there a husband here for you? Mozglyakov is empty-headed, of course, but he is the best of the lot. He is of a decent family, he has connections, he has a hundred and fifty serfs; that is better anyway than living by tricks and bribes, and God knows what shifts, that's why I turned my eyes upon him. But I swear I never had a real liking for him. I am persuaded that it was the hand of the Almighty that forewarned me. And if God were to send you even now something better—oh! what a good thing it will be that you have not pledged your word! You have not said anything positive to him today, have you, Zina?"

"Why all this pretence, mamma, when the whole thing could be said in two words?" Zina brought out irritably.

"Pretence, Zina, pretence! And you can use a word like that to your mother? But what am I saying? For a long while past you have put no faith in your mother! For a long while past you have looked on me as your enemy and not your mother."

"Oh, do leave off, mamma! Surely you and I need not dispute about words! Don't we understand each other? I should have thought it was high time we did."

"You wound me, my child! You do not believe that I am ready to do absolutely anything, anything, anything to secure your future."

Zina looked at her mother sarcastically and with annoyance.

"You don't want to marry me to that prince to *secure* my future, do you?" she asked, with a queer smile.

"I have not said a word of that, but since you have mentioned it, I will say that if it were your lot to marry the prince, it would be a great happiness for you and not at all senseless."

"And I consider that's simply nonsense!" cried Zina passionately. "Nonsense, nonsense! I also think, mamma, that you have too much romantic inspiration, you are a poetess, in the fullest sense of the word; that's what they call you here. You are continually having projects. Their impossibility and absurdity do not deter you. I had a foreboding while the prince was sitting here that you had this in your mind. When Mozglyakov began playing the fool and declaring that we ought to find a wife for the old man, I read all you were thinking in your face. I am ready to bet that you are thinking of that, and that is what you are leading up to with me. But as your incessant scheming on my behalf is beginning to bore me to death, is beginning to torture me, I beg you not to say one word about it to me; do you hear, mamma? not one word, and I should be glad if you would remember that!" She was breathless with anger.

"You are a child, Zina, a sick, irritable child," answered Marya Alexandrovna in a tearful voice full of emotion. "You speak disrespectfully to me and hurt my feelings. No mother would put up with what I endure from you every day! But you are nervous, you are ill, you are suffering, and I am a mother and, above all, a Christian. I must bear it and forgive. But one word, Zina: if I really were dreaming of that union— why do you look upon it as nonsense? To my mind Mozglyakov never spoke more sensibly than just now when he pointed out that it was essential for the prince to marry—of course not that slut Nastasya. He was talking wildly about that."

"Listen, mamma! Tell me straight out: are you questioning me like this out of curiosity, or with a motive?"

"I ask you only, why does it seem to you such nonsense?"

"Oh, how annoying! What a life!" exclaimed Zina, stamping with impatience. "I'll tell you why, if you still don't know: to say nothing of all the other absurdities—to take advantage of a wretched old man's having fallen into dotage, to deceive him, to marry him, a wreck, in order to get hold of his money

59

and then every day, every hour, to long for his death, to my mind is not simply nonsense, but so base, so base, that I can't congratulate you on such ideas, mamma!"

The silence lasted for a minute.

"Zina, do you remember what happened two years ago?" Marya Alexandrova asked suddenly.

Zina started.

"Mamma," she said in a severe voice, "you promised me solemnly never to speak of that again."

"And now I solemnly beg you, my child, to allow me only once to break that promise which I have never broken till now, Zina! The time has come for a full explanation between us. These two years of silence have been awful! It can't go on like this! . . . I am ready to beg you on my knees to let me speak. Listen, Zina, your own mother begs you on her knees! At the same time I give you my solemn promise—the promise of an unhappy mother who adores her daughter—that I will never under any circumstances whatever, even if it were a question of my life, I will never speak of it again. This shall be the last time, but now—it is essential!"

Marya Alexandrovna was calculating on her words having their full effect.

"Speak," said Zina, turning perceptibly pale.

"Thank you, Zina. Two years ago poor dear Mitya, your little brother, had a tutor . . ."

"But why do you begin in this solemn way, mamma! Why all this fine speaking, all these details, which are utterly unnecessary, which are painful, which are only too well known to both of us?" Zina cut her short with a kind of angry repulsion.

"Because, my child, I, your mother, am compelled to justify myself before you! Because I want to put it all before you from an absolutely different point of view, and not from the mistaken point of view from which you are in the habit of looking at it. In fact that you might understand better the conclusion I am

60

meaning to draw from all this. Do not imagine, my child, that I want to play with your feelings. No, Zina, you will find in me a true mother, and perhaps shedding tears at my feet, the feet of the *base woman* you have just called me, you will yourself implore the reconciliation you have so long, so haughtily rejected; that is why I wish to speak out the whole truth, Zina, the whole from the very beginning; otherwise I will be silent!"

"Speak," Zina repeated, cursing her mother's love of fine speeches from the bottom of her heart.

"I will continue, Zina: how this district school teacher, hardly more than a boy, made an impression upon you, I could never understand. I put too much confidence in your good sense, in your honourable pride, and above all, in his utter insignificance (for one must tell the whole truth), to suspect there could be anything between you. And all of a sudden you come to me and announce that you intend to marry him! Zina! It was a dagger in my heart! I uttered a shriek and fell into a swoon. But . . . you remember all that? I need not say, I thought it needful to use all my authority, which you call tyranny. Only think, a boy, the son of a sacristan hired for twelve roubles a month, a scribbler of wretched doggerel, published out of kindness in the 'Library of Good Reading,' a fellow who could talk of nothing but that cursed Shakespeare—that boy, your husband, the husband of Zinaida Moskalev! Why, it is worthy of Florian and his shepherdesses! Forgive me, Zina, but the mere remembrance moves me to frenzy! I refused him, but no authority could keep you in check. Your father could do nothing but blink his eyes, and did not even understand when I tried to explain to him. You maintained your relations with that boy, even had interviews with him, and most awful of all, you even ventured to correspond with him. Rumours were spreading all over the town. Our neighbours began stabbing me with hints: they were already in high glee, they were already blowing their trumpets, and suddenly all my predictions were fulfilled in the most flagrant way. You quarrelled over something; he showed himself utterly unworthy of you . . . the wretched boy (I cannot call him a man), and threatened to show your letters about the town. At that threat, full of indignation, you were wild with anger and gave him a slap in the face. Yes, Zina, that circumstance, too, is known to me! I know all about it, all. That very day the miserable boy showed one of your letters to that scoundrel Zaushin, and within an hour that letter was already in the hands of Natalya Dmitryevna, my deadly enemy. The same evening that madman, overcome with remorse, made an absurd attempt to poison himself. In a word, there was a most appalling scandal! That slut Nastasya ran to me in alarm with the terrible intelligence: the letter had been for a full hour in Natalya Dmitryevna's hands; within two hours the whole town would know of your disgrace! I controlled myself, I did not swoon—but with what blows you struck at my heart, Zina! That shameless hussy, that monster, Nastasya, demanded two hundred roubles, and for that sum swore to get that letter back. I myself ran through the snow in my thin slippers to the Jew Bumstein and pawned my jewel-case—a keepsake from my sainted mother! Within two hours the letter was in my hands: Nastasya had stolen it. She broke open a box and your reputation was saved—there was nothing to prove the story! But in what anxiety you made me pass that awful day! The next day I noticed, for the first time in my life, some grey hairs in my head, Zina! You have formed your own judgment now of that boy's conduct. You will agree now yourself, and perhaps with a bitter smile, that it would have been the acme of folly to entrust your future to his keeping. But from that time you have been fretting, you have been tormenting yourself, my child; you cannot forget him, or rather not him, he was always unworthy of you, but the phantom of your past happiness. That unhappy youth is lying on his death-bed now,

I am told he is in consumption, and you—angel of goodness!—you will not marry during his lifetime that you may not lacerate his feelings; for to this day he is tortured by jealousy, though I am persuaded that he never loved you with true exalted love! I know that when he heard of Mozglyakov's attentions, he spied on you, sent to find out, made inquiries. You are sparing him, my child; I have guessed your secret and God knows with what bitter tears I have wetted my pillow!"

"Oh, do drop all that, mamma!" Zina interrupted in unspeakable misery. "I think you might have left your pillow out," she she added bitingly. "You can't speak without all this declamation and flourish!"

"You do not believe me, Zina! Do not look upon me with antagonism, my child! My eyes have not been dry for these two years, but I hid my tears from you, and I swear that I, too, have greatly changed during that time! I have long understood your feelings and, I regret to say, that it is only now that I have realised all the depth of your grief. Can you blame me, my dear, for looking on this attachment as a romantic folly inspired by that cursed Shakespeare who will poke his nose where he is not wanted. What mother will blame me for my terror, for the steps I took, for the sternness of my decision? But now, now after seeing your suffering for these two years, I understand and appreciate your feelings. Believe me that I understand you, perhaps far better than you understand yourself. I am persuaded you love not him, that unnatural boy, but your golden dreams, your lost happiness, your exalted ideals. I, too, have loved, and perhaps more ardently than you. I have suffered myself; I, too, have had my exalted ideals. And so who can blame me now; and above all, can you blame me for regarding a match with the prince as the thing best fitted to save you, most essential for you in your present position?"

Zina had been listening with wonder to this long tirade,

knowing perfectly well that her mother would not take up this tone without some object. But the unexpected conclusion in her mother's last words utterly amazed her.

"Can you really propose to marry me to that prince?" she cried, looking at her mother in astonishment and almost alarm. "Then it is not a mere dream, not a project, but your firm intention. So I guessed right? And . . . and . . . and in what way will such a marriage save me and be essential in my position? And . . . and . . . and in what way is all this worked in with what you have been saying just now—with all this story?. . . I really don't understand you, mamma!"

"And I wonder how anyone can fail to understand, *mon ange!*" exclaimed Marya Alexandrovna, growing excited in her turn. "In the first place the mere fact that you will move into a different society, a different world! You will leave for ever this detestable little town, full of terrible memories for you; where you have no friend, no welcome; where you have been slandered; where all these magpies hate you for your beauty. You may even go abroad this spring to Italy, to Switzerland, to Spain; to Spain, Zina, to Spain, where there is the Alhambra and the Guadalquivir, not this wretched, miserable river here with its unseemly name. . . ."

"But excuse me, mamma, you are talking as if I were already married, or at least as though the prince had made me an offer."

"Don't trouble about that, my angel; I know what I am talking about. But—allow me to proceed. I have already mentioned the *first* point, now for the *second:* I understand, my child, with what repugnance you would give your hand to that Mozglyakov."

"I know without your telling me that I never shall be his wife!" Zina answered with heat, and her eyes flashed.

"And if you knew how well I understand your repugnance, my dear! It is an awful thing to swear before the altar of God to love one for whom you can feel no love! It is awful to

64

belong to one whom you cannot even respect! And he will have your love; it is for that he will marry you. I can tell that by the look in his eyes when you turn away from him. How awful to keep up the pretence! I have endured that trial for twenty-five years. Your father has wrecked my life. He has, so to speak, sapped my youth, and how often you have seen my tears!"

"Papa is in the country, please let him alone," answered Zina.

"I know you always take his part. Ah, Zina! My heart ached, when from motives of prudence I desired your marriage with Mozglyakov. But there would be no need to dissemble with the prince. Of course I need not say that you cannot care for him . . . with love, and indeed he is not capable of requiring such love. . . ."

"My goodness, what nonsense! But I assure you that you are mistaken from the very beginning upon the most essential point. Let me tell you that I don't want to sacrifice myself for no reason that I know of. Let me tell you that I don't want to be married to anybody, and that I shall remain single. For the last two years you have been nagging at me for not getting married. Well, you will have to make up your mind to accept it. I don't want to, and that is all! And so it shall be."

"But, Zinotchka darling, for goodness' sake don't fly into a passion before you have heard what I have to say! What a hot-headed child you are, to be sure. Allow me to look at it from my point of view, and you will agree with me at once. The prince will live for a year or two at the utmost, and to my mind it is better to be a young widow than an old maid, to say nothing of your being at his death a princess, free, wealthy, and independent! My dear, you may look with contempt on these calculations—calculations on his death! But I am a mother, and what mother would condemn me for my far-sightedness? Finally, if like an angel of goodness you still feel compassion

65

for that boy, such compassion that you are unwilling to be married so long as he lives (as I conjecture is the case), reflect that you will give him fresh courage and relieve his mind by marrying the prince! If he has a spark of common sense, he will understand, of course, that jealousy of the prince would be misplaced, absurd; he will understand that you have married from motives of prudence, from necessity. He will understand, indeed, that is—I merely mean to say, you can marry anyone you like when the prince is dead."

"To put it plainly, it comes to this: marry the prince, plunder him, reckoning on his death to marry a lover afterwards. You balance your accounts cleverly. You try to tempt me, offering me. . . . I understand you, mamma, I quite understand you! You can never resist a display of noble sentiments, even in the nastiest action. You had better have said simply and straightforwardly: 'Zina, it is base, but it is profitable, and so consent to do it!' that would be more candid, anyway."

"But why, my child, persist in looking at it from that point of view—from the point of view of deception, artfulness, self-interest? You regard my calculation as base, deceitful. But by all that is holy, what deceit is there about it, where is the baseness? Look at yourself in the glass; you are so lovely that one might give up a kingdom for your sake! And you, you a beauty, sacrifice your best years to an old man! Like a lovely star you will shed light on his declining hours; you, like the green ivy, will twine about his age; you, and not that nettle, that abominable woman, who has cast a spell on him, and from greed is sapping his existence. Do you think that his money, his princely rank, is more precious than you? Where is the deceit, where is the baseness in that? You don't know what you are saying, Zina!"

"They evidently are more precious, since I have to marry a decrepit wreck. Deceit is always deceit, mamma, whatever the object may be."

"On the contrary, my dear, on the contrary! You may look at it from a lofty, indeed from a Christian point of view, my child! You said yourself on one occasion, in a moment of frenzy, that you would like to be a sister of mercy. Your heart had suffered, had grown hard. You said (I know this) that it could not love now. If you do not believe in love, turn your feelings to another loftier subject, turn it genuinely, like a child with all faith and reverence—and God will bless you. This old man has suffered too, he is unhappy, he is persecuted; I have known him for some years and have always cherished for him an incomprehensible sympathy, akin to love, as though I had a presentiment. Be his friend, be his daughter, be perhaps even his plaything—if one is to speak plainly. But warm his heart, and you will be doing an act godly and virtuous! He is ridiculous—don't think of that. He is half a man—have compassion on him; you are a Christian! Master yourself; such deeds are done by self-mastery. To our minds it is hard to bandage wounds in a hospital; it is revolting to breathe the infected air of the sickroom. But there are angels of mercy who do that and thank God for their vocation. Here is balm for your wounded heart, occupation, self-sacrifice—and you will heal your own wounds. Where is the egotism in it, where is the baseness? But you don't believe me. You imagine, perhaps, that I am dissimulating when I talk of duty, of self-sacrifice. You can't conceive that I, a frivolous, worldly woman, can have a heart, feelings, principles. Well, refuse to believe, insult your mother, but admit that what she says is reasonable and helpful. Imagine that it is not I who am speaking but someone else; shut your eyes, turn round to the corner, imagine that some unseen voice is speaking to you. . . . What troubles you most is that it is all for the sake of money, as though it were some sale or purchase. Well, renounce the money if money is so hateful to you. Keep only what is barely necessary for yourself, and give away the rest to the poor. Help

67

him, for instance, that luckless boy lying now on his death-bed."

"He will take no help," Zina said softly, as though to herself.

"He will not take it, but his mother will take it," Marya Alexandrovna answered triumphantly. "She will take it without his knowing. You sold your earrings, your aunt's present, and helped her six months ago; I know that. I know the old woman takes in washing to keep her unhappy son."

"He will soon have no need of help."

"I know what you are hinting at, too," Marya Alexandrovna caught her up; and an inspiration, a genuine inspiration, dawned upon her. "I know what you are alluding to. They say he is in consumption and will not live long. But who says that? The other day I purposely questioned Kalist Stanislavitch; I was anxious about him, because I have a heart, Zina. Kalist Stanislavitch answered me, that the illness was, of course, serious, but that he was convinced that, so far, the poor boy was not in consumption, but that it was only a rather severe affection of the chest. Question him yourself. He told me, as a fact, that under different circumstances, especially with a change of climate and surroundings, the patient might recover. He told me that in Spain—and I had heard it before and even read it—that in Spain there is some extraordinary island, I believe it is called Malaga—like some wine, in fact—where not only persons with weak lungs, but even consumptives recover simply from the climate, and that people go there on purpose to be treated, people of rank and consequence, of course; or commercial people too, if only they are rich. But the magical Alhambra, the myrtles, the lemons, the Spaniards on their mules! That alone would make an extraordinary impression on a poetical nature. You think he will not take your help, your money for the journey? Well, deceive him, then, if you are sorry for him! Deception is pardonable when it is to save a man's life. Give him hope, even promise him your love; tell him you will marry him when you are left a widow. Anything in the world can be said in an honourable way. Your mother will not teach you anything dishonourable, Zina; you will do this to save his life, so anything is permissible! You will restore him to life through hope; he will begin to take trouble over his health, to try and cure himself, to obey the doctors. He will try to regain his health for the sake of happiness. If he recovers, even though you do not marry him, anyway he will be well again, and anyway you will have saved him, you will have brought him back to life. And indeed one may even look at him with sympathy; perhaps fate has taught him a lesson and changed him for the better, and if only he is worthy of you—marry him, if you like, when you are left a widow. You will be wealthy and independent. If you restore him to health, you can give him a position in the world—a career. Your marriage will be more excusable then than now, when it is out of the question. What would be in store for you both if you were to venture on such madness now? Universal contempt, beggary, the task of pulling the nasty urchins' ears, for that is part of his duties, the reading of Shakespeare together, staying on for ever in Mordasov; and lastly, his speedy and inevitable death. While if you restore him to health you will be restoring him for a useful, virtuous life; if you forgive him, you will make him adore you. He is fretting over his abominable action, and opening a new life to him, forgiving him, you will give him hope and reconcile him to himself. He may enter the service, may rise to a good grade; and indeed, even if he does not recover, he will die happy, at peace with himself, in your arms—for you will be able to be with him at that moment —trusting in your love, forgiven by you, in the shade of the myrtles and lemons, under the azure exotic sky! Oh, Zina! all that is in your power! There is every advantage for you in it—and all that through marriage with the prince."

Marya Alexandrovna had finished. Rather a prolonged silence followed. Zina's agitation was inexpressible.

We will not undertake to describe Zina's feelings; we cannot even conjecture them. But it seemed that Marya Alexandrovna had found the way to her heart. Not knowing what was the present state of her daughter's feelings, she had gone over every mood in which she might possibly be, and guessed that she had at last hit on the true path. She coarsely touched upon the sorest spot in Zina's heart. And, from old habit, she could not refrain from the exhibition of noble sentiments, which of course did not hoodwink Zina. "What does it matter if she does not believe me," thought Marya Alexandrovna. "If only I have made her think things over! If only I have clearly hinted at what I could not say outright!" So she argued, and she attained her object. The effect was produced. Zina listened greedily. Her cheeks glowed, her bosom heaved.

"Listen, mamma," she said resolutely at last, though the sudden pallor of her face betrayed what that resolution cost her. "Listen, mamma."

But at that moment a sudden noise in the entrance hall, and a harsh, shrill voice asking for Marya Alexandrovna, made Zina pause. Marya Alexandrovna jumped from her seat.

"Oh, my goodness!" she cried, "the devil has sent that magpie, the colonel's wife; why, I all but turned her out of the house a fortnight ago!" she added, almost in despair. "But . . . . but it is impossible not to receive her now! Impossible! She most likely has news, or she would not have dared to come. It is important, Zina! I must know. . . . We must neglect nothing now!—Oh, how grateful I am for your visit!" she cried, hastening to meet her guest. "How did you come to think of me, my precious Sofya Petrovna? What an en-chanting surprise."

Zina ran out of the room.

CHAPTER VI

THE colonel's wife, Sofya Petrovna Karpuhin, had only a moral resemblance to a magpie. Physically she was more like a sparrow. She was a little lady, about fifty, with sharp little eyes, with freckles and yellow patches all over her face. On her little dried-up body, perched on strong, thin, sparrow-like little legs, was a dark silk dress which was always rustling, for the colonel's lady could not keep still for two seconds. She was a spiteful and malignant gossip. She was mad on the fact of being a colonel's wife. She very often fought with her husband, the retired colonel, and used to scratch his face. Moreover she used to drink four glasses of vodka in the morning, and as many in the evening, and had an insane hatred for Anna Nikolaevna Antipov, who had turned her out of her house the week before, as well as for Natalya Dmitryevna Paskudin, who had assisted in the operation.

"I have only looked in for a minute, *mon ange*," she twittered. "I really ought not to have sat down. I have only come to tell you what marvellous things are going on among us. The whole town has gone off its head about that prince! Our wily ones—*vous comprenez*—are chasing him, hunting him down snatching him from one another, regaling him with champagne —you wouldn't believe it! You wouldn't believe it! How could you bring yourself to let him go? Do you know that he is at Natalya Dmitryevna's now?"

"At Natalya Dmitryevna's!" cried Marya Alexandrovna, jumping up from her seat. "Why, he was only going to see the Governor, and afterwards, perhaps, to Anna Nikolaevna's, and was not going to stay long even there!"

"Not for long, I dare say; catch him now if you can! He did not find the Governor at home, then he went to Anna Nikolaevna's, promised to dine with her, and Natalya Dmi-

71

tryevna, who is always with her nowadays, has carried him off to her house for lunch. There's your prince!"

"And what . . . about Mozglyakov? Why, he promised . . ."

"Yes, your Mozglyakov, indeed! You think a lot of him, don't you? . . . Why, he has gone with him. You see if they don't get up a game of cards there, and he loses all his money as he did last year! Yes, and they'll make the prince take a hand too, and strip him like bark. And the things she is spreading about, that Natalya! She is crying aloud that you are trying to ensnare the prince, you know, with certain objects —*vous comprenez?* She is talking to him about it. Of course he doesn't understand; he sits like a wet cat and says, 'Oh, yes! oh, yes!' at every word. And she, she brought out her Sonka— only fancy! fifteen, and she still keeps her in short skirts, only down to the knee, so you can imagine. . . . They sent for that little orphan Mashka; she is in short skirts too, only above the knee—I looked through my lorgnette . . . they put some sort of red caps with feathers on their heads—I really don't know what it was meant for! And they made the two little magpies dance the Cossack dance to the piano before the prince! Well, you know his weakness; he was melting with ecstasy. 'Contours! contours!' He looked at them through his lorgnette, and they did distinguish themselves, the magpies! They got red in the face, they twirled their legs, and it was such an exhibition that I was shocked, and that was all about it. Tfoo! Call that a dance! I've danced myself, the shawl dance, at the breaking-up party at Madame Jarnis's select boarding school —and it really was a distinguished performance. I was applauded by senators! The daughters of princes and counts were educated there! But this was simply a *cancan!* I grew hot with shame, I grew hot, hot! I simply could not sit it out! . . ."

"But . . . surely you have not been at Natalya Dmitryevna's yourself? Why, you . . ."

"Why, yes, she did insult me last week. I say that straight out to everyone. *Mais, ma chère*, I wanted to have a peep at that prince, if it was only through a crack in the door. I did go. For where else could I have seen him? I shouldn't have been to see her, if it hadn't been for that horrid old prince! Only fancy, chocolate was handed round to everyone, but not offered to me, and they did not say a word to me all the time. She did that on purpose, you know. The tub of a woman, I'll pay her out! But good-bye, *mon ange*. I am in a hurry now, a great hurry . . . I must find Akulina Panfilovna, and tell her . . . . only you may as well say good-bye to the prince now, he won't come back to you. You know he has no memory, so Anna Nikolaevna will certainly carry him off! They are all afraid that you . . . do you understand? on Zina's account."

"Quelle horreur!"

"I assure you the whole town is talking of it! Anna Niko-laevna is set on keeping him to dinner, and then to stay al-together. She is doing that to spite you, *mon ange*. I peeped into the servants' quarters; such a bustle going on there: they are preparing the dinner, such a clatter of knives. . . . They have sent for champagne. Make haste, make haste, and catch him on the road when he is on his way to her. Why, he promised to dine with you first! He is your visitor, and not hers! To think of her having the laugh of you, the sly jade, the marplot, the filthy slut! Why, she is not worth the sole of my shoe, though she is the prosecutor's wife! I am a colonel's wife myself! I was brought up at Madame Jarnis's select establishment . . . Tfoo! *Mais adieu, mon ange!* I have my own sledge waiting, or I would have gone with you. . . ."

The walking newspaper vanished. Marya Alexandrovna was all of a tremble with excitement, but her visitor's advice was extremely clear and practical. There was no reason to delay, and indeed no time to be lost. But the chief difficulty still remained. Marya Alexandrovna flew to Zina's room.

Zina, pale and troubled, was walking up and down the room, with her arms crossed and her head bowed. There were tears in her eyes, but there was a gleam of determination in the look she cast upon her mother. She made haste to hide her tears, and a sarcastic smile came on to her lips.

"Mamma," she said, before her mother could speak, "you wasted a great deal of your eloquence on me just now, far too much. But you did not blind me—I am not a child. To persuade myself that I am sacrificing myself like a sister of mercy though I have no vocation for such a life, to justify the base deeds one commits from simple egoism, with the pretence of honourable motives—all that is casuistry which cannot deceive me. Do you hear? That could not deceive me, and I want you to know that!"

"But, *mon ange*," cried Marya Alexandrovna, crestfallen.

"Do not speak, mamma. Have the patience to hear me to the end. Though I fully recognise that it is jesuitical casuistry, though I fully realise the utter baseness of such a proceeding, I fully accept your proposition—do you hear?—*fully;* and I tell you I am ready to marry the prince, and even ready to second all your efforts to induce him to marry me. With what object I do so there is no need for you to know. It is enough that I have made up my mind. I have made up my mind to everything: I will put on his boots for him; I will be his servant; I will dance to please him, to make up for my baseness to him; I will do anything in the world that he may not regret having married me! But in return for my decision, I insist that you tell me openly by what means you are going to arrange it all. Since you have begun speaking so insistently about it, you could not—I know you—have done so without having some definite plan in your head. Be open for once in your life at least. Openness is the indispensable condition! I cannot decide without knowing exactly how you intend to do it all."

Mary Alexandrovna was so much taken aback by Zina's

unexpected conclusion that for some time she stood facing her, dumb and motionless with amazement, and stared at her open-eyed. She had prepared herself to combat the obstinate romanticism of her daughter, of whose severe rectitude she stood in constant dread, and now she suddenly heard that her daughter agreed with her, and was ready to do anything, even in opposition to her principles! The whole affair was, in consequence, immensely simplified; and there was a gleam of joy in her eyes.

"Zinotchka!" she cried enthusiastically. "Zinotchka, you are my own flesh and blood!"

She could say no more, but flew to embrace her daughter.

"Oh, my goodness! I did not ask for your endearments, mamma," cried Zina, with impatient repulsion. "I don't want your raptures! I ask you for an answer to my question, and nothing more."

"But, Zina, I love you! I adore you, and you repulse me. . . . You know I am doing my best for your happiness. . . ."

And unfeigned tears glistened in her eyes. Marya Alexandrovna really did love Zina in *her own way*, and on this occasion, in her success and her excitement, she was brimming over with sentimental emotion; in spite of a certain narrowness in her outlook, Zina understood that her mother loved her and—that love was burdensome to her. She would have been more at ease, indeed, if her mother had hated her. . . .

"Well, don't be angry, mamma; I am so agitated," she said, to soothe her.

"I am not angry, I am not angry, my angel," Marya Alexandrovna twittered, reviving instantly. "Of course I know that you are agitated. Well, my dear, you insist on openness . . . certainly I will be open, entirely open, I assure you! If only you would trust me! And to begin with, I must tell you that I have not yet a definite plan—that is, in full detail, Zinotchka; and indeed I could not have; a clever girl like you will see why. I foresee some obstacles, in fact. . . . That magpie just

75

now babbled all sorts of nonsense . . . (oh, my goodness, I must make haste). You see, I am entirely open! But I swear I will attain my object," she added, with enthusiasm. "My confidence is not romancing, as you called it just now, my angel; it rests on a basis of reality. It is founded on the absolute feeble-mindedness of the prince, that is the canvas on which I can embroider what I like. The great thing is that they should not prevent me! As though those fools could outwit me!" she cried, bringing her hand down on the table, with a gleam in her eye. "That is my affair! And what is most necessary is to begin as quickly as we can, so as to settle what is most important today, if only it is possible."

"Very good, mamma; only listen to one more . . . piece of openness: do you know why I am so interested to know your plan and have no faith in it? Because I cannot rely upon myself. I have said already that I have made up my mind to this base action; but if the details of your plan are really too revolting, too dirty, I warn you that I shan't be able to endure it, and I shall fling it all up. I know that that is only an added baseness: to resolve upon vileness, and to be afraid of the filth in which it is swimming; but there is no help for it. It will inevitably be so! . . ."

"But, Zinotchka, what is there particularly vile in it, *mon ange*?" Marya Alexandrovna was protesting timidly. "It is nothing but making an advantageous marriage, and everybody does that, you know! You have only to look at it from that point of view, and it all seems perfectly honourable. . . ."

"Ah, mamma, for God's sake, don't try to deceive me! You see, I agree to anything, anything! What more do you want? Please don't be alarmed if I call things by their names. That is perhaps my only comfort now."

And a bitter smile came upon her lips.

"Well, well! that's all right, my angel; we can differ in our opinions and yet mutually respect each other. Only if you are

76

anxious about the details and are afraid they will be nasty, leave all that business to me; I assure you that not a speck of dirt shall fall on you. Should I be willing to compromise you in people's eyes? Only rely on me and everything shall be settled capitally with the utmost decorum, above all, with the utmost decorum! There shall not be the slightest scandal, and if there should be the tiniest, unavoidable, little bit of scandal—well, what of it? Why, we shall be far away then! We shan't stay here, you know! They can talk as much as they like, we can despise them! They will be envious. And they are not worth worrying about! I wonder at you, Zinotchka—but don't be angry with me—how can you, with your pride, be afraid of them?"

"Oh, mamma, I am not in the least afraid of them! You don't understand me a bit," Zina answered irritably.

"Well, well, my love, don't be angry. All I mean is that they are contriving some nasty plots every day of their lives, and here, just for once in your life . . . But how silly I am! What am I saying? It is not nasty at all! What is there nasty about it? On the contrary, it is perfectly honourable! I will prove that to you conclusively, Zina. I repeat, it all depends on how you look at it. . . ."

"Oh, do leave off, mamma, with your arguments," Zina cried wrathfully, and she stamped impatiently.

"Well, my love, I'll say no more, I'll say no more! I have said something foolish again. . . ."

A brief silence followed. Marya Alexandrovna meekly waited for Zina to speak, and looked uneasily into her eyes, as a little dog who has done wrong watches its mistress.

"I don't understand how you are going to set to work," Zina continued, with repugnance. "I feel sure that you will only meet with ignominy. I despise their opinion, but for you it will mean disgrace."

"Oh, if that's all that is worrying you, my angel, please

don't worry yourself! I beg you, I entreat you. If only we are agreed, you need not be anxious about me. Oh, if only you knew the storms I have weathered unharmed! The scrapes I have had to get out of! Well, only let me have a try. In any case we must lose no time in getting the prince *tête-à-tête*. That is the very first thing. And all the rest will depend on it! But I can foresee the rest. They will all be up in arms, but . . . that does not matter. I'll settle their business! I am frightened of Mozglyakov, too. . . ."

"Mozglyakov!" Zina pronounced with contempt.

"Why, yes, Mozglyakov; only don't you be frightened, Zinotchka! I declare I'll bring him to such a pass that he will help us of himself! You don't know me, Zinotchka! You don't know what I am equal to in an emergency! Ah, Zinotchka, darling! When I heard about the prince a little while ago, the thought flashed upon my brain even then. My whole mind seemed full of light at once. And who, who could expect that he would come to us? Why, such an opportunity might not occur once in a thousand years! Zinotchka, my angel, there is no dishonour in your marrying an old man and a broken-down cripple, but there would be in your marrying a man you could not endure, though you would *really* be his wife. And you won't be a real wife to the prince, you know. Why, it is not marriage. It is only a domestic contract! Why, of course, it will be a benefit to him, the fool! Why, it is bestowing priceless happiness on an old fool like that! Ah, how beautiful you are today, Zinotchka! Not beautiful, but a queen of beauty! Why, if I were a man I would win you half a kingdom if you wanted it! They are all asses! How resist kissing this hand!" And Marya Alexandrovna kissed her daughter's hand warmly. "Why, this is my flesh and blood! We will marry him by force, if need be, the old fool! And how we will arrange life, you and I, Zinotchka! You won't drive away your old mother, when you are in luck will you? Though we do quarrel, my

78

angel, you have never had another friend like me; anyway . . ."

"Mamma! If you have decided, perhaps it is time . . . you were doing something. You are simply wasting time here!" said Zina impatiently.

"It is time, Zina, it is. Oh, I have been letting myself chatter too long!" cried Marya Alexandrovna, catching herself up. "They are trying to entice the prince away altogether. I'll get into the sledge and set off at once. I'll drive round, call Mozglyakov out, and then . . . Yes, I'll bring him away by force, if need be! Good-bye, Zinotchka, good-bye, darling; don't grieve, have no doubts, don't be sad—above all, don't be sad. Everything will turn out splendidly; everything shall be done with dignity and decorum! It makes all the difference how you look at it. . . . Well, good-bye, good-bye."

Marya Alexandrovna made the sign of the cross over Zina, whisked out of the room, twisted and turned before the looking-glass in her own room for a brief instant, and two minutes later was being whirled along the streets of Mordasov in her sledge, which was always at the door at that hour in readiness for paying calls. Marya Alexandrovna lived *en grand*.

"No, you won't outwit me," she thought, as she sat in her sledge. "Zina consents, and that means half my task is done. And break down now! Nonsense! Ah, that Zina! She has agreed, anyway, at last! So some considerations do affect even her darling brain! I drew a tempting prospect for her! I touched her! But it is terrific how beautiful she is today! With her beauty I would have had Europe upside down to suit me. Oh, well, we'll wait and see. . . . Shakespeare will fade away when she becomes a princess and gets to know a thing or two. What does she know? Mordasov and her schoolmaster . . . H'm! . . . But what a princess she will be! I love in her that pride, that boldness. She is so unapproachable! She glances at you—it is the look of a queen. Why, how could she, how could she fail to see her advantage? She saw it

79

at last! She'll see the rest. . . . I shall be with her, of course!
In the end she will agree with me on every point! And she
won't be able to get on without me. I shall be a princess myself.
I shall be known in Petersburg. Farewell, horrid little town!
The prince will die and that boy will die, and then I will marry
her to a reigning prince. Only one thing I am afraid of: didn't
I confide too much in her? Wasn't I too open? Didn't I let
myself be carried away by my feelings? She frightens me; oh,
she frightens me!"

And Marya Alexandrovna became engrossed in her meditations; needless to say that they were of an active nature. But
as the proverb has it: "A good will does more than com-
pulsion."

Left alone, Zina spent a long time walking up and down the
room, with her arms crossed. She pondered over many things.
Often, and almost unconsciously, she repeated, "It's time, it's
time, it's high time!" What did that fragmentary exclamation
mean? More than once tears glistened on her long, silky
eyelashes. She did not think of checking them or wiping them
away. But there was no need for her mother to be anxious,
and to try to penetrate into her daughter's thoughts. Zina had
fully made up her mind, and was prepared for all the consequences.

"Wait a bit," thought Nastasya Petrovna, threading her way
out of the lumber-room on the departure of the colonel's wife.
"And I was meaning to put on a pink ribbon for the benefit
of that wretched prince, and was fool enough to believe that
he would marry me! Ah, Marya Alexandrovna, I am a slut,
I am a beggar, I take bribes of two hundred roubles, do I?
I dare say I ought to have let you off and taken nothing from a
swell like you. I took the money honourably; I took it for
the expenses connected with the job. . . . I might have had
to give a bribe myself. What do you care that I demeaned myself to break the lock with my own hands? I did the dirty

work for your benefit, while you sit with your hands in your lap! You have only to embroider on the canvas; wait a bit, I'll show you the canvas! I'll show you both whether I am a slut! You will appreciate Nastasya Petrovna and her kindness."

CHAPTER VII

BUT Marya Alexandrovna was led by her good genius. The project she was planning was a grand and daring one. To marry her daughter to a wealthy man, to a prince and to a wreck, to marry her without anyone's knowing it, taking advantage of the feeble-mindedness and defencelessness of her guest, to do this by stealth like a thief, as Marya Alexandrovna's enemies would say, was not only bold but audacious. It was of course a profitable scheme, but in case of failure the schemers would be covered with disgrace. Marya Alexandrovna knew this, but she did not despair. "You don't know what storms I have weathered unharmed," she had said to Zina, and she had spoken truly. Otherwise she would not have been much of a heroine.

There is no disputing that all this was something like highway robbery; but Marya Alexandrovna did not take much notice of that. On that score she had one wonderful and unfailing reflection: "Once married, you can't be unmarried." A simple thought, but alluring the imagination with such extraordinary advantages that the mere conception of them sent thrills and shudders all over her. Altogether she was in great excitement, and sat in her sledge as though she were on thorns. Like a woman of inspiration with an unmistakable creative gift, she had already formed a plan of action. But this plan was still a rough sketch, altogether *en grand*, and still loomed somewhat dimly before her. A mass of details and unforeseen possibilities of all sorts awaited her. But Marya Alexandrovna had confidence in herself; she was agitated, not by fear of failure—no! she longed only to begin the fray as soon as possible. Impatience, a laudable impatience, fired at at the thought of delays and obstacles. But as we are speaking of obstacles we will ask leave to explain our meaning more fully. The chief trouble Marya Alexandrovna foresaw and expected was from her excellent fellow-citizens, and especially from the highly respectable ladies of Mordasov. She knew by experience their implacable hatred for herself. She was perfectly certain, for instance, that at that moment everyone in the town probably knew of her designs, although no one had been told anything about them. She knew from bitter experience on more than one occasion, that no incident, even of the most private nature, happened in her house in the morning without being known by the evening to the humblest market-woman, the humblest individual sitting behind a counter. Of course Marya Alexandrovna, so far, had only a presentiment of trouble. But such presentiments had never deceived her. She was not deceived now. This was what had actually happened, though she knew nothing positive about it. About midday, that is just three hours after the prince's arrival in Mordasov, strange rumours were circulating about the town. No one knew where they had begun, but they spread instantly. All began assuring one another that Marya Alexandrovna had already made a match between the prince and her Zina, her portionless, twenty-three year old Zina; that Mozglyakov had been dismissed, and that it was all signed and settled. What was the cause of these rumours? Could it be that everyone knew Marya Alexandrovna so well that they instantly hit on the very centre of her secret thoughts and ideals? Neither the incongruity of such a rumour with the usual order of things, for such affairs can very rarely be settled in an hour, nor the obvious lack of any foundation for the story, for no one could discover whence it had arisen, could shake the conviction of the people of Mordasov. The rumour grew and took root with extraordinary obstinacy. What is most remarkable is that they began to circulate at the very time when Marya Alexandrovna was beginning her conversation with Zina on that very subject. So sharp are the noses of the provincials! The instinct of provincial newsmongers sometimes approaches the miraculous, and of course there is some reason for it. It is founded on the closest and most interested study of one another, pursued through many years. Every provincial lives, as it were, under a glass case. There is no possibility of concealing anything from your excellent fellow-citizens. They know you by heart, they know even what you don't know about yourself. The provincial ought, one would think, by his very nature to be a psychologist and a specialist on human nature. That is why I have been sometimes genuinely amazed at meeting in the provinces not psychologists and specialists on human nature, but a very great number of asses. But that is aside; that is a superfluous reflection.

The news was like a thunderclap. A marriage with the prince appeared to everyone so advantageous, so dazzling, that even the strangeness of the affair did not occur to anyone. We will observe one other circumstance: Zina was almost more hated than Marya Alexandrovna—why?—I cannot tell. Possibly Zina's beauty may have been partly the reason. Perhaps the fact, too, that Marya Alexandrovna was anyway recognised as one of themselves by all the ladies of Mordasov, she was a berry off the same bush. If she had vanished from the town—who knows?—they might have regretted her. She enlivened their society by her goings on. It would have been dull without her. Zina, on the contrary, behaved as if she were living in the clouds and not in Mordasov. She was somehow not on a level with these people, not their equal, and, possibly

83

without being aware of it, behaved with insufferable haughtiness in their company! And now all of a sudden, that Zina, concerning whom there was a scandalous story, that proud, that haughty Zina was becoming a millionaire and a princess, was rising to a rank and distinction. In a couple of years, when she would be a widow, she would marry a duke or maybe a gneeral, who knows, perhaps a governor (and the Governor of Mordasov was, as luck would have it, a widower with a great weakness for the fair sex). Then she would be the lady of the greatest consequence in the province, and of course the mere thought of that was insufferable, and no news could ever have aroused more indignation in Mordasov then the news of Zina's marrying the prince. Instantly a furious outcry rose on all sides. People declared that it was wicked, positively vile; that the prince was out of his mind; that the old man was being deceived, that they were taking advantage of his feeble-mindedness to deceive him, to dupe him, to cheat him; that the old man must be saved from their bloodthirsty claws; that it was robbery and immorality, and finally that other girls were just as good as Zina; and other girls might just as well marry the prince. All these objections and opinions, Marya Alexandrovna, so far, only surmised, but that was enough for her. She knew for certain that everyone, absolutely everyone, was ready to do everything possible, and even impossible, to frustrate her designs. Here they were trying to kidnap the prince so that she would have to get him back almost by force. Besides, if she did succeed in catching the prince and luring him back, she could not keep him for ever on the lead. Besides, who could guarantee that that day, within a couple of hours, the whole solemn conclave of Mordasov ladies would not be sitting in her drawing-room, would not call on her on some pretext which would make it impossible to refuse to see them. If they were refused admittance at the door, they would climb in at the window—a feat almost impossible, though it did happen in Mordasov. In short, there was not an hour, not a second to be lost, and meanwhile nothing had yet been begun. All at once an idea that was a stroke of genius flashed upon Marya Alexandrovna's brain, and was instantly matured there. Of that new idea we shall not neglect to speak in its proper place. Here we will only say that at that moment, our heroine was dashing along the streets of Mordasov full of menace and inspiration, resolving even upon actual violence should it prove necessary, in order to get the prince back. She did not yet know how it would be done and where she would meet him, but she did know positively that Mordasov would sink into the earth sooner than one jot of her present plans should fail of accomplishment.

Her first step could not have been more successful. She succeeded in waylaying the prince in the street and taking him back to dinner. If I am asked how, in spite of all her enemies' devices, she managed to insist on getting her own way, so making Anna Nikolaevna look rather a fool—I am bound to say that I regard such a question as insulting to Marya Alexandrovna. Could she fail to triumph over any Anna Nikolaevna Antipov? She simply stopped the prince on his way to her rival's house, and in spite of everything (including the protests of Mozglyakov, who was afraid of a scandal) transferred the old gentleman to her sledge. It was this that distinguished Marya Alexandrovna from her rivals, that on critical occasions she did not hesitate for fear of a scandal, taking as her motto, that success justifies everything. The prince, of course, made no great resistance, and, as usual, quickly forgot all about it and was highly delighted. At dinner he babbled away without ceasing, was exceedingly lively, made jokes and puns, began telling anecdotes which he did not finish, or jumped from one story to another without being aware of it. At Natalya Dmitryevna's he had drunk three glasses of champagne; at dinner he drank more, and was completely fuddled.

Marya Alexandrovna herself kept filling up his glass. The dinner was a very good one. The monster Nikita had not spoilt it. The lady of the house enlivened the party with the most fascinating graciousness. But the others, as though of design, seemed extraordinarily depressed. Zina maintained a sort of solemn silence. Mozglyakov was evidently put out and ate little. He was absorbed in thought, and as that was very exceptional with him, Marya Alexandrovna felt very uneasy. Nastasya Petrovna sat glum, and actually made signs to Mozglyakov which the latter entirely failed to observe. Had it not been for the enchanting suavity and vivacity of the hostess, the dinner would have been like a funeral.

Yet Marya Alexandrovna was inexpressibly excited. Zina alarmed her dreadfully with her mournful air and tear-stained eyes. And another difficulty was that, that there was need of haste, of prompt action; and that "accursed Mozglyakov" sitting on like a blockhead, troubling about nothing, and simply in the way! It was, of course, impossible to begin on such a subject before him. Marya Alexandrovna rose from the table in terrible uneasiness. What was her amazement, her delighted horror, if one may use such an expression, when, as soon as they arose from the table, Mozglyakov came up to her and suddenly, quite unexpectedly, announced—that to his great regret, of course—he was absolutely forced to take leave of them at once.

"Where are you going?" Marya Alexandrovna asked, with a note of extreme regret.

"Well, you see, Marya Alexandrovna," Mozglyakov began, with some uneasiness and even hesitation, "a very queer thing has happened to me. I really don't know how to tell you. . . . For goodness sake give me advice."

"Why, what is it?"

"My godfather Boroduev, the merchant, you know, met me today. The old fellow was quite huffy, he scolded me and said I

86

had grown proud. This is the third time I have been in Mordasov without his having a glimpse of me. 'Come to tea today,' he said. It is four o'clock now, and he drinks tea in the old-fashioned way—when he wakes up. What am I to do? It is a bore of course, Marya Alexandrovna, but think. He saved my poor father from hanging, you know, when he gambled away the government money. It was owing to that that he stood godfather to me. If I am so happy as to marry Zinaida Afanasyevna I have only a hundred and fifty serfs, while he has a million, people say, even more. He is childless. Seventy, think of it! If one pleases him he may leave one a hundred thousand in his will."

"Oh, my goodness! What are you about! Why are you delaying?" cried Marya Alexandrovna, scarcely concealing her relief. "Go to him, go to him! You must not let it slip. To be sure, I was noticing at dinner—you seemed so dull! Go, *mon ami*, go. Why, you ought to have paid a call in the morning to show that you appreciate, that you value his kindness. Ah, you young people, you young people!"

"Why, Marya Alexandrovna," cried Mozglyakov in amazement, "you yourself attacked me for that acquaintance. Why, you said that he was a peasant with a great beard, connected with innkeepers, low-class people and attorneys."

"Oh! *mon ami*! We say a great many thoughtless things. I may make mistakes like anyone else—I am not a saint. I don't remember, but I may have easily been in that mood. . . . Besides, you were not at that time paying your addresses to Zina. . . . Of course it is egoism on my part, but now I am forced to look at it from a different point of view, and what mother could blame me in the circumstances? Go, do not delay for a minute! Spend the evening with him too. . . . and, listen! Say something to him about me. Tell him that I have a great regard, a great liking, a respect for him; and do it tactfully, nicely! Oh, my goodness, why it quite went out of

87

my head! I ought to have thought to suggest it to you!"

"You have quite reassured me, Marya Alexandrovna," Mozglyakov cried, enchanted. "I swear I will obey you in everything now! Why, I was simply afraid to tell you! . . . Well, good-bye, I am off. Make my apologies to Zinaida Afanasyevna. Though I shall certainly. . . ."

"I give you my blessing, *mon ami.* Be sure you speak of me to him! He certainly is a very dear old man. I changed my opinion of him long ago. Though, indeed, I have always liked in him all those old-fashioned truly Russian ways of his. . . . *Au revoir, mon ami, au revour!*"

"Oh, what a blessing that the devil has taken him off! No, it was the hand of God helping us!" she thought, breathless with joy.

Pavel Alexandrovitch went out into the hall, and was putting on his fur coat when Nastasya Petrovna seemed suddenly to spring from nowhere. She was lying in wait for him.

"Where are you going?" she said, holding him by the arm.

"To see Boroduev my godfather, Nastasya Petrovna, who graciously stood sponsor at my christening. . . . He's a wealthy old man, he will leave me something, I must make up to him."

Pavel Alexandrovitch was in the best of spirits.

"To see Boroduev! Very well then, say good-bye to your bride," Nastasya Petrovna said, abruptly.

"How do you mean good-bye?"

"Why, what I say! You imagine she is yours already! While they are trying to marry her to the prince. I have heard it myself."

"To the prince? Mercy on us, Nastasya Petrovna!"

"Mercy on us, to be sure! Now wouldn't you like to look on and overhear? Put down your coat and come this way."

Pavel Alexandrovitch, petrified, put down his fur coat and followed Nastasya Petrovna on tiptoe; she led him to the same little lumber-room in which she had listened that morning.

"But upon my word, Nastasya Petrovna, I really don't understand."

"Oh, well, you'll understand when you bend down and listen. The farce will begin at once, no doubt."

"What farce?"

"Sh! don't speak so loud! The farce is that they are simply hoaxing you. This morning when you had gone away with the prince, Marya Alexandrovna was a whole hour persuading Zina to consent to marry this prince; she said that nothing would be easier than to get round him and force him to get married, and she pitched such a fine tale that I felt quite sick. I overheard it all from here. Zina consented. How flattering they both were to you! They look upon you simply as a fool, and Zina said straight out that nothing would induce her to marry you. I am a fool, too! I meant to pin on a pink ribbon! Listen now, listen!"

"But I say, it's the most unholy treachery, if so!" whispered Pavel Alexandrovitch, looking into Nastasya Petrovna's face in the most foolish way.

"Well, you only listen, and that's not all you'll hear."

"But listen where?"

"Why, stoop down here—to this keyhole. . . ."

"But Nastasya Petrovna . . . I . . . I am really not capable of listening at keyholes."

"Pooh, it's a bit late to think of that. It's a case of putting your honour in your pocket; since you've come you had better listen!"

"But really . . ."

"If you are incapable of it, then be made a fool of! One takes pity on you and you give yourself airs. What is it to me? I am not doing it for my own sake. I shall be gone from here before evening!"

Paveo Alexandrovitch, overcoming his scruples, stooped

down to the keyhole. His heart was beating, there was a throbbing in his temples. He scarcely understood what was happening to him.

CHAPTER VIII

"So you had a very gay time at Natalya Dmitryevna's, prince?" queried Marya Alexandrovna, surveying the field of the approaching conflict with a predatory eye, and desiring to begin the conversation as innocently as possible. Her heart was beating with excitement and anticipation.

After dinner they had taken the prince at once to the 'salon', in which he had been received that morning. All solemn functions and receptions at Marya Alexandrovna's took place in this 'salon'. She was proud of the room. The old man seemed rather limp after his six glasses of wine, and could hardly keep on his legs. But he chattered away without ceasing. His garrulousness was only intensified. Marya Alexandrovna realised that this spurt of excitement was only momentary, and that her guest, heavy from his potations, would soon be drowsy. She must seize the moment. Scanning the field of battle, she noticed with satisfaction that the lascivious old man was fixing upon Zina glances of peculiar avidity, and her maternal heart fluttered with joy.

"Ex-ceed-ing-ly gay," answered the prince, "and you know Natalya Dmitryevna is an absolutely in-com-parable woman—in-com-parable!"

Though Marya Alexandrovna was so absorbed in her great plans, yet such ringing praise of her rival stabbed her to the heart.

"Upon my word, prince," she cried, with flashing eyes, "I really don't know what to think if your Natalya Dmitryevna is an incomparable woman! You say that because you don't known our society, you don't know it at all! Why, it is a mere exhibition of fictitious qualities, of noble sentiments, a farce, an outer husk of gold. Remove that husk and you will find a perfect hell under the flowers; a perfect wasp's nest, where you will be devoured to the last bone!"

"Is it possible!" exclaimed the prince; "you surprise me!"

"But I vow that it is so! Ah, *mon prince*. Do you know, Zina, I really ought to tell the prince that absurd and undignified incident with Natalya Dmitryevna last week—do you remember? Yes, prince—it is about your vaunted Natalya Dmitreyvna, with whom you are so fascinated. Oh, my dearest prince! I vow I am not a scandalmonger! But I certainly must tell you this, simply to amuse you, to show you in a living instance, in a magnifying glass, so to speak, what people here are like. A fortnight ago Natalya Dmityevna came to see me. Coffee was served, and I went out of the room for something. I remember perfectly well how much sugar there was in my silver sugar-basin: it was quite full. I came back and looked: there were only three lumps lying at the bottom of the basin. No one had been left in the room but Natalya Dmitryevna. What do you say to that! She has a brick house of her own and heaps of money! It's an absurd, comical incident, but you can judge from that of the lofty tone of our society."

"Is it pos-si-ble!" exclaimed the prince, genuinely surprised. "What unnatural greediness! Did she eat it all up alone?"

"So you see what an *incomparable* woman she is, prince! How do you like that disgraceful incident? I believe I should have died on the spot if I had brought myself to commit such a revolting action."

"To be sure; to be sure. . . . But, you know, she really is such a *belle femme*."

"Natalya Dmitryevna! Upon my word, prince, she is a

perfect tub! Oh, prince, prince! What are you saying? I did expect better taste from you. . . ."

"To be sure, a tub . . . only, you know, she is such a fine figure . . . and that girl who da-anced, she is . . . such a good figure too. . . ."

"Sonitchka? But she is quite a child!' She is only fourteen!"

"To be sure . . . only, you know, she is so agile and she has . . . . such contours . . . too . . . they are developing, such a cha-arm-ing girl! And the other who da-an-ced with her, she is developing too. . . ."

"Ah, that is a luckless orphan, prince! She often stays with them."

"An orph-an! She is a dirty girl, though, she might wash her hands, anyway. . . . Though she was at-tra-active, too. . . ."

As he said this the prince scrutinised Zina through his lorgnette with a sort of growing avidity.

"*Mais quelle charmante personne!*" he muttered in an undertone melting with gratification.

"Zina, play us something, or, better still, sing! How she sings, prince! She is equal to a professional, a professional! And if you only knew, prince," Marya Alexandrovna went on in a low voice, when Zina had moved away to the piano with her soft swimming gait, which sent a thrill through the poor old man. "If only you knew what a daughter she is! What a loving nature she has, how tender she is with me! What feeling, what heart!"

"To be sure . . . feeling . . . and do you know, I have only known one woman in my life who could be compared with her for beau-uty," the prince interrupted, with his mouth watering. "That was Countess Nainsky, she died thirty years ago. A most fas-cin-ating woman she was, an indescribable beauty, afterwads she married her cook. . . ."

"Her cook, prince!"

"To be sure, her cook . . . a Frenchman, abroad. She got a count's title for him, abroad. He was a good-looking man, extremely well educated, with little mous-taches like this."

"And . . . and . . . how did they get on together, prince?"

"To be sure, they got on very well together. Though they separated soon afterwards. He robbed her and went off. They quarrelled about some sauce. . . ."

"Mamma, what shall I play?" asked Zina.

"You had better sing us something, Zina. How she sings, prince! Are you fond of music?"

"Oh, yes! *Charmant, charmant!* I am very fond of music. I used to know Beethoven when I was abroad."

"Beethoven! Only fancy, Zina, the prince used to know Beethoven," Marya Alexandrovna cried rapturously. "Oh, prince, did you really know Beethoven?"

"To be sure . . . we were quite fri-ends, and he always had his nose in the snuff-box. Such a funny fellow."

"Beethoven!"

"To be sure, Beethoven, but perhaps it was not Beet-hoven, though, but some other Ger-man. There are such a lot of Germans out there . . . I believe I have mix-ed them up."

"What am I to sing, mamma?" asked Zina.

"Oh, Zina! Sing that song in which there is so much chivalry, the one in which there is the lady of the castle and her troubadour. . . . Oh, prince! How I love all that age of chivalry! Those castles, those castles! That medieval life. Those troubadours, heralds, tournaments. . . . I will accompany you, Zina. Come here closer, prince! Ah, those castles, those castles!"

"To be sure . . . those castles. I love castles, too," muttered the prince rapturously, transfixing Zina with his solitary eye. "But . . . my goodness!" he exclaimed, "that so-ong, why, I know that so-ong! I heard that song long ago. . . . It brings back such memories. . . . Ah, my goodness!"

I will not undertake to describe what happened to the prince while Zina was singing. She sang an old French song, which had once been in fashion. Zina sang it beautifully. Her pure resonant contralto went straight to the heart. Her lovely face, her wonderful eyes, the wonderful delicately moulded fingers with which she turned the music, her thick brilliant black hair, her heaving bosom, her whole figure, proud, lovely, noble, all this bewitched the poor old man completely. He did not take his eyes off her while she was singing, he gasped with emotion. His aged heart, warmed by the champagne, the music, and rising memories (what man has not favourite memories?) was throbbing faster and faster, as it had not beat for ages. . . . He was ready to fall on his knees before Zina, and was almost weeping when she finished.

"*O, ma charmante enfant!*" he cried, kissing her fingers, "*vous me ravissez!* Only just now, just now I remembered. . . ." But . . . but . . . *O, ma charmante enfant. . . .*"

And the prince could not go on.

Marya Alexandrovna felt that her moment had come.

"Why are you wasting your life, prince?" she exclaimed solemnly. "What feeling, what vital energy, what spiritual riches, and to bury yourself for your whole life in solitude! To run away from people, from your friends! But it is unpardonable! Think better of it, prince! Look at life, so to speak, with a fresh eye! Evoke from your heart your memories of the past—the memories of your golden youth, of those golden days free from care; bring them back to life, restore yourself to life! Begin to live again in society among your fellows! Go abroad, go to Italy, to Spain—to Spain, prince! . . . You want someone to guide you, a heart that would love you, that would honour you and feel with you. But you have friends! Summon them, call them to you and they will flock in crowds to your side! I would be the first to throw up everything and fly at your summons. I remember our friendship,

94

prince; I would abandon my husband and follow you . . .
and, indeed, if I were younger, if I were as good and as lovely
as my daughter, I would be your travelling companion, your
friend, your wife, if that was your wish."

"And I am sure you were *une charmante personne* in your
da-ay," said the prince, blowing his nose. His eyes were moist
with tears.

"We live again in our children, prince," Marya Alexandrovna answered, with lofty feeling. "I, too, have my guardian
angel! And that is my daughter, the friend of my heart, the
partner of my thoughts, prince. She has already refused seven
offers, unwilling to part from me."

"So she would come with you when you ac-com-pan-y me
abroad? In that case I will certainly go abroad," cried the
prince, growing more animated. "I will cer-er-tain-ly go!
And if I might flatter myself with the ho-ope. . . . But she is a
fascinating, fas-cin-na-ting child! *O, ma charmante enfant!*
. . ." and the prince began kissing her hand again. The poor
man would have liked to drop on his knees before her.

"But . . . but, prince, you say: can you flatter yourself
with hope?" Marya Alexandrovna caught him up, conscious
of a fresh rush of eloquence. "But you are strange, prince.
Can you consider yourself unworthy of a woman's devotion?
It is not youth that makes a man handsome. Remember, that
you, so to speak, are a scion of the old aristocracy. You are
the embodiment of the most refined, the most chivalrous
sentiments and . . . manners! Did not Maria love Mazeppa in
his old age? I remember, I have read that Lauzun, that enchanting marquis at the court of Louis the . . . I have forgotten
which, in his declining years, when he was an old man, won the
heart of one of the leading court beauties! . . . And who has
told you that you are old? Who has instilled that idea into
you? Men like you do not grow old! You, with such wealth
of feeling, of gaiety, of wit, of vital energy, of brilliant

95

manners! Only show yourself at some spa abroad with a young wife, as beautiful as my Zina; for instance—I am not speaking of her, I only mention her for example—and you will see what a colossal sensation it will make! You a scion of the aristocracy, she—a queen of beauty! You will walk with her on your arm in triumph; she will sing in brilliant society, you, for your part, will scintillate with wit—and all the visitors at the spa will flock to look at you! All Europe will be ringing with your name, for all the newspapers, all the *feuilletons* at the watering-places, will tell the same story. . . ."

"The *feuilletons*. . . . Oh, yes; oh, yes. That's in the newspapers. . . ." muttered the prince, not understanding half Marya Alexandrovna's babble, and growing more and more limp every moment. "But . . . my chi-ild, if you are not ti-ired, sing that song you sang just now, once more."

"Oh, prince! But she has other songs better still. . . . Do you remember *L'Hirondelle*, prince? No doubt you have heard it?"

"Yes, I remember, or, rather, I have forgotten it. No, no; the same so-ong as be-fore, the same that she sang just now! I don't want *L'Hirondelle*! I want the same song. . . ." said the prince, entreating like a child.

Zina sang it over again. The prince could not restrain himself, and sank on his knees before her.

"*O, ma belle châtelaine*!" he cried, in a voice quavering with age and excitement. "*O, ma charmante châtelaine!* Oh, my sweet child! You have re-min-ded me of so much . . . of what was in the distant past. . . . I thought then that everything would be better than it was afterwards. In those days I used to sing duets . . . with the vicomtesse . . . that very song . . . and now . . . I don't know what now. . . ."

All this speech the prince uttered breathless and gasping. His tongue was perceptibly faltering. Some words were almost impossible to understand. It could only be seen that he was

96

in an extremely maudlin state; Marya Alexandrovna promptly threw oil on the flames.

"Prince! But perhaps you are falling in love with my Zina!" she cried, feeling that it was a solemn moment.

The prince's answer surpassed her highest expectations.

"I am madly in love with her," cried the old man suddenly reviving, still on his knees and trembling all over with excitement. "I am ready to devote my life to her, and if I could only ho-ope. . . . But lift me up, I feel ra-ather we-eak. . . . I . . . if I could only hope to offer her my heart, then . . . I . . . she would sing me so-ongs eve-ry day, and I could always look at her . . . always look at her. . . . Oh, my goodness!"

"Prince, prince! You offer her your hand! You want to rob me of my Zina, my darling, my angel, Zina! But I will not let you go, Zina! You will have to tear her from my arms, from the arms of her mother!" Marya Alexandrovna rushed at her daughter and folded her tightly in her arms, though she was conscious of being somewhat violently repulsed. . . . The mamma was rather overdoing it. Zina felt that in every fibre of her being, and looked on at the farce with indescribable disgust. She was silent, however, and that was all Marya Alexandrovna wanted.

"She has refused nine offers, simply to avoid being parted from her mother!" she cried. "But now, my heart forebodes separation! This morning I noticed how she looked at you. . . You have impressed her with your aristocratic ways, prince, with that refinement! . . . Oh! you are parting us; I have a presentiment of it."

"I ado-ore her!" muttered the prince, still quivering like an aspen leaf.

"And so you will forsake your mother?" exclaimed Marya Alexandrovna, dashing at her daughter once again.

Zina was in haste to put an end to the painful scene. She held out her lovely hand to the prince, and even forced herself

97

to smile. The prince took the hand with reverence and covered it with kisses.

"Only now, I be-gin to live," he muttered, gasping with ecstasy.

"Zina," Marya Alexandrovna pronounced solemnly. "Look at this man! He is the noblest, the most honourable of all the men I know! He is a medieval knight! But she knows that, prince; she knows it to my sorrow. . . . Oh, why did you come! I am giving you my treasure, my angel. Take care of her, prince! That is the earnest prayer of a mother, and what mother will censure me for my sorrow!"

"Mamma, that is enough!" whispered Zina.

"You will protect her from insult, prince. Your sword will flash in the face of any slanderer or backbiter who dare malign my Zina!"

"That is enough, mamma, or I'll . . ."

"Yes, yes, it will flash. . . ." muttered the prince. "Only now I begin to live. . . . I want the wedding to be at once, this minute . . . I . . . I want to send to Du-ha-no-vo at once. I have dia-monds there. I want to lay them at her feet."

"What fire, what fervour! What nobility of feeling!" exclaimed Marya Alexandrovna. "And you could waste yourself, waste yourself, withdrawing from the world! I shall say that a thousand times over! I am beside myself when I think of that diabolical . . ."

"How co-ould I help it, I was so fri-ghtened!" muttered the prince, whimpering and growing maudlin. "They wa-an-ted to put me in a ma-adhouse. . . . I was frightened."

"In a madhouse! Oh, the monsters! Oh, the inhuman creatures! Oh, the base treachery! Prince, I had heard that. But that was insanity on the part of those people! What for, whatever for?"

"I don't know myself, what for!" answered the old man, feeling weak, and sitting down in an easy chair. "I was at a

98

ba-all, you know, and I to-old some anecdote; and they did not li-ike it. And so there was a fuss."

"Really only for that, prince?"

"No. I played cards afterwards with Prince Pyotr Dementi-tich. I couldn't make my tricks. I had two ki-ings and three queens . . . or, rather, three queens and two ki-ings. . . . No; one ki-ing! And afterwards I had the queens . . ."

"And for that! For that! Oh, the fiendish inhumanity! You are weeping, prince! But now that will not happen again! Now I shall be at your side, my prince; I shall not part from Zina, and we shall see if they dare to say a word! . . . And indeed you know, prince, your marriage will impress them. It will put them to shame! They will see that you are still quite competent . . . that is, they will realise that such a beauty would not have married a madman! Now you can hold up your head proudly. You can look them straight in the face. . . ."

"Oh, yes; I will look them stra-aight in the face," muttered the prince, closing his eyes.

"He's nearly asleep, though," thought Marya Alexandrovna; "it is merely wasting words."

"Prince, you are agitated, I see that; you absolutely must be quiet; rest after your emotion," she said, bending over him maternally.

"Oh, yes; I should like to li-ie down a little," he said.

"Yes, yes! Calm yourself, prince! This agitation. . . . Stay I will accompany you myself. . . . I will put you to bed, myself, if need be. Why are you looking at that portrait, prince? It is the portrait of my mother, an angel, not a woman! Oh, why is she not with us now! She was a saintly woman, prince, a saintly woman! I can call her nothing else."

"A sa-aintly woman? *C'est joli.* . . . I had a mother too . . . *princesse* . . . . and only fancy, she was an ex-tra-or-din-arily fat woman. . . . But that wasn't what I meant to say. . . . I am a lit-tle tired. *Adieu, ma charmante enfant!* . . . I . . .

99

de-ligh-ted . . . today . . . tomorrow . . . But no ma-atter! *au revoir, au revoir!*" At this point he tried to wave a kiss, but slipped and almost fell down in the doorway.

"Take care, prince! Lean on my arm," cried Marya Alexandrovna.

"*Charmant, charmant!*" he muttered as he went out. "Only now I am be-gin-ning to live!"

Zina was left alone; unutterable bitterness weighed upon her heart. She felt sick with repulsion. She was ready to despise herself. Her cheeks were burning. Clenching her fists and setting her teeth, she stood motionless with bowed head. Tears of shame gushed from her eyes. . . . At that moment the door opened and Mozglyakov ran into the room.

CHAPTER IX

He had heard all, all!

He did not walk into the room, but actually ran in, pale with emotion and with fury. Zina gazed at him in amazement.

"So that's how it is," he shouted, panting. "At last I have found out what you are!"

"What I am!" repeated Zina, staring at him as though he were mad; and all at once her eyes flashed with anger. "How dare you speak like that, to me?" she cried, going up to him.

"I have heard it all!" Mozglyakov repeated solemnly, though he involuntarily drew back a step.

"You heard? You've been listening," said Zina, looking at him disdainfully.

"Yes! I've been listening. Yes, I brought myself to do a low thing, but I learned what you are, the most . . . I don't know what words to use to tell you . . . what you have shown yourself to be!" he answered, quailing more and more before Zina's eyes.

"If you have heard, what can you blame me for? What

100

right have you to blame me? What right have you to speak so rudely to me?"

"I? What right have I? And you can ask that? You are going to marry the prince, and I have no right! . . . Why, you gave me your word!"

"When?"

"How can you ask when?"

"Why, only this morning, when you were pestering me, I told you straight out that I could say nothing positive."

"But you did not drive me away, you did not refuse me altogether. So you were keeping me in reserve! So you were drawing me on!"

A look of suffering as though from an acute, piercing, internal pain came into Zina's irritated face; but she mastered her feeling.

"That I did not drive you away," she said, clearly and emphatically, though there was a scarcely perceptible quiver in her voice, "was solely through pity. You implored me yourself to take time, not to say 'no', but to get to know you better, and 'then', you said, 'then, when you are convinced that I am an honourable man, perhaps you will not refuse me.' Those were your own words when first you pressed your suit. You cannot draw back from them. You had the insolence to say just now that I drew you on. But you saw yourself my aversion when I met you today, a fortnight earlier than you promised. That aversion I did not conceal from you; on the contrary, I displayed it. You noticed it yourself, for you asked me whether I was angry with you for coming back sooner. You know one is not drawing a man on if one cannot and does *not care* to conceal one's aversion. You have had the insolence to say that I was keeping you in reserve. To that I will answer, that what I thought about you was, 'though he is not endowed with very much intelligence, he may yet be a good man, and so one might marry him.' But now I am convinced, to my relief,

101

that you are a fool, and what's more, an ill-natured fool. I have only now to wish you every happiness and *bon voyage*. Good-bye!"

Saying this, Zina turned from him and walked slowly towards the door.

Mozglyakov, guessing that all was lost, boiled with rage.

"Ah, so I am a fool," he cried, "so now I am a fool! Very well! Good-bye. But before I go away I'll tell the whole town how you and your mamma have tricked the old prince, after making him drunk! I'll tell everyone! I'll show you what Mozglyakov can do!"

Zina shuddered, and was stopping to answer; but after a moment's thought, she merely shrugged her shoulders contemptuously, and slammed the door after her.

At that moment Marya Alexandrovna appeared in the doorway. She had heard Mozglyakov's exclamation, in an instant guessed what it meant and shuddered with alarm. Mozglyakov had not gone yet, Mozglyakov near the prince, Mozglyakov would spread it all over the town, and secrecy for a short time at least was essential! Marya Alexandrovna had her own calculations. She instantly grasped the situation, and the plan for subduing Mozglyakov was already formed.

"What is the matter, *mon ami*?" she said, going up to him and holding out her hand affectionately.

"What? *mon ami*!" he cried furiously. "After what you have been plotting, you call me *mon ami*! You don't catch me, honoured madam! And do you suppose you can deceive me again?"

"I am grieved, very much grieved to see you in such a *strange* state of mind, Pavel Alexandrovitch. What an expression to use! You do not even curb your language before a lady."

"Before a lady! You . . . you may be anything you like, but not a lady!" cried Mozglyakov.

102

I don't know what he meant to express by this exclamation, but probably something very tremendous.

Marya Alexandrovna looked blandly into his face.

"Sit down," she said mournfully, motioning him to the chair on which a quarter of an hour before the prince had been reposing.

"But, do listen, Marya Alexandrovna!" cried Mozglyakov in perplexity. "You look at me as though you were not to blame in any way, but as though I had treated you badly! You can't go on like that, you know! . . . Such a tone! . . . Why, it is beyond all human endurance. . . . Do you know that?"

"My friend!" answered Marya Alexandrovna, "you must still allow me to call you that, for you have no better friend than I; my friend! You are unhappy, you are distressed, you are wounded to the heart—and so it is not to be wondered at that you speak to me in such a tone. But I am resolved to reveal to you everything, to open my whole heart, the more readily as I feel myself somewhat to blame in regard to you. Sit down, let us talk."

There was a sickly softness in Marya Alexandrovna's voice. There was a look of suffering in her face. Mozglyakov, astounded, sat down in an easy chair beside her.

"You have been listening?" she said, looking reproachfully into his face.

"Yes, I have been listening! If I hadn't listened I should have been a duffer. Anyway, I have found out all that you were plotting against me," Mozglyakov answered rudely, growing bolder and working himself into a passion.

"And you, you, with your breeding, with your principles, could bring yourself to such an action? Oh, good heavens!"

Mozglyakov positively jumped up from his chair.

"But, Marya Alexandrovna!" he cried, "it is insufferable to listen to this! Think what you have brought yourself to

103

do with your principles, and then you judge other people!"

"Another question," she said, without answering him. "Who put you up to listening, who told you, who is the spy here? That's what I want to know."

"Excuse me, but I won't tell you that."

"Very well, I shall find out for myself. I said, *Paul*, that I had treated you badly. But if you go into it all, into all the circumstances, you will see that, even if I am to blame, it is solely through a desire for your good."

"Mine? My good? That is beyond everything! I warn you, you won't delude me again! I am not such a child as that."

And he writhed in the arm-chair with such violence that it creaked.

"Please, my dear boy, keep cool, if you can. Listen to me attentively, and you will agree with everything yourself. To begin with, I intended to tell you about it at once, everything, everything, and you would have heard the whole business from me in the fullest details, without demeaning yourself to listen. That I did not explain it to you before was simply because it was only a project. It might not have come off. You see, I am being perfectly open with you. Secondly, do not blame my daughter. She loves you madly, and it cost me incredible effort to draw her away from you, and to induce her to consent to accept the prince."

"I have just had the happiness to receive the fullest proof of that *mad* love," Mozglyakov pronounced ironically.

"Very good. But how were you speaking to her? Was that the way that a lover should speak? Was that the way, indeed, for a well-bred man to speak? You wounded and irritated her!"

"It is not a question of breeding now, Marya Alexandrovna. And this morning, after you had both treated me to such honied looks, I went off with the prince and you blackguarded me behind my back! You called me names—let me tell you that. I know all about it, I know!"

"And no doubt from the same foul source?" said Marya Alexandrovna, with a contemptuous smile. "Yes, Pavel Alexandrovitch, I did disparage you, I did talk against you, and I must confess I had a hard struggle. But the very fact that I had to abuse you to her, even to slander you, that very fact proves how hard it was for me to extort her consent to abandon you! You short-sighted man! If she did not care for you, would there have been any need for me to blacken your character, to put you in an undignified and ridiculous light, to resort to such extreme measures. But you do not know everything yet! I had to use my maternal authority to eradicate you from her heart, and after incredible efforts I wrung from her only the appearance of agreement. If you were listening just now you must have noticed that she did not support me with the prince, by one word, one gesture. Throughout the whole scene she scarcely uttered a single word: she sang like an automaton. Her whole soul was aching with despondency, and it was from pity for her that, at last, I got the prince away, I am sure that she wept as soon as she was alone. When you came in here you must have noticed her tears."

Mozglyakov did, in fact, remember that when he ran into the room he had noticed that Zina was in tears.

"But you, you, why were you against me, Marya Alexandrovna?" he cried. "Why did you blacken my character? why did you slander me, as you yourself confess you did?"

"Ah, that is a different matter. If you had asked that question sensibly in the beginning, you would have had an answer to it long ago. Yes, you are right! It has all been my doing, and only mine. Don't mix Zina up in it. What was my object? I answer, in the first place, it was for Zina's sake. The prince is a man of rank and fortune, he has connections, and marrying him, Zina would make a splendid match. Besides, if he dies, perhaps before long, indeed, for we are all more or less mortal, then Zina will be a young widow, a princess, in the highest society, and perhaps very wealthy. Then she can marry anyone she likes; she would be able to make a still wealthier match. But of course she will marry the man she loves, the man she loved before, whose heart she wounded by marrying the prince. Remorse alone would force her to atone for her treatment of the man she loved before."

"H'm!" mumbled Mozglyakov, looking thoughtfully at his boots.

"And the second thing is, and I will only mention it briefly," Marya Alexandrovna went on, "for perhaps you will not understand it. You read your Shakespeare, and draw all your lofty sentiments from him, but in real life, though you are *very good*, you are too young and I am a *mother*, Pavel Alexandrovitch. Listen: I am giving Zina to the prince, partly for his sake, to save him by this marriage. I loved that noble, most kindly, chivalrously honourable old man in the past. We were friends. He is unhappy in the claws of that hellish woman. She will bring him to his grave. God is my witness that I only persuaded Zina to consent to marry the prince by putting before her all the greatness of her heroic self-sacrifice. She was carried away by the nobility of her feelings, by the fascination of an act of sacrifice. There is something chivalrous in her, too. I put before her what a lofty Christian act it was to be the prop, the comfort, the friend, the child, the lovely idol of one who has perhaps but one year yet to live. No hateful woman, no terror, no despondency should be about him in the last days of his life, but brightness, affection, love. These last declining days would seem like Paradise to him! Where is the egoism in that? Tell me pray. It is more like the noble deed of a sister of mercy than egoism!"

"So you are doing this simply for the sake of the old prince, simply as the sacrifice of a sister of mercy?" muttered Moz-glyakov in an ironical voice.

"I understand that question, Pavel Alexandrovitch, it is clear enough. You imagine, perhaps, that the interests of the prince are jesuitically intertwined with our own advantage? Well? Possibly those considerations were present in my brain, only they were not jesuitical, but unconscious. I know that you will be amazed at so open a confession, but one thing I do beg of you, Pavel Alexandrovitch: don't mix Zina up in that! She is pure as a dove; she is not calculating; she is capable of nothing but love, my sweet child! If anyone has been calcula-ting, it is I, and I alone! But in the first place, search your own conscience sternly, and tell me: who would not calculate in my position, in a case like this. We consider our interests even in the most magnanimous, even in the most disinterested of our actions, inevitably, involuntarily we consider them. No doubt we all deceive ourselves, when we assure ourselves that we are acting solely from noble motives. I don't want to deceive myself; I admit that for all the purity of my motives I was calculating. But ask yourself, am I interested on my own behalf? I want nothing, Pavel Alexandrovitch, I have lived my life. I am calculating for her sake, for the sake of my angel, for my child, and—what mother can blame me for it?"

Tears glistened in Marya Alexandrovna's eyes. Pavel Alexandrovitch listened in astonishment to this candid con-fession, and blinked incredulously.

"Well, yes, what mother would?" he said at last. "You pitch a fine tale, Marya Alexandrovna, but . . . but, you know, you gave me your word! You gave me hopes. . . . How about me? Only think! You've made me look a pretty fool, haven't you?"

"But surely you don't imagine that I haven't thought of you, *mon cher Paul;* the advantage for you in all this was so

107

immense, that it was that, indeed, that chiefly impelled me to undertake it all."

"Advantage for me!" cried Mozglyakov, completely dumbfoundered this time. "How so?"

"My goodness! Can anyone be so simple and shortsighted!" cried Marya Alexandrovna, turning up her eyes to the ceiling. "Oh, youth! youth! That is what comes of burying oneself in that Shakespeare, of dreaming, and of imagining that one is thinking for oneself when one is following the thoughts and the mind of others! You ask, my *good* Pavel Alexandrovitch, where your advantage is to be found in it. Allow me, for for the sake of clearness, to make a digression. Zina loves you —that is beyond doubt! But I have noticed that, in spite of her obvious feeling for you, she has a secret lack of confidence in you, in your good feelings, in your propensities. I have noticed that at times she behaves to you, as it were intentionally, with coldness, the result of uncertainty and lack of confidence. Have you noticed that yourself, Pavel Alexandrovitch?"

"I have noticed it, and today indeed. . . . But what do you mean to say, Marya Alexandrovna?"

"There, you see you have noticed it yourself. So I was not mistaken then. She has a strange lack of confidence in the stability of your character. I am a mother—and is it not for me to divine the secrets of my child's heart? Imagine now that instead of rushing into the room with reproaches, and even with abuse, irritating her, wounding and insulting her in her purity, her goodness and her pride, and so unwittingly confirming her suspicions of your evil propensities —imagine that you had accepted it all mildly, with tears of regret, perhaps, even, of despair, but with lofty nobility of feeling . . ."

"H'm! . . ."

"No, do not interrupt me, Pavel Alexandrovitch. I want

108

to paint the whole picture which will strike your imagination. Imagine that you had gone to her and said: 'Zinaida! I love you more than life itself, but family reasons divide us. I understand those reasons. They are for your happiness, and I do not venture to rebel against them, Zinaida! I forgive you. Be happy if you can!' And at that point you would fix your gaze upon her, the gaze of a lamb at the sacrifice, if I may so express myself—imagine all that and only think what effect such words would have had on her heart!"

"Yes, Marya Alexandrovna, let us suppose all that; I understand all that. . . . But after all, if I had said all that I should have gained nothing by it."

"No, no, no, my dear! Don't interrupt me. I want to picture the scene in every detail that it may make the right impression on you. Imagine that you meet her again a little later in the highest society; meet her at some ball, in a brilliantly lighted room, to the intoxicating strains of music, in the midst of magnificent women, and in the midst of this gay festival you alone mournful, melancholy, pale, leaning somewhere against a column (but so that you can be seen), watch her in the whirl of the ball. She dances. Around you flow the intoxicating strains of Strauss and the scintillating wit of the highest society—while you stand alone, pale and crushed by your passion. What will Zinaida feel then, do you suppose? With what eyes will she look at you. 'And I,' she will think, 'I doubted of that man who has sacrificed for me all—all, and has rent his heart for my sake.' Her old love would, of course, rise up again with irresistible force."

Marya Alexandrovna stopped to take breath. Mozglyakov wriggled in his easy chair with such violence that it creaked again. Marya Alexandrovna went on:

"For the prince's health Zina will go abroad, to Italy, to Spain—to Spain where there are myrtles, lemons, where the sky is blue, where there is the Guadalquivir; the land of love, where one cannot live without loving: the land of roses, where kisses, so to speak, float in the air. You will follow her there; you will sacrifice your past in the service, your connections, everything. There your love will begin with irresistible force; love, youth! Spain—my God! Your love of course is untainted, holy; though you will languish gazing at one another. You understand me, *mon ami*! Of course there will be base, treacherous people, monsters who will declare that you have not been tempted abroad by family feeling for a suffering old relation. I have purposely called your love untainted, because such people will perhaps give it a very different significance. But I am a mother, Pavel Alexandrovitch, and am I likely to lead you astray! . . . Of course the prince will not be in a condition to look after you both, but—what of that? Could such an abominable calumny be based on that? At last he will die, blessing his fate. Tell me: whom would Zina marry if not you? You are such a distant relation of the prince's that that can be no hindrance to your marriage. You will wed her, young, wealthy, distinguished, and, only think!—when the grandest of our noblemen would be proud to marry her. Through her you will gain a footing in the highest circles of society, through her you will gain the highest rank and position. Now you have a hundred and fifty serfs but then you will be rich; the prince will arrange everything in his will. I will see to that. And, lastly and most important, she will have gained complete confidence in you, in your heart, in your feelings, and you will become in her eyes a hero of goodness and self-sacrifice! . . . And after that you ask, where your advantage comes in? Why, you must be blind not to reflect, not to consider that advantage, when it stands not two steps from you, staring you in the face, smiling at you and crying out to you: 'Here I am, your advantage!' Pavel Alexandrovitch, upon my word!"

"Marya Alexandrovna!" cried Mozglyakov in extraordinary

excitement, "now I understand it all. I have behaved coarsely, basely and caddishly!"

He leapt up from his seat and clutched his hair.

"And unreflectingly," added Marya Alexandrovna. "Above all, unreflectingly!"

"I am an ass, Marya Alexandrovna!" he cried, almost in despair. "Now all is lost, because I loved her so madly."

"Perhaps all is not lost," said Madame Moskalev softly, as though pondering something.

"Oh, if that were possible! Help me! Teach me! Save me!"

And Mozglyakov burst into tears.

"My dear!" said Marya Alexandrovna with commiseration, giving him her hand, "you have acted from excess of ardour, from the fervour of your passion, that is, from love for her! You were in despair, you did not know what you were doing! She ought to understand all that. . . ."

"I love her to madness, and am ready to sacrifice anything to her!" cried Mozglyakov.

"I tell you what, I will set you right with her. . . ."

"Marya Alexandrovna?"

"Yes, I will undertake to do that! I will bring you together. You must tell her everything—everything as I have told it you, just now."

"Oh, God! How kind you are, Marya Alexandrovna! But . . . would it be impossible to do it at once?"

"God forbid! Oh, how inexperienced you are, my dear! She is so proud. She will take this as a fresh insult, as insolence! Tomorrow I will arrange it all; but now go away, to see that merchant, for instance . . . come in the evening, perhaps, but I would not advise you to."

"I will go away, I will! My God! You bring me back to life! But one more question. What if the prince doesn't die so soon?"

111

"Oh, my God! how naïve you are, *mon cher Paul*. On the contrary, you must pray for his health. We must, with all our hearts, hope for length of days for that dear, kind, chivalrously honourable old man. I shall be the first to pray, night and day, with tears in my eyes, for my daughter's happiness. But, alas! I fear the prince's health is hopeless. Moreover, he will have now to visit Petersburg, to take Zina into society. I fear, oh, I fear that this may be too much for him! But we will pray for the best, *cher Paul*, and the rest is—in God's Hands! . . . You are going now? I bless you, *mon ami*! Hope, be patient, be manly above all things, be manly! I never doubted the nobility of your sentiments. . . ."

She pressed his hand warmly, and Mozglyakov walked out of the room on tiptoe.

"Well, I have got rid of one fool!" she said triumphantly. "There are others left . . ."

The door opened and Zina came in. She was paler than usual. Her eyes were flashing.

"Mamma," she said, "finish it quickly or I can't endure it! It's all so vile and nasty that I am ready to run out of the house. Don't torture me, don't irritate me! I feel sick—do you hear?—sick of all this filth!"

"Zina! What is the matter with you, my angel? You . . . you have been listening!" cried Marya Alexandrovna, looking intently and uneasily at Zina.

"Yes, I have been listening. Do you want to put me to shame as you did that fool! Listen, I swear that if you go on torturing me like this, and assign to me all sorts of low parts in this low farce, I will throw it all up and make an end of it at one blow. It is enough that I have brought myself to do the vile thing that is most important. But . . . I did not know myself! I shall be stifled in this filth."

And she went out, slamming the door.

Marya Alexandrovna gazed after her and pondered.

"Haste! haste!" she cried, starting. "She is the chief trouble, the chief danger, and if all these scoundrels won't let us alone, if they spread it all over the town—as they probably have done by now—all is lost! She will never endure the hubbub and will refuse. At all costs we must take the prince into the country, and promptly too! I will fly off first myself, will haul along my blockhead and bring him here, he must make himself useful at last; meanwhile the old man will have had his sleep out, and we will set off."

She rang the bell.

"The horses?" she asked the servant who came in.

"They have been ready a long while," answered the footman.

The horses had been ordered at the moment when Marya Alexandrovna was taking the prince upstairs.

She dressed, but first ran into Zina to tell her in rough outline her decision and to give her some instructions. But Zina could not listen to her. She was lying on her bed, with her face in her pillow, and her white arms bare to the elbows; she was shedding tears and tearing her long, exquisite hair. At moments she shuddered all over as though a cold shiver were running over her limbs. Marya Alexandrovna began talking, but Zina did not even lift her head.

After standing for some time beside her, Marya Alexandrovna went out in confusion, and to vent her feelings, got into the carriage and told her coachman to drive as fast as he could.

"It's a nuisance that Zina overheard it,' she thought as she got into the carriage. "I brought Mozglyakov round with the same words that I used with her. She is proud, and perhaps was wounded. . . . Hm! But the great thing, the great thing is to make haste and settle it all before they have got wind of it! It's a pity! Well, and what if by ill luck the fool is not at home!"

And at the mere thought of that she was overcome with a

fury that boded nothing pleasant to Afanasy Matveyitch; she could hardly sit still for impatience. The horses whirled her along full speed.

CHAPTER X

THE carriage flew along. We mentioned before that an idea that was a stroke of genius had flashed into Mary Alexandrovna's brain that morning when she was hunting over the town for the prince. We promised to refer to that idea in its proper place. But the reader knows it already. The idea was to kidnap the prince in her turn, and to carry him off as quickly as possible to their estate in the neighbourhood, where the blissful Afanasy Matveyitch flourished in tranquillity. There is no disguising the fact that Marya Alexandrovna was more and more overcome by an inexplicable uneasiness. This does happen at times to real heroes at the very moment when they are attaining their object. Some instinct suggested to her that it was dangerous to remain at Mordasov. "But once we are in the country," she thought, "the whole town may be upside down for all I care!" Of course, no time was to be lost even in the country. Anything might happen—anything, absolutely anything; though, of course, we put no faith in the rumours, circulated later about my heroine by her enemies, that at this juncture she was actually afraid of the police. In short she saw that she must get the marriage of Zina and the prince solemnised as quickly as possible. She had the means for doing so at hand. The village priest could celebrate the nuptials in their own home. The ceremony might actually be performed the day after tomorrow; in the last resort, even tomorrow. There were cases of weddings within two hours of the betrothal! They could present the haste, the absence of festivities, of betrothal, of bridesmaids, to the prince as essen-

114

tially *comme il faut;* they could impress upon him that it would be more in keeping with decorum and aristocratic style. In fact, it might all be made to appear as a romantic adventure, and so the most susceptible chord in the prince's heart would be struck. If all else failed, they could always make him drunk or, still better, keep him in a state of perpetual drunkenness. And afterwards, come what may, Zina would anyway be a princess! Even if they did not get off afterwards without a scandal—in Petersburg or Moscow, for instance, where the prince had relations—even that had its consolations. In the first place, all that was in the future; and in the second, Marya Alexandrovna believed that in the best society scarcely anything ever happened without a scandal, especially in the matrimonial line; that this was, in fact, *chic*, though the scandals of the best society were, she imagined, necessarily all of a special stamp—on a grand scale, something after the style of *Monte Cristo* or *Les Mémoires du Diable.* That, in fact, Zina need only show herself in the best society, and her mamma need only be there to support her, and everyone—absolutely everyone—would instantly be conquered, and that not one of all those countesses and princesses would be capable of withstanding the sousing which Marya Alexandrovna alone was capable of giving them, collectively or individually, in true Mordasov style. In consequence of these reflections, Marya Alexandrovna was now flying to her country seat to fetch Afanasy Matveyitch, whose presence, she calculated, was now indispensable. Indeed, to take the prince to the country would mean taking him to see Afanasy Matveyitch, whose acquaintance the prince might not be anxious to make. If Afanasy Matveyitch were to give the invitation it would put quite a different complexion upon it. Moreover, the arrival of an elderly and dignified paterfamilias in a white cravat and a dress-coat, with a hat in his hand, who had come from distant parts at once on hearing about the prince, might produce a

115

very agreeable effect, might even flatter the *amour-propre* of the latter. It would be difficult to refuse an invitation so pressing and so ceremonious, thought Marya Alexandrovna. At last the carriage had driven the two and a half miles, and Sofron, the coachman, pulled up his horses at the front door of a rambling wooden building of one storey, somewhat dilapidated and blacked by age, with a long row of windows, and old lime trees standing round it on all sides. This was the country house and summer residence of Marya Alexandrovna. Lights were already burning in the house.

"Where is the blockhead?" cried Marya Alexandrovna, bursting into the rooms like a hurricane. "What is that towel here for? Ah! he has been drying himself! Have you been to the baths again? And he is for ever swilling his tea! Well, why are you staring at me like that, you perfect fool? Why hasn't his hair been cut? Grishka! Grishka! Grishka! Why haven't you cut your master's hair, as I told you to last week?"

As she went into the room Marya Alexandrovna intended to greet her spouse far more gently, but seeing that he had just come from the bath-house and was sipping his tea with great enjoyment, she could not refrain from the bitterest indignation. And, indeed, her cares and anxieties were only equalled by the blissful quietism of the useless and incompetent Afanasy Matveyitch; the contrast instantly stung her to the heart. Meanwhile the blockhead, or to speak more respectfully, he who was called the blockhead, sat behind the samovar, and in senseless panic gazed at his better half with open mouth and round eyes, almost petrified by her appearance. The drowsy and clumsy figure of Grishka blinking at this scene was thrust in from the entry.

"He wouldn't let me, that is why I didn't cut it," he said in a grumbling and husky voice. "A dozen times I went up to him with the scissors, and said, 'The mistress will be coming

116

directly, and then we shall both catch it; and what shall we do then?' 'No,' he said; 'wait a little. I am going to curl it on Sunday, so I must have my hair long.'"

"What? So he curls his hair. So you have begun curling your hair while I am away? What new fashion is this? Why, does it suit you—does it suit your wooden head? My goodness, how untidy it is here! What is this smell? I am asking you, you monster, what is this horrid smell here?" shouted his wife, scolding her innocent and completely flabbergasted husband more and more angrily.

"Mo . . . mother!" muttered her panic-stricken spouse, gazing with imploring eyes at his domineering tyrant, and not getting up from his seat. "Mo . . . mother! . . ."

"How often have I knocked into your ass's head that I am not to be called 'mother'? Mother, indeed, to you, a pigmy! How dare you use such a mode of address to a refined lady, whose proper place is in the best society, instead of beside an ass like you!"

"But . . . but you know, Marya Alexandrovna, you are my lawful wedded wife, and so I speak to you . . . as to my wife," Afanasy Matveyitch protested, and at the same moment put up both hands to his head to protect his hair.

"Oh, you ugly creature! Oh, you aspen post! Was anything ever more stupid than your answer? Lawful wedded wife? Lawful wedded wife, indeed, nowadays! Does anybody in good society make use of that stupid clerical, that revoltingly vulgar expression, '*lawful wedded*'? And how dare you remind me that I am your wife, when I am doing my best, my very utmost, to forget it! Why are you putting your hands over your head? Look what his hair is like! Sopping, absolutely sopping! It won't be dry for another three hours! How can I take him now—how can I let people see him! What's to be done now?"

And Marya Alexandrovna wrung her hands in fury, running

117

backwards and forwards in the room. The trouble, of course, was a small one, and could easily be set right; but the fact was that Marya Alexandrovna could not control her all-conquering and masterful spirit. She felt an irresistible craving to be constantly venting her wrath upon Afanasy Matveyitch, for tyranny is a habit which becomes an irresistible craving. And we all know what a contrast some refined ladies of a certain position are capable of at home behind the scenes; and it is just that contrast I wish to reproduce. Afanasy Matveyitch watched his wife's evolution with a tremor, and positively broke into a perspiration as he looked at her.

"Grishka," she cried at last, "dress your master at once: his dress-coat, his trousers, his white tie, his waistcoat. Look sharp! But where is his hair-brush? Where is the brush?"

"Mother! Why, I have just come from the bath; I shall catch cold if I drive to the town. . . ."

"You won't catch cold!"

"But my hair is wet. . . ."

"Well, we will dry it directly. Grishka, take the hair-brush; brush him till he is dry. Harder, harder, harder! That's it! That's it!"

At this command the zealous and devoted Grishka began brushing his master's hair with all his might, clutching him by the shoulder to get a more convenient grip, and pressing him down to the sofa. Afanasy Matveyitch frowned and almost wept.

"Now come here! Lift him up, Grishka! Where is the pomatum? Bend down, bend down, you good-for-nothing; bend down, you sluggard!"

And Marya Alexandrovna set to work to pomade her husband's head with her own hands, ruthlessly tugging at his thick, grizzled locks, which, to his sorrow, he had not had cut. Afanasy Matveyitch cleared his throat, gasped, but did not scream, and endured the whole operation submissively.

"You have sucked the life-blood out of me, you sloven!" said Marya Alexandrovna. "Bend down more, bend down!"

"How have I sucked your life-blood, mother?" mumbled her husband, bending his head as far as he could.

"Blockhead! He doesn't understand allegory! Now comb your hair; and you, dress him, and look sharp!"

Our heroine sat down in an easy chair and kept an inquisitorial watch on the whole ceremony of arraying Afanasy Matveyitch. Meanwhile he succeeded in getting his breath and recovering himself a little, and when the tying of his cravat was reached he even ventured to express an opinion of his own on the style and beauty of the knot. Finally, putting on his dress-coat, the worthy man was restored to cheerfulness, and looked at himself in the glass with some respect.

"Where are you taking me, Marya Alexandrovna?" he said, prinking before the looking-glass.

Marya Alexandrovna could not believe her ears. "Hear him! Oh, you dummy! How dare you ask me where I am taking you!"

"Mother, but, you know, one must know. . . ."

"Hold your tongue! Only I tell you if you call me 'mother' once more, especially where we are going now, you shall be cut off tea for a month!"

The panic-stricken husband held his tongue.

"Ugh! Not a single decoration has he gained, the sloven!" she went on, looking at Afanasy Matveyitch's black coat contemptuously.

At last her husband was offended.

"It's the government gives decorations, mother; and I am a councillor and not a sloven," he said, with honourable indignation.

"What, what, what? So you have learnt to argue out here! Ah, you peasant! Ah, you sniveller! It's a pity I haven't time to see to you, or I'd . . . But I shan't forget it later on.

119

Give him his hat, Grishka! Give him his overcoat! While I'm away get these three rooms ready; get the green corner room ready, too. Fetch your brooms instantly! Take the covers off the looking-glasses, off the clocks, too, and within an hour let everything be ready; and put on your swallow-tail yourself and give the servants gloves! Do you hear, Grishka, do you hear?"

They got into the carriage. Afanasy Matveyitch was puzzled and wondering. Meanwhile Marya Alexandrovna was deliberating how she could most intelligently knock into her husband's brain certain admonitions indispensable in his present position. But her husband anticipated her.

"Do you know, Marya Alexandrovna, I had a most original dream this morning," he informed her quite unexpectedly, in the midst of silence on both sides.

"Phoo! you confounded dummy! Goodness knows what I thought you were going to say! Some stupid dream! How dare you interrupt me with your loutish dreams! Original! Do you understand what original means? Listen: I tell you for the last time, if you dare to say one word today about your dream or anything else, I'll . . . I don't know what I'll do to you! Listen attentively. Prince K. has come to stay with me. Do you remember Prince K.?"

"I remember him, mother, I remember him. What has he come for?"

"Be quiet; that is not your business. You must, as master of the house, invite him, with special politeness, to stay with us in the country. That is what I am taking you for. We shall set off and drive back today. But if you dare to utter one single word the whole evening, or tomorrow, or the day after tomorrow, or at any time, I'll set you to herd the geese for a whole year! Don't say anything, not a single word. That's the whole of your duty. Do you understand?"

"But if I am asked a question?"

"Never mind, hold your tongue."

"But you know it's impossible to hold one's tongue all the while, Marya Alexandrovna."

"In that case, answer in monosyllables; something, for instance, such as '*H'm!*' or something of that kind, to show you are a sensible man and think before you speak."

"H'm!"

"Understand me: I am taking you because you have heard about the prince, and, delighted at his visit, have hastened to pay your respects to him and to ask him to visit you in the country. Do you understand?"

"H'm!"

"None of your h'mming now, you idiot! You answer me."

"Very good, mother, it shall all be as you say. Only why am I to invite the prince?"

"What, what? Arguing again! What business is it of yours what for? And how dare you ask questions about it?"

"But I keep wondering, mother, how I am to invite him if I hold my tongue, as you tell me."

"I will speak for you, and you've simply got to bow—do you hear? to bow—and hold your hat in your hand. Do you understand?"

"I understand, moth . . . Marya Alexandrovna."

"The prince is extremely witty. If he says anything, even though it is not to you, you must respond to everything with a bright and good-humoured smile. Do you understand?"

"H'm!"

"H'mming again! Don't say 'H'm!' to me. Answer simply and directly. Do you hear?"

"I hear, Marya Alexandrovna; of course I hear. And I am saying 'H'm!' to practise saying it, as you told me. Only I keep wondering about the same thing, mother: how it is to be. If the prince says anything, you tell me to look at him and smile. Well, but if he asks me something?"

121

"You slow-witted dolt! I have told you already: hold your tongue. I will answer for you; you simply look at him and smile."

"Why, but he'll think I am dumb," grumbled Afanasy Matveyitch.

"As though that mattered! Let him think it; you'll conceal the fact that you are a fool, anyway."

"H'm! . . . But what if other people ask me some question?"

"Nobody will ask you; no one will be there. But in case—which God forbid!—somebody does come in, and if anybody does ask you a question, or say something to you, you must answer at once by a sarcastic smile. Do you know what is meant by a sarcastic smile?"

"It means witty, doesn't it, mother?"

"I'll teach you to be witty, you blockhead! And who would ask a fool like you to be witty? A mocking smile—don't you understand?—mocking and contemptuous."

"H'm!"

"Oh, I do feel uneasy about this blockhead!" Marya Alexandrovna murmured to herself. "He certainly has taken a vow to be the death of me! It really would have been better not to have brought him at all."

Absorbed in such reflections, in regret and anxiety, Marya Alexandrovna was continually popping her head out of the window and urging on the coachman. The horses raced along, but still it seemed too slow for her. Afanasy Matveyitch sat silently in his corner, inwardly repeating his lesson. At last the carriage drove into the town and stopped at Marya Alexandrovna's house. But our heroine had hardly had time to alight at the front door, when all at once she saw driving up to the house a two-seated sledge with a hood—the very sledge in which Anna Nikolaevna Antipov usually drove about. In the sledge were sitting two ladies. One of them was, of course, Anna Nikolaevna herself, the other Natalya Dmitryevna, who had of late been her devoted friend and follower. Marya Alexandrovna's heart sank. But before she had time to cry out, another carriage drove up—a sledge, in which there was evidently another visitor. There was a sound of joyful exclamations:

"Marya Alexandrovna! And with Afanasy Matveyitch, too! You have just arrived? Where from? How lucky! And we have come to spend the whole evening! What a surprise!"

The visitors sprang out at the front door, and chattered like swallows. Marya Alexandrovna could not believe her eyes or her ears.

"I'll see you further," she thought to herself. "It looks like a plot! I must inquire into it. But . . . you won't outwit me, you magpies. . . . You wait a bit. . . ."

CHAPTER XI

As Mozglyakov left Marya Alexandrovna, he was apparently quite comforted. She had completely inflamed his imagination. He did not go to see Boroduev, feeling that he wanted to be alone. A perfect flood of heroic and romantic dreams would not let him rest. He dreamed of a solemn explanation with Zina, then of generous tears of forgiveness on his part, pallor and despair at the gorgeous ball in Petersburg, Spain, the Guadalquivir, love and the dying prince joining their hands on his death-bed. Then his lovely wife devoted to him and for ever lost in admiration of his heroism and lofty feelings; incidentally, on the quiet, the attentions of some countess belonging to the best society into which he would certainly be brought by his marriage with Zina, the window of Prince K.; a post as vice-governor, money—in fact, everything so eloquently described by Marya Alexandrovna passed once more through his gratified soul, caressing and attracting it, and, above all, flattering his vanity. But—and I really don't know how to explain it—as he began to be wearied by these raptures, the extremely vexatious reflection occurred to him: that all this was, in any case, in the future, while now anyway he had been made a fool of. When this thought came into his mind, he noticed that he had wandered a long way into some solitary and unfamiliar suburb of Mordasov. It had grown dark. In the streets, with their rows of little houses sunk into the earth, there was a savage barking of·the dogs which abound in provincial towns in alarming numbers, precisely in those quarters where there is nothing to guard and nothing to steal. Snow was beginning to fall and melting as it fell. From time to time he met a belated workman or a peasant woman in a sheep skin and high boots. All this, for some unknown reason, began to irritate Pavel Alexandrovitch—a very bad sign, for when things are going well everything strikes us in a charming and attractive light. Pavel Alexandrovitch could not help remembering that hitherto he had always been a leading figure in Mordasov. He had been highly gratified when in every house he had heard it hinted that he was an eligible *parti* and had been congratulated on that distinction. He was actually proud of being an eligible young man. And now he would appear before everyone as on the shelf! There would be laughter at his expense. Of course he could not enlighten them, he could not talk to them about Petersburg ballrooms with columns, and about the Guadalquivir! Thinking of all this, full of dejection and regret, he stumbled at last upon a thought which had for a long while been rankling unnoticed in his heart: "Was it all true? Would it all come to pass as Marya Alexandrovna had described it?" At that point he remembered very opportunely that Marya Alexandrovna was a very designing woman, that however worthy of general respect she might be, she was gossiping and lying from morning till night; that in getting rid of him now, she probably had her own reasons, and that drawing

124

fancy pictures of the future was a thing that anybody could do. He thought of Zina, too, recalled her parting look at him, which expressed anything rather than concealed passion; and therewith appropriately remembered that an hour before she had called him a fool. At that recollection Pavel Alexandrovitch stopped short as though rooted to the spot, and flushed with shame till the tears came into his eyes. As ill-luck would have it, the next minute he had an unpleasant adventure: he stepped back and went flying from the wooden pavement into a heap of snow. While he was floundering in the snow a pack of dogs, which had been pursuing him with their barking for some time, flew at him on all sides. One of them, the smallest and most aggressive, hung on to him, fastening its teeth into his fur coat. Fighting off the dogs, swearing aloud, and even cursing his fate, Pavel Alexandrovitch, with a torn coat and insufferable despondency in his heart, reached the corner of the street and only then realised that he had lost his way. We all know that a man who has lost his way in an unknown part of the town, especially at night, can never walk straight along the streets. Some unknown force seems at every moment to impel him to turn down every side street he comes to on his way. Following this system, Pavel Alexandrovitch was soon hopelessly lost. "Deuce take all these exalted notions!" he said to himself, spitting with anger. "And the devil himself take you with your lofty feelings and your Guadalquivirs!" I cannot say that Mozglyakov was attractive at that moment. After wandering about for a couple of hours, he arrived exhausted and harassed at Marya Alexandrovna's front door. He was surprised at seeing a number of carriages. "Can there be visitors, can it be an evening party?" he thought. "What's the object of it?" Questioning a servant he met, and learning that Mary Alexandrovna had been to their country house and had brought back with her Afanasy Matveyitch in a white cravat, and that the prince was awake but had not yet come downstairs to join the visitors, Pavel Alexandrovitch went upstairs to his 'uncle' without saying a word to anyone. He was at the moment in that state of mind when a man of weak character is capable of committing some horrible, malignant and nasty action from revenge, without considering that he may have to regret it all his life afterwards.

Going upstairs, he saw the prince sitting in an easy chair before his travelling dressing-case, with an absolutely bald head, though he had his 'imperial' and whiskers on. The wig was in the hands of his grey-haired old valet and favourite, Ivan Pahomitch. Pahomitch was combing it with an air of deep reflection and respect. As for the prince, he presented a very sorry spectacle, having hardly recovered from his recent potations. He was sitting, as it were, all of a heap, blinking, crumpled and out of sorts, and he looked at Mozglyakov as though he did not recognise him.

"How are you feeling, uncle?" asked Mozglyakov.

"What! . . . That's you," said his 'uncle' at last. "I've had a little nap, my boy. Oh, my goodness!" he cried, suddenly reviving, "why, I . . . haven't got my wi-ig on."

"Don't disturb yourself, uncle. I . . . I will help you, if you like."

"But now you've learnt my secret! I said we ought to lo-ock the door. Come, my dear, you must give me your wo-ord of honour at once that you won't give away my secret and won't tell anyone that my hair is fa-alse."

"Upon my word, uncle! Can you think me capable of anything so base!" cried Mozglyakov, anxious to please the old gentleman, with . . . ulterior aims.

"Oh, yes; oh, yes! And as I see you are an honourable man, so be it, I will surprise you . . . and will tell you all my secrets. How do you like my mous-taches, my dear?"

"They are superb, uncle! Marvellous! How can you have preserved them so long?"

"Don't deceive yourself, my dear, they are ar-ti-fi-cial," said the prince, looking with triumph at Pavel Alexandrovitch.

"Is it possible? I can hardly believe it. And the whiskers? Confess, uncle, you must darken them?"

"Darken them? They are not dyed, they are artificial."

"Artificial? No, uncle, you may say what you like, but I don't believe it. You are laughing at me!"

"*Parole d'honneur, mon ami*!" the prince cried triumphantly; "and only fan-cy, everyone is de-ceived, like you. Even Stepanida Matveyevna cannot believe it, though she sometimes fi-xes them on herself. But, I am sure, my boy, you will keep my secret. Give me your word of honour. . . ."

"On my word of honour, uncle, I will keep it. I ask you again, can you think me capable of anything so base?"

"Oh, my dear, what a fall I have had while you were away to-day. Feofil upset me out of the carriage again."

"Upset you again! When?"

"We were on our way to the mon-as-tery. . . ."

"I know, uncle, this morning."

"No, no, two hours ago, not more. I set off to the monastery and he upset me. How frigh-tened I was, even now my heart isn't right."

"But you've been asleep, uncle!" said Mozglyakov, wondering.

"Oh, yes, I've been asleep . . . and afterwards I drove out, though indeed . . . though perhaps I . . . oh, how strange it is!"

"I assure you, uncle, that you have been dreaming it! You have been quietly dozing ever since dinner."

"Really?" and the prince pondered. "Oh, yes, perhaps I really did dream it, though I remember everything I dreamed. At first I dreamt of a very dreadful bull with horns; and then I dreamt of some pub-lic pro-se-cu-tor who seemed to have ho-orns, too. . . ."

127

"I suppose that was Nikolay Vassilitch Antipov, uncle?"

"Oh, yes, perhaps it was he; and then I dreamt of Napoleon Bonaparte. Do you know, my dear, they all tell me that I am like Napoleon Bonaparte . . . and in profile I am strikingly like some pope of old days! What do you think, my dear, am I like a pope?"

"I think you are more like Napoleon, uncle."

"Oh, yes, full face. I think so myself, too, my dear. And I dreamt about him, when he was on the island, and you know he was so talkative, so springhtly, such a jo-olly fel-low that he quite amused me."

"Are you speaking of Napoleon, uncle?" said Pavel Alex-androvitch, looking at the old man reflectively. A strange idea was beginning to dawn upon his mind, an idea which he could not yet define clearly to himself.

"Oh, yes, of Na-po-leon. We were discussing philosophy to-gether. And do you know, my dear, that I am really sorry the En-glish treated him so harshly. Of course, if he had not been kept on the chain he would have been attacking people again. He was a desperate man, but still I am sorry for him. I wouldn't have treated him so. I would have put him upon an un-in-habited island. . . ."

"Why on an uninhabited one?" asked Mozglyakov absent-mindedly.

"Well, perhaps, on an in-habited one; but inhabited only by sensible people. And I would have got up entertainments of all sorts for him: a theatre, concerts, ballets, and all at the government expense. I would have let him go for walks under supervision, of course, or else he would have slipped away at once. He was very fond of little pies. Well, I would have made him little pies every day. I would have looked after him like a father, so to speak. He would have re-pen-ted in my care. . . ."

Mozglyakov listened absent-mindedly to the babble of the

old man not yet fully awake, and bit his nails with impatience. He wanted to turn the conversation upon marriage, though he scarcely yet knew why; and unbounded anger was surging in his heart. All at once the old man cried out in surprise:

"Oh, *mon ami*! Why, I forgot to tell you. Only fancy, I made a pro-po-sal today."

"A proposal uncle!" cried Mozglyakov, waking up.

"Why, yes, a pro-po-sal. Pahomitch, are you going? Very good. *C'est une charmante personne.* . . . But . . . I confess, my dear boy, I acted thought-less-ly. I only se-ee that now. Oh, dear me!"

"But excuse me, uncle, when did you make this proposal?"

"I own, my dear boy, that I really don't quite know when it was. Didn't I dream it, perhaps? Ah, how queer it is, though!"

Mozglyakov shuddered with delight. A new idea flashed upon his mind.

"But who was it you made an offer to, and when did you make it, uncle?" he repeated impatiently.

"The daughter of the house, *mon ami . . . cette belle personne.* . . . I have for-got-ten her name, though. Only you see, my dear, I really can't get ma-arried. What am I to do now?"

"Yes, it will certainly be your ruin if you get married. But allow me to ask you one question, uncle. You seem to be convinced that you really have made an offer?"

"Oh, yes. . . . I am sure of it."

"But what if you have dreamed it all, just as you dreamed you had been upset out of your carriage a second time?"

"Oh, my goodness! Perhaps this really was a dream, too! So that I really don't know how to behave with them. How is one to find out for certain, my dear boy, whether I did make a proposal or not? But now fancy what a position I am in?"

"Do you know, uncle, I fancy there is no need to find out."

"How so?"

"I feel sure that you dreamed it."

129

"I think so, too, my dear, especially as I often have dreams of that sort."

"There you see, uncle. Remember that you had a little wine at lunch, and then again at dinner, and in the end. . . ."

"Oh, yes, my dear; it very like-ly was due to that."

"Besides, uncle, however exhilarated you may have been, you couldn't possibly under any circumstances have made such a nonsensical proposal in reality. As far as I know you, uncle, you are a man of the greatest good sense, and . . ."

"Oh, yes; oh, yes."

"Only consider one point: if your relations, who have nothing but ill-will for you in any case, were to hear of it, what would happen then?"

"Oh, my goodness!" cried the prince in alarm, "what would happen then?"

"Upon my word! Why, they would all cry out in chorus, that you were out of your mind when you did it, that you had gone mad, that you must be put under restraint, that you had been taken advantage of, and perhaps they would put you somewhere under supervision."

Mozglyakov knew what would frighten the prince most.

"Oh, my God!" cried the prince, trembling like a leaf. "Could they possibly shut me up?"

"And then only think, uncle, could you possibly have made such an imprudent offer when you were awake? You understand your own interests. I assure you solemnly that it was all a dream."

"It cer-tain-ly must have been a dream, it cer-tain-ly must!" the prince repeated in a panic. "Oh, how sensibly you've thought it out, my de-ear boy! I am sincerely grateful to you for setting me right."

"I am awfully glad, uncle, that I have met you today. Only fancy, if I had not been here you might really have been muddled, have thought that you were engaged, and have gone

130

down to them as though you were. Think how dangerous!"

"Oh, yes . . . yes, dangerous."

"Remember that young lady is three-and-twenty; nobody wants to marry her, and all at once you, a man of wealth and rank, appear as a suitor! Why, they would snatch at the idea at once, would assure you you were engaged, and would force you perhaps into marriage. And they would calculate on the possibility of your dying before long."

"Really?"

"And remember, uncle, a man of your qualities . . ."

"Oh, yes, with my qualities . . ."

"With your intelligence, with your politeness . . ."

"Oh, yes, with my intelligence, yes! . . ."

"And last, but not least, you are a prince. What a splendid match you might make if, for some reason, you really did want to marry! Only think what your relations would say!"

"Oh, my dear, why they would be the death of me! I have endured such treachery, such ill-treatment at their hands. . . . Would you believe it, I suspect they wanted to put me into a lu-na-tic asylum. Upon my word, my dear, wasn't that absurd? Why, what could I have done there . . . in a lu-na-tic asylum?"

"Quite so, uncle, and so I won't leave your side when you go downstairs. There are visitors there now."

"Visitors? Oh, my goodness!"

"Don't be uneasy, uncle, I will keep with you."

"But how grate-ful I am to you, my dear, you are simply my saviour! But do you know, I think I had better go away."

"Tomorrow morning, uncle, at seven o'clock tomorrow morning. But today you can take leave of everyone and tell them you are going away."

"I will certainly go away . . . to Father Misail. . . . But my dear boy—what if they do make a match of it?"

"Don't be afraid, uncle, I shall be with you, and whatever

131

they say to you, whatever they hint at, you say straight out that it was all a dream, as it certainly was. . . ."

"Oh, yes, it cer-tain-ly must have been a dream. Only do you know, my dear, it was a most en-chan-ting dream! She is wonderfully good-looking, and do you know, such a figure. . . ."

"Well, farewell, uncle. I am going downstairs, and you. . . ."

"What! Are you going to leave me alone?" cried the prince in alarm.

"No, uncle, we'll both go down but separately; I'll go first, and then you. That will be better."

"Oh, ve-ry well. And by the way, I must jot down an idea."

"Quite so, uncle, jot down your idea and then come down, don't delay. Tomorrow morning. . . ."

"And tomorrow morning to Father Misail, cer-tain-ly to Father Misail! *Charmant, charmant*! But do you know, my dear, she is won-der-ful-ly good-looking . . . such contours . . . and if I really had to be married . . ."

"God preserve you, uncle."

"Oh, yes, God preserve me! . . . Well, good-bye, my dear, I'll come directly . . . only I will just jot down. *À propos*, I have been meaning to ask you for a long time. Have you read the memoirs of Casanova?"

"Yes, I have, uncle, why?"

"Oh, well . . . I have forgotten now what I meant to say. . . ."

"You will think of it later, uncle. Good-bye for the present!"

"Good-bye, my dear, good-bye. Though it really was a fascinating dream, a fa-as-cin-a-ting dream! . . ."

132

CHAPTER XII

"WE'VE all come to see you, all of us' and Praskovya Ilyinitchna is coming too, and Luiza Karlovna meant to come too," twittered Anna Nikolaevna, walking into the *salon* and looking about her greedily.

She was a rather pretty little lady, dressed expensively but in gaudy colours, and very well aware that she was pretty. She fancied that the prince was hidden somewhere in a corner with Zina.

"And Katerina Petrovna is coming, and Felisata Mihalovna meant to be here too," added Natalya Dmitryevna, the lady of colossal proportions, remarkably like a grenadier, whose appearance had so delighted the prince.

She had on an extraordinary small pink hat perched on the back of her head. For the last three weeks she had been the devoted friend of Anna Nikolaevna, whose good graces she had long been trying to win, and whom, to judge by appearances, she could have swallowed up at one gulp, bones and all.

"I won't speak of the delight, I may call it, of seeing you both here and in the evening too," Marya Alexandrovna chanted, recovering from her first stupefaction. "But tell me, please, what miracle has brought you to me tonight, when I quite despaired of such an honour."

"Oh, my goodness, Marya Alexandrovna, what a forgetful lady you are!" said Natalya Dmitryevna in honied accents, mincing and speaking in a bashful and squeaky voice which was a very curious contrast to her appearance.

"*Mais ma charmante,*" twittered Anna Nikolaevna, "we must, you know, we really must complete our arrangements for these theatricals. Only today Pyotr Mihalovitch said to Kalist Stanislavitch that he was very much disappointed that it was not coming off well, and that we did nothing but fall out over it. So we met together this evening and thought:

133

let us go to Marya Alexandrovna's and settle it all right away. Natalya Dmitryevna let the others know. They are all coming. So we will talk it all over together and all will go well. We won't let them say that we do nothing but quarrel, will we, *mon ange*?" she added playfully, kissing Marya Alexandrovna. "Oh, my goodness! Zinaida Afanasyevna! Why, you grow prettier every day!"

Anna Nikolaevna flew to shower kisses on Zina.

"Indeed, she has nothing else to do but grow prettier," Natalya Dmitryevna added in sugary accents, rubbing her huge hands.

"The devil take them! I did not think about those theatricals! They have been sharp, the magpies!" Marya Alexandrovna murmured, beside herself with fury.

"Especially, my angel, since that darling prince is staying with you. You know there used to be a theatre at Duhanovo in the time of the late owners. We have made inquiries already and know that all the old scenery, the curtain, and even the costumes are put away somewhere. The prince called on me today, and I was so surprised at seeing him that I quite forgot to speak of it. Now we will introduce the subject of the theatre, you must help us, and the prince will order all the old trappings to be sent us. For who is there here you can trust to make anything like scenery? And what is more, we want to interest the prince in our theatricals. He must subscribe, you see it is for charity. Perhaps he will even take a part —he is so sweet and obliging. Then it will be a wonderful success."

"Of course he will take a part. Why, he can be made to play any part," Natalya Dmitryevna added with vast significance.

Anna Nikolaevna had not misinformed Marya Alexandrovna: ladies kept arriving every minute. Marya Alexandrovna hardly had time to receive them and utter the exclamations demanded on such occasions by propriety and the rules of *comme il faut*.

I will not undertake to describe all the visitors. I will only mention that each one wore a look of extraordinary wiliness. Anticipation and a sort of wild impatience was expressed on every face. Some of the ladies had come with the express object of witnessing an extraordinary and scandalous scene, and would have been exceedingly wroth if they had had to drive home again without having seen it. On the surface they behaved with the utmost amiability, but Marya Alexandrovna resolutely prepared herself for the attack. There was a shower of questions about the prince; they sounded most natural, yet each seemed to contain an allusion or innuendo. Tea was brought in; everyone sat down. One group took possession of the piano. On being asked to play and sing, Zina answered that she did not feel quite well. The paleness of her face confirmed her words. Sympathetic inquiries were showered upon her, and the ladies even seized the opportunity to ask questions and drop hints. They inquired about Mozglyakov, too, and addressed these inquiries to Zina. Marya Alexandrovna displayed ten times her usual energy at that moment; she saw everything that was going on in every corner of the room, heard what was said by each one of her visitors, though there were nearly a dozen of them, and answered every question immediately, without hesitating for a word. She was trembling for Zina and was surprised that she did not go away, as she had always done before on such occasions. She kept her eye, too, on Afanasy Matveyitch. Everybody always made fun of him in order to pique Marya Alexandrovna through her husband. On this occasion it might be possible to learn something from the simple-minded and open-hearted Afanasy Matveyitch. Marya Alexandrovna looked with anxiety at the way in which her husband was being besieged. Moreover, to every question he answered "H'm," with an expression so unhappy and unnatural that it might well have driven her to fury.

"Marya Alexandrovna, Afanasy Matveyitch won't talk to us at all!" cried one bold, sharp-eyed little lady, who was afraid of nobody and never embarrassed by anything. "Do tell him to be more polite with ladies."

"I really don't know what has come over him today," answered Marya Alexandrovna, interrupting her conversation with Anna Nikolaevna and Natalya Dmitryevna, with a gay smile. "He certainly is uncommunicative! He has scarcely said a word to me. Why don't you answer Felisata Mihalovna, *Athanase*? What did you ask him?"

"But . . . but . . . you know, mother, you told me yourself . . ." Afanasy Matveyitch began muttering in his surprise and confusion. At that moment he was standing by the lighted fire, with his hands thrust into his waistcoat in a picturesque attitude which he had chosen for himself. He was sipping tea. The ladies' questions so embarrassed him that he blushed like a girl. When he began justifying himself, he caught such a terrible glance from his infuriated wife that he almost lost consciousness from terror. Not knowing what to do, anxious to put himself right and regain respect, he took a gulp at his tea; but the tea was too hot. Having taken it so hastily he burnt himself terribly, dropped the cup, spluttered and choked so violently that he had to go out of the room to the surprise of all present. In fact, everything was clear. Marya Alexandrovna realised that her visitors knew all about it and had met together with the worst intentions. The position was dangerous. They might talk to the feeble-minded old man and turn him from his purpose even in her presence. They might even take the prince away from her, set him against her that very evening, and entice him away with them. She might expect anything. But fate had another ordeal in store for her; the door opened, and she beheld Mozglyakov, whom she had believed to be at Boroduev's and did not in the least expect that

136

evening. She started as though something had stabbed her.

Mozglyakov stopped in the doorway and looked round at everyone a little confused. He was not able to control his emotion, which was clearly apparent in his face.

"Oh, my goodness, Pavel Alexandrovitch!" cried several voices.

"Oh, my goodness! Why, it is Pavel Alexandrovitch. How was it you told us he had gone to Boroduev's, Marya Alexandrovna? We were told you were hiding at Boroduev's, Pavel Alexandrovitch!" Natalya Dmitryevna piped.

"Hiding?" repeated Mozglyakov, with a rather wry smile. 'It is a strange expression! Excuse me, Natalya Dmitryevna! I don't conceal myself from anyone, and I don't want to conceal anybody else, either," he added, looking significantly at Marya Alexandrovna.

Marya Alexandrovna was in a tremor.

"Can the blockhead be mutinous?" she wondered, looking searchingly at Mozglyakov. "No, that will be worse than anyanything. . . ."

"Is it true, Pavel Alexandrovitch, that they have given you the sack . . . at your office, I mean, of course?" the impudent Felisata Mihalovna asked pertly, sarcastically looking him straight in the face.

"The sack? What sack? I am simply transferring from one branch to another. I have a post in Petersburg," Mozglyakov answered coldly.

"Oh, I congratulate you, then," Felisata Mihalovna went on. "We were positively scared when we heard you were trying to get a post in Mordasov. The posts here can't be relied upon, Pavel Alexandrovitch, there is no keeping them."

"It is only as a teacher in the district school that you might find a vacancy," observed Natalya Dmitryevna.

The hint was so obvious and so crude that Anna Nikolaevna, confused, gently nudged her malicious friend with her foot.

137

"Do you imagine that Pavel Alexandrovitch would be willing to take the place of a wretched teacher?" put in Felisata Mihalovna.

But Pavel Alexandrovitch could not find an answer. He turned round and jostled against Afanasy Matveyitch, who held out his hand to him. Mozglyakov very stupidly did not take his hand, but gave him a low and ironical bow. Exceedingly irritated, he went up to Zina, and looking angrily into her face, muttered:

"This is all thanks to you. Wait a bit, I'll show you this very evening whether I am a fool."

"Why put it off? One can see that now," Zina answered aloud, looking her former suitor up and down with an air of aversion.

Moaglyakov turned away hurriedly, frightened by her loud voice.

"Have you been to see Boroduev?" Marya Alexandrovna ventured to inquire at last.

"No, I have been seeing uncle."

"Uncle? So you have just been with the prince, then?"

"Oh, my goodness! Then the prince is awake? And we were told that he was still resting," added Natalya Dmitryevna, with a malignant look at Marya Alexandrovna.

"Don't trouble about the prince, Natalya Dmitryevna," answered Mozglyakov; "he is awake, and now, thank God, he has all his senses about him. This morning he was given too much wine; first when he was with you, and afterwards here, till his head, never over-strong, was completely muddled. But now, thank God, we have had a little talk, and he has recovered his common sense. He will be here directly to take leave of you, Marya Alexandrovna, and thank you for all your hospitality. Tomorrow at daybreak we are setting off together to the monastery, and then I shall certainly escort him back to Duhanovo myself, to avoid a second accident like that of

138

today; and then I shall hand him over to Stepanida Matveyevna, who by that time will certainly be back from Moscow and will not let him go on his travels a second time—I can answer for that."

As he said this, Mozglyakov looked spitefully at Marya Alexandrovna. She was sitting as though petrified with amazement. I admit with grief that my heroine was, perhaps for the first time in her life, cowed.

"So he is going away at daybreak tomorrow! How's that?" said Natalya Dmitryevna, addressing Marya Alexandrovna.

"How is that?" the visitors were heard saying naïvely. "Why, we heard that . . . why, that's very odd."

But their hostess did not know what answer to make. Suddenly the general attention was diverted in the most strange and eccentric way. In the adjoining room a strange noise was heard, and abrupt exclamations, and all at once, utterly unexpectedly, Sofya Petrovna Karpuhin dashed into Marya Alexandrovna's *salon*. Sofya Petrovna was unquestionably the most eccentric lady in Mordasov, so eccentric that it had even been decided of late not to receive her in society. It must be observed, too, that regularly every evening at seven o'clock it was her habit to take a nip of something—for the sake of her stomach, as she explained—and after it, she was a rule in an emancipated state of mind, to put it mildly. She was in that state of mind now at the moment when she so unexpectedly burst in upon Marya Alexandrovna.

"So this is the way Marya Alexandrovna," she shouted to be heard all over the room. "So this is the way you treat me! Don't disturb yourself, I have only come for a minute, I won't sit down. I've come on purpose to find out whether it is true what I am told! So you have balls, banquets, a betrothal party, but Sofya Petrovna must sit at home and knit a stocking! You've asked the whole town, but not me! Though this morning I was your friend and *mon ange* when I came to

139

...ll you what they were doing with the prince at Natalya Dmitryevna's. And now here's Natalya Dmitryevna, whom you were abusing like a pickpocket, and who was abusing you, paying you a visit. Don't disturb yourself, Natalya Dmitryevna. I don't want your chocolate *à la sante*, at twopence a stick. I have better to drink at home! Tfoo!"

"One can see you have," observed Natalya Dmitryevna.

"But upon my word, Sofya Petrovna," cried Marya Alexandrovna, flushing with vexation, "what is the matter with you? Do control yourself at least."

"Don't trouble about me, Marya Alexandrovna, I know all about it, all about it!" cried Sofya Petrovna in her harsh, shrill voice. She was surrounded by the other visitors, who seemed to be enjoying this unexpected scene. "I have found out all about it. Your Nastasya ran round and told me the whole story. You pounced on this wretched prince, made him drunk, and made him propose to your daughter whom nobody wants to marry now, and you imagine that you've become a fine bird now yourself—a duchess in lace! Tfoo! Don't disturb yourself, I am a colonel's wife myself. I don't care if you don't invite me to your betrothal party. I have mixed with better people than you. I have dined with Countess Zalihvatsky. The head commisssary, Kurotchkin, paid me his addresses. As though I wanted your invitation! Tfoo!"

"Come, Sofya Petrovna," answered Marya Alexandrovna, losing patience, "I must tell you, this is not the way to burst into a lady's house, especially in *such a condition*, and if you do not relieve me of your presence and your eloquent remarks, I shall promptly take steps to get rid of you."

"I know you will tell your nasty servants to turn me out! Don't excite yourself, I can find the way for myself. Good-bye; make any marriage you like. And you, Natalya Dmitryevna, don't laugh at me, if you please; I don't care a damn about your chocolate! Though I am not invited here, I don't go dancing jigs to amuse princes. What are you laughing at, Anna Nikolaevna? Sushilov has broken his leg; they've just carried him home! And you, Felisata Mihalovna, if you don't tell your bare-legged Matryoshka to drive your cow home in good time so she's not mooing under my window every day, I will break her legs. Good-bye, Marya Alexandrovna, good luck to you! Tfoo!"

Sofya Petrovna vanished. The visitors laughed. Marya Alexandrovna was thrown into extreme embarrassment.

"I think the lady has had a little too much," Natalya Dmitryevna brought out in her sugary voice.

"But what insolence!"

"*Quelle abominable femme!*"

"How funny she was, though!"

"Ah, what shocking things she said!"

"But what was it she said about a betrothal party? What betrothal party? Felisata Mihalovna asked sarcastically.

"But this is awful!" Marya Alexandrovna burst out at last. "It is these monsters who scatter these absurd rumours by handfuls! It is not so strange, Felisata Mihalovna, that such ladies are to be found in our midst, no; what is more surprising is that these ladies are sought after, are listened to, are encouraged, are believed, are . . ."

"The prince! the prince!" all voices cried suddenly at once.

"Oh, my goodness! *Le cher prince!*"

"Oh, thank goodness. Now we shall find out all the details," Felisata Mihalovna whispered to her neighbour.

CHAPTER XIII

THE prince came in with a honied smile on his lips. The alarm which Mozglyakov had inspired in his chicken heart entirely disappeared at the sight of the ladies. He melted at once like a sweetmeat. The ladies greeted him with shrill cries of delight. Ladies always made a great deal of our old friend, and were very familiar with him. He was able to afford them incredible entertainment. Felisata Mihalovna had declared that morning (not in earnest, of course) that she was ready to sit on his knee, if that would give him any pleasure, "because he was a darling, darling old man, sweet beyond all bounds!" Marya Alexandrovna transfixed him with her eyes, trying to read something from his face and to divine from it the way out of her critical position. It was evident that Mozglyakov had said horrible things about her, and that her plans were in jeopardy. But nothing could be read from the prince's face. He was the same as he had been that morning and as he always was.

"Ah, my goodness, here is the prince! We have been waiting and waiting for you," cried several of the ladies.

"With impatience, prince, with impatience!" piped others.

"That's extremely flat-ter-ing," lisped the prince, sitting down at the table on which the samovar was boiling. The ladies immediately surrounded him. Anna Nikolaevna and Natalya Dmitryevna were the only ones left by the side of Marya Alexandrovna. Afanasy Matveyitch smiled respectfully. Mozglyakov smiled too, and with a defiant air looked at Zina, who, without taking the slightest notice of him, went and sat down by her father near the fire.

"Oh, prince, is it true what they say, that you are leaving us ?" pipedFelisata Mihalovna.

"Oh, yes, *mesdames*, I am going away, I want to go abro-oad im-med-iately."

"Abroad, prince, abroad!" they all cried in chorus. "What an idea!"

"Abro-oad," repeated the prince, prinking. "And do you know, I want to go abroad particularly for the sake of the new ideas."

"How do you mean for the sake of the new ideas? New

dịeas about what?" said the ladies, exchanging glances with one another.

"Oh, yes, for the sake of the new ideas," repeated the prince, with an air of the deepest conviction. "Everyone now goes abroad for the sake of the new i-deas, and so I, too, want to gain ne-ew i-ideas."

"Don't you want, perhaps, to enter a masonic lodge, uncle?" put in Mozglyakov, who evidently wished to impress the ladies by his wit and his ease.

"Oh, yes, my dear, you are quite right," the old man answered unexpectedly. "In old days I reall-y did belong to a masonic lodge abroad, and I, too, had a number of noble ideas. I intended, indeed, at that time to do a great deal for the en-lighten-ment of the peo-ple, and I quite decided at Frankfurt to set free my man Sidor whom I had brought with me from Russia. But to my surprise he ran away from me himself. He was an ex-treme-ly odd man. Afterwards I met him in Pa-ris, such a swell, with whiskers, he was walking along the boule-vard with a mamselle. He looked at me, gave me a nod, and the mamselle with him was such a brisk, sharp-eyed, alluring creature . . ."

"Come, uncle! Why, you'll be setting all your peasants free next, if you go abroad this time," cried Mozglyakov, laughing loudly.

"You have gu-essed perfectly right, my dear boy, what I desire to do," the prince answered without hesitation. "I do want to set them all fre-ee."

"But upon my word, prince, they will all run away from you directly, and then where will you get your money?" cried Felisata Mihalovna.

"Of course they would all run away," Anna Nikolaevna echoed, with a note of alarm.

"Oh, dear me, do you really think they would run away?" cried the prince in astonishment.

143

"They would run away, they would all run away at once and would leave you alone," Natalya Dmitryevna confirmed.

"Oh, dear me! Well, then I shall not se-et them free. But of course I did not mean it."

"So much the better, uncle," Mozglyakov said approvingly.

Till then, Marya Alexandrovna had been listening and watching in silence. It seemed to her that the prince had entirely forgotten her, and that that was not natural.

"Allow me, prince," she began in a loud and dignified voice, "to introduce my husband, Afanasy Matveyitch. He came expressly from our country house as soon as he heard you were staying with us."

Afanasy Matveyitch smiled and looked dignified. It seemed to him as though he were being praised.

"Ah, I am delighted," said the prince, "A-fa-nasy Matveyitch! To be sure, I believe I remember something. A-fa-nasy Mat-ve-yitch. To be sure, that is the gentleman in the country. *Charmant, charmant*, delighted. My dear!" cried the prince, turning to Mozglyakov. "Why, that's the very man, do you remember, who was in that rhyme this morning. How did it go? 'The husband's on the stair, and the wife has gone.' . . . Oh, yes, the wife has gone away to some town."

"Oh, prince, why that's true; 'The husband's on the stair, while wife has gone to Tver,' the very vaudeville the actors played here last year," Felisata Mihalovna put in.

"Oh, yes, precisely: To Tver; I always forget. *Charmant, charmant!* So you are that very man? Extremely glad to make your ac-quaint-ance," said the prince, holding out his hand to the smiling Afanasy Matveyitch without getting up from his chair. "Well, I hope you are well?"

"H'm. . . ."

"He is quite well, prince, quite well," Marya Alexandrovna answered hurriedly.

"Oh, yes, one can see he is quite well. And are you always in

144

the country? Well, I am delighted. Why, what red che-eeks he has and how he keeps laughing!"

Afanasy Matveyitch continued smiling, bowing, and even scraping with his foot. But at the prince's last observation he could not restrain himself, and all of a sudden, apropos of nothing, in the most foolish way burst into a loud laugh. Everybody laughed. The ladies squealed with delight. Zina flushed and with flashing eyes looked at Marya Alexandrovna, who in her turn was bursting with anger. It was high time to change the conversation.

"How did you sleep, prince?" she asked in a honied voice, at the same time turning a menacing look upon Afanasy Matveyitch to indicate that he should take himself off as quickly as possible.

"Oh, I had a very good sleep," answered the prince; "and do you know, I had a most en-chan-ting dream, an en-chan-ting dream!"

"A dream! I love to hear people tell their dreams," cried Felisata Mihalovna.

"And I, too, I love it!" added Natalya Dmitryevna.

"An en-chan-ting dream!" repeated the prince, with a mawkish smile; "but the dream is a dead secret!"

"How so, prince, do you really mean you can't tell it us? It must have been a wonderful dream!" observed Anna Nikolaevna.

"A dead secret," repeated the prince, gleefully tantalising the ladies' curiosity.

"Oh, then it must be very interesting!" cried the ladies.

"I bet that the prince dreamed that he fell on his knees before some beautiful young lady and made her an offer of marriage!" cried Felisata Mihalovna. "Come, prince, own up, that that's right! Darling prince, confess!"

"Confess, prince, confess," the others chimed in on all sides.

The prince listened triumphantly and ecstatically to all their outcries. The ladies' supposition flattered his vanity extremely, and he almost licked his lips.

"Though I said that my dream was a dead secret," he answered at last, "yet I must admit, madam, that to my great surprise, you have guessed al-most per-fect-ly right."

"Guessed right!" cried Felisata Mihalovna rapturously. "Well, prince! Well, now you absolutely must tell us who the beautiful young lady was!"

"You must tell us!"

"Does she live in these parts?"

"Darling prince, do tell us! You must tell us, whatever happens!" they cried on all sides.

"*Mesdames, mesdames*! . . . If you are so very in-sis-tent to know, I can only tell you one thing, that it was the most fas-ci-na-ting and, I may say, the most vir-tu-ous young lady I know," mumbled the prince, melting like wax.

"Most fascinating and . . . someone living here! Who could it be?" the ladies kept asking, exchanging significant glances and winking at one another.

"Of course, the one who is considered the chief belle here," said Natalya Dmitryevna, rubbing her huge red hands and looking with her cat-like eyes at Zina. All the others looked at Zina with her.

"Well, prince, if you have such dreams, why don't you get married in reality?" asked Felisata Mihalovna, with a significant look at the others.

"What a splendid match we would make for you!" another lady put in.

"Prince, darling! do get married!" piped a third.

"Get married, get married!" they cried on all sides. "Why shouldn't you get married?"

"Oh, yes, why not get married," the prince assented, completely confused by these outcries.

146

"Uncle!" cried Mozglyakov.

"Oh, yes, my dear, I un-der-stand. I meant to tell you, *mesdames*, that I am not able to get married and that, when I have spent a delightful evening with our fascinating hostess, I shall set off tomorrow to Father Misail at the monastery, and then I am going straight abroad so as to keep up with the progress of European enlightenment."

Zina turned pale and looked at her mother with inexpressible misery. But Marya Alexandrovna had already made up her mind. Hitherto she had only been waiting, testing things, though she did realise that her project was ruined and that her enemies had circumvented her successfully. At last she grasped the whole position, she made up her mind at one blow to crush the many-headed hydra. She got up from her easy chair majestically and with resolute steps approached the table, scanning with haughty eyes her pigmy foes. There was the light of inspiration in that look. She determined to impress, to disconcert all these venomous scandalmongers, to squash Mozglyakov as though he were a beetle, and by one bold resolute stroke to recapture all her lost influence over the imbecile prince. Exceptional audacity was of course needed; but Marya Alexandrovna had no lack of audacity!

"*Mesdames*," she began solemnly and with dignity (Marya Alexandrovna was particularly fond of a solemn manner), "*mesdames*, I have been listening for some time to your conversation, to your gay and witty jests, and I think it is time for me to put in my word. You know we have met together this evening—quite by chance (and I am so glad, so glad of it) . . . I should never have brought myself of my own accord to announce to you an important family secret and to publish it abroad sooner than the most ordinary feeling of decorum would dictate. Especially I must beg the forgiveness of my dear guest; but I fancied that he himself, by indirect hints at the very circumstance, gives me to understand that a formal and

147

ceremonious announcement of our family secret will not be disagreeable, that, in fact, he desires this announcement . . . . Is it not so, prince, I am not mistaken?"

"Oh, yes, you are not mistaken . . . and I am delighted!" said the prince, without the faintest idea of what she was talking about.

For the sake of greater effect, Marya Alexandrovna stopped to take breath and looked round at the whole company. All the visitors were listening to her words with spiteful and uneasy curiosity. Mozglyakov started. Zina flushed crimson and got up from her chair. Afanasy Matveyitch, in anticipation of something extraordinary, blew his nose to be ready for anything.

"Yes, *mesdames*, I am ready joyfully to confide to you my family secret. After dinner today the prince, captivated by the beauty and . . . virtues of my daughter, did her the honour of offering her his hand. Prince!" she concluded in a voice quivering with tears and emotion, "dear prince, you must not, you cannot by angry with me for my indiscretion! Nothing but my great joy as a mother could have torn from my heart this precious secret before the fitting time, and . . . what mother could blame me in this case."

I cannot find words to describe the effect produced by Marya Alexandrovna's unexpected outburst. Everyone seemed as though petrified with amazement. The treacherous visitors, who had thought they would frighten Marya Alexandrovna by their knowledge of her secret, had expected to crush her by the premature disclosure of that secret, who had expected to torment her, at first simply by allusions, were dumbfounded by such audacious candour. Such fearless audacity was a sure sign of power. "Then was the prince really going to marry Zina of his own free will? Then had they not allured him, made him drunk, deceived him? Then he was not being forced into marriage in an underhand, dishonest way? Then Marya Alexandrovna was not afraid of anybody? Then it would be impossible to prevent the marriage since the prince was not being forced into it?" For a moment there was a sound of whispering which turned at once into shrill ries of delight. Natalya Dmitryevna was the first to embrace Marya Alexandrovna; Anna Nikolaevna followed her exmaple, and after her Felisata Mihalovna. They all jumped up from their seats, they were all thrown into confusion, some of the ladies were pale from spite. They began to congratulate the embarrassed Zina; they even fastened on Afanasy Matveyitch. Marya Alexandrovna held out her arms in a picturesque attitude, and almost by force enfolded her daughter in her embrace. The prince alone looked on at the scene with strange surprise, though he went on smiling as before. The scene pleased him in a way, however. At the sight of the mother embracing the daughter, he took out his handkerchief and wiped his eyes in which there gleamed a tear. Of course people rushed to congratulate him too.

"We congratulate you, prince! We congratulate you!" the ladies cried on all sides.

"So you are going to get married?"

"So you are really going to get married?"

"Darling prince, so you are going to get married?"

"Oh, yes; oh, yes," answered the prince, extremely delighted with their raptures and their congratulations. "And I must say, that nothing gives me more pleasure than your kind sympathy, which I shall ne-ever forget, ne-ever forget. *Charmant! charmant!* You've brought tears into my eyes."

"Kiss me, prince," Felisata Mihalovna cried, louder than all the rest.

"And I must say," the prince went on, interrupted on all sides, "I am most of all surprised that Marya I-van-ov-na, our honoured hostess, has guessed my dream with such ex-tra-or-di-nary insight. It is as though she had dreamed it instead of me. Ex-tra-or-di-nary insight! Ex-tra-or-di-nary insight!"

"Oh, prince, the dream again?"

"Come, confess, prince, confess!" they all cried, surrounding him.

"Yes, prince, there is no need for concealment, the time has come to reveal our secret!" Marya Alexandrovna said sternly and resolutely. "I understand your subtle allegory, the enchanting delicacy with which you tried to hint to me your desire to make public your engagement. Yes, *mesdames*, it is true: this afternoon the prince went down on his knees to my daughter, and not in a dream but reality, and made her a formal offer."

"Exactly as though it were real and actually with the very same circumstances," repeated the prince. "*Mademoiselle*," he said, turning with marked courtesy to Zina, who had not yet recovered from her amazement, "*mademoiselle*! I swear that I would never had made so bold as to pronounce your name if others had not ut-tered it before me. It was a fascinating dream, a fa-sci-na-ting dream, and I am doubly happy· that I am now permitted to tell it to you. *Charmant, charmant! . . .*"

"But upon my word how is this? He is still talking about a dream," whispered Anna Nikolaevna to Marya Alexandrovna, who was somewhat fluttered and had turned a little pale.

Alas! There was an ache and a tremor in Marya Alexandrovna's heart already, apart from those warning words.

"How is this?" whispered the ladies, looking at one another.

"Why, prince," began Marya Alexandrovna, with a wry and sickly smile. "I protest, you surprise me! What is this strange idea about a dream? I confess I thought till now that you were jesting, but . . . if it is a joke, it is rather an inappropriate one. . . . I should desire, I should wish to put it down to your absent-mindedness, but . . ."

"Perhaps it really is the result of his absent-mindedness," hissed Natalya Dmitryevna.

"Oh, yes, perhaps it is absent-mindedness," the prince assented, still not fully grasping what they were trying to get out of him. "And only fancy, I must tell you an a-nec-dote. In Petersburg I was invited to a fu-ne-ral to some people, *maison bourgeoise, mais honnête*, and I muddled it up and thought it was a nameday party. The nameday party had been the week before. I got ready a bouquet of camelias for the lady whose nameday it was. I go in and what do I see, a respectable, dignified man lying on the table, so that I was quite sur-prised. I simply did not know what to do with myself and the bou-quet."

"Come, prince, this is not a time for anecdotes!" Marya Alexandrovna interrupted with vexation. "Of course my daughter has no need to run after suitors, but this afternoon, beside that piano, you made her a proposal. I did not invite you to do so. . . . I was, I may say, astounded. . . . I was, of course, struck by one idea at the time, and I put it all off till you should wake. But I am a mother . . . she is my daughter. . . . You spoke yourself just now of a dream, and I thought that you wished, under the guise of allegory, to tell us of your engagement. I know very well that you will be dissuaded . . . and I suspect who it is . . . but . . . explain yourself, prince, make haste and explain satisfactorily. You cannot jest like this with a respectable family."

"Oh, no, one cannot jest like this with a respectable family," the prince assented mechanically, though he was beginning to be a little uneasy.

"But that is no answer, prince, to my question. I beg you to give a definite answer; repeat at once, repeat before everyone that you did make my daughter an offer this afternoon."

"Oh, yes, I am ready to repeat it, though I have already told the whole story, and Felisata Yakovlevna guessed my dream exactly."

"It was not a dream, it was not a dream!" cried Marya Alexandrovna in exasperation. "It was not a dream, it was reality, prince; reality—do you hear?—reality!"

"Reality!" cried the prince, getting up from his chair in his surprise. "Well, my dear, it is just as you foretold upstairs!" he added, turning to Mozglyakov. "But I assure you, honoured Marya Stepanovna, that you are in error! I am quite persuaded that I only dreamed it."

"Lord have mercy upon us!" cried Marya Alexandrovna.

"Don't upset yourself, Marya Alexandrovna," Natalya Dmitryevna put in. "Perhaps the prince has forgotten. . . . He will remember."

"I wonder at you, Natalya Dmitryevna," retorted Marya Alexandrovna indignantly. "Can such things be forgotten? Can one forget it? Upon my word, prince, are you laughing at us? Or you are, perhaps, playing the part of a profligate beau of the days of the Regency depicted by Dumas. Some Faire-la-cour or Lauzun? But apart from that not being in keeping with your years, I assure you that you will not succeed in it. My daughter is not a vicomtesse. Here, this afternoon, on this spot she sang to you, and carried away by her singing you dropped on your knees and made her an offer! Can I be dreaming? Can I be sleeping? Speak, prince: am I awake or sleeping?"

"Oh, yes . . . or rather, perhaps, no . . ." answered the bewildered prince. "I mean, that I believe I am not dreaming now. You see, I was asleep this afternoon, and so I had a dream that in my sleep . . . "

"Tfoo, my goodness, what does it mean? Not asleep—asleep, dreaming—not dreaming! Why, goodness knows what it means. Are you raving, prince?"

"Oh, yes, goodness knows . . . though I believe I'm utterly at sea now," said the prince, turning uneasy glances around him.

152

"But how could you have dreamed it?" Marya Alexandrovna insisted in distress, "when I tell you your own dream in such detail, though you had not yet told anyone of us about it!"

"But perhaps the prince did tell somebody," said Natalya Dmitryevna.

"Oh, yes, perhaps I did tell somebody," the prince repeated, utterly bewildered.

"Here's a farce," whispered Felisata Mihalovna to her neighbour.

"Good heavens, this is past all endurance!" cried Marya Alexandrovna, wringing her hands in a frenzy. "She sang to you, she sang a ballad! Did you dream that too?"

"Oh, yes; yes, indeed, I fancy she did sing a ballad," the prince muttered meditatively.

And his face lightened up at some sudden recollection.

"My dear," he cried, addressing Mozglyakov, "I forgot to tell you just now that there really was a ballad, and there were continually castles in that ballad, so that it seemed as if there were a great many castles; and then there was a troubadour! Oh, yes, I remember it all. . . . So that I even shed tears. . . . And now I am puzzled, it seems as if that really did happen and was not a dream."

"I must say, uncle," answered Mozglyakov, speaking as calmly as he could, though his voice quivered from some emotion, "I must say it seems to me that it is very easy to account for that and make it fit in. I believe you really did listen to singing. Zinaida Afanasyevna sings beautifully. After dinner you were brought in here and Zinaida Afanasyevna sang the ballad to you. I was not there at the time, but you were probably touched by its recalling old days; perhaps remembering that very vicomtesse with whom you used once to sing ballads, and about whom you told us this morning. And then afterwards when you went to bed, in consequence of

153

your pleasant impressions you dreamed that you were in love and had made an offer."

Marya Alexandrovna was positively petrified by this audacity.

"Ah, my dear, that is just as it really was!" cried the prince, delighted. "It was just in consequence of those pleasant impressions. I certainly remember the ballad being sung to me, and it was because of that, that in my dream I wanted to get married. And it is true about the vicomtesse too. . . . Oh, how clever of you, my dear, to see it all! Well, now I am quite convinced that I dreamed all that! Marya Vassilyevna! I assure you that you are mistaken! It was a dream. Otherwise I should not be playing with your estimable feelings. . . ."

"Ah, now I see clearly who has been at work in this!" cried Marya Alexandrovna, beside herself with fury, addressing Mozglyakov. "It is you, you sir; you dishonourable man, it is all your doing. You have muddled this unhappy imbecile, because you were refused! But you shall pay for this insult, you blackguard! You shall pay for it. You shall pay for it!"

"Marya Alexandrovna!" cried Mozglyakov, turning as red as a crab. "Your words are so . . . I really don't know what to say of your words. . . . No well-bred lady would allow herself. . . . I am defending my kinsman, anyway. You must admit that to ensnare him like this . . ."

"Oh, yes, to ensnare like this . . ." the prince chimed in, trying to hide behind Mozglyakov.

"Afanasy Matveyitch!" shrieked Marya Alexandrovna, in an unnatural voice. " Don't you hear how we are being outraged and dishonoured? Or have you lost all sense of your duties? Are you not the head of your family, but a repulsive wooden post? Why do you keep blinking? Any other husband would long ago have washed out such an insult to his family in blood! . . ."

"Wife," Afanasy Matveyitch began with dignity, proud that

154

he was needed at last. "Wife! Didn't you perhaps dream it all, and afterwards when you woke up, you muddled it all to suit yourself! . . ."

But Afanasy Matveyitch was not destined to give full expression to his witty surmise. To that point the visitors had restrained themselves and had treacherously assumed an air of demure dignity. But at this point a loud burst of laughter that could not be restrained resounded through the room. Marya Alexandrovna, forgetting all propriety, rushed at her husband, probably with the intention of immediately scratching his eyes out. But she was restrained by force. Natalya Dmitryevna took advantage of the occasion to add just one drop more of venom.

"Oh, Marya Alexandrovna, perhaps that is just how it was, and you are upsetting yourself," she said, in a most honeyed voice.

"What was? How was it?" cried Marya Alexandrovna, not yet fully understanding it.

"Oh, Marya Alexandrovna, you know it sometimes does happen."

"What happens? Do you want to drive me crazy?"

"Perhaps you really did dream it?"

"Dream it, I? Dream it! And you dare to tell me that to my face?"

"Well, perhaps that is really how it was," responded Felisata Mihalovna.

"Oh, yes, perhaps that is how it really was," the prince, too, muttered.

"He too, he too! Lord have mercy on us!" cried Marya Alexandrovna, clasping her hands.

"How you do upset yourself, Marya Alexandrovna! Remember that dreams are sent us from on high. If it is God's will, there is none can oppose Him, and we are all in His Hands. It's no use being angry about it."

"Oh, yes, it's no good being angry about it," the prince chimed in.

"Do you take me for a lunatic?" Marya Alexandrovna articulated faintly, gasping from wrath. This was beyond human endurance. She hastily sought a chair and sank into a swoon. A hubbub followed.

"It was to do the correct thing that she fainted," Natalya Dmitryevna whispered to Anna Nikolaevna.

But at that instant, at the moment when the general bewilderment was greatest and the position was at its tensest, a person who had hitherto remained silent suddenly stepped forward—and immediately the whole character of the scene was changed. . . .

CHAPTER XIV

ZINAIDA AFANASYEVNA was, speaking generally, of an extremely romantic disposition. I don't know whether this was, as Marya Alexandrovna maintained, due to too much reading of "that fool Shakespeare" with "her wretched little schoolmaster". But never in the course of her life at Mordasov had Zina permitted herself such an extraordinary romantic or rather heroic action as the one which we are just about to describe.

Pale, with a look of determination in her eyes, but almost shaking with excitement, wonderfully lovely in her indignation, she stepped forward. Scanning the whole company with a slow, challenging look in the midst of the sudden silence, she turned to her mother, who at her first movement had promptly recovered from her swoon and opened her eyes.

"Mamma," said Zina, "why keep up deception? Why defile ourselves further by lying? It has all been made so foul that it is not worth taking degrading pains to cover up that foulness!"

"Zina, Zina! What is the matter with you? Think what you

156

are doing!" cried Marya Alexandrovna, leaping up from her chair.

"I told you, I told you beforehand, mamma, that I could not bear all this disgrace," Zina went on. "Is it necessary to degrade oneself even more, to defile oneself still further? But do you know, mamma, that I take it all upon myself, for I am more to blame than anyone. I, I by consenting, set this vile . . . intrigue . . . going! You are a mother; you love me, you meant to secure my happiness, in your own way, according to your own ideas. You may be forgiven; but I, I, never."

"Zina, surely you don't mean to speak? . . . Oh, my God! I foresaw that that dagger would stab me to the heart!"

"Yes, mamma, I shall speak out. I am disgraced, you . . . we are all disgraced! . . ."

"You are exaggerating, Zina! You are not yourself, and don't understand what you are saying! And what is the use of telling it? There is no sense in it. . . . The disgrace is not ours. I will show at once that the disgrace is not ours."

"No, mamma," cried Zina, with an angry quiver in her voice, "I will not remain silent longer before these people, whose opinion I despise and who have come to jeer at us. I will not endure insult from them; not one of them has the right to throw dirt at me. They are all ready any minute to do thirty times worse than you or I! Dare they, can they be our judges? . . ."

"That's a nice thing! Do you hear what she says? What does it mean? It's insulting us!" was heard on all sides.

"The young lady simply does not know what she is saying," said Natalya Dmitryevna.

We may observe in parenthesis that Natalya Dmitryevna's remark was a true one. If Zina did not consider those ladies worthy to judge her, what was the object of rushing into such publicity, into such confessions before them? Zinaida Afanasyevna was, in fact, extremely hasty, such was the opinion of the best heads in Mordasov later on. Everything could have been set right, everything could have been smoothed over. It is true that Marya Alexandrovna, too, had damaged their position that evening by her hastiness and presumption. They need only have derided the imbecile old gentleman and have sent him about his business. But as though of design, Zina, contrary to all good sense and Mordasov prudence, addressed herself to the prince.

"Prince," she said to the old man, who was so impressed by her at that moment that he got up from his chair as a sign of respect. "Prince, forgive me, forgive us. We deceived you! We drew you on . . ."

"Oh, will you be silent, unhappy girl!" Marya Alexandrovna cried in a frenzy.

"Madam, madam! *Ma charmante enfant . . .*" muttered the prince, much impressed.

But Zina's proud, impulsive and extremely idealistic character carried her at that instant far away from every propriety demanded by the reality of the position. She even forgot her mother, who was writhing in agony at her confession.

"Yes, we both deceived you, prince; mamma, by determining to make you marry me, and I, by consenting to it. You were given too much wine, I consented to sing and play a part before you. We, as Pavel Alexandrovitch has expressed it, have tricked you when you were weak and helpless, tricked you for the sake of your fortune, for the sake of your rank. All this was horribly base and I repent of it. But I swear to you, prince, that it was from no base impulse that I brought myself to that base act. I meant . . . but what am I saying, it is twice as base to justify oneself for a thing like that! But I assure you, prince, that if I had taken anything from you, I would have paid for it by being your plaything, your handmaid, your dancing girl, your slave. . . . I had vowed it, and would have kept my vow!"

A lump in her throat prevented her from going on. All the visitors seemed petrified and listened with their eyes starting out of their heads. Zina's strange and, to them, utterly unintelligible outbreak completely perplexed them; only the prince was touched to tears, though he did not understand half of what Zina was saying.

"But I will marry you, *ma belle enfant*, if you wi-ish it so much," he muttered, "and it will be a gre-at honour to me! Only I assure you that it real-ly was like a dream. . . . Why, I dream all sorts of things. Why are you so tro-oubled? I really don't understand it at all, *mon ami*," he went on, addressing Mozglyakov. "You explain to me, please. . . ."

"And you, Pavel Alexandrovitch," said Zina, turning too to Mozglyakov, "you, on whom I once brought myself to look as my future husband, you who have now so cruelly revenged yourself on me, can you really have joined with these people to torture me and cover me with ignominy? And you told me you loved me! But it is not for me to preach to you, I am more to blame than you. . . . I have injured you, for I really did lure you on with promises, and my statements were lies and a tissue of falsehoods! I never loved you, and if I had brought myself to marry you it would simply have been to get away from here, from this accursed town, and to escape from all this corruption. . . . But, I swear to you, that if I had married you I would have made you a good and faithful wife. . . . You have cruelly revenged yourself on me, and if that flatters your pride . . ."

"Zinaida Afanasyevna!" cried Mozglyakov.

"If you still harbour a feeling of hatred for me . . ."

"Zainaida Afanasyevna! !"

"If you ever," said Zina, stifling her tears, "if you ever did love me! ! !"

"Zinaida Afanasyevna! ! !"

"Zina, Zina, my daughter," wailed Marya Alexandrovna.

"I am a scoundrel, Zinaida Afanasyevna. I am a scoundrel and nothing else," declared Mozglyakov, and general excitement followed. Cries of surprise and indignation were raised, but Mozglyakov stood as though rooted to the spot, incapable of thought or speech.

For weak and shallow characters accustomed to habitual subordination who have dared at last to be moved to wrath and to protest, in short, to be resolute and consistent, there is always a line—a limit—to their resolution and consistency, which is soon reached. Their protest is apt at first to be most vigorous. Their energy even approaches frenzy. They fling themselves against obstacles as though with closed eyes, and always take upon themselves burdens beyond their strength. But reaching a certain point, the frenzied man, as though frightened at himself, stops short, dumbfounded with the awful question, "What is this that I have done?" Then at once he grows limp, whimpers, asks for explanations, drops on his knees, begs forgiveness, implores that all shall be as before, only quickly, as quickly as possible. . . . This is almost exactly what happened now with Mozglyakov. After having been beside himself with fury, having invited trouble which now he ascribed entirely to himself alone, having satisfied his vanity and indignation and beginning to hate himself for it, he stopped short, conscience-stricken, before Zina's unexpected outbreak. Her last words crushed him completely. To rush from one extreme to another was the work of a minute.

"I am an ass, Zinaida Afanasyevna!" he cried, in a rush of frantic penitence. "No! What's an ass? An ass would be nothing. I am incomparably worse than an ass! But I will show you, Zinaida Afanasyevna, I will show you that even an ass may be an honourable man! . . . . Uncle! I deceived you. It was I, I deceived you! You were not asleep; you really did make an offer, and I, I, like a scoundrel, out of revenge for having been refused, persuaded you that it had all been a dream."

"Wonderfully interesting things are coming out," whispered Natalya Dmitryevna in Anna Nikolaevna's ear.

"My dear," answered the prince, "ple-ease calm yourself; you really frighten me with your shouting. I assure you that you are mis-ta-ken. . . . I am ready to be married by all means if it is necessary; but, you know, you assured me your-self that it was only a dream. . . ."

"Oh, how can I convince you! Tell me how to convince him! Uncle, uncle! You know it's an important matter, most important, affecting family honour. Reflect! Consider!"

"My dear, certainly I will re-flect. Stay, let me recall it all in order. At first I dreamed of my coachman, Fe-o-fi-il . . ."

"Oh! it is not a question of Feofil now, uncle."

"Oh, well, I suppose it is not a question of him now. Then there was Na-po-le-on, and then we seemed to be drinking tea and a lady came and ate up all the sugar."

"But, uncle"—Mozglyakov bawled in the confusion of his mind—"why, it was Marya Alexandrovna herself told us that this morning about Natalya Dmitryevna! Why, I was here and heard it myself? I was hiding and looking at you through the keyhole. . . ."

"What, Marya Alexandrovna," Natalya Dmitryevna broke in; "so you told the prince too that I stole the sugar out of your sugar-basin! So I come to steal your sugar, do I?"

"Get away with you!" cried Marya Alexandrovna, reduced to despair.

"No, I won't go away, Marya Alexandrovna. Don't dare to speak to me like that! . . . . So I stole your sugar, did I? I have been hearing for a long time that you tell such nasty stories about me. Sofya Petrovna gave me an exact account of it. . . . So I steal your sugar, do I?"

"But, *mesdames*," cried the prince, "it was only a dream,

161

you know. Why, I dream all sorts of things. . . ."

"Cursed tub," Marya Alexandrovna muttered in an undertone.

"So I am a tub, am I!" shrieked Natalya Dmitryevna. "And who are you? I have known for ever so long that you called me a tub. I have got a husband, anyway, while you've got a fool. . . ."

"Oh, yes, I remember there was a tub too," muttered the prince, unconsciously recalling his conversation with Marya Alexandrovna that morning.

"So you're insulting a lady too? How dare you, prince, insult a lady? If I am a tub, you have no legs . . ."

"Who? I have no legs?"

"Yes, indeed, no legs and no teeth either, so that's what you are."

"Yes, and only one eye, too," shouted Marya Alexandrovna.

"You have stays instead of ribs," said Natalya Dmitryevna.

"Your face is worked by springs."

"You've no hair! . . ."

"And the idiot has a false moustache," cried Marya Alexandrovna.

"Do at least leave me my nose, Marya Stepanovna," cried the prince, overwhelmed by such sudden candour. "My dear! Was it you gave me away? Did you tell them that my hair was false?"

"Uncle!"

"No, my dear, I really can't stay here any longer. Take me away . . . *quelle société*! What have you brought me to, my goodness?"

"Imbecile, scoundrel!" cried Marya Alexandrovna.

"Oh dear!" said the poor prince. "I've forgotten for the minute why I came here, but I shall re-mem-ber di-rect-ly. Take me away, dear boy, or they will te-ar me to pieces! Meanwhile . . . I must at once no-ote down a new idea. . . ."

162

"Let us go, uncle, it is not too late; I will take you at once to an hotel and I will go with you. . . ."

"Oh, yes, to an ho-tel. *Adieu, ma charmante enfant.* . . . You alone . . . you alone . . . are good and vir-tu-ous. You are an hon-ou-rable girl. Come along, my dear boy. Oh, dear; oh, dear!"

But I will not describe the conclusion of the unpleasant scene which took place on the prince's departure. The visitors dispersed with shrill scoldings and abuse. Marya Alexandrovna was left at last alone in the midst of the ruins of her former glory. Alas! Power, glory, consequence—all had vanished in that one evening. Marya Alexandrova realised that she could never rise to her former height. Her despotic rule over local society which had lasted long years was annihilated for ever. What was left her now? To be philosophical? But she was not philosophical. She was in a paroxysm of rage all night. Zina was dishonoured, there would be endless gossip and scandal! Horrors!

As a faithful historian I ought to mention that from this frenzy the chief sufferer was Afanasy Matveyitch, who took refuge at last in the lumber-room, and stayed there freezing till morning; at last the morning came, but it brought nothing good. Misfortunes never come singly.

CHAPTER XV

If destiny once begins to pursue someone with misfortune there is no end to its blows. That has been noticed long ago. Was the shame and disgrace of the previous day not enough for Marya Alexandrovna? No! Fate was preparing something more, something better.

Before ten o'clock in the morning a strange and almost incredible rumour was suddenly all over the town, welcomed by all with the most spiteful and venomous glee—as we generally do welcome any extraordinary scandal connected with any of our neighbours. "To be so lost to all shame and conscience!" people cried on all sides; "to demean herself to such a degree, to disregard all decorum, so utterly to cast off all restraint!" and so on, and so on.

This was what had happened, however. Early in the morning, a little before six o'clock, a poor and pitiful-looking old woman in tears and despair ran up to Marya Alexandrovna's house and besought the maidservant to wake the young lady immediately, only the young lady, and in secret, so that Marya Alexandrovna should in no way hear of it: Zina, pale and shattered, ran out to the old woman at once. The latter fell at her feet, kissed them, bathed them with her tears, and besought her to come with her to her sick Vasya, who had been so bad, so bad all night that he might perhaps not last through the day. The old woman, sobbing, told Zina that Vasya himself begged her to go for a last farewell before he died, implored her by all the holy angels, by all that had been in the past, and said that if she did not come he would die in despair. Zina at once resolved to go, though yielding to this entreaty would obviously confirm all the old malicious gossip about the intercepted letter, about her scandalous behaviour, and so on. Saying nothing to her mother, she threw on a cloak and at once hastened with the old woman right across the town to one of the poorest quarters of Mordasov, to the most out-of-the-way street, in which there was a little dilapidated house, with little slits for windows, fallen aslant, as it were sunken into the ground and almost buried under huge drifts of snow.

In this little house, in a little, low-pitched, musty room in which the huge stove filled up half the floor space, a young man was lying covered with an old greatcoat, on an unpainted wooden bed with a mattress as thin as a pancake. His face was pale and exhausted, his eyes glittered with a feverish glow,

164

his hands were thin and dry as sticks, his breathing was laboured and husky. It could be seen that he had once been handsome; but disease had disfigured the delicate features of his handsome face, which was terrible and pitiful to look at, as the face of a consumptive, or rather of a dying man, always is. His old mother, who had been for a whole year, almost to the last hour, hoping for her Vasya's recovery, saw at last that he was not long for this world. She stood over him now crushed with grief, but tearless, clasping her hands and gazing at him as though she could never look at him enough; and though she knew it, she could not grasp that in a few days her Vasya, the apple of her eye, would be covered by the frozen earth out yonder under the snowdrifts in the wretched graveyard. But Vasya was not looking at her at that moment. His whole face, wasted and marked by suffering, was full of bliss. He saw before him, at last, her of whom he had been dreaming, asleep and awake, for the last year and a half in the long, dreary nights of his sickness. He saw that she had forgiven him, coming to him like the angel of the Lord as he lay at death's door. She was pressing his hands, was weeping over him, smiling at him, looking at him again with her wonderful eyes and—and all the past, never to return, rose up in the dying man's soul. Life glowed again in his heart, and seemed at parting from him as though it would make the sufferer feel how hard it was to part.

"Zina," he said, "Zinotchka! Don't weep over me, don't mourn, don't grieve, don't remind me that I shall soon die. I shall look at you—yes, as I am looking at you now—I shall feel that our souls are together again, that you have forgiven me; I shall kiss your hands again as in old days, and die, perhaps, without noticing death! You have grown thin, Zinotchka! My angel, with what kindness you are looking at me now. And do you remember how you used to laugh in old days? Do you remember? . . . . Ah, Zina, I will not ask your forgiveness, I do not want to remember what happened, because, Zina, because though you have forgiven me I shall never forgive myself. There have been long nights, Zina, long, sleepless nights, awful nights, and in those nights on this bed I thought for long hours over many things, and made up my mind long ago that it is better for me to die; yes, by God, it is better! . . . I am not fit for life, Zinotchka!"

Zina was weeping and mutely pressing his hands as though she would check his words.

"Why are you crying, my angel?" the sick man went on; "because I am dying—only for that? But you know all the past has been dead and buried long ago! You are cleverer than I, you are more pure-hearted, and so you have known a long time that I am a bad man. Can you still love me? And what it has cost me to endure the thought that you know I am a bad and shallow man. And how much pride there was in that, perhaps honourable pride . . . I don't know. Oh, my dear, all my life has been a dream. I was always dreaming, for ever dreaming, but did not live. I was proud, I despised the herd; and in what was I superior to other people? I don't know. Purity of heart, generosity of feeling? But all that was dreaming, Zina, when we read Shakespeare together; but when it came to action I showed my purity and generosity of feeling."

"Hush!" said Zina, "hush! . . . All that is not so, it is useless . . . you are killing yourself."

"Why do you stop me, Zina? I know you have forgiven me, and perhaps you forgave me long ago; but you judged me—and understood the sort of man I am; that is what torments me. I am unworthy of your love, Zina! You were honest and you went to your mother and said that you would marry me and no one else, and you would have kept your word because with you words were not apart from action. While I, I! when it came to action. . . . Do you know, Zina, I did not understand then what you would be sacrificing in marrying me!

166

did not even understand that marrying me you might die of starvation. I never even thought of it; I only thought that you would marry me, a great poet (a future one, that is). I would not understand the reasons you brought forward begging me to put off our marriage; I tormented you, bullied you, reproached you, despised you, and it came at last to my threatening you with that letter. I was not even a scoundrel at that moment. I was simply a worm! Oh, how you must have despised me! Yes, it is well that I am dying! It is well that you did not marry me! I should have understood nothing of your sacrifice, I should have tormented you, I should have worried you over our poverty; the years would have passed, and who knows!—Perhaps I should have grown to hate you, as a hindrance in my life. Now it is better. Now at least my bitter tears have purified my heart. Ah, Zinotchka! love me a little as you used to love me once . . . in this last hour at least. . . . I know, of course, that I do not deserve your love, but . . . but. . . . Oh, my angel!"

Several times in the course of this speech, Zina, sobbing herself, tried to stop him. But he did not listen to her; he was tormented by a longing to express himself, and he went on speaking, though with difficulty, gasping in a hoarse and choking voice.

"If you hadn't met me, if you hadn't loved me, you would have lived!" said Zina. "Oh, why, why did we meet!"

"No, my darling, do not reproach yourself with my dying," the sick man went on. "I am the only person to blame for everything! How much vanity there was in it! Romantic foolishness! Have they told you my foolish history, Zina? You see, two years ago there was a convict here, a criminal and murderer; but when it came to punishment, he turned out to be the most cowardly creature. Knowing that they would not flog a sick man, he got hold of some spirit, put tobacco in it and drank it. He was attacked with such violent sickness,

167

vomiting blood, and it lasted so long, that it affected his lungs. He was moved to the hospital, and within a few months he died of rapid consumption. Well, my angel, I thought of that convict that very day . . . you know, after that note . . . and made up my mind to destroy myself in the same way; but why do you think I chose consumption? Why didn't I strangle myself or drown myself? Was I afraid of immediate death? Perhaps it was that; but I keep fancying, Zinotchka, that even in this I could not lay aside romantic foolishness! Anyway, I had in my mind at the time the thought: how picturesque it would be, here I should lie in bed dying of consumption, while you would be distressed and unhappy at having sent me into consumption; you would come to me confessing yourself guilty, would fall on your knees before me. . . . I should forgive you, should die in your arms. It was silly, Zinotchka, silly, wasn't it?"

"Don't speak of it!" said Zina; "don't say that! You are not like that. Let us rather remember something else, that was good and happy in our past!"

"It is bitter to me, my darling, that is why I talk of it. I haven't seen you for a year and a half. I should like to open my heart to you now. You know ever since then I have been utterly alone, and I think there has not been one moment when I have not thought of you, my precious one. And do you know what, Zinotchka? How I longed to do something, to deserve that you should change your opinion of me! Until lately I did not believe that I should die. You know I was not laid up at first, for a long time I was walking about after my lungs were affected. And what absurd projects I had! I dreamed, for instance, of becoming all at once a great poet and publishing in the *Notes of the Fatherland* a poem unlike anything in the world. I thought of pouring into it all my feelings, all my soul, so that wherever you might be, I should be with you, always reminding you of me with my poem, and the very best of my dreams was that you would think at last and say, 'No! he is not such a bad man as I thought!' It was stupid, Zinotchka, wasn't it?"

"No, no, Vasya, no!" said Zina.

She fell on his breast and kissed his hands.

"And how jealous I was of you all this time! I believe I should have died if I had heard of your marriage. I sent, I kept watch on you, I spied. . . . She was constantly going" (and he nodded towards his mother). "You did not love Mozglyakov, did you, Zinotchka? Oh, my angel! Will you remember me when I am dead? I know you will remember; but years will pass, the heart will grow harder, you will grow cold, there will be winter in your soul, and you will forget me, Zinotchka! . . ."

"No, no, never! I shall not marry. . . . You are my first . . . and mine for ever. . . ."

"Everything dies, Zinotchka, even memories. . . . And our noble feelings die. Commonsense takes their place. What is the use of repining? Make use of life, Zina, Live long, live happily. Love someone else, if you can love; there is no loving the dead! Only think of me from time to time; do not remember what was bad, forgive the bad; but you know there was good, too, in our love, Zinotchka. Oh, golden days that never can return! . . . Listen, my angel, I always loved the evening hour of sunset. Think of me sometimes at that hour! Oh, no, no! Why die? Oh, how I long to come back to life again! Remember, my dear, remember, remember that time. It was spring then, the sun was shining so brightly, the flowers were in blossom, it was like a holiday all round us; and now look, look!"

And with a wasted hand the poor fellow pointed to the dingy, frozen window. Then he clutched Zina's hands, pressed them to his eyes and sobbed bitterly, bitterly. His sobs almost lacerated his racked breast.

169

And the whole day he was sobbing in anguish and misery. Zina did her best to comfort him, but she was half dead with misery. She told him that she would never forget him, and that she would never love another man as she loved him. He believed her, smiled, kissed her hands, but memories of the past only kindled fresh suffering in his soul. So passed the whole day. Meanwhile Marya Alexandrovna in alarm sent a dozen times to Zina entreating her to return home and not to ruin herself completely in public opinion. At last, when it was getting dark, almost beside herself with horror, she made up her mind to go to Zina herself. Calling her daughter out into the other room, she besought her almost on her knees "to turn aside this last worst dagger from her heart". Zina went out to her feeling ill, her head was burning. She listened and did not understand her mother. Marya Alexandrovna went away at last in despair, for Zina was determined to stay the night in the dying man's house. She did not leave his bedside all night. But the sick-man grew worse and worse. The day came at last, but there was no hope that the sufferer would live through it. The old mother seemed frantic, she walked about as though she could not take it in, giving her son medicines which he would not take. His agony lasted a long time. He could not speak, and only incoherent, husky sounds broke from his throat. Up to the very last moment he gazed at Zina, still sought her with his eyes, and when the light in his eyes was beginning to grow dim, he still, with a straying, uncertain hand, felt for her hand to press it in his. Meanwhile the short winter day was passing. And when the last farewell gleam of sunshine gilded the solitary frozen window of the little room, the soul of the sufferer parted from his exhausted body and floated after that last ray. The old mother, seeing her adored boy lying dead before her, clasped her hands, uttered a shriek, and threw herself upon his breast.

"It is you, you snake in the grass, have been his ruin! You

170

accursed girl, with your ill deeds have parted us and been his undoing."

But Zina did not hear her. She stood over the dead man as though she had lost all comprehension. At last she bent down, made the sign of the cross over him, kissed him, and walked mechanically out of the room. Her eyes were burning, her head was going round. Her agonising experiences, her two nights without sleep, almost deprived her of reason. She vaguely felt that all her past had been, as it were, torn out of her heart, and that a new life was beginning, gloomy and menacing. But before she had gone ten paces, Mozglyakov seemed to spring out of the earth before her; he seemed to be purposely lying in wait for her at that spot.

"Zinaida Afanasyevna," he began in a timorous whisper, looking nervously around him, for it was hardly dark yet, "Zinaida Afanasyevna, of course I am an ass. That is, if you like I am not an ass now, for you see, anyway, I have behaved honourably. But still I am sorry for having been an ass. . . . I am afraid I am muddled, Zinaida Afanasyevna, but that is due to all sorts of reasons . . ."

Zina gazed at him almost unconsciously, and went on her way in silence. As it was difficult for two to go abreast on the raised wooden pavement, and as Zina did not move aside, Pavel Alexandrovitch jumped off the pavement and ran by her side below, peeping up continually into her face.

"Zinaida Afanasyevna," he went on, "I have reflected, and if you are willing, I am prepared to renew my offer. I am ready to forget everything, Zinaida Afanasvevna, the whole disgrace, and to forgive it, but only on one condition: so long as we are here—let it all be kept secret. You will go away from here as soon as possible; I shall follow you secretly; we will be married in some remote place so that no one shall see it, and then at once we will go to Petersburg, travelling with posting horses, so you should only take a little portmanteau. Eh? Do you agree,

Zinaida Afanasyevna? Tell me quickly! I can't wait about, we might be seen together."

Zina made no answer, she only looked at Mozglyakov; but the look was such that he understood at once, took off his hat, bowed himself off, and vanished at the first turning into a side street.

"What is the meaning of it?" he thought. "That evening, the day before yesterday, she was all softness and sentiment, and took all the blame on herself? She changes from day to day, it seems!"

And meanwhile one event was following another in Mordasov. A tragic circumstance had occurred. After being driven to the hotel by Mozglyakov, the old prince was taken ill the same night, and dangerously ill. The people of Mordasov heard the news next morning. Kalist Stanislavitch scarcely left his bedside. In the evening there was a consultation of all the Mordasov doctors. The invitations to request their attendance were written in Latin. But in spite of the Latin the prince had already lost consciousness, was delirious, kept asking Kalist Stanislavitch to sing him a ballad, and talking about wigs; at times he seemed frightened and cried out. The doctors decided that the hospitality of Mordasov had set up inflammation of the stomach, which had somehow passed (probably on the journey) to the brain. They admitted the possibility also of some moral shock. They summed up in conclusion by saying that the prince had been for a long time past predisposed to death, and so would certainly die. On the last point they were not mistaken, for three days later the poor old man died at the hotel. This was a great shock to the people of Mordasov. No one had expected the affair to take such a serious turn. They flocked in crowds to the hotel where the dead body was lying; they discussed and debated, nodded their heads, and ended by severely censuring "the luckless prince's murderers", understanding, of course, by that term, Marya Alexandrovna and her daughter. Everyone felt that this affair from its extremely scandalous character might easily gain an unpleasant publicity, would perhaps reach far-away parts, and all sorts of possibilities were talked over and discussed. All this time Mozglyakov was in the greatest fuss and flurry, and at last his head was in a perfect whirl. He was in that state of mind when he saw Zina. His position was certainly difficult. He had brought the prince into the town, he had moved him to the hotel, and now he did not know what to do with the dead man, where to bury him, whom to inform of his death! Should the body be taken to Duhanovo? Besides, he considered himself a nephew. He trembled with apprehension that he might be blamed for the venerable old man's death. "Very likely there will be talk of it in Petersburg in the best society!" he thought with a shudder. He could not extract advice of any sort from his Mordasov acquaintances; they were all overcome by sudden consternation, they rushed away from the dead body and left Mozglyakov in gloomy isolation. But all at once the scene was completely transformed. Early the next morning a new visitor arrived in the town. Of this visitor all Mordasov instantly began talking, but they spoke of him mysteriously in a whisper, staring at him out of every chink and every window when he drove along the High Street on his way to the governor's. Even Pyotr Mihalovitch seemed overawed, and did not know what tone to take with his visitor. The visitor was no other than the renowned Prince Shtchepetilov, a relative of the old prince's, a man still youngish, about thirty-five, with shoulder-knots and the epaulets of a colonel. The sight of those shoulder-knots struck awe into the hearts of all subordinate officials. The police-master, for instance, completely lost his head—in a moral sense, of course; physically he put in an appearance, though it was a very stiff and constrained appearance. It was at last learned that Prince Shtchepetilov had come from Petersburg, calling on the way at Duhanovo. Finding no one at

Duhanovo, he flew off in pursuit of his uncle to Mordasov, where he had been thunderstruck by the news of the old man's death and the rumours concerning the circumstances attending it. Pyotr Mihalovitch was actually a little nervous as he gave the necessary explanations; and indeed everyone in Mordasov had a guilty air. Moreover, the visitor had such a stern, such a dissatisfied face, though one would have thought it impossible to be dissatisfied with the fortune he was inheriting. He at once took everything into his own hands; Mozglyakov promptly and with shame effaced himself before the real, not self-styled, nephew and vanished—no one knew where. It was decided to move the dead body at once to the monastery, where a requiem service was arranged. All the directions were given by the old prince's kinsman briefly, drily, and sternly, but with tact and decorum. Next day all the town assembled at the monastery to hear the requiem service. An absurd rumour was current among the ladies that Marya Alexandrovna would appear at the church in person, and on her knees before the coffin would pray aloud for forgiveness, and that this all had to be in accordance with the law. All this, of course, proved to be nonsense, and Marya Alexandrovna did not come to the church. We forgot to say that immediately after Zina's return to the house, her mother decided that very evening to move to their country-house, considering it impossible to remain longer in the town. There she listened anxiously from her seclusion to the rumours from the town, sent to find out about the new arrival, and was all the time in a state of fever. The road from the monastery to Duhavono passed less than three-quarters of a mile from her windows, and so Marya Alexandrovna could command a convenient view of the long procession which stretched from the monastery to Duhavono after the service. The coffin was upon a high hearse; and after it stretched a long string of carriages escorting it to the point where the road turns off to the town. And that gloomy hearse could be seen a long

174

way further, a black patch against the white snow-covered plain, moving slowly with becoming dignity. But Marya Alexandrovna could not look at it long, she walked away from the window.

A week later she moved to Moscow with her daughter and Afanasy Matveyitch, and a month later the news reached Mordasov that Marya Alexandrovna's country house as well as her town house were for sale. And so this *comme-il-faut* lady was lost to Mordasov for ever! Even this could not pass without ill-natured jibes. It was asserted, for instance, that Afanasy Matveyitch was being sold with their country place. . . . One year passed and then a second, and Marya Alexandrovna was almost forgotten. Alas! that is how it always is in life! It was said, however, that she had bought another country place, and had moved to another provincial town, where, of course, she had already taken control of everything; that Zina was still unmarried, that Afanasy Matveyitch. . . . However, it is hardly worth while to repeat these rumours, they were all very untrustworthy.

Three years have passed since I wrote the last line of the first part of my Mordasov chronicle, and who would have supposed that I should have occasion to open my manuscript again and to add another piece of news to my story? Well, here it is! I will begin with Pavel Alexandrovitch Mozglyakov. When he disappeared from Mordasov he went straight to Petersburg, where he successfully obtained the post in the service that had long been promised him. He soon forgot all the incidents at Mordasov, threw himself into the vortex of social life on Vassilyevsky Island and had a gay time of it, flirted, kept up with the times, fell in love, made an offer, swallowed another refusal, and before he had digested it, was led by idleness and the frivolity of his character to get for himself a post on an expedition which was being sent to one of the remotest borders of our

175

boundless fatherland, for inspection or for some other object, I don't know for certain what. The party successfully traversed all the forests and deserts, and at last, after long peregrinations, arrived in the chief town of that remote region to call on the governor-general. He was a tall, lean, stern general, an old military man, who had been often wounded in battle, and had two stars and a white cross on his breast. He received the expedition with dignity and decorum, and invited all the officials to a ball which was to be given that very evening on the occasion of the nameday of the governor's wife. Pavel Alexandrovitch was very much pleased. Attiring himself in his Petersburg suit in which he intended to produce an effect, he walked with a free and easy air into the big reception hall, but he was at once somewhat taken aback at the sight of the numbers of thick and plaited epaulets and civilian uniforms with stars on their breasts. He had to pay his respects to the governor's wife, of whom he had heard that she was young and very good-looking. He went up to her, indeed, with aplomb, but was suddenly petrified with amazement. Before him stood Zina in a resplendent ball-dress and diamonds, looking proud and haughty. She completely failed to recognise Pavel Alexandrovitch. Her eyes glided over his face and at once turned to someone else. Astounded, Pavel Alexandrovitch moved to one side, and in the crowd came into collision with a timid young official who seemed to be frightened at finding himself at the governor's ball. Pavel Alexandrovitch immediately began to question him, and learned the most interesting facts. He learned that the governor had married two years ago, when he had visited Moscow, and that he had married a very wealthy young lady of a distinguished family; that the governor's wife "was awfully good-looking, even one might say a beauty of the first order, but that she behaved extremely proudly, and only danced with generals"; that at the present ball there were in all nine generals, their own and visitors, including the actual civil councillors; "that the governor's wife had a mamma who lived with her, and that this mamma belonged to the highest society, and was very clever," but that the mamma herself was completely dominated by the daughter, while the general himself simply doted on his spouse. Mozglyakov faltered a question about Afanasy Matveyitch, but they had no conception of his existence in "the remote region". Regaining his confidence a little, Mozglyakov walked about the rooms and soon saw Marya Alexandrovna, gorgeously attired, brandishing a costly fan and talking with animation to a personage of the fourth class. Round her clustered several ladies evidently anxious to propitiate her, and Marya Alexandrovna was apparently very gracious to all of them. Mozglyakov ventured to introduce himself. Marya Alexandrovna seemed a little startled, but almost instantly recovered herself. She graciously condescended to recognise Pavel Alexandrovitch, questioned him about Petersburg acquaintances, asked him why he was not abroad. To Mordasov she made no allusion whatever, as though such a place had no existence on earth. At last, after mentioning the name of a distinguished Petersburg prince and inquiring after his health, though Mozglyakov had no acquaintance whatever with the prince in question, she turned imperceptibly to a grand personage who was approaching, whose grey locks were fragrant with scent, and a minute later had completely forgotten Pavel Alexandrovitch, though he remained standing before her. With his hat in his hand and a sarcastic smile on his face, Mozglyakov returned to the great hall. Considering for some unknown reasons that he was insulted and even wounded, he resolved not to dance. A morose and absent expression and a biting Mephistophelean smile never left his face the whole evening. He leaned in a picturesque attitude against a column (as luck would have it, there were columns in the hall), and during the whole ball, that is for several hours together, he remained standing at the same place watching Zina. But alas!

177

all his antics, all his striking attitudes, his disillusioned air and all the rest of it were thrown away. Zina completely failed to observe him. At last, enraged and with legs aching from long standing, hungry because as an unhappy lover he could not remain to supper, he returned to his lodgings quite worn out and feeling as though he had been beaten by someone. For a long while he did not go to bed, recalling the past which he had so long forgotten. Next morning new instructions arrived, and with relief Mozglyakov succeeded in being entrusted with the execution of them. He felt positively lighter-hearted as he drove out of the town. Snow was lying like a dazzling shroud over the boundless, deserted plain. In the distance on the very horizon stretched dark forests.

The mettlesome horses dashed along, flinging the powdery snow with their hoofs. The sledge bell tinkled, Pavel Alexandrovitch sank into thought, and then into dreams, and then into a sweet sleep. He woke at the third posting station, feeling fresh and well, with quite different thoughts in his mind.

A Novel in Nine Letters

I

(FROM PYOTR IVANITCH TO IVAN PETROVITCH)

DEAR SIR AND MOST PRECIOUS FRIEND, IVAN PETROVITCH,

For the last two days I have been, I may say, in pursuit of you, my friend, having to talk over most urgent business with you, and I cannot come across you anywhere. Yesterday, while we were at Semyon Alexeyitch's, my wife made a very good joke about you, saying that Tatyana Petrovna and you were a pair of birds always on the wing. You have not been married three months and you already neglect your domestic hearth. We all laughed heartily—from our genuine kindly feeling for you, of course—but, joking apart, my precious friend, you have given me a lot of trouble. Semyon Alexeyitch said to me that you might be going to the ball at the Social Union's club! Leaving my wife with Semyon Alexeyitch's good lady, I flew off to the Social Union. It was funny and tragic! Fancy my position! Me at the ball—and alone, without my wife! Ivan Andreyitch meeting me in the porter's lodge and seeing me alone, at once concluded (the rascal!) that I had a passion for dances, and taking me by the arm, wanted to drag me off by force to a dancing class, saying that it was too crowded at the Social Union, that an ardent sprit had not room to turn, and that his head ached from the patchouli and mignonette. I found neither you, nor Tatyana Petrovna. Ivan Andreyitch vowed and declared that you would be at *Woe from Wit*, at the Alexandrinsky theatre.

I flew off to the Alexandrinsky theatre: you were not there either. This morning I expected to find you at Tchistoganov's—

no sign of you there. Tchistoganov sent to the Perepalkins'—
the same thing there. In fact, I am quite worn out; you can
judge how much trouble I have taken! Now I am writing
to you (there is nothing else I can do). My business is by no
means a literary one (you understand me?) ; it would be better
to meet face to face, it is extremely necessary to discuss something with you and as quickly as possible, and so I beg you to
come to us today with Tatyana Petrovna to tea and for a
chat in the evening. My Anna Mihalovna will be extremely
pleased to see you. You will truly, as they say, oblige me to
my dying day. By the way, my precious friend—since I have
taken up my pen I'll go into all I have against you—I have a
slight complaint I must make; in fact, I must reproach you,
my worthy friend, for an apparently very innocent little trick
which you have played at my expense. . . . You are a rascal,
a man without conscience. About the middle of last month,
you brought into my house an acquaintance of yours, Yevgeny
Nikolaitch; you vouched for him by your friendly and, for me,
of course, sacred recommendation; I rejoiced at the opportunity of receiving the young man with open arms, and when I
did so I put my head in a noose. A noose it hardly is, but it has
turned out a pretty business. I have not time now to explain,
and indeed it is an awkward thing to do in writing, only a very
humble request to you, my malicious friend: could you not
somehow very delicately, in passing, drop a hint into the young
man's ear that there are a great many houses in the metropolis
besides ours? It's more than I can stand, my dear fellow!
We fall at your feet, as our friend Semyonovitch says. I will
tell you all about it when we meet. I don't mean to say that the
young man has sinned against good manners, or is lacking in
spiritual qualities, or is not up to the mark in some other way.
On the contrary, he is an amiable and pleasant fellow; but wait,
we shall meet; meanwhile if you see him, for goodness' sake
whisper a hint to him, my good friend. I would do it myself,

180

but you know what I am, I simply can't, and that's all about it. You introduced him. But I will explain myself more fully this evening, anyway. Now good-bye. I remain, etc.

P.S.—My little boy has been ailing for the last week, and gets worse and worse every day; he is cutting his poor little teeth. My wife is nursing him all the time, and is depressed, poor thing. Be sure to come, you will give us real pleasure, my precious friend.

II

(FROM IVAN PETROVITCH TO PYOTR IVANITCH)

DEAR SIR, PYOTR IVANITCH!

I got your letter yesterday, I read it and was perplexed. You looked for me, goodness knows where, and I was simply at home. Till ten o'clock I was expecting Ivan Ivanitch Tolokonov. At once on getting your letter I set out with my wife, I went to the expense of taking a cab, and reached your house about half-past six. You were not at home, but we were met by your wife. I waited to see you till half-past ten, I could not stay later. I set off with my wife, went to the expense of a cab again, saw her home, and went on myself to the Perepalkins', thinking I might meet you there, but again I was out in my reckoning. When I got home I did not sleep all night, I felt uneasy; in the morning I drove round to you three times, at nine, at ten and at eleven; three times I went to the expense of a cab, and again you left me in the lurch.

I read your letter and was amazed. You write about Yevgeny Nikolaitch, beg me to whisper some hint and do not tell me what about. I commend your caution, but all letters are not alike, and I don't give documents of importance to my wife

181

for curl-papers. I am puzzled, in fact, to know with what motive you wrote all this to me. However, if it comes to that, why should I meddle in the matter? I don't poke my nose into other people's business. You can be not at home to him; I only see that I must have a brief and decisive explanation with you, and, moreover, time is passing. And I am in straits and don't know what to do if you are going to neglect the terms of our agreement. A journey for nothing; a journey costs something, too, and my wife's whining for me to get her a velvet mantle of the latest fashion. About Yevgeny Nikolaitch I hasten to mention that when I was at Pavel Semyonovitch Perepalkin's yesterday I made inquiries without loss of time. He has five hundred serfs in the province of Yaroslav, and he has expectations from his grandmother of an estate of three hundred serfs near Moscow. How much money he has I cannot tell; I think you ought to know that better. I beg you once for all to appoint a place where I can meet you. You met Ivan Andreyitch yesterday, and you write that he told you that I was at the Alexandrinsky theatre with my wife. I write, that he is a liar, and it shows how little he is to be trusted in such cases, that only the day before yesterday he did his grandmother out of eight hundred roubles. I have the honour to remain, etc.

P.S.—My wife is going to have a baby; she is nervous about it and feels depressed at times. At the theatre they sometimes have fire-arms going off and sham thunderstorms. And so for fear of a shock to my wife's nerves I do not take her to the theatre. I have no great partiality for the theatre myself.

III

MY PRECIOUS FRIEND, IVAN PETROVITCH,

      I am to blame, to blame, a thousand times to blame, but I hasten to defend myself. Between five and six yesterday, just as we were talking of you with the warmest affection, a messenger from Uncle Stepan Alexeyitch galloped up with the news that my aunt was very bad. Being afraid of alarming my wife, I did not say a word of this to her, but on the pretext of other urgent business I drove off to my aunt's house. I found her almost dying. Just at five o'clock she had had a stroke, the third she has had in the last two years. Karl Fyodoritch, their family doctor, told us that she might not live through the night. You can judge of my position, dearest friend. We were on our legs all night in grief and anxiety. It was not till morning that, utterly exhausted and overcome by moral and physical weakness, I lay down on the sofa; I forgot to tell them to wake me, and only woke at half-past eleven. My aunt was better. I drove home to my wife. She, poor thing, was quite worn out expecting me. I snatched a bite of something, embraced my little boy, reassured my wife and set off to call on you. You were not at home. At your flat I found Yevgeny Nikolaitch. When I got home I took up a pen, and here I am writing to you. Don't grumble and be cross to me, my true friend. Beat me, chop my guilty head off my shoulders, but don't deprive me of your affection. From your wife I learned that you will be at the Slavyanovs' this evening. I will certainly be there. I look forward with the greatest impatience to seeing you.

                               I remain, etc.

P.S.—We are in perfect despair about our little boy. Karl Fyodoritch prescribes rhubarb. He moans. Yesterday he did not know anyone. This morning he did know us, and began lisping papa, mamma, boo. . . . My wife was in tears the whole morning.

IV

(FROM IVAN PETROVITCH TO PYOTR IVANITCH)

MY DEAR SIR, PYOTR IVANITCH!

I am writing to you, in your room, at your bureau; and before taking up my pen, I have been waiting for more than two and a half hours for you. Now allow me to tell you straight out, Pyotr Ivanitch, my frank opinion about this shabby incident. From your last letter I gathered that you were expected at the Slavyanovs', that you were inviting me to go there; I turned up, I stayed for five hours and there was no sign of you. Why, am I to be made a laughing-stock to people, do you suppose? Excuse me, my dear sir . . . I came to you this morning, I hoped to find you, not imitating certain deceitful persons who look for people, God knows where, when they can be found at home at any suitably chosen time. There is no sign of you at home. I don't know what restrains me from telling you now the whole harsh truth. I will only say that I see you seem to be going back on your bargain regarding our agreement. And only now reflecting on the whole affair, I cannot but confess that I am absolutely astounded at the artful workings of your mind. I see clearly now that you have been cherishing your unfriendly design for a long time. This supposition of mine is confirmed by the fact that last week in an almost unpardonable way you took possession of that letter of yours addressed to me, in which you laid down yourself, though rather vaguely and incoherently, the terms of our

184

agreement in regard to a circumstance of which I need not remind you. You are afraid of documents, you destroy them, and you try to make a fool of me. But I won't allow myself to made a fool of, for no one has ever considered me one hitherto, and everyone has thought well of me in that respect. I am opening my eyes. You try and put me off, confuse me with talk of Yevgeny Nikolaitch, and when with your letter of the seventh of this month, which I am still at a loss to understand, I seek a personal explanation from you, you make humbugging appointments, while you keep out of the way. Surely you do not suppose, sir, that I am not equal to noticing all this? You promised to reward me for my services, of which you are very well aware, in the way of introducing various persons, and at the same time, and I don't know how you do it, you contrive to borrow money from me in considerable sums without giving a receipt, as happened no longer ago than last week. Now, having got the money, you keep out of the way, and what's more, you repudiate the service I have done you in regard to Yevgeny Nikolaitch. You are probably reckoning on my speedy departure to Simbirsk, and hoping I may not have time to settle your business. But I assure you solemnly and testify on my word of honour that if it comes to that, I am prepared to spend two more months in Petersburg expressly to carry through my business, to attain my objects, and to get hold of you. For I, too, on occasion know how to get the better of people. In conclusion, I beg to inform you that if you do not give me a satisfactory explanation today, first in writing, and then personally face to face, and do not make a fresh statement in your letter of the chief points of the agreement existing between us, and do not explain fully your views in regard to Yevgeny Nikolaitch, I shall be compelled to have recourse to measures that will be highly unpleasant to you, and indeed repugnant to me also.

Allow me to remain, etc.

185

V

(FROM PYOTR IVANITCH TO IVAN PETROVITCH)

November 11.

MY DEAR AND HONOURED FRIEND, IVAN PETROVITCH!

I was cut to the heart by your letter. I wonder you were not ashamed, my dear but unjust friend, to behave like this to one of your most devoted friends. Why be in such a hurry, and without explaining things fully, wound me with such insulting suspicions? But I hasten to reply to your charges. You did not find me yesterday, Ivan Petrovitch, because I was suddenly and quite unexpectedly called away to a death-bed. My aunt, Yefimya Nikolaevna, passed away yesterday evening at eleven o'clock in the night. By the general consent of the relatives I was selected to make the arrangements for the sad and sorrowful ceremony. I had so much to do that I had not time to see you this morning, nor even to send you a line. I am grieved to the heart at the misunderstanding which has arisen between us. My words about Yevgeny Nikolaitch uttered casually and in jest you have taken in quite a wrong sense and have ascribed to them a meaning deeply offensive to me. You refer to money and express your anxiety about it. But without wasting words I am ready to satisfy all your claims and demands, though I must remind you that the three hundred and fifty roubles I had from you last week were in accordance with a certain agreement and not by way of a loan. In the latter case there would certainly have been a receipt. I will not condescend to discuss the other points mentioned in your letter. I see that it is a misunderstanding. I see it is your habitual hastiness, hot temper and obstinacy. I know that your good-heartedness and open character will not allow doubts to persist in your heart, and that you will be, in fact, the

186

first to hold out your hand to me. You are mistaken, Ivan Petrovitch, you are greatly mistaken!

Although your letter has deeply wounded me, I should be prepared even today to come to you and apologise, but I have been since yesterday in such a rush and flurry that I am utterly exhausted and can scarcely stand on my feet. To complete my troubles, my wife is laid up; I am afraid she is seriously ill. Our little boy, thank God, is better; but I must lay down my pen, I have a mass of things to do and they are urgent. Allow me, my dear friend, to remain, etc.

VI

(FROM IVAN PETROVITCH TO PYOTR IVANITCH)

November 14.

DEAR SIR, PYOTR IVANITCH!

I have been waiting for three days, I tried to make a profitable use of them—meanwhile I feel that politeness and good manners are the greatest of ornaments for everyone. Since my last letter of the tenth of this month, I have neither by word nor deed reminded you of my existence, partly in order to allow you undisturbed to perform the duty of a Christian in regard to your aunt, partly because I needed the time for certain considerations and investigations in regard to a business you know of. Now I hasten to explain myself to you in the most thoroughgoing and decisive manner.

I frankly confess that on reading your first two letters I seriously supposed that you did not understand what I wanted; that was how it was that I rather sought an interview with you and explanations face to face. I was afraid of writing, and blamed myself for lack of clearness in the expression of my thoughts on paper. You are aware that I have not the advantages of education and good manners, and that I shun a hollow show of gentility because I have learned from bitter experience how misleading appearances often are, and that a snake sometimes lies hidden under flowers. But you understood me; you did not answer me as you should have done because, in the treachery of your heart, you had planned beforehand to be faithless to your word of honour and to the friendly relations existing between us. You have proved this absolutely by your abominable conduct towards me of late, which is fatal to my interests, which I did not expect and which I refused to believe till the present moment. From the very beginning of our acquaintance you captivated me by your clever manners, by the subtlety of your behaviour, your knowledge of affairs and the advantages to be gained by association with you. I imagined that I had found a true friend and well-wisher. Now I recognise clearly that there are many people who under a flattering and brilliant exterior hide venom in their hearts, who use their cleverness to weave snares for their neighbour and for unpardonable deception, and so are afraid of pen and paper, and at the same time use their fine language not for the benefit of their neighbour and their country, but to drug and bewitch the reason of those who have entered into business relations of any sort with them. Your treachery to me, my dear sir, can be clearly seen from what follows.

In the first place, when, in the clear and distinct terms of my letter, I described my position, sir, and at the same time asked you in my first letter what you meant by certain expressions and intentions of yours, principally in regard to Yevgeny Niko-laitch, you tried for the most part to avoid answering and, confounding me by doubts and suspicions, you calmly put the subject aside. Then after treating me in a way which cannot be described by any seemly word, you began writing that you were wounded. Pray, what am I to call that, sir? Then when every minute was precious to me and when you had set me running after you all over the town, you wrote, pretending personal friendship, letters in which, intentionally avoiding all mention of business, you spoke of utterly irrelevant matters; to wit, of the illnesses of your good lady for whom I have, in any case, every respect, and of how your baby had been dosed with rhubarb and was cutting a tooth. All this you alluded to in every letter with a disgusting regularity that was insulting to me. Of course I am prepared to admit that a father's heart may be torn by the sufferings of his babe, but why make mention of this when something different, far more important and interesting, was needed? I endured it in silence, but now when time has elapsed I think it my duty to explain myself. Finally, treacherously deceiving me several times by making humbugging appointments, you tried, it seems, to make me play the part of a fool and a laughing-stock for you, which I never intend to be. Then after first inviting me and thoroughly deceiving me, you informed me that you were called away to your suffering aunt who had had a stroke, precisely at five o'clock as you stated with shameful exactitude. Luckily for me, sir, in the course of these three days I have succeeded in making inquiries and have learnt from them that your aunt had a stroke on the day before the seventh not long before midnight. From this fact I see that you have made use of sacred family relations in order to deceive persons in no way concerned with them. Finally, in your last letter you mention the death of your relative as though it had taken place precisely at the time when I was to have visited you to consult about various business matters. But here the vileness of your arts and calculations exceeds all belief, for from trustworthy information which I was able by a lucky chance to obtain just in the nick of time, I have found out that your aunt died twenty-four hours later than the time you so impiously fixed for her decease in your letter. I shall never have done if I enumerate all the signs by which I have discovered your treachery in regard to me. It is sufficient, indeed, for any impartial observer that in every letter you style me, your true friend, and call me all sorts of polite names, which you do, to the best of my belief, for no other object than to put my conscience to sleep.

I have come now to your principal act of deceit and treachery in regard to me, to wit, your continual silence of late in regard to everything concerning our common interests, in regard to your wicked theft of the letter in which you stated, though in language somewhat obscure and not perfectly intelligible to me, our mutual agreements, your barbarous forcible loan of three hundred and fifty roubles which you borrowed from me as your partner without giving any receipt, and finally, your abominable slanders of our common acquaintance, Yevgeny Nikolaitch. I see clearly now that you meant to show me that he was, if you will allow me to say so, like a billy-goat, good for neither milk nor wool, that he was neither one thing nor the other, neither fish nor flesh, which you put down as a vice in him in your letter of the sixth instant. I knew Yevgeny Nikolaitch as a modest and well-behaved young man, whereby he may well attract, gain and deserve respect in society. I know also that every evening for the last fortnight you've put into your pocket dozens and sometimes even hundreds of roubles, playing games of chance with Yevgeny Nikolaitch. Now you disavow all this, and now only refuse to compensate me for what I have suffered, but have even appropriated money belonging to me, tempting me by suggestions that I should be partner in the affair, and luring me with various advantages which were to accrue. After having appropriated, in a most illegal way, money of mine and of Yevgeny Nikolaitch's, you decline to compensate me, resorting for that object to calumny with which you have unjustifiably blackened in my eyes a man whom I, by my efforts and exertions, introduced into your house. While on the contrary, from what I hear from your friends, you are still almost slobbering over him, and give out to the whole world that he is your dearest friend, though there is no one in the world such a fool as not to guess at once what your designs are aiming at and what your friendly relations really mean. I should say that they mean deceit, treachery, forgetfulness of human duties and proprieties, contrary to the law of God and vicious in every way. I take myself as a proof and example. In what way have I offended you and why have you treated me in this godless fashion?

I will end my letter. I have explained myself. Now in conclusion. If, sir, you do not in the shortest possible time after receiving this letter return me in full, first, the three hundred and fifty roubles I gave you, and, secondly, all the sums that should come to me according to your promise, I will have recourse to every possible means to compel you to return it, even to open force, secondly to the protection of the laws, and finally I beg to inform you that I am in possession of facts, which, if they remain in the hands of your humble servant, may ruin and disgrace your name in the eyes of all the world. Allow me to remain, etc.

VII

(FROM PYOTR IVANITCH TO IVAN PETROVITCH)

November 15.

IVAN PETROVITCH!

When I received your vulgar and at the same time queer letter, my impulse for the first minute was to tear it into shreds, but I have preserved it as a curiosity. I do, however, sincerely regret our misunderstandings and unpleasant relations. I did not mean to answer you. But I am compelled by necessity. I must in these lines inform you that it would be very unpleasant for me to see you in my house at any time; my wife feels the same; she is in delicate health and the smell of tar upsets her. My wife sends your wife the book, *Don Quixote de la Mancha*, with her sincere thanks. As for the goloshes you say you left behind here on your last visit, I must regretfully inform you that they are nowhere to be found. They are still being looked for; but if they do not turn up, then I will buy you a new pair.

I have the honour to remain your sincere friend,

VIII

On the sixteenth of November, Pyotr Ivanitch received by post two letters addressed to him. Opening the first envelope, he took out a carefully folded note on pale pink paper. The handwriting was his wife's. It was addressed to Yevgeny Nikolaitch and dated November the second. There was nothing else in the envelope. Pyotr Ivanitch read:

DEAR EUGÈNE,

Yesterday was utterly impossible. My husband was at home the whole evening. Be sure to come tomorrow punctually at eleven. At half-past ten my husband is going to Tsarskoe and not coming back till evening. I was in a rage all night. Thank you for sending me the information and the correspondence. What a lot of paper. Did she really write all that? She has style though; many thanks, dear; I see that you love me. Don't be angry, but, for goodness sake, come tomorrow.

A.

Pyotr Ivanitch tore open the other letter:

PYOTR IVANITCH,

I should never have set foot again in your house anyway; you need not have troubled to soil paper about it.

Next week I am going to Simbirsk Yevgeny Nikolaitch

192

remains your precious and beloved friend. I wish you luck, and don't trouble about the goloshes.

<h1 style="text-align:center">IX</h1>

On the seventeenth of November Ivan Petrovitch received by post two letters addressed to him. Opening the first letter, he took out a hasty and carelessly written note. The handwriting was his wife's; it was addressed to Yevgeny Nikolaitch, and dated August the fourth. There was nothing else in the envelope. Ivan Petrovitch read:

Good-bye, good-bye, Yevgeny Nikolaitch! The Lord reward you for this too. May you be happy, but my lot is bitter, terribly bitter! It is your choice. If it had not been for my aunt I should not have put such trust in you. Do not laugh at me nor at my aunt. Tomorrow is our wedding. Aunt is relieved that a good man has been found, and that he will take me without a dowry. I took a good look at him for the first time today. He seems good-natured! They are hurrying me. Farewell, farewell. . . . My darling!! Think of me sometimes; I shall never forget you. Farewell! I sign this last like my first letter, do you remember?

TATYANA.

The second letter was as follows:

IVAN PETROVITCH,

Tomorrow you will receive a new pair of goloshes. It is not my habit to filch from other men's pockets, and I am not fond of picking up all sorts of rubbish in the streets.

Yevgeny Nikolaitch is going to Simbursk in a day or two on his grandfather's business, and he has asked me to find a travelling companion for him; wouldn't you like to take him with you?

193

An Unpleasant Predicament

THIS unpleasant business occurred at the epoch when the regeneration of our beloved fatherland and the struggle of her valiant sons towards new hopes and destinies was beginning with irresistible force and with a touchingly naïve impetuosity. One winter evening in that period, between eleven and twelve o'clock, three highly respectable gentlemen were sitting in a comfortable and even luxuriously furnished room in a handsome house of two storeys on the Petersburg Side, and were engaged in a staid and edifying conversation on a very interesting subject. These three gentlemen were all of generals' rank. They were sitting round a little table, each in a soft and handsome armchair, and as they talked, they quietly and luxuriously sipped champagne. The bottle stood on the table on a silver stand with ice round it. The fact was that the host, a privy councillor called Stepan Nikiforovitch Nikiforov, an old bachelor of sixty-five, was celebrating his removal into a house he had just bought, and as it happened, also his birthday, which he had never kept before. The festivity, however, was not on a very grand scale; as we have seen already, there were only two guests, both of them former colleagues and former subordinates of Mr. Nikiforov; that is, an actual civil councillor called Semyon Ivanovitch Shipulenko, and another actual civil councillor, Ivan Ilyitch Pralinsky. They had arrived to tea at nine o'clock, then had begun upon the wine, and knew that at exactly half-past eleven they would have to set off home. Their host had all his life been fond of regularity. A few words about him.

He had begun his career as a petty clerk with nothing to back him, had quietly plodded on for forty-five years, knew very well what to work towards, had no ambition to draw the stars down from heaven, though he had two stars already, and particularly disliked expressing his own opinion on any subject. He was honest, too, that is, it had not happened to him to do anything particularly dishonest; he was a bachelor because he was an egoist; he had plenty of brains, but he could not bear showing his intelligence; he particularly disliked slovenliness and enthusiasm, regarding it as moral slovenliness; and towards the end of his life had become completely absorbed in a voluptuous, indolent comfort and systematic solitude. Though he sometimes visited people of a rather higher rank than his own, yet from his youth up he could never endure entertaining visitors himself; and of late he had, if he did not play a game of patience, been satisfied with the society of his dining-room clock, and would spend the whole evening dozing in his armchair, listening placidly to its ticking under its glass case on the chimneypiece. In appearance he was closely shaven and extremely proper-looking, he was well-preserved, looking younger than his age; he promised to go on living many years longer, and closely followed the rules of the highest good breeding. His post was a fairly comfortable one: he had to preside somewhere and to sign something. In short, he was regarded as a first-rate man. He had only one passion, or more accurately, one keen desire: that was, to have his own house, and a house built like a gentleman's residence, not a commercial investment. His desire was at last realised! He looked out and bought a house on the Petersburg Side, a good way off, it is true, but it had a garden and was an elegant house. The new owner decided that it was better for being a good way off: he did not like entertaining at home, and for driving to see anyone or to the office he had a handsome carriage of a chocolate hue, a coachman, Mihey, and two little but strong

195

and handsome horses. All this was honourably acquired by the careful frugality of forty years, so that his heart rejoiced over it.

This was how it was that Stepan Nikiforovitch felt such pleasure in his placid heart that he actually invited two friends to see him on his birthday, which he had hitherto carefully concealed from his most intimate acquaintances. He had special designs on one of these visitors. He lived in the upper storey of his new house, and he wanted a tenant for the lower half, which was built and arranged in exactly the same way. Stepan Nikiforovitch was reckoning upon Semyon Ivanovitch Shipulenko, and had twice that evening broached the subject in the course of conversation. But Semyon Ivanovitch made no response. The latter, too, was a man who had doggedly made a way for himself in the course of long years. He had black hair and whiskers, and a face that always had a shade of jaundice. He was a married man of morose disposition who liked to stay at home; he ruled his household with a rod of iron; in his official duties he had the greatest self-confidence. He, too, knew perfectly well what goal he was making for, and better still, what he never would reach. He was in a good position, and he was sitting tight there. Though he looked upon the new reforms with a certain distaste, he was not particularly agitated about them: he was extremely self-confident, and listened with a shade of ironical malice to Ivan Ilyitch Pralinsky expatiating on new themes. All of them had been drinking rather freely, however, so that Stepan Nikiforovitch himself condescended to take part in a slight discussion with Mr. Pralinsky concerning the latest reforms. But we must say a few words about his Excellency, Mr. Pralinsky, especially as he is the chief hero of the present story.

The actual civil councillor Ivan Ilyitch Pralinsky had only been "his Excellency" for four months; in short, he was a young general. He was young in years, too—only forty-three, no more—and he looked and liked to look even younger. He was a tall, handsome man, he was smart in his dress, and prided himself on its solid, dignified character; with great aplomb he displayed an order of some consequence on his breast. From his earliest childhood he had known how to acquire the airs and graces of aristocratic society, and being a bachelor, dreamed of a wealthy and even aristocratic bride. He dreamed of many other things, though he was far from being stupid. At times he was a great talker, and even liked to assume a parliamentary pose. He came of a good family. He was the son of a general, and brought up in the lap of luxury; in his tender childhood he had been dressed in velvet and fine linen, had been educated at an aristocratic school, and though he acquired very little learning there he was successful in the service, and had worked his way up to being a general. The authorities looked upon him as a capable man, and even expected great things from him in the future. Stepan Nikiforovitch, under whom Ivan Ilyitch had begun his career in the service, and under whom he had remained until he was made a general, had never considered him a good business man and had no expectations of him whatever. What he liked in him was that he belonged to a good family, had property—that is, a big block of buildings, let out in flats, in charge of an overseer—was connected with persons of consequence, and what was more, had a majestic bearing. Stepan Nikiforovitch blamed him inwardly for excess of imagination and instability. Ivan Ilyitch himself felt at times that he had too much *amour-propre* and even sensitiveness. Strange to say, he had attacks from time to time of morbid tenderness of conscience and even a kind of faint remorse. With bitterness and a secret soreness of heart he recognised now and again that he did not fly so high as he imagined. At such moments he sank into despondency, especially when he was suffering from hæmorrhoids, called his life *une existence manquée*, and ceased—privately, of course—

to believe even in his parliamentary capacities, calling himself a talker, a maker of phrases; and though all that, of course, did him great credit, it did not in the least prevent him from raising his head again half an hour later, and growing even more obstinately, even more conceitedly self-confident, and assuring himself that he would yet succeed in making his mark, and that he would be not only a great official but a statesman whom Russia would long remember. He actually dreamed at times of monuments. From this it will be seen that Ivan Ilyitch aimed high, though he hid his vague hopes and dreams deep in his heart, even with a certain trepidation. In short, he was a good-natured man and a poet at heart. Of late years these morbid moments of disillusionment had begun to be more frequent. He had become peculiarly irritable, ready to take offence, and was apt to take any contradiction as an affront. But reformed Russia gave him great hopes. His promotion to general was the finishing touch. He was roused; he held his head up. He suddenly began talking freely and eloquently. He talked about the new ideas, which he very quickly and unexpectedly made his own and professed with vehemence. He sought opportunities for speaking, drove about the town, and in many places succeeded in gaining the reputation of a desperate Liberal, which flattered him greatly. That evening, after drinking four glasses, he was particularly exuberant. He wanted on every point to confute Stepan Nikiforovitch, whom he had not seen for some time past, and whom he had hitherto always respected and even obeyed. He considered him for some reason reactionary, and fell upon him with exceptional heat. Stepan Nikiforovitch hardly answered him, but only listened slyly, though the subject interested him. Ivan Ilyitch got hot, and in the heat of the discussion sipped his glass more often than he ought to have done. Then Stepan Nikiforovitch took the bottle and at once filled his glass again, which for some reason seemed to offend Ivan Ilyitch, especially as

Semyon Ivanovitch Shipulenko, whom he particularly despised and indeed feared on account of his cynicism and ill-nature, preserved a treacherous silence and smiled more frequently than was necessary. "They seem to take me for a schoolboy," flashed across Ivan Ilyitch's mind.

"No, it was time, high time," he went on hotly. "We have put it off too long, and to my thinking humanity is the first consideration, humanity with our inferiors, remembering that they, too, are men. Humanity will save everything and bring out all that is . . ."

"He-he-he-he!" was heard from the direction of Semyon Ivanovitch.

"But why are you giving us such a talking to?" Stepan Nikiforovitch protested at last, with an affable smile. "I must own, Ivan Ilyitch, I have not been able to make out so far, what you are maintaining. You advocate humanity. That is love of your fellow-creatures, isn't it?"

"Yes, if you like. I . . ."

"Allow me! As far as I can see, that's not the only thing. Love of one's fellow-creatures has always been fitting. The reform movement is not confined to that. All sorts of questions have arisen relating to the peasantry, the law courts, economics, government contracts, morals and . . . and . . . and those questions are endless, and all together may give rise to great upheavals, so to say. That is what we have been anxious about, and not simply humanity. . . ."

"Yes, the thing is a bit deeper than that," observed Semyon Ivanovitch.

"I quite understand, and allow me to observe, Semyon Ivanovitch, that I can't agree to being inferior to you in depth of understanding," Ivan Ilyitch observed sarcastically and with excessive sharpness. "However, I will make so bold as to assert, Stepan Nikiforovitch, that you have not understood me either. . . ."

199

"No, I haven't."

"And yet I maintain and everywhere advance the idea that humanity and nothing else with one's subordinates, from the official in one's department down to the copying clerk, from the copying clerk down to the house serf, from the servant down to the peasant—humanity, I say, may serve, so to speak, as the corner-stone of the coming reforms and the reformation of things in general. Why? Because. Take a syllogism. I am human, consequently I am loved. I am loved, so confidence is felt in me. There is a feeling of confidence, and so there is trust. There is trust, and so there is love . . . that is, no, I mean to say that if they trust me they will believe in the reforms, they will understand, so to speak, the essential nature of them, will, so to speak, embrace each other in a moral sense, and will settle the whole business in a friendly way, fundamentally. What are you laughing at, Semyon Ivanovitch? Can't you understand?"

Stepan Nikiforovitch raised his eyebrows without speaking; he was surprised.

"I fancy I have drunk a little too much" said Semyon Ivanovitch sarcastically, "and so I am a little slow of comprehension. Not quite all my wits about me."

Ivan Ilyitch winced.

"We should break down," Stepan Nikiforovitch pronounced suddenly, after a slight pause of hesitation.

"How do you mean we should break down?" asked Ivan Ilyitch, surprised at Stepan Nikiforovitch's abrupt remark.

"Why, we should break under the strain." Stepan Nikiforovitch evidently did not care to explain further.

"I suppose you are thinking of new wine in old bottles?" Ivan Ilyitch replied, not without irony. "Well, I can answer for myself, anyway."

At that moment the clock struck half-past eleven.

"One sits on and on, but one must go at last," said Semyon

Ivanovitch, getting up. But Ivan Ilyitch was before him; he got up from the table and took his sable cap from the chimney-piece. He looked as though he had been insulted.

"So how is it to be, Semyon Ivanovitch? Will you think it over?" said Stepan Nikiforovitch, as he saw the visitors out.

"About the flat, you mean? I'll think it over, I'll think it over."

"Well, when you have made up your mind, let me know as soon as possible."

"Still on business?" Mr. Pralinsky observed affably, in a slightly ingratiating tone, playing with his hat. It seemed to him as though they were forgetting him.

Stepan Nikiforovitch raised his eyebrows and remained mute, as a sign that he would not detain his visitors. Semyon Ivanovitch made haste to bow himself out.

"Well . . . after that what is one to expect . . . if you don't understand the simple rules of good manners . . ." Mr. Pralinsky reflected to himself, and held out his hand to Stepan Nikiforovitch in a particularly offhand way.

In the hall Ivan Ilyitch wrapped himself up in his light, expensive fur coat; he tried for some reason not to notice Semyon Ivanovitch's shabby raccoon, and they both began descending the stairs.

"The old man seemed offended," said Ivan Ilyitch to the silent Semyon Ivanovitch.

"No, why?" answered the latter with cool composure.

"Servile flunkey," Ivan Ilyitch thought to himself.

They went out at the front door. Semyon Ivanovitch's sledge with a grey ugly horse drove up.

"What the devil! What has Trifon done with my carriage?" cried Ivan Ilyitch, not seeing his carriage.

The carriage was nowhere to be seen. Stepan Nikiforovitch's servant knew nothing about it. They appealed to Varlam, Semyon Ivanovitch's coachman, and received the answer that

201

he had been standing there all the time and that the carriage had been there, but now there was no sign of it.

"An unpleasant predicament," Mr. Shipulenko pronounced. "Shall I take you home?"

"Scoundrelly people!" Mr. Pralinsky cried with fury. "He asked me, the rascal, to let him go to a wedding close here in the Petersburg Side; some crony of his was getting married, deuce take her! I sternly forbade him to absent himself, and now I'll bet he has gone off there."

"He certainly has gone there, sir," observed Varlam; "but he promised to be back in a minute, to be here in time, that is."

"Well, there it is! I had a presentiment that this would happen! I'll give it to him!"

"You'd better give him a good flogging once or twice at the police station, then he will do what you tell him," said Semyon Ivanovitch, as he wrapped the rug round him.

"Please don't you trouble, Semyon Ivanovitch!"

"Well, won't you let me take you along?"

"*Merci, bon voyage.*"

Semyon Ivanovitch drove off, while Ivan Ilyitch set off on foot along the wooden pavement, conscious of a rather acute irritation.

"Yes, indeed I'll give it to you now, you rogue! I am going on foot on purpose to make you feel it, to frighten you! He will come back and hear that his master has gone off on foot . . . the blackguard!"

Ivan Ilyitch had never abused anyone like this, but he was greatly angered, and besides, there was a buzzing in his head. He was not given to drink, so five or six glasses soon affected him. But the night was enchanting. There was a frost, but it was remarkably still and there was no wind. There was a clear, starry sky. The full moon was bathing the earth in soft silver light. It was so lovely that after walking some fifty paces

Ivan Ilyitch almost forgot his troubles. He felt particularly pleased. People quickly change from one mood to another when they are a little drunk. He was even pleased with the ugly little wooden houses of the deserted street.

"It's really a capital thing that I am walking," he thought; "it's a lesson to Trifon and a pleasure to me. I really ought to walk oftener. And I shall soon pick up a sledge on the Great Prospect. It's a glorious night. What little houses they all are! I suppose small fry live here, clerks, tradesmen, perhaps. . . . That Stepan Nikiforovitch! What reactionaries they all are, those old fogies! Fogies, yes, *c'est le mot*. He is a sensible man, though; he has that *bon sens*, sober, practical understanding of things. But they are old, old. There is a lack of . . . what is it? There is a lack of something. . . . 'We shall break down.' What did he mean by that? He actually pondered when he said it. He didn't understand me a bit. And yet how could he help understanding? It was more difficult not to understand it than to understand it. The chief thing is that I am convinced, convinced in my soul. Humanity . . . the love of one's kind. Restore a man to himself, revive his personal dignity, and then . . . when the ground is prepared, get to work. I believe that's clear? Yes! Allow me, your Excellency; take a syllogism, for instance: we meet, for instance, a clerk, a poor, downtrodden clerk. 'Well . . . who are you?' Answer: 'A clerk.' Very good, a clerk; further: 'What sort of clerk are you?' Answer: 'I am such and such a clerk,' he says. 'Are you in the service?' 'I am.' 'Do you want to be happy?' 'I do.' 'What do you need for happiness?' 'This and that.' 'Why?' 'Because . . .' and there the man understands me with a couple of words, the man's mine, the man is caught, so to speak, in a net, and I can do what I like with him, that is, for his good. Horrid man that Semyon Ivanovitch! And what a nasty phiz he has! . . . 'Flog him in the police station,' he said that on purpose. No, you are talking rubbish; you can flog, but I'm

203

not going to; I shall punish Trifon with words, I shall punish him with reproaches, he will feel it. As for flogging, h'm! . . . it is an open question, h'm! . . . What about going to Emerance? Oh, damnation take it, the cursed pavement!" he cried out, suddenly tripping up. "And this is the capital. Enlightenment! One might break one's leg. H'm! I detest that Semyon Ivanovitch; a most revolting phiz. He was chuckling at me just now when I said they would embrace each other in a moral sense. Well, and they will embrace each other, and what's that to do with you? I am not going to embrace you; I'd rather embrace a peasant. . . . If I meet a peasant, I shall talk to him. I was drunk, though, and perhaps did not express myself properly. Possibly I am not expressing myself rightly now. . . . H'm! I shall never touch wine again. In the evening you babble, and next morning you are sorry for it. After all, I am walking quite steadily. . . . But they are all scoundrels, anyhow!"

So Ivan Ilyitch meditated incoherently and by snatches, as he went on striding along the pavement. The fresh air began to affect him, set his mind working. Five minutes later he would have felt soothed and sleepy. But all at once, scarcely two paces from the Great Prospect, he heard music. He looked round. On the other side of the street, in a very tumbledown-looking long wooden house of one storey, there was a great fête, there was the scraping of violins, and the droning of a double bass, and the squeaky tooting of a flute playing a very gay quadrille tune. Under the windows stood an audience, mainly of women in wadded pelisses with kerchiefs on their heads; they were straining every effort to see something through a crack in the shutters. Evidently there was a gay party within. The sound of the thud of dancing feet reached the other side of the street. Ivan Ilyitch saw a policeman standing not far off, and went up to him.

"Whose house is that, brother?" he asked, flinging his

expensive fur coat open, just far enough to allow the policeman to see the imposing decoration on his breast.

"It belongs to the registration clerk Pseldonimov," answered the policeman, drawing himself up instantly, discerning the decoration.

"Pseldonimov? Bah! Pseldonimov! What is he up to? Getting married?"

"Yes, your Honour, to a daughter of a titular councillor, Mlekopitaev, a titular councillor . . . used to serve in the municipal department. That house goes with the bride."

"So that now the house is Pseldonimov's and not Mleko-pitaev's?"

"Yes, Pseldonimov's, your Honour. It was Mlekopitaev's, but now it is Pseldonimov's."

"H'm! I am asking you, my man, because I am his chief. I am a general in the same office in which Pseldonimov serves."

"Just so, your Excellency."

The policeman drew himself up more stiffly than ever, while Ivan Ilyitch seemed to ponder. He stood still and meditated. . . .

Yes, Pseldonimov really was in his department and in his own office; he remembered that. He was a little clerk with a salary of ten roubles a month. As Mr. Pralinsky had received his department very lately he might not have remembered precisely all his subordinates, but Pseldonimov he remembered just because of his surname. It had caught his eyes from the very first, so that at the time he had had the curiosity to look with special attention at the possessor of such a surname. He remembered now a very young man with a long hooked nose, with tufts of flaxen hair, lean and ill-nourished, in an impossible uniform, and with unmentionables so impossible as to be actually unseemly; he remembered how the thought had flashed through his mind at the time: shouldn't he give the poor fellow ten roubles for Christmas, to spend on his wardrobe? But as the poor fellow's face was too austere, and his expression extremely unprepossessing, even exciting repulsion, the good-natured idea somehow faded away of itself, so Pseldonimov did not get his tip. He had been the more surprised when this same Pseldonimov had not more than a week before asked for leave to be married. Ivan Ilyitch remembered that he had somehow not had time to go into the matter, so that the matter of the marriage had been settled offhand, in haste. But yet he did remember exactly that Pseldonimov was receiving a wooden house and four hundred roubles in cash as dowry with his bride. The circumstance had surprised him at the time; he remembered that he had made a slight jest over the juxtaposition of the names Pseldonimov and Mlekopitaev. He remembered all that clearly.

He recalled it, and grew more and more pensive. It is well known that whole trains of thought sometimes pass through our brains instantaneously as though they were sensations without being translated into human speech, still less into literary language. But we will try to translate these sensations of our hero's, and present to the reader at least the kernel of them, so to say, what was most essential and nearest to reality in them. For many of our sensations when translated into ordinary language seem absolutely unreal. That is why they never find expression, though everyone has them. Of course Ivan Ilyitch's sensations and thoughts were a little incoherent. But you know the reason.

"Why," flashed through his mind, "here we all talk and talk, but when it comes to action—it all ends in nothing. Here, for instance, take this Pseldonimov: he has just come from his wedding full of hope and excitement, looking forward to his wedding feast. . . . This is one of the most blissful days of his life. . . . Now he is busy with his guests, is giving a banquet, a modest one, poor, but gay and full of genuine gladness. . . . What if he knew that at this very moment I, I, his superior, his chief, am standing by his house listening to the music? Yes, really how would he feel? No, what would he feel if I suddenly walked in? H'm! . . . Of course at first he would be frightened, he would be dumb with embarrassment. . . . I should be in his way, and perhaps should upset everything. Yes, that would be so if any other general went in, but not I. . . . That's a fact, anyone else, but not I. . . .

"Yes, Stepan Nikiforovitch! You did not understand me just now, but here is an example ready for you.

"Yes, we all make an outcry about acting humanely, but we are not capable of heroism, of fine actions.

"What sort of heroism? This sort. Consider: in the existing relations of the various members of society, for me, for me, after midnight to go in to the wedding of my subordinate, a registration clerk, at ten roubles the month—why, it would mean embarrassment, a revolution, the last days of Pompeii, a nonsensical folly. No one would understand it. Stepan Nikiforovitch would die before he understood it. Why, he said we should break down. Yes, but that's you old people, inert, paralytic people; but I shan't break down, I will transform the last day of Pompeii to a day of the utmost sweetness for my subordinate, and a wild action to an action normal, patriarchal, lofty and moral. How? Like this. Kindly listen. . . .

"Here . . . I go in, suppose; they are amazed, leave off dancing, look wildly at me, draw back. Quite so, but at once I speak out: I go straight up to the frightened Pseldonimov, and with a most cordial, affable smile, in the simplest words, I say: 'This is how it is, I have been at his Excellency Stepan Nikiforovitch's. I expect you know, close here in the neighbourhood. . . .' Well, then, lightly, in a laughing way, I shall tell him of my adventure with Trifon. From Trifon I shall pass on to say how I walked here on foot. . . . 'Well, I heard music, I inquired of a policeman, and learned, brother, that it was your wedding. Let me go in, I thought, to my subordinate's; let me see how my clerks enjoy themselves and . . . celebrate

207

their wedding. I suppose you won't turn me out?' Turn me out! What a word for a subordinate! How the devil could he dream of turning me out! I fancy that he would be half crazy, that he would rush headlong to seat me in an arm-chair, would be trembling with delight, would hardly know what he was doing for the first minute!

"Why, what can be simpler, more elegant than such an action? Why did I go in? That's another question! That is, so to say, the moral aspect of the question. That's the pith.

"H'm, what was I thinking about, yes!

"Well, of course they will make me sit down with the most important guest, some titular councillor or a relation who's a retired captain with a red nose. Gogol describes these eccentrics so capitally. Well, I shall make acquaintance, of course, with the bride, I shall compliment her, I shall encourage the guests. I shall beg them not to stand on ceremony. To enjoy themselves, to go on dancing. I shall make jokes, I shall laugh; in fact, I shall be affable and charming. I am always affable and charming when I am pleased with myself. . . . H'm . . . the point is that I believe I am still a little, well, not drunk exactly, but . . .

"Of course, as a gentleman I shall be quite on an equality with them, and shall not expect any especial marks of . . . But morally, morally, it is a different matter; they will understand and appreciate it. . . . My actions will evoke their nobler feelings. . . . Well, I shall stay for half an hour . . . even for an hour; I shall leave, of course, before supper; but they will be bustling about, baking and roasting, they will be making low bows, but I will only drink a glass, congratulate them and refuse supper. I shall say—'business'. And as soon as I pronounce the word 'business', all of them will at once have sternly respectful faces. By that I shall delicately remind them that there is a difference between them and me. The earth and the sky. It is not that I want to impress that on them, but it must be done . . . it's even essential in a moral sense, when all is said and done. I shall smile at once, however, I shall even laugh, and then they will all pluck up courage again. . . . I shall jest a little again with the bride; h'm! . . . I may even hint that I shall come again in just nine months to stand god-father, he-he! And she will be sure to be brought to bed by then. They multiply, you know, like rabbits. And they will all roar with laughter and the bride will blush; I shall kiss her feelingly on the forehead, even give her my blessing . . . and next day my exploit will be known at the office. Next day I shall be stern again, next day I shall be exacting again, even implacable, but they will all know what I am like. They will know my heart, they will know my essential nature: 'He is stern as chief, but as a man he is an angel!' And I shall have conquered them; I shall have captured them by one little act which would never have entered your head; they would be mine; I should be their father, they would be my children. . . . Come now, your Excellency Stepan Nikiforovitch, go and do likewise. . . .

"But do you know, do you understand, that Pseldonimov will tell his children how the General himself feasted and even drank at his wedding! Why you know those children would tell their children, and those would tell their grandchildren as a most sacred story that a grand gentleman, a statesman (and I shall be all that by then) did them the honour, and so on, and so on. Why, I am morally elevating the humiliated, I restore him to himself. . . . Why, he gets a salary of ten roubles a month! . . . If I repeat this five or ten times, or something of the sort, I shall gain popularity all over the place. . . . My name will be printed on the hearts of all, and the devil only knows what will come of that popularity! . . ."

These, or something like these, were Ivan Ilyitch's reflections, (a man says all sorts of things sometimes to himself, gentlemen, especially when he is in rather an eccentric condition).

All these meditations passed through his mind in something like half a minute, and of course he might have confined himself to these dreams and, after mentally putting Stepan Nikiforovitch to shame, have gone very peacefully home and to bed. And he would have done well. But the trouble of it was that the moment was an eccentric one.

As ill-luck would have it, at that very instant the self-satisfied faces of Stepan Nikiforovitch and Semyon Ivanovitch suddenly rose before his heated imagination.

"We shall break down!" repeated Stepan Nikiforovitch, smiling disdainfully.

"He-he-he," Semyon Ivanovitch seconded him with his nastiest smile.

"Well, we'll see whether we do break down!" Ivan Ilyitch said resolutely, with a rush of heat to his face.

He stepped down from the pavement and with resolute steps went straight across the street towards the house of his registration clerk Pseldonimov.

His star carried him away. He walked confidently in at the open gate and contemptuously thrust aside with his foot the shaggy, husky little sheep-dog who flew at his legs with a hoarse bark, more as a matter of form than with any real intention. Along a wooden plank he went to the covered porch which led like a sentry-box to the yard, and by three decaying wooden steps he went up to the tiny entry. Here, though a tallow candle or something in the way of a night-light was burning somewhere in a corner, it did not prevent Ivan Ilyitch from putting his left foot just as it was, in its golosh, into a galantine which had been stood out there to cool. Ivan Ilyitch bent down, and looking with curiosity, he saw that there were two other dishes of some sort of jelly and also two shapes apparently of blanc-mange. The squashed galantine embarrassed him, and for one brief instant the thought flashed through his mind, whether he

210

should not slink away at once. But he considered this too low. Reflecting that no one would have seen him, and that they would never think he had done it, he hurriedly wiped his golosh to conceal all traces, fumbled for the felt-covered door, opened it and found himself in a very little ante-room. Half of it was literally piled up with greatcoats, wadded jackets, cloaks, capes, scarves and goloshes. In the other half the musicians had been installed; two violins, a flute, and a double bass, a band of four, picked up, of course, in the street. They were sitting at an unpainted wooden table, lighted by a single tallow candle, and with the utmost vigour were sawing out the last figure of the quadrille. From the open door into the drawing-room one could see the dancers in the midst of dust, tobacco smoke and fumes. There was a frenzy of gaiety. There were sounds of laughter, shouts and shrieks from the ladies. The gentlemen stamped like a squadron of horses. Above all the Bedlam there rang out words of command from the leader of the dance, probably an extremely free and easy, and even unbuttoned gentleman: "Gentlemen advance, ladies' chain, set to partners!" and so on, and so on. Ivan Ilyitch in some excitement cast off his coat and goloshes, and with his cap in his hand went into the room. He was no longer reflecting, however.

For the first minute nobody noticed him; all were absorbed in dancing the quadrille to the end. Ivan Ilyitch stood as though entranced, and could make out nothing definite in the chaos. He caught glimpses of ladies' dresses, of gentlemen with cigarettes between their teeth. He caught a glimpse of a lady's pale blue scarf which flicked him on the nose. After the wearer a medical student, with his hair blown in all directions on his head, pranced by in wild delight and jostled violently against him on the way. He caught a glimpse, too, of an officer of some description, who looked half a mile high. Someone in an unnaturally shrill voice shouted, "O-o-oh, Pseldonimov!" as the speaker flew by stamping. It was sticky under Ivan Ilyitch's feet; evidently the floor had been waxed. In the room, which was a very small one, there were about thirty people.

But a minute later the quadrille was over, and almost at once the very thing Ivan Ilyitch had pictured when he was dreaming on the pavement took place.

A stifled murmur, a strange whisper passed over the whole company, including the dancers, who had not yet had time to take breath and wipe their perspiring faces. All eyes, all faces began quickly turning towards the newly arrived guest. Then they all seemed to draw back a little and beat a retreat. Those who had not noticed him were pulled by their coats or dresses and informed. They looked round and at once beat a retreat with the others. Ivan Ilyitch was still standing at the door without moving a step forward, and between him and the company there stretched an ever widening empty space of floor strewn with countless sweetmeat wrappings, bits of paper and cigarette-ends. All at once a young man in a uniform, with a shock of flaxen hair and a hooked nose, stepped timidly out into that empty space. He moved forward, hunched up, and looked at the unexpected visitor exactly with the expression with which a dog looks at its master when the latter has called him up and is going to kick him.

"Good evening, Pseldonimov, do you know me?" said Ivan Ilyitch, and felt at the same minute that he had said this very awkwardly; he felt, too, that he was perhaps doing something horribly stupid at that moment.

"You-our Ex-cel-len-cy!" muttered Pseldonimov.

"To be sure. . . . I have called in to see you quite by chance, my friend, as you can probably imagine. . . ."

But evidently Pseldonimov could imagine nothing. He stood with staring eyes in the utmost perplexity.

"You won't turn me out, I suppose. . . . Pleased or not, you must make a visitor welcome. . . ." Ivan Ilyitch went on, feeling that he was confused to a point of unseemly feebleness;

212

that he was trying to smile and was utterly unable; that the humorous reference to Stepan Nikiforovitch and Trifon was becoming more and more impossible. But as ill luck would have it, Pseldonimov did not recover from his stupefaction, and still gazed at him with a perfectly idiotic air. Ivan Ilyitch winced, he felt that in another minute something incredibly foolish would happen.

"I am not in the way, am I? . . . I'll go away," he faintly articulated, and there was a tremor at the right corner of his mouth.

But Pseldonimov had recovered himself.

"Good heavens, your Excellency . . . the honour . . ." he muttered, bowing hurriedly. "Graciously sit down, your Excellency. . . ." And recovering himself still further, he motioned him with both hands to a sofa before which a table had been moved away to make room for the dancing.

Ivan Ilyitch felt relieved and sank on the sofa; at once someone flew to move the table up to him. He took a cursory look round and saw that he was the only person sitting down, all the others were standing, even the ladies. A bad sign. But it was not yet time to reassure and encourage them. The company still held back, while before him, bending double, stood Pseldonimov, utterly alone, still completely at a loss and very far from smiling. It was horrid; in short, our hero endured such misery at that moment that his Haroun al-Raschid-like descent upon his subordinates for the sake of principle might well have been reckoned an heroic action. But suddenly a little figure made its appearance beside Pseldonimov, and began bowing. To his inexpressible pleasure and even happiness, Ivan Ilyitch at once recognised him as the head clerk of his office, Akim Petrovitch Zubikov, and though, of course, he was not acquainted with him, he knew him to be a businesslike and exemplary clerk. He got up at once and held out his hand to Akim Petrovitch— his whole hand, not two fingers. The latter took it in both of his with the deepest respect. The general was triumphant, the situation was saved.

And now indeed Pseldonimov was no longer, so to say, the second person, but the third. It was possible to address his remarks to the head clerk in his necessity, taking him for an acquaintance and even an intimate one, and Pseldonimov meanwhile could only be silent and be in a tremor of reverence. So that the proprieties were observed. And some explanation was essential, Ivan Ilyitch felt that; he saw that all the guests were expecting something, that the whole household was gathered together in the doorway, almost creeping, climbing over one another in their anxiety to see and hear him. What was horrid was that the head clerk in his foolishness remained standing.

"Why are you standing?" said Ivan Ilyitch, awkwardly motioning him to a seat on the sofa beside him.

"Oh, don't trouble. . . . I'll sit here." And Akim Petrovitch hurriedly sat down on a chair, almost as it was being put for him by Pseldonimov, who remained obstinately standing.

"Can you imagine what happened," addressing himself exclusively to Akim Petrovitch in a rather quavering, though free and easy voice. He even drawled out his words, with special emphasis on some syllables, pronounced the vowel *ah* like *eh*; in short, felt and was conscious that he was being affected but could not control himself: some external force was at work. He was painfully conscious of many things at that moment.

"Can you imagine, I have only just come from Stepan Nikiforovitch Nikiforov's, you have heard of him perhaps, the privy councillor. You know . . . on that special committee. . . ."

Akim Petrovitch bent his whole person forward respectfully: as much as to say, "Of course we have heard of him."

"He is your neighbour now," Ivan Ilyitch went on, for one instant for the sake of ease and good manners addressing

214

Pseldonimov, but he quickly turned away again, on seeing from the latter's eyes that it made absolutely no difference to him.

"The old fellow, as you know, has been dreaming all his life of buying himself a house. . . . Well, and he has bought it. And a very pretty house too. Yes. . . . And to-day was his birthday and he had never celebrated it before, he used even to keep it secret from us, he was too stingy to keep it, he-he. But now he is so delighted over his new house, that he invited Semyon Ivanovitch Shipulenko and me, you know."

Akim Petrovitch bent forward again. He bent forward zealously. Ivan Ilyitch felt somewhat comforted. It had struck him, indeed, that the head clerk possibly was guessing that he was an indispensable *point d'appui* for his Excellency at that moment. That would have been more horrid than anything.

"So we sat together, the three of us, he gave us champagne, we talked about problems . . . even dis-pu-ted. . . . He-he!"

Akim Petrovitch raised his eyebrows respectfully.

"Only that is not the point. When I take leave of him at last —he is a punctual old fellow, goes to bed early, you know, in his old age—I go out. . . . My Trifon is nowhere to be seen! I am anxious, I make inquiries. 'What has Trifon done with the carriage?' It comes out that, hoping I should stay on, he had gone off to the wedding of some friend of his, or sister maybe. . . . Goodness only knows. Somewhere here on the Petersburg Side. And took the carriage with him while he was about it."

Again for the sake of good manners the general glanced in the direction of Pseldonimov. The latter promptly gave a wriggle, but not at all the sort of wriggle the general would have liked. "He has no sympathy, no heart," flashed through his brain.

"You don't say so!" said Akim Petrovitch, greatly impressed. A faint murmur of surprise ran through all the crowd.

"Can you fancy my position. . . ." (Ivan Ilyitch glanced at

them all). "There was nothing for it, I set off on foot, I thought I would trudge to the Great Prospect, and there find some cabby . . . he-he!"

"He-he-he!" Akim Petrovitch echoed. Again a murmur, but this time on a more cheerful note, passed through the crowd. At that moment the chimney of a lamp on the wall broke with a crash. Someone rushed zealously to see to it. Pseldonimov started and looked sternly at the lamp, but the general took no notice of it, and all was serene again.

"I walked . . . and the night was so lovely, so still. All at once I heard a band, stamping, dancing. I inquired of a police-man; it is Pseldonimov's wedding. Why, you are giving a ball to all Petersburg Side, my friend. Ha-ha." He turned to Pseldonimov again.

"He-he-he! To be sure," Akim Petrovitch responded. There was a stir among the guests again, but what was most foolish was that Pseldonimov, though he bowed, did not even now smile, but seemed as though he were made of wood. "Is he a fool or what?" thought Ivan Ilyitch. "He ought to have smiled at that point, the ass, and everything would have run easily." There was a fury of impatience in his heart.

"I thought I would go in to see my clerk. He won't turn me out I expect . . . pleased or not, one must welcome a guest. You must please excuse me, my dear fellow. If I am in the way, I will go . . . I only came in to have a look. . . ."

But little by little a general stir was beginning.

Akim Petrovitch looked at him with a mawkishly sweet expression as though to say, "How could your Excellency be in the way?" all the guests stirred and began to display the first symptoms of being at their ease. Almost all the ladies sat down. A good sign and a reassuring one. The boldest spirits among them fanned themselves with their handkerchiefs. One of them in a shabby velvet dress said something with intentional loudness. The officer addressed by her would have liked to

216

answer her as loudly, but seeing that they were the only ones speaking aloud, he subsided. The men, for the most part government clerks, with two or three students among them, looked at one another as though egging each other on to unbend, cleared their throats, and began to move a few steps in different directions. No one, however, was particularly timid, but they were all restive, and almost all of them looked with a hostile expression at the personage who had burst in upon them, to destroy their gaiety. The officer, ashamed of his cowardice, began to edge up to the table.

"But I say, my friend, allow me to ask you your name," Ivan Ilyitch asked Pseldonimov.

"Porfiry Petrovitch, your Excellency," answered the latter, with staring eyes as though on parade.

"Introduce me, Porfiry Petrovitch, to your bride. . . . Take me to her . . . I . . ."

And he showed signs of a desire to get up. But Pseldonimov ran full speed to the drawing-room. The bride, however, was standing close by at the door, but as soon as she heard herself mentioned, she hid. A minute later Pseldonimov led her up by the hand. The guests all moved aside to make way for them. Ivan Ilyitch got up solemnly and addressed himself to her with a most affable smile.

"Very, very much pleased to make your acquaintance," he pronounced with a most aristocratic half-bow, "and especially on such a day. . . ."

He gave a meaning smile. There was an agreeable flutter among the ladies.

"*Charmée*," the lady in the velvet dress pronounced, almost aloud.

The bride was a match for Pseldonimov. She was a thin little lady not more than seventeen, pale, with a very small face and a sharp little nose. Her quick, active little eyes were not at all embarrassed; on the contrary, they looked at him steadily and even with a shade of resentment. Evidently Pseldonimov was marrying her for her beauty. She was dressed in a white muslin dress over a pink slip. Her neck was thin, and she had a figure like a chicken's with the bones all sticking out. She was not equal to making any response to the general's affability.

"But she is very pretty," he went on, in an undertone, as though addressing Pseldonimov only, though intentionally speaking so that the bride could hear.

But on this occasion, too, Pseldonimov again answered absolutely nothing, and did not even wriggle. Ivan Ilyitch fancied that there was something cold, suppressed in his eyes, as though he had something peculiarly malignant in his mind. And yet he had at all costs to wring some sensibility out of him. Why, that was the object of his coming.

"They are a couple, though!" he thought.

And he turned again to the bride, who had seated herself beside him on the sofa, but in answer to his two or three questions he got nothing but "yes" or "no", and hardly that.

"If only she had been overcome with confusion," he thought to himself, "then I should have begun to banter her. But as it is, my position is impossible."

And as ill-luck would have it, Akim Petrovitch, too, was mute; though this was only due to his foolishness, it was still unpardonable.

"My friends! Haven't I perhaps interfered with your enjoyment?" he said, addressing the whole company.

He felt that the very palms of his hands were perspiring.

"No . . . don't trouble, your Excellency; we are beginning directly, but now . . . we are getting cool," answered the officer.

The bride looked at him with pleasure; the officer was not old, and wore the uniform of some branch of the service. Pseldonimov was still standing in the same place, bending forward, and it seemed as though his hooked nose stood out further than ever. He looked and listened like a footman

218

standing with the greatcoat on his arm, waiting for the end of his master's farewell conversation. Ivan Ilyitch made this comparison himself. He was losing his head; he felt that he was in an awkward position, that the ground was giving way under his feet, that he had got in somewhere and could not find his way out, as though he were in the dark.

Suddenly the guests all moved aside, and a short, thick-set, middle-aged woman made her appearance, dressed plainly though she was in her best, with a big shawl on her shoulders, pinned at her throat, and on her head a cap to which she was evidently unaccustomed. In her hands she carried a small round tray on which stood a full but uncorked bottle of champagne and two glasses, neither more nor less. Evidently the bottle was intended for only two guests.

The middle-aged lady approached the general.

"Don't look down on us, your Excellency," she said, bowing. "Since you have deigned to do my son the honour of coming to his wedding, we beg you graciously to drink to the health of the young people. Do not disdain us; do us the honour."

Ivan Ilyitch clutched at her as though she were his salvation. She was by no means an old woman—forty-five or forty-six, not more; but she had such a good-natured, rosy-cheeked, such a round and candid Russian face, she smiled so good-humouredly, bowed so simply, that Ivan Ilyitch was almost comforted and began to hope again.

"So you are the mo-other of your so-on?" he said, getting up from the sofa.

"Yes, my mother, your Excellency," mumbled Pseldonimov, craning his long neck and thrusting forward his long nose again.

"Ah! I am delighted—de-ligh-ted to make your acquaintance."

"Do not refuse us, your Excellency."

"With the greatest pleasure."

The tray was put down. Pseldonimov dashed forward to pour out the wine. Ivan Ilyitch, still standing, took the glass.

"I am particularly, particularly glad on this occasion, that I can . . ." he began, "that I can . . . testify before all of you . . . In short, as your chief . . . I wish you, madam" (he turned to the bride), "and you, friend Porfiry, I wish you the fullest, completest happiness for many long years."

And he positively drained the glass with feeling, the seventh he had drunk that evening. Pseldonimov looked at him gravely and even sullenly. The general was beginning to feel an agonising hatred of him.

"And that scarecrow" (he looked at the officer), "keeps obtruding himself. He might at least have shouted 'hurrah!' and it would have gone off, it would have gone off . . ."

"And you too, Akim Petrovitch, drink a glass to their health," added the mother, addressing the head clerk. "You are his superior, he is under you. Look after my boy, I beg you as a mother. And don't forget us in the future, our good, kind friend, Akim Petrovitch."

"How nice these old Russian women are," thought Ivan Ilyitch. "She has livened us all up. I have always loved the democracy . . ."

At that moment another tray was brought to the table; it was brought in by a maid wearing a crackling cotton dress that had never been washed, and a crinoline. She could hardly grasp the tray in both hands, it was so big. On it there were numbers of plates of apples, sweets, fruit meringues and fruit cheeses, walnuts and so on, and so on. The tray had been till then in the drawing-room for the delectation of all the guests, and especially the ladies. But now it was brought to the general alone.

"Do not disdain our humble fare, your Excellency. What we have we are pleased to offer," the old lady repeated, bowing.

220

"Delighted!" said Ivan Ilyitch, and with real pleasure took a walnut and cracked it between his fingers. He had made up his mind to win popularity at all costs.

Meantime the bride suddenly giggled.

"What is it?" asked Ivan Ilyitch with a smile, encouraged by this sign of life.

"Ivan Kostenkinitch, here, makes me laugh," she answered, looking down.

The general distinguished, indeed, a flaxen-headed young man, exceedingly good-looking, who was sitting on a chair at the other end of the sofa, whispering something to Madame Pseldonimov. The young man stood up. He was apparently very young and very shy.

"I was telling the lady about a 'dream book', your Excellency," he muttered as though apologising.

"About what sort of 'dream book'?" asked Ivan Ilyitch condescendingly.

"There is a new 'dream book', a literary one. I was telling the lady that to dream of Mr. Panaev means spilling coffee on one's shirt front."

"What innocence!" thought Ivan Ilyitch, with positive annoyance.

Though the young man flushed very red as he said it, he was incredibly delighted that he had said this about Mr. Panaev.

"To be sure, I have heard of it . . ." responded his Excellency.

"No, there is something better than that," said a voice quite close to Ivan Ilyitch. "There is a new encyclopædia being published, and they say Mr. Kraevsky will write articles . . . and satirical literature."

This was said by a young man who was by no means embarrassed, but rather free and easy. He was wearing gloves and a white waistcoat, and carried a hat in his hand. He did not dance, and looked condescending, for he was on the staff of a satirical paper called *The Firebrand*, and gave himself airs accordingly. He had come casually to the wedding, invited as an honoured guest of the Pseldonimovs', with whom he was on intimate terms and with whom only a year before he had lived in very poor lodgings, kept by a German woman. He drank vodka, however, and for that purpose had more than once withdrawn to a snug little back room to which all the guests knew their way. The general disliked him extremely.

"And the reason that's funny," broke in joyfully the flaxen-headed young man, who had talked of the shirt front and at whom the young man on the comic paper looked with hatred in consequence, "it's funny, your Excellency, because it is supposed by the writer that Mr. Kraevsky does not know how to spell, and thinks that 'satirical' ought to be written with a 'y' instead of an 'i'."

But the poor young man scarcely finished his sentence; he could see from his eyes that the general knew all this long ago, for the general himself looked embarrassed, and evidently because he knew it. The young man seemed inconceivably ashamed. He succeeded in effacing himself completely, and remained very melancholy all the rest of the evening. But to make up for that the young man on the staff of the *Firebrand* came up nearer, and seemed to be intending to sit down somewhere close by. Such free and easy manners struck Ivan Ilyitch as rather shocking.

"Tell me, please, Porfiry," he began, in order to say something, "why—I have always wanted to ask you about it in person—why you are called Pseldonimov instead of Pseudonimov? Your name surely must be Pseudonimov."

"I cannot inform you exactly, your Excellency," said Pseldonimov.

"It must have been that when his father went into the service they made a mistake in his papers, so that he has remained now Pseldonimov," put in Akim Petrovitch. "That does happen."

222

"Un-doubted-ly," the general said with warmth, "un-doubted-ly; for only think, Pseudonimov comes from the literary word pseudonym, while Pseldonimov means nothing."

"Due to foolishness," added Akim Petrovitch.

"You mean what is due to foolishness?"

"The Russian common people in their foolishness often alter letters, and sometimes pronounce them in their own way. For instance, they say nevalid instead of invalid."

"Oh, yes, nevalid, he-he-he . . ."

"Mumber, too, they say, your Excellency," boomed out the tall officer, who had long been itching to distinguish himself in some way.

"What do you mean by mumber?"

"Mumber instead of number, your Excellency."

"Oh, yes, mumber . . . instead of number. . . . To be sure, to be sure . . . He-he-he!" Ivan Ilyitch had to do a chuckle for the benefit of the officer too.

The officer straightened his tie.

"Another thing they say is nigh by," the young man on the comic paper put in. But his Excellency tried not to hear this. His chuckles were not at everybody's disposal.

"Nigh by, instead of near," the young man on the comic paper persisted, in evident irritation.

Ivan Ilyitch looked at him sternly.

"Come, why persist?" Pseldonimov whispered to him

"Why, I was talking. Mayn't one speak?" the latter pro-tested in a whisper; but he said no more and with secret fury walked out of the room.

He made his way straight to the attractive little back room where, for the benefit of the dancing gentlemen, vodka of two sorts, salt fish, caviare cut into slices and a bottle of very strong sherry of Russian make had been set early in the evening on a little table, covered with a Yaroslav cloth. With anger in his heart he was pouring himself out a glass of vodka, when suddenly the medical student with the dishevelled locks, the foremost dancer and cutter of capers at Pseldonimov's ball, rushed in. He fell on the decanter with greedy haste.

"They are just going to begin!" he said rapidly, helping himself. "Come and look, I am going to dance a solo on my head; after supper I shall risk the fish dance. It is just the thing for the wedding. So to speak, a friendly hint to Pseldonimov. She's a jolly creature that Kleopatra Semyonovna, you can venture on anything you like with her."

"He's a reactionary," said the young man on the comic paper gloomily, as he tossed off his vodka.

"Who is a reactionary?"

"Why, the personage before whom they set those sweet-meats. He's a reactionary, I tell you."

"What nonsense!" muttered the student, and he rushed out of the room, hearing the opening bars of the quadrille.

Left alone, the young man on the comic paper poured himself out another glass to give himself more assurance and independence; he drank and ate a snack of something, and never had the actual civil councillor Ivan Ilyitch made for himself a bitterer foe more implacably bent on revenge than was the young man on the staff of the *Firebrand* whom he had so slighted, especially after the latter had drunk two glasses of vodka. Alas! Ivan Ilyitch suspected nothing of the sort. He did not suspect another circumstance of prime importance either, which had an influence on the mutual relations of the guests and his Excellency. The fact was that though he had given a proper and even detailed explanation of his presence at his clerk's wedding, this explanation did not really satisfy any-one, and the visitors were still embarrassed. But suddenly everything was transformed as though by magic, all were re-assured and ready to enjoy themselves, to laugh, to shriek, to dance, exactly as though the unexpected visitor were not in the room. The cause of it was a rumour, a whisper, a report which

spread in some unknown way that the visitor was not quite
. . . it seemed—was, in fact, "a little top-heavy". And though
this seemed at first a horrible calumny, it began by degrees to
appear to be justified; suddenly everything became clear. What
was more, they felt all at once extraordinarily free. And it was
just at this moment that the quadrille for which the medical
student was in such haste, the last before supper, began.

And just as Ivan Ilyitch meant to address the bride again,
intending to provoke her with some innuendo, the tall officer
suddenly dashed up to her and with a flourish dropped on one
knee before her. She immediately jumped up from the sofa,
and whisked off with him to take her place in the quadrille.
The officer did not even apologise, and she did not even glance
at the general as she went away; she seemed, in fact, relieved to
escape.

"After all she has a right to be," thought Ivan Ilyitch, "and
of course they don't know how to behave." "Hm! Don't you
stand on ceremony, friend Porfiry," he said, addressing Pseldonimov. "Perhaps you have . . . arrangements to make . . . or
something . . . please don't put yourself out." "Why does he
keep guard over me?" he thought to himself.

Pseldonimov, with his long neck and his eyes fixed intently
upon him, began to be insufferable. In fact, all this was not
the thing, not the thing at all, but Ivan Ilyitch was still far from
admitting this.

The quadrille began.

"Will you allow me, your Excellency?" asked Akim Petrovitch, holding the bottle respectfully in his hands and preparing
to pour from it into his Excellency's glass.

"I . . . I really don't know, whether . . ."

But Akim Petrovitch, with reverent and radiant face, was
already filling the glass. After filling the glass, he proceeded,
writhing and wriggling, as it were stealthily, as it were furtively,

to pour himself out some, with this difference, that he did not fill his own glass to within a finger length of the top, and this seemed somehow more respectful. He was like a woman in travail as he sat beside his chief. What could he talk about, indeed? Yet to entertain his Excellency, was an absolute duty since he had the honour of keeping him company. The champagne served as a resource, and his Excellency, too, was pleased that he had filled his glass—not for the sake of the champagne, for it was warm and perfectly abominable, but just morally pleased.

"The old chap would like to have a drink himself," thought Ivan Ilyitch, "but he doesn't venture till I do. I mustn't prevent him. And indeed it would be absurd for the bottle to stand between us untouched."

He took a sip, anyway it seemed better than sitting doing nothing.

"I am here," he said, with pauses and emphasis, "I am here, you know, so to speak, accidentally, and, of course, it may be . . . that some people would consider . . . it unseemly for me to be at such . . . a gathering."

Akim Petrovitch said nothing, but listened with timid curiosity.

"But I hope you will understand, with what object I have come. . . . I haven't really come simply to drink wine . . . he-he!"

Akim Petrovitch tried to chuckle, following the example of his Excellency, but again he could not get it out, and again he made absolutely no consolatory answer.

"I am here . . . in order, so to speak, to encourage . . . to show, so to speak, a moral aim," Ivan Ilyitch continued, feeling vexed at Akim Petrovitch's stupidity, but he suddenly subsided into silence himself. He saw that poor Akim Petrovitch had dropped his eyes as though he were in fault. The general in some confusion made haste to take another sip from his glass,

226

and Akim Petrovitch clutched at the bottle as though it were his only hope of salvation and filled the glass again.

"You haven't many resources," thought Ivan Ilyitch, looking sternly at poor Akim Petrovitch. The latter, feeling that stern general-like eye upon him, made up his mind to remain silent for good and not to raise his eyes. So they sat beside each other for a couple of minutes—two sickly minutes for Akim Petrovitch.

A couple of words about Akim Petrovitch. He was a man of the old school, as meek as a hen, reared from infancy to obsequious servility, and at the same time a good-natured and even honourable man. He was a Petersburg Russian; that is, his father and his father's father were born, grew up and served in Petersburg and had never once left Petersburg. That is quite a special type of Russian. They have hardly any idea of Russia, though that does not trouble them at all. Their whole interest is confined to Petersburg and chiefly the place in which they serve. All their thoughts are concentrated on preference for farthing points, on the shop, and their month's salary. They don't know a single Russian custom, a single Russian song except 'Lutchinushka', and that only because it is played on the barrel organs. However, there are two fundamental and invariable signs by which you can at once distinguish a Petersburg Russian from a real Russian. The first sign is the fact that Petersburg Russians, all without exception, speak of the newspaper as the *Academic News* and never call it the *Petersburg News*. The second and equally trustworthy sign is that Petersburg Russians never make use of the word 'breakfast', but always call it 'Frühstück' with especial emphasis on the first syllable. By these radical and distinguishing signs you can tell them apart; in short, this is a humble type which has been formed during the last thirty-five years. Akim Petrovitch, however, was by no means a fool. If the general had asked him a question about anything in his own province he would have answered and kept up a conversation; as it was, it was unseemly for a subordinate even to answer such questions as these, though Akim Petrovitch was dying from curiosity to know something more detailed about his Excellency's real intentions.

And meanwhile Ivan Ilyitch sank more and more into meditation and a sort of whirl of ideas; in his absorption he sipped his glass every half-minute. Akim Petrovitch at once zealously filled it up. Both were silent. Ivan Ilyitch began looking at the dances, and immediately something attracted his attention. One circumstance even surprised him. . . .

The dances were certainly lively. Here people danced in the simplicity of their hearts to amuse themselves and even to romp wildly. Among the dancers few were really skilful, but the unskilled stamped so vigorously that they might have been taken for agile ones. The officer was among the foremost; he particularly liked the figures in which he was left alone, to perform a solo. Then he performed the most marvellous capers. For instance, standing upright as a post, he would suddenly bend over to one side, so that one expected him to fall over; but with the next step he would suddenly bend over in the opposite direction at the same acute angle to the floor. He kept the most serious face and danced in the full conviction that everyone was watching him. Another gentleman, who had had rather more than he could carry before the quadrille, dropped asleep beside his partner so that his partner had to dance alone. The young registration clerk, who had danced with the lady in the blue scarf through all the figures and through all the five quadrilles which they had danced that evening, played the same prank the whole time: that is, he dropped a little behind his partner, seized the end of her scarf, and as they crossed over succeeded in imprinting some twenty kisses on the scarf. His partner sailed along in front of him, as though she noticed nothing. The medical student really did dance on his head, and excited frantic enthusiasm, stamping, and shrieks of delight. In short, the absence of constraint was very marked. Ivan Ilyitch, whom the wine was beginning to affect, began by smiling, but by degrees a bitter doubt began to steal into his heart; of course he liked free and easy manners and unconventionality. He desired, he had even inwardly prayed for free and easy manners, when they had all held back, but now that unconventionality had gone beyond all limits. One lady, for instance, the one in the shabby dark blue velvet dress, bought fourth-hand, in the sixth figure pinned her dress so as to turn it into—something like trousers. This was the Kleopatra Semyonovna with whom one could venture to do anything, as her partner, the medical student, had expressed it. The medical student defied description: he was simply a Fokin. How was it? They had held back and now they were so quickly emancipated! One might think it nothing, but this transformation was somehow strange; it indicated something. It was as though they had forgotten Ivan Ilyitch's existence. Of course he was the first to laugh, and even ventured to applaud. Akim Petrovitch chuckled respectfully in unison, though, indeed, with evident pleasure and no suspicion that his Excellency was beginning to nourish in his heart a new gnawing anxiety.

"You dance capitally, young man," Ivan Ilyitch was obliged to say to the medical student as he walked past him.

The student turned sharply towards him, made a grimace, and bringing his face close into unseemly proximity to the face of his Excellency, crowed like a cock at the top of his voice. This was too much. Ivan Ilyitch got up from the table. In spite of that, a roar of inexpressible laughter followed, for the crow was an extraordinarily good imitation, and the whole performance was utterly unexpected. Ivan Ilyitch was still standing in bewilderment, when suddenly Pseldonimov himself made his appearance, and with a bow, began begging him to come to supper. His mother followed him.

"Your Excellency," she said, bowing, "do us the honour, do not disdain our humble fare."

"I . . . I really don't know," Ivan Ilyitch was beginning. "I did not come with that idea . . . I . . . meant to be going . . ."

He was, in fact, holding his hat in his hands. What is more, he had at that very moment taken an inward vow at all costs to depart at once and on no account whatever to consent to remain, and . . . he remained. A minute later he led the procession to the table. Pseldinomov and his mother walked in front, clearing the way for him. They made him sit down in the seat of honour, and again a bottle of champagne, opened but not begun, was set beside his plate. By way of *hors d'œuvre* there were salt herrings and vodka. He put out his hand, poured out a large glass of vodka and drank it off. He had never drunk vodka before. He felt as though he were rolling down a hill, were flying, flying, flying, that he must stop himself, catch at something, but there was no possibility of it.

His position was certainly becoming more and more eccentric. What is more, it seemed as though fate were mocking at him. God knows what had happened to him in the course of an hour or so. When he went in he had, so to say, opened his arms to embrace all humanity, all his subordinates; and here not more than an hour had passed and in all his aching heart he felt and knew that he hated Pseldonimov and was cursing him, his wife and his wedding. What was more, he saw from his face, from his eyes alone, that Pseldonimov himself hated him, that he was looking at him with eyes that almost said: "If only you would take yourself off, curse you! Foisting yourself on us!" All this he had read for some time in his eyes.

Of course as he sat down to table, Ivan Ilyitch would sooner have had his hand cut off than have owned, not only aloud, but even to himself, that this was really so. The moment had not fully arrived yet. There was still a moral vacillation. But his heart, his heart . . . it ached! It was clamouring for

230

freedom, for air, for rest. Ivan Ilyitch was really too good-natured.

He knew, of course, that he ought long before to have gone away, not merely to have gone away but to have made his escape. That all this was not the same, but had turned out utterly different from what he had dreamed of on the pavement.

"Why did I come? Did I come here to eat and drink?" he asked himself as he tasted the salt herring. He even had attacks of scepticism. There was at moments a faint stir of irony in regard to his own fine action at the bottom of his heart. He actually wondered at times why he had come in.

But how could he go away? To go away like this without having finished the business properly was impossible. What would people say? They would say that he was frequenting low company. Indeed it really would amount to that if he did not end it properly. What would Stepan Nikiforovitch, Semyon Ivanovitch say (for of course it would be all over the place by to-morrow)? what would be said in the offices, at the Shembels', at the Shubins'? No, he must take his departure in such a way that all should understand why he had come, he must make clear his moral aim. . . . And meantime the dramatic moment would not present itself. "They don't even respect me," he went on, thinking. "What are they laughing at? They are as free and easy as though they had no feeling. . . . But I have long suspected that all the younger generation are without feeling! I must remain at all costs! They have just been dancing, but now at table they will all be gathered together. . . . I will talk about questions, about reforms, about the greatness of Russia. . . . I can still win their enthusiasm! Yes! Perhaps nothing is yet lost. . . . Perhaps it is always like this in reality. What should I begin upon with them to attract them? What plan can I hit upon? I am lost, simply lost. . . . And what is it they want, what is it they require? . . . I see they are laughing together there. Can it be at me, merciful

231

heavens! But what is it I want . . . why is it I am here, why don't I go away, why do I go on persisting?" . . . He thought this, and a sort of shame, a deep unbearable shame, rent his heart more and more intensely.

But everything went on in the same way, one thing after another.

Just two minutes after he had sat down to the table one terrible thought overwhelmed him completely. He suddenly felt that he was horribly drunk, that is, not as he was before, but hopelessly drunk. The cause of this was the glass of vodka which he had drunk after the champagne, and which had immediately produced an effect. He was conscious, he felt in every fibre of his being that he was growing hopelessly feeble. Of course his assurance was greatly increased, but consciousness had not deserted him, and it kept crying out: "It is bad, very bad and, in fact, utterly unseemly!" Of course his unstable drunken reflections could not rest long on one subject; there began to be apparent and unmistakably so, even to himself, two opposite sides. On one side there was swaggering assurance, a desire to conquer, a disdain of obstacles and a desperate confidence that he would attain his object. The other side showed itself in the aching of his heart, and a sort of gnawing in his soul. "What would they say? How would it all end? What would happen to-morrow, to-morrow, to-morrow?" . . .

He had felt vaguely before that he had enemies in the company. "No doubt that was because I was drunk," he thought with agonising doubt. What was his horror when he actually, by unmistakable signs, convinced himself now that he really had enemies at the table, and that it was impossible to doubt of it.

"And why—why?" he wondered.

At the table there were all the thirty guests, of whom several were quite tipsy. Others were behaving with a careless and sinister independence, shouting and talking at the top of their voices, bawling out the toasts before the time, and pelting the ladies with pellets of bread. One unprepossessing personage in a greasy coat had fallen off his chair as soon as he sat down, and remained so till the end of supper. Another one made desperate efforts to stand on the table, to propose a toast, and only the officer, who seized him by the tails of his coat, moderated his premature ardour. The supper was a pell-mell affair, although they had hired a cook who had been in the service of a general; there was the galantine, there was tongue and potatoes, there were rissoles with green peas, there was, finally, a goose, and last of all blancmange. Among the drinks were beer, vodka and sherry. The only bottle of champagne was standing beside the general, which obliged him to pour it out for himself and also for Akim Petrovitch, who did not venture at supper to officiate on his own initiative. The other guests had to drink the toasts in Caucasian wine or anything else they could get. The table was made up of several tables put together, among them even a card-table. It was covered with many tablecloths, amongst them one coloured Yaroslav cloth; the gentlemen sat alternately with the ladies. Pseldonimov's mother would not sit down to the table; she bustled about and supervised. But another sinister female figure, who had not shown herself till then, appeared on the scene, wearing a reddish silk dress, with a very high cap on her head and a bandage round her face for toothache. It appeared that this was the bride's mother, who had at last consented to emerge from a back room for supper. She had refused to appear till then owing to her implacable hostility to Pseldonimov's mother, but to that we will refer later. This lady looked spitefully, even sarcastically, at the general, and evidently did not wish to be presented to him. To Ivan Ilyitch this figure appeared suspicious in the extreme. But apart from her,

233

several other persons were suspicious and inspired involuntary apprehension and uneasiness. It even seemed that they were in some sort of plot together against Ivan Ilyitch. At any rate it seemed so to him, and throughout the whole supper he became more and more convinced of it. A gentleman with a beard, some sort of free artist, was particularly sinister; he even looked at Ivan Ilyitch several times, and then turning to his neighbour, whispered something. Another person present was unmistakably drunk, but yet, from certain signs, was to be regarded with suspicion. The medical student, too, gave rise to unpleasant expectations. Even the officer himself was not quite to be depended on. But the young man on the comic paper was blazing with hatred, he lolled in his chair, he looked so haughty and conceited, he snorted so aggressively! And though the rest of the guests took absolutely no notice of the young journalist, who had contributed only four wretched poems to the *Firebrand*, and had consequently become a Liberal and evidently, indeed, disliked him, yet when a pellet of bread aimed in his direction fell near Ivan Ilyitch, he was ready to stake his head that it had been thrown by no other than the young man in question.

All this, of course, had a pitiable effect on him.

Another observation was particularly unpleasant. Ivan Ilyitch became aware that he was beginning to articulate indistinctly and with difficulty, that he was longing to say a great deal, but that his tongue refused to obey him. And then he suddenly seemed to forget himself, and worst of all he would suddenly burst into a loud guffaw of laughter, *à propos* of nothing. This inclination quickly passed off after a glass of champagne which Ivan Ilyitch had not meant to drink, though he had poured it out and suddenly drunk it quite by accident. After that glass he felt at once almost inclined to cry. He felt that he was sinking into a most peculiar state of sentimentality; he began to be again filled with love, he loved everyone, even

234

Pseldonimov, even the young man on the comic paper. He suddenly longed to embrace all of them, to forget everything and to be reconciled. What is more, to tell them everything openly, all, all; that is, to tell them what a good, nice man he was, with what wonderful talents. What services he would do for his country, how good he was at entertaining the fair sex, and above all, how progressive he was, how humanely ready he was to be indulgent to all, to the very lowest; and finally in conclusion to tell them frankly all the motives that had impelled him to turn up at Pseldonimov's uninvited, to drink two bottles of champagne and to make him happy with his presence.

"The truth, the holy truth and candour before all things! I will capture them by candour. They will believe me, I see it clearly; they actually look at me with hostility, but when I tell them all I shall conquer them completely. They will fill their glasses and drink my health with shouts. The officer will break his glass on his spur. Perhaps they will even shout hurrah! Even if they want to toss me after the Hussar fashion I will not oppose them, and indeed it would be very jolly! I will kiss the bride on her forehead; she is charming. Akim Petrovitch is a very nice man, too. Pseldonimov will improve, of course, later on. He will acquire, so to speak, a society polish. . . . And although, of course, the younger generation has not that delicacy of feeling, yet . . . yet I will talk to them about the contemporary significance of Russia among the European States. I will refer to the peasant question, too; yes, and . . . and they will all like me and I shall leave with glory! . . ."

These dreams were, of course, extremely agreeable, but what was unpleasant was that in the midst of these roseate anticipations, Ivan Ilyitch suddenly discovered in himself another unexpected propensity, that was to spit. Anyway saliva began running from his mouth apart from any will of his own. He observed this on Akim Petrovitch, whose cheek he spluttered upon and who sat not daring to wipe it off from respectfulness.

Ivan Ilyitch took his dinner napkin and wiped it himself, but this immediately struck him himself as so incongruous, so opposed to all common sense, that he sank into silence and began wondering. Though Akim Petrovitch emptied his glass, yet he sat as though he were scalded. Ivan Ilyitch reflected now that he had for almost a quarter of an hour been talking to him about some most interesting subject, but that Akim Petrovitch had not only seemed embarrassed as he listened, but positively frightened. Pseldonimov, who was sitting one chair away from him, also craned his neck towards him, and bending his head sideways, listened to him with the most unpleasant air. He actually seemed to be keeping a watch on him. Turning his eyes upon the rest of the company, he saw that many were looking straight at him and laughing. But what was strangest of all was, that he was not in the least embarrassed by it; on the contrary, he sipped his glass again and suddenly began speaking so that all could hear:

"I was saying just now," he began as loudly as possible, "I was saying just now, ladies and gentlemen, to Akim Petrovitch, that Russia . . . yes, Russia . . . in short, you understand, that I mean to s-s-say . . . Russia is living, it is my profound conviction, through a period of hu-hu-manity . . ."

"Hu-hu-manity . . ." was heard at the other end of the table.

"Hu-hu . . ."

"Tu-tu!"

Ivan Ilyitch stopped. Pseldonimov got up from his chair and began trying to see who had shouted. Akim Petrovitch stealthily shook his head, as though admonishing the guests. Ivan Ilyitch saw this distinctly, but in his confusion said nothing.

"Humanity!" he continued obstinately; "and this evening . . . and only this evening I said to Stepan Niki-ki-forovitch . . . yes . . . that . . . that the regeneration, so to speak, of things . . ."

236

"Your Excellency!" was heard a loud exclamation at the other end of the table.

"What is your pleasure?" answered Ivan Ilyitch, pulled up short and trying to distinguish who had called to him.

"Nothing at all, your Excellency. I was carried away, continue! Con-ti-nue!" the voice was heard again.

Ivan Ilyitch felt upset.

"The regeneration, so to speak, of those same things."

"Your Excellency!" the voice shouted again.

"What do you want?"

"How do you do!"

This time Ivan Ilyitch could not restrain himself. He broke off his speech and turned to the assailant who had disturbed the general harmony. He was a very young lad, still at school, who had taken more than a drop too much, and was an object of great suspicion to the general. He had been shouting for a long time past, and had even broken a glass and two plates, maintaining that this was the proper thing to do at a wedding. At the moment when Ivan Ilyitch turned towards him, the officer was beginning to pitch into the noisy youngster.

"What are you about? Why are you yelling? We shall turn you out, that's what we shall do."

"I don't mean you, your Excellency, I don't mean you. Continue!" cried the hilarious schoolboy, lolling back in his chair. "Continue, I am listening, and am very, ve-ry, ve-ry much pleased with you! Praise-wor-thy, praisewor-thy!"

"The wretched boy is drunk," said Pseldonimov in a whisper.

"I see that he is drunk, but . . ."

"I was just telling a very amusing anecdote, your Excellency!" began the officer, "about a lieutenant in our company who was talking just like that to his superior officers; so this young man is imitating him now. To every word of his superior officers he said 'praiseworthy, praiseworthy!' He was turned out of the army ten years ago on account of it."

237

"Wha-at lieutenant was that?"

"In our company, your Excellency, he went out of his mind over the word praiseworthy. At first they tried gentle methods, then they put him under arrest. . . . His commanding officer admonished him in the most fatherly way, and he answered, 'praiseworthy, praiseworthy!' And strange to say, the officer was a fine-looking man, over six feet. They meant to court-martial him, but then they perceived that he was mad."

"So . . . a schoolboy. A schoolboy's prank need not be taken seriously. For my part I am ready to overlook it. . . ."

"They held a medical inquiry, your Excellency."

"Upon my word, but he was alive, wasn't he?"

"What! Did they dissect him?"

A loud and almost universal roar of laughter resounded among the guests, who had till then behaved with decorum. Ivan Ilyitch was furious.

"Ladies and gentlemen!" he shouted, at first scarcely stammering, "I am fully capable of apprehending that a man is not dissected alive. I imagined that in his derangement he had ceased to be alive . . . that is, that he had died . . . that is, I mean to say . . . that you don't like me . . . and yet I like you all. . . . Yes, I like Por . . . Porfiry . . . I am lowering myself by speaking like this. . . ."

At that moment Ivan Ilyitch spluttered so that a great dab of saliva flew on to the tablecloth in a most conspicuous place. Pseldonimov flew to wipe it off with a table-napkin. This last disaster crushed him completely.

"My friends, this is too much," he cried in despair.

"The man is drunk, your Excellency," Pseldonimov prompted him again.

"Porfiry, I see that you . . . all . . . yes! I say that I hope . . . yes, I call upon you all to tell me in what way have I lowered myself?"

Ivan Ilyitch was almost crying.

238

"Your Excellency, good heavens!"

"Porfiry, I appeal to you. . . . Tell me, when I came . . . yes . . . yes, to your wedding, I had an object. I was aiming at moral elevation. . . . I wanted it to be felt. . . . I appeal to all: am I greatly lowered in your eyes or not?"

A deathlike silence. That was just it, a deathlike silence, and to such a downright question. "They might at least shout at this minute!" flashed through his Excellency's head. But the guests only looked at one another. Akim Petrovitch sat more dead than alive, while Pseldonimov, numb with terror, was repeating to himself the awful question which had occurred to him more than once already.

"What shall I have to pay for all this to-morrow?"

At this point the young man on the comic paper, who was very drunk but who had hitherto sat in morose silence, addressed Ivan Ilyitch directly, and with flashing eyes began answering in the name of the whole company.

"Yes," he said in a loud voice, "yes, you have lowered yourself. Yes, you are a reactionary . . . re-ac-tion-ary!"

"Young man, you are forgetting yourself! To whom are you speaking, so to express it?" Ivan Ilyitch cried furiously, jumping up from his seat again.

"To you; and secondly, I am not a young man. . . . You've come to give yourself airs and try to win popularity."

"Pseldonimov, what does this mean?" cried Ivan Ilyitch.

But Pseldonimov was reduced to such horror that he stood still like a post and was utterly at a loss what to do. The guests, too, sat mute in their seats. All but the artist and the schoolboy, who applauded and shouted, "Bravo, bravo!"

The young man on the comic paper went on shouting with unrestrained violence:

"Yes, you came to show off your humanity! You've hindered the enjoyment of everyone. You've been drinking champagne without thinking that it is beyond the means of a clerk at ten roubles a month. And I suspect that you are one of those high officials who are a little too fond of the young wives of their clerks! What is more, I am convinced that you support State monopolies. . . . Yes, yes, yes!"

"Pseldonimov, Pseldonimov," shouted Ivan Ilyitch, holding out his hands to him. He felt that every word uttered by the comic young man was a fresh dagger at his heart.

"Directly, your Excellency; please do not distrub yourself!" Pseldonimov cried energetically, rushing up to the comic young man, seizing him by the collar and dragging him away from the table. Such physical strength could indeed not have been expected from the weakly-looking Pseldonimov. But the comic young man was very drunk, while Pseldonimov was perfectly sober. Then he gave him two or three cuffs in the back, and thrust him out of the door.

"You are all scoundrels!" roared the young man of the comic paper. "I will caricature you all to-morrow in the *Firebrand*."

They all leapt up from their seats.

"Your Excellency, your Excellency!" cried Pseldonimov, his mother and several others, crowding round the general; "your Excellency, do not be disturbed!"

"No, no," cried the general, "I am annihilated. . . . I came . . . I meant to bless you, so to speak. And this is how I am paid, for everything, everything! . . ."

He sank on to a chair as though unconscious, laid both his arms on the table, and bowed his head over them, straight into a plate of blancmange. There is no need to describe the general horror. A minute later he got up, evidently meaning to go out, gave a lurch, stumbled against the leg of a chair, fell full length on the floor and snored. . . .

This is what is apt to happen to men who don't drink when they accidentally take a glass too much. They preserve their consciousness to the last point, to the last minute, and then fall to the ground as though struck down. Ivan Ilyitch lay on the floor absolutely unconscious. Pseldonimov clutched at his hair and sat as though petrified in that position. The guests made haste to depart, commenting each in his own way on the incident. It was about three o'clock in the morning.

The worst of it was that Pseldonimov's circumstances were far worse than could have been imagined, in spite of the un-attractiveness of his present surroundings. And while Ivan Ilyitch is lying on the floor and Pseldonimov is standing over him tearing his hair in despair, we will break off the thread of our story and say a few explanatory words about Porfiry Petrovitch Pseldonimov.

Not more than a month before his wedding he was in a state of hopeless destitution. He came from a province where his father had served in some department and where he had died while awaiting his trial on some charge. When five months before his wedding, Pseldonimov, who had been in hopeless misery in Petersburg for a whole year before, got his berth at ten roubles a month, he revived both physically and mentally, but he was soon crushed by circumstances again. There were only two Pseldonimovs left in the world, himself and his mother, who had left the province after her husband's death. The mother and son barely existed in the freezing cold, and sus-tained life on the most dubious substances. There were days when Pseldonimov himself went with a jug to the Fontanka for water to drink. When he got his place he succeeded in settling with his mother in a 'corner'. She took in washing, while for four months he scraped together every farthing to get himself boots and an overcoat. And what troubles he had to endure at his office; his superior approached him with the question: "How long was it since he had had a bath?" There was a rumour about him that under the collar of his uniform there were nests of bugs. But Pseldonimov was a man of strong

241

character. On the surface he was mild and meek; he had the merest smattering of education, he was practically never heard to talk of anything. I do not know for certain whether he thought, made plans and theories, had dreams. But on the other hand there was being formed within him an instinctive, furtive, unconscious determination to fight his way out of his wretched circumstances. He had the persistence of an ant. Destroy an ants' nest, and they will begin at once re-erecting it; destroy it again, and they will begin again without wearying. He was a constructive house-building animal. One could see from his brow that he would make his way, would build his nest, and perhaps even save for a rainy day. His mother was the only creature in the world who loved him, and she loved him beyond everything. She was a woman of resolute character, hard-working and indefatigable, and at the same time good-natured. So perhaps they might have lived in their corner for five or six years till their circumstances changed, if they had not come across the retired titular councillor Mlekopitaev, who had been a clerk in the treasury and had served at one time in the provinces, but had latterly settled in Petersburg and had established himself there with his family. He knew Pseldo-nimov, and had at one time been under some obligation to his father. He had a little money, not a large sum, of course, but there it was; how much it was no one knew, not his wife, nor his elder daughter, nor his relations. He had two daughters, and as he was an awful bully, a drunkard, a domestic tyrant, and in addition to that an invalid, he took it into his head one day to marry one of his daughters to Pseldonimov: "I knew his father," he would say, "he was a good fellow and his son will be a good fellow." Mlekopitaev did exactly as he liked, his word was law. He was a very queer bully. For the most part he spent his time sitting in an arm-chair, having lost the use of his legs from some disease which did not, however, prevent him from drinking vodka. For days together he would be drinking and swearing. He was an ill-natured man. He always wanted to have someone whom he could be continually tormenting. And for that purpose he kept several distant relations: his sister, a sickly and peevish woman; two of his wife's sisters, also ill-natured and very free with their tongues, and his old aunt, who had through some accident a broken rib; he kept another dependent also, a Russianised German, for the sake of her talent for entertaining him with stories from the *Arabian Nights*. His sole gratification consisted in jeering at all these unfortunate women and abusing them every minute with all his energies; though the latter, not excepting his wife, who had been born with toothache, dared not utter a word in his presence. He set them at loggerheads at one another, inventing and fostering spiteful backbiting and dissensions among them, and then laughed and rejoiced seeing how they were ready to tear one another to pieces. He was very much delighted when his elder daughter, who had lived in great poverty for ten years with her husband, an officer of some sort, and was at last left a widow, came to live with him with three little sickly children. He could not endure her children, but as her arrival had increased the material upon which he could work his daily experiments, the old man was very much pleased. All these ill-natured women and sickly children, together with their tormentor, were crowded together in a wooden house on Petersburg Side, and did not get enough to eat because the old man was stingy and gave out to them money a farthing at a time, though he did not grudge himself vodka; they did not get enough sleep because the old man suffered from sleeplessness and insisted on being amused. In short, they all were in misery and cursed their fate. It was at that time that Mlekopitaev's eye fell upon Pseldonimov. He was struck by his long nose and submissive air. His weakly and unprepossessing younger daughter had just reached the age of seventeen. Though she had at one time attended a

German school, she had acquired scarcely anything but the alphabet. Then she grew up rickety and anæmic in fear of her crippled drunken father's crutch, in a Bedlam of domestic backbiting, eavesdropping and scolding. She had never had any friends or any brains. She had for a long time been eager to be married. In company she sat mute, but at home with her mother and the women of the household she was spiteful and cantankerous. She was particularly fond of pinching and smacking her sister's children, telling tales of their pilfering bread and sugar, and this led to endless and implacable strife with her elder sister. Her old father himself offered her to Pseldonimov. Miserable as the latter's position was, he yet asked for a little time to consider. His mother and he hesitated for a long time. But with the young lady there was to come as dowry a house, and though it was a nasty little wooden house of one storey, yet it was property of a kind. Moreover, they would give with her four hundred roubles, and how long it would take him to save it up himself! "What am I taking the man into my house for?" shouted the drunken bully. "In the first place because you are all females, and I am sick of female society. I want Pseldonimov, too, to dance to my piping. For I am his benefactor. And in the second place I am doing it because you are all cross and don't want it, so I'll do it to spite you. What I have said, I have said! And you beat her, Porfiry, when she is your wife; she has been possessed of seven devils ever since she was born. You beat them out of her, and I'll get the stick ready."

Pseldonimov made no answer, but he was already decided. Before the wedding his mother and he were taken into the house, washed, clothed, provided with boots and money for the wedding. The old man took them under his protection possibly just because the whole family was prejudiced against them. He positively liked Pseldonimov's mother, so that he actually restrained himself and did not jeer at her. On the other hand, he made Pseldonimov dance the Cossack dance a week before the wedding.

"Well, that's enough. I only wanted to see whether you remembered your position before me or not," he said at the end of the dance. He allowed just enough money for the wedding, with nothing to spare, and invited all his relations and acquaintances. On Pseldonimov's side there was no one but the young man who wrote for the *Firebrand*, and Akim Petrovitch, the guest of honour. Pseldonimov was perfectly aware that his bride cherished an aversion for him, and that she was set upon marrying the officer instead of him. But he put up with everything, he had made a compact with his mother to do so. The old father had been drunk and abusive and foul-tongued the whole of the wedding day and during the party in the evening. The whole family took refuge in the back rooms and were crowded there to suffocation. The front rooms were devoted to the dance and the supper. At last when the old man fell asleep dead drunk at eleven o'clock, the bride's mother, who had been particularly displeased with Pseldonimov's mother that day, made up her mind to lay aside her wrath, become gracious and join the company. Ivan Ilyitch's arrival had turned everything upside down. Madame Mlekopitaev was overcome with embarrassment, and began grumbling that she had not been told that the general had been invited. She was assured that he had come uninvited, but was so stupid as to refuse to believe it. Champagne had to be got. Pseldonimov's mother had only one rouble, while Pseldonimov himself had not one farthing. He had to grovel before his ill-natured mother-in-law, to beg for the money for one bottle and then for another. They pleaded for the sake of his future position in the service, for his career, they tried to persuade her. She did at last give from her own purse, but she forced Pseldonimov to swallow such a cupful of gall and bitterness that more than once he ran into the room where the nuptial couch had been prepared, and madly clutching at his hair and trembling all over with impotent rage, he buried his head in the bed destined for the joys of paradise. No, indeed, Ivan Ilyitch had no notion of the price paid for the two bottles of Jackson he had drunk that evening. What was the horror, the misery and even the despair of Pseldonimov when Ivan Ilyitch's visit ended in this unexpected way. He had a prospect again of no end of misery, and perhaps a night of tears and outcries from his peevish bride, and upbraidings from her unreasonable relations. Even apart from this his head ached already, and there was dizziness and mist before his eyes. And here Ivan Ilyitch needed looking after, at three o'clock at night he had to hunt for a doctor or a carriage to take him home, and a carriage it must be, for it would be impossible to let an ordinary cabby take him home in that condition. And where could he get the money even for a carriage? Madame Mlekopitaev, furious that the general had not addressed two words to her, and had not even looked at her at supper, declared that she had not a farthing. Possibly she really had not a farthing. Where could he get it? What was he to do? Yes, indeed, he had good cause to tear his hair.

Meanwhile Ivan Ilyitch was moved to a little leather sofa that stood in the dining-room. While they were clearing the tables and putting them away, Pseldonimov was rushing all over the place to borrow money, he even tried to get it from the servants, but it appeared that nobody had any. He even ventured to trouble Akim Petrovitch who had stayed after the other guests. But good-natured as he was, the latter was reduced to such bewilderment and even alarm at the mention of money that he uttered the most unexpected and foolish phrases:

"Another time, with pleasure," he muttered, "but now . . . you really must excuse me. . . ."

And taking his cap, he ran as fast as he could out of the house. Only the good-natured youth who had talked about

246

the dream book was any use at all; and even that came to nothing. He, too, stayed after the others, showing genuine sympathy with Pseldonimov's misfortunes. At last Pseldonimov, together with his mother and the young man, decided in consultation not to send for a doctor, but rather to fetch a carriage and take the invalid home, and meantime to try certain domestic remedies till the carriage arrived, such as moistening his temples and his head with cold water, putting ice on his head, and so on. Pseldonimov's mother undertook this task. The friendly youth flew off in search of a carriage. As there were not even ordinary cabs to be found on the Petersburg Side at that hour, he went off to some livery stables at a distance to wake up the coachmen. They began bargaining, and declared that five roubles would be little to ask for a carriage at that time of night. They agreed to come, however, for three. When at last, just before five o'clock, the young man arrived at Pseldonimov's with the carriage, they had changed their minds. It appeared that Ivan Ilyitch, who was still unconscious, had become so seriously unwell, was moaning and tossing so terribly, that to move him and take him home in such a condition was impossible and actually unsafe. "What will it lead to next?" said Pseldonimov, utterly disheartened. What was to be done? A new problem arose: if the invalid remained in the house, where should he be moved and where could they put him? There were only two bedsteads in the house: one large double bed in which old Mlekopitaev and his wife slept, and another double bed of imitation walnut which had just been purchased and was destined for the newly married couple. All the other inhabitants of the house slept on the floor side by side on feather beds, for the most part in bad condition and stuffy, anything but presentable in fact, and even of these the supply was insufficient; there was not one to spare. Where could the invalid be put? A feather bed might perhaps have been found—it might in the last resort have been pulled from

247

under someone, but where and on what could a bed have been made up? It seemed that the bed must be made up in the drawing-room, for that room was the furthest from the bosom of the family and had a door into the passage. But on what could the bed be made? Surely not upon chairs. We all know that beds can only be made up on chairs for schoolboys when they come home for the week-end, and it would be terribly lacking in respect to make up a bed in that way for a personage like Ivan Ilyitch. What would be said next morning when he found himself lying on chairs? Pseldonimov would not hear of that. The only alternative was to put him on the bridal couch. This bridal couch, as we have mentioned already, was in a little room that opened out of the dining-room, on the bed-stead was a double mattress actualy newly bought first-hand, clean sheets, four pillows in pink calico covered with frilled muslin cases. The quilt was of pink satin, and it was quilted in patterns. Muslin curtains hung down from a golden ring overhead, in fact it was all just as it should be, and the guests who had all visited the bridal chamber had admired the decora-tion of it; though the bride could not endure Pseldonimov, she had several times in the course of the evening run in to have a look at it on the sly. What was her indignation, her wrath, when she learned that they meant to move an invalid, suffering from something not unlike a mild attack of cholera, to her bridal couch! The bride's mother took her part, broke into abuse and vowed she would complain to her husband next day, but Pseldonimov asserted himself and insisted: Ivan Ilyitch was moved into the bridal chamber, and a bed was made up on chairs for the young people. The bride whimpered, would have liked to pinch him, but dared not disobey; her papa had a crutch with which she was very familiar, and she knew that her papa would call her to account next day. To console her they carried the pink satin quilt and the pillows in muslin cases into the drawing-room. At that moment the youth arrived with the carriage, and was horribly alarmed that the carriage was not wanted. He was left to pay for it himself, and he never had as much as a ten-kopeck piece. Pseldonimov explained that he was utterly bankrupt. They tried to parley with the driver. But he began to be noisy and even to batter on the shutters. How it ended I don't know exactly. I believe the youth was carried off to Peski by way of a hostage to Fourth Rozhdensky Street, where he hoped to rouse a student who was spending the night at a friend's, and to try whether he had any money. It was going on for six o'clock in the morning when the young people were left alone and shut up in the drawing-room. Pseldonimov's mother spent the whole night by the bedside of the sufferer. She installed herself on a rug on the floor and covered herself with an old coat, but could not sleep because she had to get up every minute: Ivan Ilyitch had a terrible attack of colic. Madame Pseldonimov, a woman of courage and greatness of soul, undressed him with her own hands, took off all his things, looked after him as if he were her own son, and spent the whole night carrying basins, etc., from the bedroom across the passage and bringing them back again empty. And yet the misfortunes of that night were not yet over.

Not more than ten minutes after the young people had been shut up alone in the drawing-room, a piercing shriek was suddenly heard, not a cry of joy, but a shriek of the most sinister kind. The screams were followed by a noise, a crash, as though of the falling of chairs, and instantly there burst into the still dark room a perfect crowd of exclaiming and frightened women, attired in every kind of *déshabillé*. These women were the bride's mother, her elder sister, abandoning for the moment the sick children, and her three aunts, even the one with a broken rib dragged herself in. Even the cook was there, and the German lady who told stories, whose own feather bed, the best in the house, and her only property, had been forcibly dragged from under her for the young couple, trailed in together with the others. All these respectable and sharp-eyed ladies had, a quarter of an hour before, made their way on tiptoe from the kitchen across the passage, and were listening in the ante-room, devoured by unaccountable curiosity. Meanwhile someone lighted a candle, and a surprising spectacle met the eyes of all. The chairs supporting the broad feather bed only at the sides had parted under the weight, and the feather bed had fallen between them on the floor. The bride was sobbing with anger, this time she was mortally offended. Pseldonimov, morally shattered, stood like a criminal caught in a crime. He did not even attempt to defend himself. Shrieks and exclamations sounded on all sides. Pseldonimov's mother ran up at the noise, but the bride's mamma on this occasion got the upper hand. She began by showering strange and for the most part quite undeserved reproaches, such as: "A nice husband you are, after this. What are you good for after such a disgrace?" and so on; and at last carried her daughter away from her husband, undertaking to bear the full responsibility for doing so with her ferocious husband, who would demand an explanation. All the others followed her out exclaiming and shaking their heads. No one remained with Pseldonimov except his mother, who tried to comfort him. But he sent her away at once.

He was beyond consolation. He made his way to the sofa and sat down in the most gloomy confusion of mind just as he was, barefooted and in nothing but his night attire. His thoughts whirled in a tangled criss-cross in his mind. At times he mechanically looked about the room where only a little while ago the dancers had been whirling madly, and in which the cigarette smoke still lingered. Cigarette-ends and sweetmeat papers still littered the slopped and dirty floor. The wreck of the nuptial couch and the overturned chairs bore witness to the transitoriness of the fondest and surest earthly hopes and

250

dreams. He sat like this almost an hour. The most oppressive thoughts kept coming into his mind, such as the doubt: What was in store for him in the office now? He recognised with painful clearness that he would have, at all costs, to exchange into another department; that he could not possibly remain where he was after all that had happened that evening. He thought, too, of Mlekopitaev, who would probably make him dance the Cossack dance next day to test his meekness. He reflected, too, that though Mlekopitaev had given fifty roubles for the wedding festivities, every farthing of which had been spent, he had not thought of giving him the four hundred roubles yet, no mention had been made of it, in fact. And, indeed, even the house had not been formally made over to him. He thought, too, of his wife who had left him at the most critical moment of his life, of the tall officer who had dropped on one knee before her. He had noticed that already; he thought of the seven devils which according to the testimony of her own father were in possession of his wife, and of the crutch in readiness to drive them out. . . . Of course he felt equal to bearing a great deal, but destiny had let loose such surprises upon him that he might well have doubts of his fortitude. So Pseldonimov mused dolefully. Meanwhile the candle-end was going out, its fading light, falling straight upon Pseldonimov's profile, threw a colossal shadow of it on the wall, with a drawn-out neck, a hooked nose, and with two tufts of hair sticking out on his forehead and the back of his head. At last, when the air was growing cool with the chill of early morning, he got up, frozen and spiritually numb, crawled to the feather bed that was lying between the chairs, and without rearranging anything, without putting out the candle-end, without even laying the pillow under his head, fell into a leaden, deathlike sleep, such as the sleep of men condemned to flogging on the morrow must be.

. . .

251

On the other hand, what could be compared with the agonising night spent by Ivan Ilyitch Pralinsky on the bridal couch of the unlucky Pseldonimov! For some time, headache, vomiting and other most unpleasant symptoms did not leave him for one second. He was in the torments of hell. The faint glimpses of consciousness that visited his brain, lighted up such an abyss of horrors, such gloomy and revolting pictures, that it would have been better for him not to have returned to consciousness. Everything was still in a turmoil in his mind, however. He recognised Pseldonimov's mother, for instance, heard her gentle admonitions, such as : "Be patient, my dear; be patient, good sir, it won't be so bad presently." He recognised her, but could give no logical explanation of her presence beside him. Revolting phantoms haunted him, most frequently of all he was haunted by Semyon Ivanitch; but looking more intently, he saw that it was not Semyon Ivanitch but Pseldonimov's nose. He had visions, too, of the free-and-easy artist, and the officer and the old lady with her face tied up. What interested him most of all was the gilt ring which hung over his head, through which the curtains hung. He could distinguish it distinctly in the dim light of the candle-end which lighted up the room, and he kept wondering inwardly: What was the object of that ring, why was it there, what did it mean? He questioned the old lady several times about it, but apparently did not say what he meant; and she evidently did not understand it, however much he struggled to explain. At last by morning the symptoms had ceased and he fell into a sleep, a sound sleep without dreams. He slept about an hour, and when he woke he was almost completely conscious, with an insufferable headache, and a disgusting taste in his mouth and on his tongue, which seemed turned into a piece of cloth. He sat up in the bed, looked about him, and pondered. The pale light of morning peeping through the cracks of the shutters in a narrow streak, quivered on the wall. It was about seven o'clock in the morning. But when Ivan Ilyitch suddenly grasped the position and recalled all that had happened to him since the evening; when he remembered all his adventures at supper, the failure of his magnanimous action, his speech at table; when he realised all at once with horrifying clearness all that might come of this now, all that people would say and think of him; when he looked round and saw to what a mournful and hideous condition he had reduced the peaceful bridal couch of his clerk— oh, then such deadly shame, such agony overwhelmed him, that he uttered a shriek, hid his face in his hands and fell back on the pillow in despair. A minute later he jumped out of bed, saw his clothes carefully folded and brushed on a chair beside him, and seizing them, and as quickly as he could, in desperate haste began putting them on, looking round and seeming terribly frightened at something. On another chair close by lay his greatcoat and fur cap, and his yellow gloves were in his cap. He meant to steal away secretly. But suddenly the door opened and the elder Madame Pseldonimov walked in with an earthenware jug and basin. A towel was hanging over her shoulder. She set down the jug, and without further conversation told him that he must wash.

"Come, my good sir, wash; you can't go without washing...."

And at that instant Ivan Ilyitch recognised that if there was one being in the whole world whom he need not fear, and before whom he need not feel ashamed, it was that old lady. He washed. And long afterwards, at painful moments of his life, he recalled among other pangs of remorse all the circumstances of that waking, and that earthenware basin, and the china jug filled with cold water in which there were still floating icicles, and the oval cake of soap at fifteen kopecks, in pink paper with letters embossed on it, evidently bought for the bridal pair though it fell to Ivan Ilyitch to use it, and the old lady with the linen towel over her left shoulder. The cold water refreshed him, he dried his face, and without even thanking his sister of mercy, he snatched up his hat, flung over his shoulders the coat handed to him by Pseldonimov, and crossing the passage and the kitchen where the cat was already mewing, and the cook sitting up in her bed staring after him with greedy curiosity, ran out into the yard, into the street, and threw himself into the first sledge he came across. It was a frosty morning. A chilly yellow fog still hid the house and everything. Ivan Ilyitch turned up his collar. He thought that everyone was looking at him, that they were all recognising him, all. . . .

For eight days he did not leave the house or show himself at the office. He was ill, wretchedly ill, but more morally than physically. He lived through a perfect hell in those days, and they must have been reckoned to his account in the other world. There were moments when he thought of becoming a monk and entering a monastery. There really were. His imagination, indeed, took special excursions during that period. He pictured subdued subterranean singing, an open coffin, living in a solitary cell, forests and caves; but when he came to himself he recognised almost at once that all this was dreadful nonsense and exaggeration, and was ashamed of this nonsense. Then began attacks of moral agony on the theme of his *existence manquée*. Then shame flamed up again in his soul, took complete possession of him at once, consumed him like fire and re-opened his wounds. He shuddered as pictures of all sorts rose before his mind. What would people say about him, what would they think when he walked into his office? what a whisper would dog his steps for a whole year, ten years, his whole life! His story would go down to posterity. He sometimes fell into such dejection that he was ready to go straight off to Semyon Ivanovitch and ask for his forgiveness and friendship. He did not even justify himself, there was no limit to his blame of himself. He could find no extenuating circumstances, and was ashamed of trying to.

254

He had thoughts, too, of resigning his post at once and devoting himself to human happiness as a simple citizen, in solitude. In any case he would have completely to change his whole circle of acquaintances, and so thoroughly as to eradicate all memory of himself. Then the thought occurred to him that this, too, was nonsense, and that if he adopted greater severity with his subordinates it might all be set right. Then he began to feel hope and courage again. At last, at the expiration of eight days of hesitation and agonies, he felt that he could not endure to be in uncertainty any longer, and *un beau matin* he made up his mind to go to the office.

He had pictured a thousand times over his return to the office as he sat at home in misery. With horror and conviction he told himself that he would certainly hear behind him an ambiguous whisper, would see ambiguous faces, would intercept ominous smiles. What was his surprise when nothing of the sort happened. He was greeted with respect; he was met with bows; everyone was grave; everyone was busy. His heart was filled with joy as he made his way to his own room.

He set to work at once with the utmost gravity, he listened to some reports and explanations, settled doubtful points. He felt as though he had never explained knotty points and given his decisions so intelligently, so judiciously as that morning. He saw that they were satisfied with him, that they respected him, that he was treated with respect. The most thin-skinned sensitiveness could not have discovered anything.

At last Akim Petrovitch made his appearance with some document. The sight of him sent a stab to Ivan Ilyitch's heart, but only for an instant. He went into the business with Akim Petrovitch, talked with dignity, explained things, and showed him what was to be done. The only thing he noticed was that he avoided looking at Akim Petrovitch for any length of time, or rather Akim Petrovitch seemed afraid of catching his eye.

but at last Akim Petrovitch had finished and began to collect his papers.

"And there is one other matter," he began as dryly as he could, "the clerk Pseldonimov's petition to be transferred to another department. His Excellency Semyon Ivanovitch Shipulenko has promised him a post. He begs your gracious assent, your Excellency."

"Oh, so he is being transferred," said Ivan Ilyitch, and he felt as though a heavy weight had rolled off his heart. He glanced at Akim Petrovitch, and at that instant their eyes met. "Certainly, I for my part . . . I will use," answered Ivan Ilyitch; "I am ready."

Akim Petrovitch evidently wanted to slip away as quickly as he could. But in a rush of generous feeling Ivan Ilyitch determined to speak out. Apparently some inspiration had come to him again.

"Tell him," he began, bending a candid glance full of profound meaning upon Akim Petrovitch, "tell Pseldonimov that I feel no ill-will, no, I do not! . . . That on the contrary I am ready to forget all that is past, to forget it all. . . ."

But all at once Ivan Ilyitch broke off, looking with wonder at the strange behaviour of Akim Petrovitch, who suddenly seemed transformed from a sensible person into a fearful fool. Instead of listening and hearing Ivan Ilyitch to the end, he suddenly flushed crimson in the silliest way, began with positively unseemly haste making strange little bows, and at the same time edging towards the door. His whole appearance betrayed a desire to sink through the floor, or more accurately, to get back to his table as quickly as possible. Ivan Ilyitch, left alone, got up from his chair in confusion; he looked in the looking-glass without noticing his face.

"No, severity, severity and nothing but severity," he whispered almost unconsciously, and suddenly a vivid flush overspread his face. He felt suddenly more ashamed, more

256

weighed down than he had been in the most insufferable moments of his eight days of tribulation. "I did break down!" he said to himself, and sank helplessly into his chair.

Another Man's Wife

or

The Husband Under the Bed

An Extraordinary Adventure

I

"BE so kind, sir . . . allow me to ask you . . ."

The gentleman so addressed started and looked with some alarm at the gentleman in raccoon furs who had accosted him so abruptly at eight o'clock in the evening in the street. We all know that if a Petersburg gentleman suddenly in the street speaks to another gentleman with whom he is unacquainted, the second gentleman is invariably alarmed.

And so the gentleman addressed started and was somewhat alarmed.

"Excuse me for troubling you," said the gentleman in raccoon, "but I . . . I really don't know . . . you will pardon me, no doubt; you see, I am a little upset. . . ."

Only then the young man in the wadded overcoat observed that this gentleman in the raccoon furs certainly was upset. His wrinkled face was rather pale, his voice was trembling. He was evidently in some confusion of mind, his words did not flow easily from his tongue, and it could be seen that it cost him a terrible effort to present a very humble request to a personage possibly his inferior in rank or condition, in spite of the urgent necessity of addressing his request to somebody. And indeed the request was in any case unseemly, undignified, strange, coming from a man who had such a dignified fur coat,

258

such a respectable jacket of a superb dark green colour, and such distinguished decorations adorning that jacket. It was evident that the gentleman in raccoon was himself confused by all this, so that at last he could not stand it, but made up his mind to suppress his emotion and politely to put an end to the unpleasant position he had himself brought about.

"Excuse me, I am not myself: but it is true you don't know me . . . forgive me for disturbing you; I have changed my mind."

Here, from politeness, he raised his hat and hurried off.

"But allow me . . ."

The little gentleman had, however, vanished into the darkness, leaving the gentleman in the wadded overcoat in a state of stupefaction.

"What a queer fellow!" thought the gentleman in the wadded overcoat. After wondering as was only natural, and recovering at last from his stupefaction, he bethought him of his own affairs, and began walking to and fro, staring intently at the gates of a house with an endless numbers of storeys. A fog was beginning to come on, and the young man was somewhat relieved at it, for his walking up and down was less noticeable in the fog, though indeed no one could have noticed him but some cabman who had been waiting all day without a fare.

"Excuse me!"

The young man started again; again the gentleman in raccoon was standing before him.

"Excuse me again . . ." he began, "but you . . . you are no doubt an honourable man! Take no notice of my social position . . . but I am getting muddled . . . look at it as man to man . . . you see before you, sir, a man craving a humble favour. . . ."

"If I can. . . . What do you want?"

"You imagine, perhaps, that I am asking for money," said

the mysterious gentleman, with a wry smile, laughing hysterically and turning pale.

"Oh, dear, no."

"No, I see that I am tiresome to you! Excuse me, I cannot bear myself; consider that you are seeing a man in an agitated condition, almost of insanity, and do not draw any conclusion. . . ."

"But to the point, to the point," responded the young man, nodding his head encouragingly and impatiently.

"Now think of that! A young man like you reminding me to keep to the point, as though I were some heedless boy! I must certainly be doting! . . . How do I seem to you in my degrading position? Tell me frankly."

The young man was overcome with confusion, and said nothing.

"Allow me to ask you openly: have you not seen a lady? That is all that I have to ask you," the gentleman in the raccoon coat said resolutely at last.

"Lady?"

"Yes, a lady."

"Yes, I have seen . . . but I must say lots of them have passed. . . ."

"Just so," answered the mysterious gentleman, with a bitter smile. "I am muddled, I did not mean to ask that; excuse me, I meant to say, haven't you seen a lady in a fox fur cape, in a dark velvet hood and a black veil?"

"No, I haven't noticed one like that . . . no, I think I haven't seen one."

"Well, in that case, excuse me!"

The young man wanted to ask a question, but the gentleman in raccoon vanished again; again he left his patient listener in a state of stupefaction.

"Well, the devil take him!" thought the young man in the wadded overcoat, evidently troubled.

With annoyance he turned up his beaver collar, and began cautiously walking to and fro again before the gates of the house of many storeys. He was raging inwardly.

"Why doesn't she come out?" he thought. "It will soon be eight o'clock."

The town clock struck eight.

"Oh, devil take you!"

"Excuse me! . . ."

"Excuse me for speaking like that . . . but you came upon me so suddenly that you quite frightened me," said the young man, frowning and apologising.

"Here I am again. I must strike you as tiresome and queer."

"Be so good as to explain at once, without more ado; I don't know what it is you want. . . ."

"You are in a hurry. Do you see, I will tell you everything openly, without wasting words. It cannot be helped. Circumstances sometimes bring together people of very different characters. . . . But I see you are impatient, young man. . . . So here . . . though I really don't know how to tell you: I am looking for a lady (I have made up my mind to tell you all about it). You see, I must know where that lady has gone. Who she is—I imagine there is no need for you to know her name, young man."

"Well, well, what next?"

"What next? But what a tone you take with me! Excuse me, but perhaps I have offended you by calling you young man, but I had nothing . . . in short, if you are willing to do me a very great service, here it is: a lady—that is, I mean a gentlewoman of a very good family, of my acquaintance . . . I have been commissioned . . . I have no family, you see . . ."

"Oh!"

"Put yourself in my position, young man (ah, I've done it again; excuse me, I keep calling you young man). Every minute is precious. . . . Only fancy, that lady . . . but cannot you tell me who lives in this house?"

"But . . . lots of people live here."

"Yes, that is, you are perfectly right," answered the gentleman in raccoon, giving a slight laugh for the sake of good manners. "I feel I am rather muddled. . . . But why do you take that tone? You see, I admit frankly that I am muddled, and however haughty you are, you have seen enough of my humiliation to satisfy you. . . . I say a lady of honourable conduct, that is, of light tendencies—excuse me, I am so confused; it is as though I were speaking of literature—Paul de Kock is supposed to be of light tendencies, and all the trouble comes from Paul de Kock, you see. . . ."

The young man looked compassionately at the gentleman in raccoon, who seemed in a hopeless muddle and pausing, stared at him with a meaningless smile and with a trembling hand for no apparent reason gripped the lappet of his wadded overcoat.

"You ask who lives here?" said the young man, stepping back a little.

"Yes; you told me lots of people live here."

"Here . . . I know that Sofya Ostafyevna lives here, too," the young man brought out in a low and even commiserating tone.

"There, you see, you see! You know something, young man?"

"I assure you I don't, I know nothing . . . I judged from your troubled air . . ."

"I have just learned from the cook that she does come here; but you are on the wrong tack, that is, with Sofya Ostafyevna . . . she does not know her . . ."

"No? Oh . . . I beg your pardon, then. . . ."

"I see this is of no interest to you, young man," said the queer man, with bitter irony.

"Listen," said the young man, hesitating. "I really don't

understand why you are in such a state, but tell me frankly, I suppose you are being deceived?" The young man smiled approvingly. "We shall understand one another, anyway," he added, and his whole person loftily betrayed an inclination to make a half-bow.

"You crush me! But I frankly confess that is just it . . . but it happens to everyone! . . . I am deeply touched by your sympathy. To be sure, among young men . . . though I am not young; but you know, habit, a bachelor life, among bachelors, we all know . . ."

"Oh, yes, we all know, we all know! But in what way can I be of assistance to you?"

"Why, look here: admitting a visit to Sofya Ostafyevna . . . though I don't know for a fact where the lady has gone, I only know that she is in that house; but seeing you walking up and down, and I am walking up and down on the same side myself, I thought . . . you see, I am waiting for that lady . . . I know that she is there. I should like to meet her and explain to her how shocking and improper it is! . . . In fact, you understand me . . ."

"H'm! Well?"

"I am not acting for myself; don't imagine it; it is another man's wife! Her husband is standing over there on the Voznesensky Bridge; he wants to catch her, but he doesn't dare; he is still loath to believe it, as every husband is." (Here the gentleman in raccoon made an effort to smile.) "I am a friend of his; you can see for yourself I am a person held in some esteem; I could not be what you take me for."

"Oh, of course. Well, well!"

"So, you see, I am on the look out for her. The task has been entrusted to me (the unhappy husband!). But I know that the young lady is sly (Paul de Kock for ever under her pillow); I am certain she scurries off somewhere on the sly. . . . I must confess the cook told me she comes here; I rushed off like a madman as soon as I heard the news; I want to catch her. I have long had suspicions, and so I wanted to ask you; you are walking here . . . you—you—I don't know . . ."

"Come, what is it you want?"

"Yes . . . I have not the honour of your acquaintance; I do not venture to inquire who and what you may be. . . . Allow me to introduce myself, anyway; glad to meet you! . . ."

The gentleman, quivering with agitation, warmly shook the young man's hand.

"I ought to have done this to begin with," he added, "but I have lost all sense of good manners."

The gentleman in raccoon could not stand still as he talked; he kept looking about him uneasily, fidgeted with his feet, and like a drowning man clutched at the young man's hand.

"You see," he went on, "I meant to address you in a friendly way. . . . Excuse the freedom. . . . I meant to ask you to walk along the other side and down the side street, where there is a back entrance. I, too, on my side, will walk from the front entrance, so that we cannot miss her; I'm afraid of missing her by myself; I don't want to miss her. When you see her, stop her and shout to me. . . . But I'm mad! Only now I see the foolishness and impropriety of my suggestion! . . ."

"No, why, no! It's all right! . . ."

"Don't make excuses for me; I am so upset. I have never been in such a state before. As though I were being tried for my life! I must own indeed—I will be straightforward and honourable with you, young man; I actually thought you might be the lover."

"That is, to put it simply, you want to know what I am doing here?"

"You are an honourable man, my dear sir. I am far from supposing that you are *he*, I will not insult you with such a suspicion; but . . . give me your word of honour that you are not the lover. . . ."

264

"Oh, very well, I'll give you my word of honour that I am a lover, but not of your wife; otherwise I shouldn't be here in the street, but should be with her now!"

"Wife! Who told you she was my wife, young man? I am a bachelor, I—that is, I am a lover myself. . . ."

"You told me there is a husband on Voznesensky Bridge. . . ."

"Of course, of course, I am talking too freely; but there are other ties! And you know, young man, a certain lightness of character, that is . . ."

"Yes, yes, to be sure, to be sure. . . ."

"That is, I am not her husband at all. . . ."

"Oh, no doubt. But I tell you frankly that in reassuring you now, I want to set my own mind at rest, and that is why I am candid with you; you are upsetting me and in my way. I promise that I will call you. But I most humbly beg you to move further away and let me alone. I am waiting for someone too."

"Certainly, certainly, I will move further off. I respect the passionate impatience of your heart. Oh, how well I understand you at this moment!"

"Oh, all right, all right. . . ."

"Till we meet again! . . . But excuse me, young man, here I am again . . . I don't know how to say it . . . give me your word of honour once more, as a gentleman, that you are not her lover."

"Oh, mercy on us!"

"One more question, the last: do you know the surname of the husband of your . . . that is, I mean the lady who is the object of your devotion?"

"Of course I do; it is not your name, and that is all about it."

"Why, how do you know my name?"

"But, I say, you had better go; you are losing time; she might go away a thousand times. Why, what do you want? Your lady's in a fox cape and a hood, while mine is wearing a plaid cloak and a pale blue velvet hat. . . . What more do you want? What else?"

"A pale blue velvet hat! She has a plaid cloak and a pale blue velvet hat!" cried the pertinacious man, instantly turning back again.

"Oh, hang it all! Why, that may well be. . . . And, indeed, my lady does not come here!"

"Where is she, then—your lady?"

"You want to know that? What is it to you?"

"I must own, I am still . . ."

"Tfoo! Mercy on us! Why, you have no sense of decency, none at all. Well, my lady has friends here, on the third storey looking into the street. Why, do you want me to tell you their names?"

"My goodness, I have friends too, on the third storey, and their windows look on to the street. . . . General . . ."

"General!"

"A general. If you like I will tell you what general: well, then . . . General Polovitsyn."

"You don't say so! No, that is not the same! (Oh, damnation, damnation!)."

"Not the same?"

"No, not the same."

Both were silent, looking at each other in perplexity.

"Why are you looking at me like that?" exclaimed the young man, shaking off his stupefaction and air of uncertainty with vexation.

The gentleman was in a fluster.

"I . . . I must own . . ."

"Come, allow me, allow me; let us talk more sensibly now. It concerns us both. Explain to me . . . whom do you know there?"

"You mean, who are my friends?"

"Yes, your friends. . . ."

266

"Well, you see . . . you see! . . . I see from your eyes that I have guessed right!"

"Hang it all! No, no, hang it all! Are you blind? Why, I am standing here before you, I am not with her. Oh, well! I don't care, whether you say so or not!"

Twice in his fury the young man turned on his heel with a contemptuous wave of his hand.

"Oh, I meant nothing, I assure you. As an honourable man I will tell you all about it. At first my wife used to come here alone. They are relatives of hers; I had no suspicions; yesterday I met his Excellency: he told me that he had moved three weeks ago from here to another flat, and my wi . . . that is, not mine, but somebody else's (the husband's on the Voznesensky Bridge) . . . that lady had told me that she was with them the day before yesterday, in this flat I mean . . . and the cook told me that his Excellency's flat had been taken by a young man called Bobynitsyn. . . ."

"Oh, damn it all, damn it all! . . ."

"My dear sir, I am in terror, I am in alarm!"

"Oh, hang it! What is it to me that you are in terror and in alarm? Ah! Over there . . . someone flitted by . . . over there. . . ."

"Where, where? You just shout, 'Ivan Andreyitch,' and I will run. . . ."

"All right, all right. Oh, confound it! Ivan Andreyitch!"

"Here I am," cried Ivan Andreyitch, returning, utterly breathless. "What is it, what is it? Where?"

"Oh, no, I didn't mean anything . . . I wanted to know what this lady's name is."

"Glaf . . ."

"Glafira?"

"No, not Glafira. . . . Excuse me, I cannot tell you her name."

As he said this the worthy man was as white as a sheet.

"Oh, of course it is not Glafira, I know it is not Glafira, and mine's not Glafira; but with whom can she be?"

"Where?"

"There! Oh, damn it, damn it!" (The young man was in such a fury that he could not stand still.)

"There, you see! How did you know that her name was Glafira?"

"Oh, damn it all, really! To have a bother with you, too! Why, you say—that yours is not called Glafira! . . ."

"My dear sir, what a way to speak!"

"Oh, the devil! As though that mattered now! What is she? Your wife?"

"No—that is, I am not married. . . . But I would not keep flinging the devil at a respectable man in trouble, a man, I will not say worthy of esteem, but at any rate a man of education. You keep saying, 'The devil, the devil!'"

"To be sure, the devil take it; so there you are, do you understand?"

"You are blinded by anger, and I say nothing. Oh, dear, who is that?"

"Where?"

There was a noise and a sound of laughter; two pretty girls ran down the steps; both the men rushed up to them.

"Oh, what manners! What do you want?"

"Where are you shoving?"

"They are not the right ones!"

"Aha, so you've pitched on the wrong ones! Cab!"

"Where do you want to go, mademoiselle?"

"To Pokrov. Get in, Annushka; I'll take you."

"Oh, I'll sit on the other side; off! Now, mind you drive quickly."

The cab drove off.

"Where did they come from?"

"Oh, dear, oh, dear! Hadn't we better go there?"

"Where?"

"Why, to Bobynitsyn's. . . ."

"No, that's out of the question."

"Why?"

"I would go there, of course, but then she would tell me some other story; she would . . . get out of it. She would say that she had come on purpose to catch me with someone, and I should get into trouble."

"And, you know, she may be there! But you—I don't know for what reason—why, you might go to the general's. . . ."

"But, you know, he has moved!"

"That doesn't matter, you know. She has gone there; so you go, too—don't you understand? Behave as though you didn't know the general had gone away. Go as though you had come to fetch your wife, and so on."

"And then?"

"Well, and then find the person you want at Bobynitsyn's. Tfoo, damnation take you, what a senseless . . ."

"Well, and what is it to you, my finding? You see, you see!"

"What, what, my good man? What? You are on the same old tack again. Oh, Lord have mercy on us! You ought to be ashamed, you absurd person, you senseless person!"

"Yes, but why are you so interested? Do you want to find out . . ."

"Find out what? What? Oh, well, damnation take you! I have no thoughts for you now; I'll go alone. Go away; get along; look out; be off!"

"My dear sir, you are almost forgetting yourself!" cried the gentleman in raccoon in despair.

"Well, what of it? What if I am forgetting myself?" said the young man, setting his teeth and stepping up to the gentleman in raccoon in a fury. "What of it? Forgetting myself before whom?" he thundered, clenching his fists.

"But allow me, sir . . ."

"Well, who are you, before whom I am forgetting myself? What is your name?"

"I don't know about that, young man; why do you want my name? . . . I cannot tell it you. . . . I'd better come with you. Let us go; I won't hang back; I am ready for anything. . . . But I assure you I deserve greater politeness and respect! You ought never to lose your self-possession, and if you are upset about something—I can guess what about—at any rate there is no need to forget yourself. . . . You are still a very, very young man! . . ."

"What is it to me that you are old? There's nothing wonderful in that! Go away. Why are you dancing about here?"

"How am I old? Of course, in position; but I am not dancing about. . . ."

"I can see that. But get away with you."

"No, I'll stay with you; you cannot forbid me; I am mixed up in it, too; I will come with you. . . ."

"Well, then, keep quiet, keep quiet, hold your tongue. . . ."

They both went up the steps and ascended the stairs to the third storey. It was rather dark.

"Stay; have you got matches?"

"Matches! What matches?"

"Do you smoke cigars?"

"Oh, yes, I have, I have; here they are, here they are; here, stay. . . ." The gentleman in raccoon rummaged in a fluster.

"Tfoo, what a senseless . . . damnation! I believe this is the door. . . ."

"This, this, this?"

"This, this, this . . . Why are you bawling? Hush! . . ."

"My dear sir, overcoming my feelings, I . . . you are a reckless fellow, so there! . . ."

The light flared up.

"Yes, so it is; here is the brass plate. This is Bobynitsyn's; do you see Bobynitsyn?"

"I see it, I see it."

"Hu-ush!"

"Why, has it gone out?"

"Yes, it has."

"Should we knock?"

"Yes, we must," responded the gentleman in raccoon.

"Knock, then."

"No, why should I? You begin, you knock!"

"Coward!"

"You are a coward yourself!"

"G-et a-way with you!"

"I almost regret having confided my secret to you; you . . ."

"I—what about me?"

"You take advantage of my distress; you see that I am upset. . . ."

"But do I care? I think it's ridiculous, that's all about it!"

"Why are you here?"

"Why are you here, too? . . ."

"Delightful morality!" observed the gentleman in raccoon, with indignation.

"What are you saying about morality? What are you?"

"Well, it's immoral!"

"What? . . ."

"Why, to your thinking, every deceived husband is a noodle!"

"Why, are you the husband? I thought the husband was on Voznesensky Bridge? So what is it to you? Why do you meddle?"

"I do believe that you are the lover! . . ."

"Listen: if you go on like this I shall be forced to think you are a noodle! That is, do you know who?"

"That is, you mean to say that I am the husband," said the gentleman in raccoon, stepping back as though he were scalded with boiling water.

"Hush, hold your tongue. Do you hear? . . ."

"It is she."

"No!"

"Tfoo, how dark it is!"

There was a hush; a sound was audible in Bobynitsyn's flat.

"Why should we quarrel, sir?" whispered the gentleman in raccoon.

"But you took offence yourself, damn it all!"

"But you drove me out of all patience."

"Hold your tongue!"

"You must admit that you are a very young man."

"Hold your tongue!"

"Of course I share your idea, that a husband in such a position is a noodle."

"Oh, will you hold your tongue? Oh!..."

"But why such savage persecution of the unfortunate husband?..."

"It is she!"

But at that moment the sound ceased.

"It is she!"

"It is, it is, it is! But why are you—you worrying about it? It is not your trouble!"

"My dear sir, my dear sir," muttered the gentleman in raccoon, turning pale and gulping, "I am, of course, greatly agitated ... you can see for yourself my abject position; but now it's night, of course, but to-morrow ... though indeed we are not likely to meet to-morrow, though I am not afraid of meeting you—and besides, it is not I, it is my friend on the Voznesensky Bridge; it really is he! It is his wife, it is somebody else's wife. Poor fellow! I assure you, I know him very intimately; if you will allow me I will tell you all about it. I am a great friend of his, as you can see for yourself, or I shouldn't be in such a state about him now—as you see for yourself. Several times I said to him: 'Why are you getting married, dear boy? You have position, you have means, you

272

are highly respected. Why risk it all at the caprice of coquetry? You must see that.' 'No, I am going to be married,' he said; 'domestic bliss.' . . . Here's domestic bliss for you! In old days he deceived other husbands . . . now he is drinking the cup . . . you must excuse me, but this explanation was absolutely necessary. . . . He is an unfortunate man, and is drinking the cup—now! . . ." At this point the gentleman in raccoon gave such a gulp that he seemed to be sobbing in earnest.

"Ah, damnation take them all! There are plenty of fools. But who are you?"

The young man ground his teeth in anger.

"Well, you must admit after this that I have been gentlemanly and open with you . . . and you take such a tone!"

"No, excuse me . . . what is your name?"

"Why do you want to know my name? . . ."

"Ah!"

"I cannot tell you my name. . . ."

"Do you know Shabrin?" the young man said quickly.

"Shabrin!!!"

"Yes, Shabrin! Ah!!!" (Saying this, the gentleman in the wadded overcoat mimicked the gentleman in raccoon.) "Do you understand?"

"No, what Shabrin?" answered the gentleman in raccoon, in a fluster. "He's not Shabrin; he is a very respectable man! I can excuse your discourtesy, due to the tortures of jealousy."

"He's a scoundrel, a mercenary soul, a rogue that takes bribes, he steals government money! He'll be had up for it before long!"

"Excuse me," said the gentleman in raccoon, turning pale, "you don't know him; I see that you don't know him at all."

"No, I don't know him personally, but I know him from others who are in close touch with him."

"From what others, sir? I am agitated, as you see. . . ."

"A fool! A jealous idiot! He doesn't look after his wife! That's what he is, if you like to know!"

"Excuse me, young man, you are grievously mistaken. . . ."

"Oh!"

"Oh!"

A sound was heard in Bobynitsyn's flat. A door was opened, voices were heard.

"Oh, that's not she! I recognise her voice; I understand it all now, this is not she!" said the gentleman in raccoon, turning as white as a sheet.

"Hush!"

The young man leaned against the wall.

"My dear sir, I am off. It is not she, I am glad to say."

"All right! Be off, then!"

"Why are you staying, then?"

"What's that to you?"

The door opened, and the gentleman in raccoon could not refrain from dashing headlong downstairs.

A man and a woman walked by the young man, and his heart stood still. . . . He heard a familiar feminine voice and then a husky male voice, utterly unfamiliar.

"Never mind, I will order the sledge," said the husky voice.

"Oh, yes, yes; very well, do. . . ."

"It will be here directly."

The lady was left alone.

"Glafira! Where are your bows?" cried the young man in the wadded overcoat, clutching the lady's arm.

"Oh, who is it? It's you, Tvorogov? My goodness! What are you doing here?"

"Who is it you have been with here?"

"Why, my husband. Go away, go away; he'll be coming out directly . . . from . . . in there . . . from the Polovitsyns'. Go away; for goodness' sake, go away."

"It's three weeks since the Polovitsyns moved! I know all about it!"

"*Aïe!*" The lady dashed downstairs. The young man overtook her.

"Who told you?" asked the lady.

"Your husband, madam, Ivan Andreyitch; he is here before you, madam. . . ."

Ivan Andreyitch was indeed standing at the front door.

"*Aïe*, it's you," cried the gentleman in raccoon.

"Ah! *C'est vous,*" cried Glafira Petrovna, rushing up to him with unfeigned delight. "Oh, dear, you can't think what has been happening to me. I went to see the Polovitsyns; only fancy . . . you know they are living now by Izmailovsky Bridge; I told you, do you remember? I took a sledge from there. The horses took fright and bolted, they broke the sledge, and I was thrown out about a hundred yards from here; the coachman was taken up; I was in despair. Fortunately Monsieur Tvorogov . . ."

"What!"

Monsieur Tvorogov was more like a fossil than like Monsieur Tvorogov.

"Monsieur Tvorogov saw me here and undertook to escort me; but now you are here, and I can only express my warm gratitude to you, Ivan Ilyitch. . . ."

The lady gave her hand to the stupefied Ivan Ilyitch, and almost pinched instead of pressing it.

"Monsieur Tvorogov, an acquaintance of mine; it was at the Skorlupovs' ball we had the pleasure of meeting; I believe I told you; don't you remember, Koko?"

"Oh, of course, of course! Ah, I remember," said the gentleman in raccoon addressed as Koko. "Delighted, delighted!" And he warmly pressed the hand of Monsieur Tvorogov.

"Who is it? What does it mean? I am waiting . . . "said a husky voice.

275

Before the group stood a gentleman of extraordinary height; he took out a lorgnette and looked intently at the gentleman in the raccoon coat.

"Ah, Monsieur Bobynitsyn!" twittered the lady. "Where have you come from? What a meeting! Only fancy, I have just had an upset in a sledge . . . but here is my husband! Jean! Monsieur Bobynitsyn, at the Karpovs' ball. . . ."

"Ah, delighted, very much delighted! . . . But I'll take a carriage at once, my dear."

"Yes, do, Jean, do; I still feel frightened; I am all of a tremble, I feel quite giddy. . . . At the masquerade to-night," she whispered to Tvorogov. . . . "Good-bye, good-bye, Mr. Bobynitsyn! We shall meet to-morrow at the Karpovs' ball, most likely."

"No, excuse me, I shall not be there to-morrow; I don't know about to-morrow, if it is like this now. . . ." Mr. Bobynitsyn muttered something between his teeth, made a scrape with his huge boot, got into his sledge and drove away.

A carriage drove up; the lady got into it. The gentleman in the raccoon coat stopped, seemed incapable of making a movement and gazed blankly at the gentleman in the wadded coat. The gentleman in the wadded coat smiled rather foolishly.

"I don't know . . ."

"Excuse me, delighted to make your acquaintance," answered the young man, bowing with curiosity and a little intimidated.

"Delighted, delighted! . . ."

"I think you have lost your golosh. . . ."

"I—oh, yes, thank you, thank you. I keep meaning to get rubber ones."

"The foot gets so hot in rubbers," said the young man, apparently with immense interest.

"*Jean!* Are you coming?"

"It does make it hot. Coming directly, darling; we are

276

having an interesting conversation! Precisely so, as you say, it does make the foot hot. . . . But excuse me, I . . ."

"Oh, certainly."

"Delighted, very much delighted to make your acquaintance! . . ."

The gentleman in raccoon got into the carriage, the carriage set off, the young man remained standing looking after it in astonishment.

II

THE following evening there was a performance of some sort at the Italian opera. Ivan Andreyitch burst into the theatre like a bomb. Such furore, such a passion for music had never been observed in him before. It was known for a positive fact, anyway, that Ivan Andreyitch used to be exceeding fond of a nap for an hour or two at the Italian opera; he even declared on several occasions how sweet and pleasant it was. "Why, the prima donna," he used to say to his friends, "mews a lullaby to you like a little white kitten." But it was a long time ago, last season, that he used to say this; now, alas! even at home Ivan Andreyitch did not sleep at nights. Nevertheless he burst into the crowded opera-house like a bomb. Even the conductor started suspiciously at the sight of him, and glanced out of the corner of his eye at his side-pocket in the full expectation of seeing the hilt of a dagger hidden there in readiness. It must be observed that there were at that time two parties, each supporting the superior claims of its favourite prima donna. They were called the ——*sists* and the ——*nists*. Both parties were so devoted to music, that the conductors actually began to be apprehensive of some startling manifestation of the passion for the good and the beautiful embodied in the two prima donnas. This was how it was that, looking at this youthful dash into the parterre of a grey-haired senior (though, indeed, he was not actually grey-haired, but a man about fifty, rather bald, and altogether of respectable appearance), the conductor could not help recalling the lofty judgment of Hamlet Prince of Denmark upon the evil example set by age to youth, and, as we have mentioned above, looking out of the corner of his eye at the gentleman's side-pocket in the expectation of seeing a dagger. But there was a pocket-book and nothing else there.

Darting into the theatre, Ivan Andreyitch instantly scanned all the boxes of the second tier, and, oh—horror! His heart stood still, she was here! She was sitting in the box! General Polovitsyn, with his wife and sister-in-law, was there too. The general's adjutant—an extremely alert young man, was there too; there was a civilian too. . . . Ivan Andreyitch strained his attention and his eyesight, but—oh, horror! The civilian treacherously concealed himself behind the adjutant and remained in the darkness of obscurity.

She was here, and yet she had said she would not be here!

It was this duplicity for some time displayed in every step Glafira Petrovna took which crushed Ivan Andreyitch. This civilian youth reduced him at last to utter despair. He sank down in his stall utterly overwhelmed. Why? one may ask. It was a very simple matter. . . .

It must be observed that Ivan Andreyitch's stall was close to the baignoire, and to make matters worse the treacherous box in the second tier was exactly above his stall, so that to his intense annoyance he was utterly unable to see what was going on over his head. At which he raged, and got as hot as a samovar. The whole of the first act passed unnoticed by him, that is, he did not hear a single note of it. It is maintained that what is good in music is that musical impressions can be made to fit any mood. The man who rejoices finds joy in its strains, while he who grieves finds sorrow in it; a regular tempest was howling in Ivan Andreyitch's ears. To add to his vexation, such terrible voices were shouting behind him, before him and on both sides of him, that Ivan Andreyitch's heart was torn. At last the act was over. But at the instant when the curtain was falling, our hero had an adventure such as no pen can describe.

It sometimes happens that a playbill flies down from the upper boxes. When the play is dull and the audience is yawning this is quite an event for them. They watch with particular interest the flight of the extremely soft paper from the upper gallery, and take pleasure in watching its zigzagging journey down to the very stalls, where it infallibly settles on some head which is quite unprepared to receive it. It is certainly very interesting to watch the embarrassment of the head (for the head is invariably embarrassed). I am indeed always in terror over the ladies' opera-glasses which usually lie on the edge of the boxes; I am constantly fancying that they will fly down on some unsuspecting head. But I perceive that this tragic observation is out of place here, and so I shall send it to the columns of those newspapers which are filled with advice, warnings against swindling tricks, against unconscientiousness, hints for getting rid of beetles if you have them in the house, recommendations of the celebrated Mr. Princhipi, sworn foe of all beetles in the world, not only Russian but even foreign, such as Prussian cockroaches, and so on.

But Ivan Andreyitch had an adventure, which has never hitherto been described. There flew down on his—as already stated, somewhat bald—head, not a playbill; I confess I am actually ashamed to say what did fly down upon his head, because I am really loath to remark that on the respectable and bare—that is, partly hairless—head of the jealous and irritated Ivan Andreyitch there settled such an immoral object as a scented love-letter. Poor Ivan Andreyitch, utterly unprepared for this unforeseen and hideous occurrence, started as

279

though he had caught upon his head a mouse or some other wild beast.

That the note was a love-letter, of that there could be no mistake. It was written on scented paper, just as love-letters are written in novels, and folded up so as to be treacherously small so that it might be slipped into a lady's glove. It had probably fallen by accident at the moment it had been handed to her. The playbill might have been asked for, for instance, and the note, deftly folded in the playbill, was being put into her hands; but an instant, perhaps an accidental, nudge from the adjutant, extremely adroit in his apologies for his awkwardness, and the note had slipped from a little hand that trembled with confusion, and the civilian youth, stretching out his impatient hand, received instead of the note the empty playbill, and did not know what to do with it. A strange and unpleasant incident for him, no doubt, but you must admit that for Ivan Andreyitch it was still more unpleasant.

"*Prédestiné*," he murmured, breaking into a cold sweat and squeezing the note in his hands, "*prédestiné*' The bullet finds the guilty man," the thought flashed through his mind. "No, that's not right! In what way am I guilty? But there is another proverb, 'Once out of luck, never out of trouble.' . . ."

But it was not enough that there was a ringing in his ears and a dizziness in his head at this sudden incident. Ivan Andreyitch sat petrified in his chair, as the saying is, more dead than alive. He was persuaded that his adventure had been observed on all sides, although at that moment the whole theatre began to be filled with uproar and calls of encore. He sat overwhelmed with confusion, flushing crimson and not daring to raise his eyes, as though some unpleasant surprise, something out of keeping with the brilliant assembly had happened to him. At last he ventured to lift his eyes.

"Charmingly sung," he observed to a dandy sitting on his left side.

The dandy, who was in the last stage of enthusiasm, clapping his hands and still more actively stamping with his feet, gave Ivan Andreyitch a cursory and absent-minded glance, and immediately putting up his hands like a trumpet to his mouth, so as to be more audible, shouted the prima donna's name. Ivan Andreyitch, who had never heard such a roar, was delighted. "He has noticed nothing!" he thought, and turned round; but the stout gentleman who was sitting behind him had turned round too, and with his back to him was scrutinising the boxes through his opera-glass. "He is all right too!" thought Ivan Andreyitch. In front, of course, nothing had been seen. Timidly and with a joyous hope in his heart, he stole a glance at the baignoire, near which was his stall, and started with the most unpleasant sensation. A lovely lady was sitting there who, holding her handkerchief to her mouth and leaning back in her chair, was laughing as though in hysterics.

"Ugh, these women!" murmured Ivan Andreyitch, and treading on people's feet, he made for the exit.

Now I ask my readers to decide, I beg them to judge between me and Ivan Andreyitch. Was he right at that moment? The Grand Theatre, as we all know, contains four tiers of boxes and a fifth row above the gallery. Why must he assume that the note had fallen from one particular box, from that very box and no other? Why not, for instance, from the gallery where there are often ladies too? But passion is an exception to every rule, and jealousy is the most exceptional of all passions.

Ivan Andreyitch rushed into the foyer, stood by the lamp, broke the seal and read:

"To-day immediately after the performance, in G. Street at the corner of X. Lane, K. buildings, on the third floor, the first on the right from the stairs. The front entrance. Be there, *sans faute*; for God's sake."

Ivan Andreyitch did not know the handwriting, but he had no doubt it was an assignation. "To track it out, to catch it

281

and nip the mischief in the bud," was Ivan Andreyitch's first idea. The thought occurred to him to unmask the infamy at once on the spot; but how could it be done? Ivan Andreyitch even ran up to the second row of boxes, but judiciously came back again. He was utterly unable to decide where to run. Having nothing clear he could do, he ran round to the other side and looked through the open door of somebody else's box at the opposite side of the theatre. Yes, it was so, it was! Young ladies and young men were sitting in all the seats vertically one above another in all the five tiers. The note might have fallen from all tiers at once, for Ivan Andreyitch suspected all of them of being in a plot against him. But nothing made him any better, no probabilities of any sort. The whole of the second act he was running up and down all the corridors and could find no peace of mind anywhere. He would have dashed into the box office in hope of finding from the attendant there the names of the persons who had taken boxes on all the four tiers, but the box office was shut. At last there came an outburst of furious shouting and applause. The performance was over. Calls for the singers began, and two voices from the top gallery were particularly deafening—the leaders of the opposing factions. But they were not what mattered to Ivan Andreyitch. Already thoughts of what he was to do next flitted through his mind. He put on his overcoat and rushed off to G. Street to surprise them there, to catch them unawares, to unmask them, and in general to behave somewhat more energetically than he had done the day before. He soon found the house, and was just going in at the front door, when the figure of a dandy in an overcoat darted forward right in front of him, passed him and went up the stairs to the third storey. It seemed to Ivan Andreyitch that this was the same dandy, though he had not been able at the time to distinguish his features in the theatre. His heart stood still. The dandy was two flights of stairs ahead of him. At last he heard a door opened on the third floor, and opened without the ringing of a bell, as though the visitor were expected. The young man disappeared into the flat. Ivan Andreyitch mounted to the third floor, before there was time to shut the door. He meant to stand at the door, to reflect prudently on his next step, to be rather cautious, and then to determine upon some decisive course of action; but at that very minute a carriage rumbled up to the entrance, the doors were flung open noisily, and heavy footsteps began ascending to the third storey to the sound of coughing and clearing of the throat. Ivan Andreyitch could not stand his ground, and walked into the flat with all the majesty of an injured husband. a servant-maid rushed to meet him much agitated, then a man-servant appeared. But to stop Ivan Andreyitch was impossible. He flew in like a bomb, and crossing two dark rooms, suddenly found himself in a bedroom facing a lovely young lady, who was trembling all over with alarm and gazing at him in utter horror as though she could not understand what was happening around her. At that instant there was a sound in the adjoining room of heavy footsteps coming straight towards the bedroom; they were the same footsteps that had been mounting the stairs.

"Goodness! It is my husband!" cried the lady, clasping her hands and turning whiter than her dressing-gown.

Ivan Andreyitch felt that he had come to the wrong place, that he had made a silly, childish blunder, that he had acted without due consideration, that he had not been sufficiently cautious on the landing. But there was no help for it. The door was already opening, already the heavy husband, that is if he could be judged by his footsteps, was coming into the room. . . . I don't know what Ivan Andreyitch took himself to be at that moment! I don't know what prevented him from confronting the husband, telling him that he had made a mistake, confessing that he had unintentionally behaved in the most unseemly way, making his apologies and vanishing—not of course with flying colours, not of course with glory, but at any rate departing in an open and gentlemanly manner. But no, Ivan Andreyitch again behaved like a boy, as though he considered himself a Don Juan or a Lovelace! He first hid himself behind the curtain of the bed, and finally, feeling utterly dejected and hopeless, he dropped on the floor and senselessly crept under the bed. Terror had more influence on him than reason, and Ivan Andreyitch, himself an injured husband, or at any rate a husband who considered himself such, could not face meeting another husband, but was afraid to wound him by his presence. Be this as it may, he found himself under the bed, though he had no idea how it had come to pass. But what was most surprising, the lady made no opposition. She did not cry out on seeing an utterly unknown elderly gentleman seek a refuge under her bed. Probably she was so alarmed that she was deprived of all power of speech.

The husband walked in gasping and clearing his throat, said good-evening to his wife in a singsong, elderly voice, and flopped into an easy chair as though he had just been carrying up a load of wood. There was a sound of a hollow and prolonged cough. Ivan Andreyitch, transformed from a ferocious tiger to a lamb, timid and meek as a mouse before a cat, scarcely dared to breathe for terror, though he might have known from his own experience that not all injured husbands bite. But this idea did not enter his head, either from lack of consideration or from agitation of some sort. Cautiously, softly, feeling his way he began to get right under the bed so as to lie more comfortably there. What was his amazement when with his hand he felt an object which, to his intense amazement, stirred and in its turn seized his hand! Under the bed there was another person!

"Who's this?" whispered Ivan Andreyitch.

"Well, I am not likely to tell you who I am," whispered the

strange man. "Lie still and keep quiet, if you have made a mess of things!"

"But, I say! . . ."

"Hold your tongue!"

And the extra gentleman (for one was quite enough under the bed) the extra gentleman squeezed Ivan Andreyitch's hand in his fist so that the latter almost shrieked with pain.

"My dear sir . . ."

"Sh!"

"Then don't pinch me so, or I shall scream."

"All right, scream away, try it on."

Ivan Andreyitch flushed with shame. The unknown gentleman was sulky and ill-humoured. Perhaps it was a man who had suffered more than once from the persecutions of fate, and had more than once been in a tight place; but Ivan Andreyitch was a novice and could not breathe in his constricted position. The blood rushed to his head. However, there was no help for it; he had to lie on his face. Ivan Andreyitch submitted and was silent.

"I have been to see Pavel Ivanitch, my love," began the husband. "We sat down to a game of preference. Khee-khee-khee!" (he had a fit of coughing.) "Yes . . . khee! So my back . . . khee! Bother it . . . khee-khee-khee!"

And the old gentleman became engrossed in his cough.

"My back," he brought out at last with tears in his eyes, "my spine began to ache. . . . A damned hæmorrhoid, I can't stand nor sit . . . or sit. Akkhee-khee-khee!" . . .

And it seemed as though the cough that followed was destined to last longer than the old gentleman in possession of it. The old gentleman grumbled something in its intervals, but it was utterly impossible to make out a word.

"Dear sir, for goodness' sake, move a little," whispered the unhappy Ivan Andreyitch.

"How can I? There's no room."

285

"But you must admit that it is impossible for me. It is the first time that I have found myself in such a nasty position."

"And I in such unpleasant society."

"But, young man! . . ."

"Hold your tongue!"

"Hold my tongue? You are very uncivil, young man. . . . If I am not mistaken, you are very young; I am your senior."

"Hold your tongue!"

"My dear sir! You are forgetting yourself. You don't know to whom you are talking!"

"To a gentleman lying under the bed."

"But I was taken by surprise . . . a mistake, while in your case, if I am not mistaken, immorality . . ."

"That's where you are mistaken."

"My dear sir! I am older than you, I tell you. . . ."

"Sir, we are in the same boat, you know. I beg you not to take hold of my face!"

"Sir, I can't tell one thing from another. Excuse me, but I have no room."

"You shouldn't be so fat!"

"Heavens! I have never been in such a degrading position."

"Yes, one couldn't be brought more low."

"Sir, sir! I don't know who you are, I don't understand how this came about; but I am here by mistake; I am not what you think. . . ."

"I shouldn't think about you at all if you didn't shove. But hold your tongue, do!"

"Sir, if you don't move a little I shall have a stroke; you will have to answer for my death, I assure you. . . . I am a respectable man, I am the father of a family. I really cannot be in such a position! . . ."

"You thrust yourself into the position. Come, move a little! I've made room for you, I can't do more!"

"Noble young man! Dear sir! I see I was mistaken about

you," said Ivan Andreyitch, in a transport of gratitude for the space allowed him, and stretching out his cramped limbs. "I understand your constricted condition, but there's no help for it. I see you think ill of me. Allow me to redeem my reputation in your eyes, allow me to tell you whom I am. I have come here against my will, I assure you; I am not here with the object you imagine. . . . I am in a terrible fright."

"Oh, do shut up! Understand that if we are overheard it will be the worse for us. Sh! . . . He is talking."

The old gentleman's cough did, in fact, seem to be over.

"I tell you what, my love," he wheezed in the most lachrymose chant, "I tell you what, my love . . . khee-khee! Oh, what an affliction! Fedosey Ivanovitch said to me: 'You should try drinking yarrow tea,' he said to me; do you hear, my love?"

"Yes, dear."

"Yes, that was what he said, 'You should try drinking yarrow tea,' he said. I told him I had put on leeches. But he said, 'No, Alexandr Demyanovitch, yarrow tea is better, it's a taxative, I tell you' . . . Khee-khee. Oh, dear! What do you think, my love? Khee! Oh, my God! Khee-khee! Had I better try yarrow tea? . . . Khee-khee-khee! Oh . . . Khee!" and so on.

"I think it would be just as well to try that remedy," said his wife.

"Yes, it would be! 'You may be in consumption,' he said. Khee-khee! And I told him it was gout and irritability of the stomach . . . Khee-khee! But he would have it that it might be consumption. What do you think . . . khee-khee! What do you think, my love; is it consumption?"

"My goodness, what are you talking about?"

"Why, consumption! You had better undress and go to bed now, my love . . . khee-khee! I've caught a cold in my head to-day."

287

"Ouf!" said Ivan Andreyitch. "For God's sake, do move a little."

"I really don't know what is the matter with you; can't you lie still? . . ."

"You are exasperated against me, young man, you want to wound me, I see that. You are, I suppose, this lady's lover?"

"Shut up!"

"I will not shut up! I won't allow you to order me about! You are, no doubt, her lover. If we are discovered I am not to blame in any way; I know nothing about it."

"If you don't hold your tongue," said the young man, grinding his teeth, "I will say that you brought me here. I'll say that you are my uncle who has dissipated his fortune. Then they won't imagine I am this lady's lover, anyway."

"Sir, you are amusing yourself at my expense. You are exhausting my patience."

"Hush, or I will make you hush! You are a curse to me. Come, tell me what you are here for? If you were not here I could lie here somehow till morning, and then get away."

"But I can't lie here till morning. I am a respectable man, I have family ties, of course. . . . What do you think, surely he is not going to spend the night here?"

"Who?"

"Why, this old gentleman. . . ."

"Of course he will. All husbands aren't like you. Some of them spend their nights at home."

"My dear sir, my dear sir!" cried Ivan Andreyitch, turning cold with terror, "I assure you I spend my nights at home too, and this is the first time; but, my God, I see you know me. Who are you, young man? Tell me at once, I beseech you, from disinterested friendship, who are you?"

"Listen, I shall resort to violence . . ."

"But allow me, allow me, sir, to tell you, allow me to explain all this horrid business."

288

"I won't listen to any explanation. I don't want to know anything about it. Be silent or . . ."

"But I cannot. . . ."

A slight skirmish took place under the bed, and Ivan Andre-yitch subsided.

"My love, it sounds as though there were cats hissing."

"Cats! What will you imagine next?"

Evidently the lady did not know what to talk to her husband about. She was so upset that she could not pull herself together. Now she started and pricked up her ears.

"What cats?"

"Cats, my love. The other day I went into my study, and there was the tom-cat in my study, and hissing shoo-shoo-shoo! I said to him: 'What is it, pussy?' and he went shoo-shoo-shoo again, as though he were whispering. I thought, 'Merciful heavens! isn't he hissing as a sign of my death?' "

"What nonsense you are talking to-day! You ought to be ashamed, really!"

"Never mind, don't be cross, my love. I see, you don't like to think of my dying; I didn't mean it. But you had better undress and get to bed, my love, and I'll sit here while you go to bed."

"For goodness' sake, leave off; afterwards . . ."

"Well, don't be cross, don't be cross: but really I think there must be mice here."

"Why, first cats and then mice, I really don't know what is the matter with you."

"Oh, I am all right. . . . Khee . . . I . . . khee! Never mind . . . khee-khee-khee-khee! Oh! Lord have mercy on me . . . khee."

"You hear, you are making such an upset that he hears you," whispers the young man.

"But if you knew what is happening to me. My nose is bleeding."

"Let it bleed. Shut up. Wait till he goes away."

"But, young man, put yourself in my place. Why, I don't know with whom I am lying."

"Would you be any better off if you did? Why, I don't want to know your name. By the way, what is your name?"

"No; what do you want with my name? . . . I only want to explain the senseless way in which . . ."

"Hush . . . he is speaking again. . . ."

"Really, my love, there is whispering."

"Oh, no, it's the cotton wool in your ears has got out of place."

"Oh, by the way, talking of the cotton wool, do you know that upstairs . . . khee-khee . . . upstairs . . . khee-khee . . ." and so on.

"Upstairs!" whispered the young man. "Oh, the devil! I thought that this was the top storey; can it be the second?"

"Young man," whispered Ivan Andreyitch, "what did you say? For goodness' sake why does it concern you? I thought it was the top storey too. Tell me, for God's sake, is there another storey?"

"Really someone is stirring," said the old man, leaving off coughing at last.

"Hush! Do you hear?" whispered the young man, squeezing Ivan Andreyitch's hands.

"Sir, you are holding my hands by force. Let me go!"

"Hush!"

A slight struggle followed and then there was a silence again.

"So I met a pretty woman . . ." began the old man.

"A pretty woman!" interrupted his wife.

"Yes. . . . I thought I told you before that I met a pretty woman on the stairs, or perhaps I did not mention it? My memory is weak. Yes, St. John's wort . . . khee!"

"What?"

"I must drink St. John's wort; they say it does good . . . khee-khee-khee! It does good!"

"It was you interrupted him," said the young man, grinding his teeth again.

"You said, you met some pretty woman to-day?" his wife went on.

"Eh?"

"Met a pretty woman?"

"Who did?"

"Why, didn't you?"

"I? When?"

"Oh, yes! . . ."

"At last! What a mummy! Well!" whispered the young man, inwardly raging at the forgetful old gentleman.

"My dear sir, I am trembling with horror. My God, what do I hear? It's like yesterday, exactly like yesterday! . . ."

"Hush!"

"Yes, to be sure! I remember, a sly puss, such eyes . . . in a blue hat . . ."

"In a blue hat! *Aïe, aïe!*"

"It's she! She has a blue hat! My God!" cried Ivan Andreyitch.

"She? Who is she?" whispered the young man, squeezing Ivan Andreyitch's hands.

"Hush!" Ivan Andreyitch exhorted in his turn. "He is speaking."

"Ah, my God, my God!"

"Though, after all, who hasn't a blue hat?"

"And such a sly little rogue," the old gentleman went on. "She comes here to see friends. She is always making eyes. And other friends come to see those friends too. . . ."

"Foo! how tedious!" the lady interrupted. "Really, how can you take interest in that?"

"Oh, very well, very well, don't be cross," the old gentleman

291

responded in a wheedling chant. "I won't talk if you don't care to hear me. You seem a little out of humour this evening."

"But how did you get here?" the young man began.

"Ah, you see, you see! Now you are interested, and before you wouldn't listen!"

"Oh, well, I don't care! Please don't tell me. Oh, damnation take it, what a mess!"

"Don't be cross, young man; I don't know what I am saying. I didn't mean anything; I only meant to say that there must be some good reason for your taking such an interest. . . . But who are you, young man? I see you are a stranger, but who are you? Oh, dear, I don't know what I am saying!"

"Ugh, leave off, please!" the young man interrupted, as though he were considering something.

"But I will tell you all about it. You think, perhaps, that I will not tell you. That I feel resentment against you. Oh, no! Here is my hand. I am only feeling depressed, nothing more. But for God's sake, first tell me how you came here yourself? Through what chance? As for me, I feel no ill-will; no, indeed, I feel no ill-will, here is my hand. I have made it rather dirty, it is so dusty here; but that's nothing, when the feeling is true."

"Ugh, get away with your hand! There is no room to turn, and he keeps thrusting his hand on me!"

"But, my dear sir, but you treat me, if you will allow me to say so, as though I were an old shoe," said Ivan Andreyitch in a rush of the meekest despair, in a voice full of entreaty. "Treat me a little more civilly, just a little more civilly, and I will tell you all about it! We might be friends; I am quite ready to ask you home to dinner. We can't lie side by side like this, I tell you plainly. You are in error, young man, you do not know. . . ."

"When was it he met her?" the young man muttered, evidently in violent emotion. "Perhaps she is expecting me now. . . . I'll certainly get away from here!"

"She? Who is she? My God, of whom are you speaking, young man? You imagine that upstairs . . . My God, my God! Why am I punished like this?"

Ivan Andreyitch tried to turn on his back in his despair.

"Why do you want to know who she is? Oh, the devil, whether it was she or not, I will get out."

"My dear sir! What are you thinking about? What will become of me?" whispered Ivan Andreyitch, clutching at the tails of his neighbour's dress coat in his despair.

"Well, what's that to me? You can stop here by yourself. And if you won't, I'll tell them that you are my uncle, who has squandered all his property, so that the old gentleman won't think that I am his wife's lover."

"But that is utterly impossible, young man; it's unnatural I should be your uncle. Nobody would believe you. Why, a baby wouldn't believe it," Ivan Andreyitch whispered in despair.

"Well, don't babble then, but lie as flat as a pancake! Most likely you will stay the night here and get out somehow to-morrow; no one will notice you. If one creeps out, it is not likely they would think there was another one here. There might as well be a dozen. Though you are as good as a dozen by yourself. Move a little, or I'll get out."

"You wound me, young man. . . . What if I have a fit of coughing? One has to think of everything."

"Hush!"

"What's that? I fancy I hear something going on upstairs again," said the old gentleman, who seemed to have had a nap in the interval.

"Upstairs?"

"Do you hear, young man? I shall get out."

"Well, I hear."

"My goodness! Young man, I am going."

"Oh, well, I am not, then! I don't care. If there is an upset

293

I don't mind! But do you know what I suspect? I believe you are an injured husband—so there."

"Good heavens, what cynicism! . . . Can you possibly suspect that? Why a husband? . . . I am not married."

"Not married? Fiddlesticks!"

"I may be a lover myself!"

"A nice lover."

"My dear sir, my dear sir! Oh, very well, I will tell you the whole story. Listen to my desperate story. It is not I—I am not married. I am a bachelor like you. It is my friend, a companion of my youth. . . . I am a lover. . . . He told me that he was an unhappy man. 'I am drinking the cup of bitterness,' he said; 'I suspect my wife.' 'Well,' I said to him reasonably, 'why do you suspect her?' . . . But you are not listening to me. Listen, listen! 'Jealousy is ridiculous,' I said to him; 'jealousy is a vice!' . . . 'No,' he said; 'I am an unhappy man! I am drinking . . . that is, I suspect my wife.' 'You are my friend,' I said; 'you are the companion of my tender youth. Together we culled the flowers of happiness, together we rolled in feather-beds of pleasure.' My goodness, I don't know what I am saying. You keep laughing, young man. You'll drive me crazy."

"But you are crazy now. . . ."

"There, I knew you would say that . . . when I talked of being crazy. Laugh away, laugh away, young man. I did the same in my day; I, too, went astray! Ah, I shall have inflammation of the brain!"

"What is it, my love? I thought I heard someone sneeze," the old man chanted. "Was that you sneezed, my love?"

"Oh, goodness!" said his wife.

"Tch!" sounded from under the bed.

"They must be making a noise upstairs," said his wife, alarmed, for there certainly was a noise under the bed.

"Yes, upstairs!" said the husband. "Upstairs, I told you

294

just now, I met a . . . khee-khee . . . that I met a young swell with moustaches—oh, dear, my spine!—a young swell with moustaches."

"With moustaches! My goodness, that must have been you," whispered Ivan Andreyitch.

"Merciful heavens, what a man! Why, I am here, lying here with you! How could he have met me? But don't take hold of my face."

"My goodness, I shall faint in a minute."

There certainly was a loud noise overhead at this moment.

"What can be happening there?" whispered the young man.

"My dear sir! I am in alarm, I am in terror, help me."

"Hush!"

"There really is a noise, my love; there's a regular hubbub. And just over your bedroom, too. Hadn't I better send up to inquire?"

"Well, what will you think of next?"

"Oh, well, I won't; but really, how cross you are to-day! . . ."

"Oh, dear, you had better go to bed."

"Liza, you don't love me at all."

"Oh, yes, I do! For goodness' sake, I am so tired."

"Well, well; I am going!"

"Oh, no, no; don't go!" cried his wife; "or, no, better go!"

"Why, what is the matter with you! One minute I am to go, and the next I'm not! Khee-khee! It really is bedtime, khee-khee! The Panafidins' little girl . . . khee-khee . . . their little girl . . . khee . . . I saw their little girl's Nuremburg doll . . . khee-khee. . . ."

"Well, now it's dolls!"

"Khee-khee . . . a pretty doll . . . khee-khee."

"He is saying good-bye," said the young man; "he is going, and we can get away at once. Do you hear? You can rejoice!"

"Oh, God grant it!"

"It's a lesson to you. . . ."

"Young man, a lesson for what! . . . I feel it . . . but you are young, you cannot teach me."

"I will, though. . . . Listen."

"Oh, dear, I am going to sneeze! . . ."

"Hush, if you dare."

"But what can I do, there is such a smell of mice here: I can't help it. Take my handkerchief out of my pocket; I can't stir. . . . Oh, my God, my God, why am I so punished?"

"Here's your handkerchief! I will tell you what you are punished for. You are jealous. Goodness knows on what grounds, you rush about like a madman, burst into other people's flats, create a disturbance . . ."

"Young man, I have not created a disturbance."

"Hush!"

"Young man, you can't lecture to me about morals, I am more moral than you."

"Hush!"

"Oh, my God—oh, my God!"

"You create a disturbance, you frighten a young lady, a timid woman who does not know what to do for terror, and perhaps will be ill; you disturb a venerable old man suffering from a complaint and who needs repose above everything—and all this what for? Because you imagine some nonsense which sets you running all over the neighbourhood! Do you understand what a horrid position you are in now?"

"I do very well, sir! I feel it, but you have not the right . . ."

"Hold your tongue! What has right got to do with it? Do you understand that this may have a tragic ending? Do you understand that the old man, who is fond of his wife, may go out of his mind when he sees you creep out from under the bed? But no, you are incapable of causing a tragedy! When you crawl out, I expect everyone who looks at you will laugh. I should like to see you in the light; you must look very funny."

"And you. You must be funny, too, in that case. I should like to have a look at you too."

"I dare say you would!"

"You must carry the stamp of immorality, young man."

"Ah! you are talking about morals, how do you know why I'm here? I am here by mistake, I made a mistake in the storey. And the deuce knows why they let me in, I suppose she must have been expecting someone (not you, of course). I hid under the bed when I heard your stupid footsteps, when I saw the lady was frightened. Besides, it was dark. And why should I justify myself to you. You are a ridiculous, jealous old man, sir. Do you know why I don't crawl out? Perhaps you imagine I am afraid to come out? No, sir, I should have come out long ago, but I stay here for compassion for you. Why, what would you be taken for, if I were not here? You'd stand facing them, like a post, you know you wouldn't know what to do. . . ."

"Why like that object? Couldn't you find anything else to compare me with, young man? Why shouldn't I know what to do? I should know what to do."

"Oh, my goodness, how that wretched dog keeps barking!"

"Hush! Oh, it really is. . . . That's because you keep jabbering. You've waked the dog, now there will be trouble."

The lady's dog, who had till then been sleeping on a pillow in the corner, suddenly awoke, sniffed strangers and rushed under the bed with a loud bark.

"Oh, my God, what a stupid dog!" whispered Ivan Andreyitch; "it will get us all into trouble. Here's another affliction!"

"Oh, well, you are such a coward, that it may well be so."

"Ami, Ami, come here," cried the lady; "*ici, ici*." But the dog, without heeding her, made straight for Ivan Andreyitch.

"Why is it Amishka keeps barking?" said the old gentleman. "There must be mice or the cat under there. I seem to hear a sneezing . . . and pussy had a cold this morning."

297

"Lie still," whispered the young man. "Don't twist about! Perhaps it will leave off."

"Sir, let go of my hands, sir! Why are you holding them?"

"Hush! Be quiet!"

"But mercy on us, young man, it will bite my nose. Do you want me to lose my nose?"

A struggle followed, and Ivan Andreyitch got his hands free. The dog broke into volleys of barking. Suddenly it ceased barking and gave a yelp.

"*Aïe!*" cried the lady.

"Monster! what are you doing?" cried the young man. "You will be the ruin of us both! Why are you holding it? Good heavens, he is strangling it! Let it go! Monster! You know nothing of the heart of women if you can do that! She will betray us both if you strangle the dog."

But by now Ivan Andreyitch could hear nothing. He had succeeded in catching the dog, and in a paroxysm of self-preservation had squeezed its throat. The dog yelled and gave up the ghost.

"We are lost!" whispered the young man.

"Amishka! Amishka," cried the lady. "My God, what are they doing with my Amishka? Amishka! Amishka! *Ici!* Oh, the monsters! Barbarians! Oh, dear, I feel giddy!"

"What is it, what is it?" cried the old gentleman, jumping up from his easy chair. "What is the matter with you, my darling? Amishka! here, Amishka! Amishka! Amishka!" cried the old gentleman, snapping with his fingers and clicking with his tongue, and calling Amishka from under the bed. "Amishka, *ici, ici*. The cat cannot have eaten him. The cat wants a thrashing, my love, he hasn't had a beating for a whole month, the rogue. What do you think? I'll talk to Praskovya Zaharyevna. But, my goodness, what is the matter, my love? Oh, how white you are! Oh, oh, servants, servants!" and the old gentleman ran about the room.

298

"Villains! Monsters!" cried the lady, sinking on the sofa.

"Who, who, who?" cried the old gentleman.

"There are people there, strangers, there under the bed! Oh, my God, Amishka, Amishka, what have they done to you?"

"Good heavens, what people? Amishka. . . . Servants, servants, come here! Who is there, who is there?" cried the old gentleman, snatching up a candle and bending down under the bed. "Who is there?"

Ivan Andreyitch was lying more dead than alive beside the breathless corpse of Amishka, but the young man was watching every movement of the old gentleman. All at once the old gentleman went to the other side of the bed by the wall and bent down. In a flash the young man crept out from under the bed and took to his heels, while the husband was looking for his visitors on the other side.

"Good gracious!" exclaimed the lady, staring at the young man. "Who are you? Why, I thought . . ."

"That monster's still there," whispered the young man. "He is guilty of Amishka's death!"

"*Aïe.*" shrieked the lady, but the young man had already vanished from the room.

"*Aïe.* There is someone here. Here are somebody's boots!" cried the husband, catching Ivan Andreyitch by the leg.

"Murderer, murderer!" cried the lady. "Oh, Ami! Ami!"

"Come out, come out!" cried the old gentleman, stamping on the carpet with both feet; "come out. Who are you? Tell me who you are! Good gracious, what a queer person!"

"Why, it's robbers! . . ."

"For God's sake, for God's sake," cried Ivan Andreyitch, creeping out, "for God's sake, your Excellency, don't call the servants! Your Excellency, don't call anyone. It is quite unnecessary. You can't kick me out! . . . I am not that sort of person. I am a different case. Your Excellency, it has all been due to a mistake! I'll explain directly, your Excellency," exclaimed Ivan Andreyitch, sobbing and gasping. "It's all my wife that is not my wife, but somebody else's wife. I am not married, I am only . . . It's my comrade, a friend of youthful days."

"What friend of youthful days?" cried the old gentleman, stamping. "You are a thief, you have come to steal . . . and not a friend of youthful days."

"No, I am not a thief, your Excellency; I am really a friend of youthful days. . . . I have only blundered by accident, I came into the wrong place."

"Yes, sir, yes; I see from what place you've crawled out."

"Your Excellency! I am not that sort of man. You are mistaken. I tell you, you are cruelly mistaken, your Excellency. Only glance at me, look at me, and by signs and tokens you will see that I can't be a thief. Your Excellency! Your Excellency!" cried Ivan Andreyitch, folding his hands and appealing to the young lady. "You are a lady, you will understand me. . . . It was I who killed Amishka. . . . But it was not my fault. . . . It was really not my fault. . . . It was all my wife's fault. I am an unhappy man, I am drinking the cup of bitterness!"

"But really, what has it to do with me that you are drinking the cup of bitterness? Perhaps it's not the only cup you've drunk. It seems so, to judge from your condition. But how did you come here, sir?" cried the old gentleman, quivering with excitement, though he certainly was convinced by certain signs and tokens that Ivan Andreyitch could not be a thief. "I ask you: how did you come here? You break in like a robber . . ."

"Not a robber, your Excellency. I simply came to the wrong place; I am really not a robber! It is all because I was jealous. I will tell you all about it, your Excellency, I will confess it all frankly, as I would to my own father; for at your venerable age I might take you for a father."

300

"What do you mean by venerable age?"

"Your Excellency! Perhaps I have offended you? Of course such a young lady . . . and your age . . . it is a pleasant sight, your Excellency, it really is a pleasant sight such a union . . . in the prime of life. . . . But don't call the servants, for God's sake, don't call the servants . . . servants would only laugh. . . . I know them . . . that is, I don't mean that I am only acquainted with footmen, I have a footman of my own, your Excellency, and they are always laughing . . . the asses! Your Highness . . . I believe I am not mistaken, I am addressing a prince. . . ."

"No, I am not a prince, sir, I am an independent gentleman. . . . Please do not flatter me with your 'Highness'. How did you get here, sir? How did you get here?"

"Your Highness, that is, your Excellency. . . . Excuse me, I thought that you were your Highness. I looked . . . I imagined . . . it does happen. You are so like Prince Korotkouhov whom I have had the honour of meeting at my friend Mr. Pusyrev's. . . . You see, I am acquainted with princes, too, I have met princes, too, at the houses of my friends; you cannot take me for what you take me for. I am not a thief. Your Excellency, don't call the servants; what will be the good of it if you do call them?"

"But how did you come here?" cried the lady. "Who are you?"

"Yes, who are you?" the husband chimed in. "And, my love, I thought it was pussy under the bed sneezing. And it was he. Ah, you vagabond! Who are you? Tell me!"

And the old gentleman stamped on the carpet again.

"I cannot speak, your Excellency, I am waiting till you are finished, I am enjoying your witty jokes. As regards me, it is an absurd story, your Excellency; I will tell you all about it. It can all be explained without more ado, that is, I mean, don't call the servants, your Excellency! Treat me in a gentlemanly way. . . . It means nothing that I was under the bed, I have

301

not sacrificed my dignity by that. It is a most comical story, your Excellency!" cried Ivan Andreyitch, addressing the lady with a supplicating air. "You, particularly, your Excellency, will laugh! You will behold upon the scene a jealous husband. You see, I abase myself, I abase myself of my own free will. I did indeed kill Amishka, but . . . my God, I don't know what I am saying!"

"But how, how did you get here?"

"Under cover of night, your Excellency, under cover of night. . . . I beg your pardon! Forgive me, your Excellency! I humbly beg your pardon! I am only an injured husband, nothing more! Don't imagine, your Excellency, that I am a lover! I am not a lover! Your wife is virtue itself, if I may venture so to express myself. She is pure and innocent!"

"What, what? What did you have the audacity to say?" cried the old gentleman, stamping his foot again. "Are you out of your mind or not? How dare you talk about my wife?"

"He is a villain, a murderer who has killed Amishka," wailed the lady, dissolving into tears. "And then he dares! . . ."

"Your Excellency, your Excellency! I spoke foolishly," cried Ivan Andreyitch in a fluster. "I was talking foolishly, that was all! Think of me as out of my mind. . . . For goodness' sake, think of me as out of my mind. . . . I assure you that you will be doing me the greatest favour. I would offer you my hand, but I do not venture to. . . . I was not alone, I was an uncle. . . . I mean to say that you cannot take me for the lover. . . . Goodness! I have put my foot in it again. . . . Do not be offended, your Excellency," cried Ivan Andreyitch to the lady. "You are a lady, you understand what love is, it is a delicate feeling. . . . But what am I saying? I am talking nonsense again; that is, I mean to say that I am an old man— that is, a middle-aged man, not an old man; that I cannot be your lover; that a lover is a Richardson—that is, a Lovelace. . . . I am talking nonsense, but you see, your Excellency, that

302

I am a well-educated man and know something of literature. You are laughing, your Excellency. I am delighted, delighted that I have *provoked* your mirth, your Excellency. Oh, how delighted I am that I have provoked your mirth."

"My goodness, what a funny man!" cried the lady, exploding with laughter.

"Yes, he is funny, and in such a mess," said the old man, delighted that his wife was laughing. "He cannot be a thief, my love. But how did he come here?"

"It really is strange, it really is strange, it is like a novel! Why! At the dead of night, in a great city, a man under the bed. Strange, funny! Rinaldo-Rinaldini after a fashion. But this is no matter, no matter, your Excellency. I will tell you all about it. . . . And I will buy you a new lapdog, your Excellency. . . . A wonderful lapdog! Such a long coat, such short little legs, it can't walk more than a step or two: it runs a little, gets entangled in its own coat, and tumbles over. One feeds it on nothing but sugar. I will bring you one, I will certainly bring you one."

"Ha-ha-ha-ha-ha!" The lady was rolling from side to side with laughter. "Oh, dear, I shall have hysterics! Oh, how funny he is!"

"Yes, yes! Ha-ha-ha! Khee-khee-khee! He is funny and he is in a mess—khee-khee-khee!"

"Your Excellency, your Excellency, I am now perfectly happy. I would offer you my hand, but I do not venture to, your Excellency. I feel that I have been in error, but now I am opening my eyes. I am certain my wife is pure and innocent! I was wrong in suspecting her."

"Wife—his wife!" cried the lady, with tears in her eyes through laughing.

"He married? Impossible! I should never have thought it," said the old gentleman.

"Your Excellency, my wife—it is all her fault; that is, it is my fault: I suspected her; I knew that an assignation had been arranged here—here upstairs; I intercepted a letter, made a mistake about the storey and got under the bed. . . ."

"He-he-he-he!"

"Ha-ha-ha-ha!"

"Ha-ha-ha-ha!" Ivan Andreyitch began laughing at last. "Oh, how happy I am! Oh, how wonderful to see that we are all so happy and harmonious! And my wife is entirely innocent. That must be so, your Excellency!"

"He-he-he! Khee-khee! Do you know, my love, who it was?" said the old man at last, recovering from his mirth.

"Who? Ha-ha-ha."

"She must be the pretty woman who makes eyes, the one with the dandy. It's she, I bet that's his wife!"

"No, your Excellency, I am certain it is not she; I am perfectly certain."

"But, my goodness! You are losing time," cried the lady, leaving off laughing. "Run, go upstairs. Perhaps you will find them."

"Certainly, your Excellency, I will fly. But I shall not find anyone, your Excellency; it is not she, I am certain of it beforehand. She is at home now. It is all my fault! It is simply my jealousy, nothing else. . . . What do you think? Do you suppose that I shall find them there, your Excellency?"

"Ha-ha-ha!"

"He-he-he! Khee-khee!"

"You must go, you must go! And when you come down, come in and tell us!" cried the lady; "or better still, to-morrow morning. And do bring her too, I should like to make her acquaintance."

"Good-bye, your Excellency, good-bye! I will certainly bring her, I shall be very glad for her to make your acquaintance. I am glad and happy that it has all ended so and has turned out for the best."

304

"And the lapdog! Don't forget it: be sure to bring the lapdog!"

"I will bring it, your Excellency, I will certainly bring it," responded Ivan Andreyitch, darting back into the room, for he had already made his bows and withdrawn. "I will certainly bring it. It is such a pretty one. It is just as though a confectioner had made it of sweetmeats. And it's such a funny little thing—gets entangled in its own coat and falls over. It really is a lapdog! I said to my wife: 'How is it, my love, it keeps tumbling over?' 'It is such a little thing,' she said. As though it were made of sugar, of sugar, your Excellency! Good-bye, your Excellency, very, very glad to make your acquaintance, very glad to make your acquaintance!"

Ivan Andreyitch bowed himself out.

"Hey, sir! Stay, come back," cried the old gentleman, after the retreating Ivan Andreyitch.

The latter turned back for the third time.

"I still can't find the cat, didn't you meet him when you were under the bed?"

"No, I didn't, your Excellency. Very glad to make his acquaintance, though, and I shall look upon it as an honour . . ."

"He has a cold in his head now, and keeps sneezing and sneezing. He must have a beating."

"Yes, your Excellency, of course; corrective punishment is essential with domestic animals."

"What?"

"I say that corrective punishment is necessary, your Excellency, to enforce obedience in the domestic animals."

"Ah! . . . Well, good-bye, good-bye, that is all I had to say."

Coming out into the street, Ivan Andreyitch stood for a long time in an attitude that suggested that he was expecting to have a fit in another minute. He took off his hat, wiped the cold sweat from his brow, screwed up his eyes, thought a minute, and set off homewards.

What was his amazement when he learned at home that Glafira Petrovna had come back from the theatre a long, long time before, that she had toothache, that she had sent for the doctor, that she had sent for leeches, and that now she was lying in bed and expecting Ivan Andreyitch.

Ivan Andreyitch slapped himself on the forehead, told the servant to help him wash and to brush his clothes, and at last ventured to go into his wife's room.

"Where is it you spend your time? Look what a sight you are! What do you look like? Where have you been lost all this time? Upon my word, sir; your wife is dying and you have to be hunted for all over the town. Where have you been? Surely you have not been tracking me, trying to disturb a rendezvous I am supposed to have made, though I don't know with whom. For shame, sir, you are a husband! People will soon be pointing at you in the street."

"My love . . ." responded Ivan Andreyitch.

But at this point he was so overcome with confusion that he had to feel in his pocket for his handkerchief and to break off in the speech he was beginning, because he had neither words, thoughts or courage. . . . What was his amazement, horror and alarm when with his handkerchief fell out of his pocket the corpse of Amishka. Ivan Andreyitch had not noticed that when he had been forced to creep out from under the bed, in an access of despair and unreasoning terror he had stuffed Amishka into his pocket with a far-away idea of burying the traces, concealing the evidence of his crime, and so avoiding the punishment he deserved.

"What's this?" cried his spouse; "a nasty dead dog! Goodness! where has it come from? . . . What have you been up to? . . . Where have you been? Tell me at once where have you been?"

"My love," answered Ivan Andreyitch, almost as dead as Amishka, "my love . . ."

But here we will leave our hero—till another time, for a new and quite different adventure begins here. Some day we will describe all these calamities and misfortunes, gentlemen. But you will admit that jealousy is an unpardonable passion, and what is more, it is a positive misfortune.

The Heavenly Christmas Tree

I AM a novelist, and I suppose I have made up this story. I write "I suppose", though I know for a fact that I have made it up, but yet I keep fancying that it must have happened somewhere at some time, that it must have happened on Christmas Eve in some great town in a time of terrible frost.

I have a vision of a boy, a little boy, six years old or even younger. This boy woke up that morning in a cold damp cellar. He was dressed in a sort of little dressing-gown and was shivering with cold. There was a cloud of white steam from his breath, and sitting on a box in the corner, he blew the steam out of his mouth and amused himself in his dullness watching it float away. But he was terribly hungry. Several times that morning he went up to the plank bed where his sick mother was lying on a mattress as thin as a pancake, with some sort of bundle under her head for a pillow. How had she come here? She must have come with her boy from some other town and suddenly fallen ill. The landlady who let the 'corners' had been taken two days before to the police station, the lodgers were out and about as the holiday was so near, and the only one left had been lying for the last twenty-four hours dead drunk, not having waited for Christmas. In another corner of the room a wretched old woman of eighty, who had once been a children's nurse but was now left to die friendless, was moaning and groaning with rheumatism, scolding and grumbling at the boy so that he was afraid to go near her corner. He had got a drink of water in the outer room, but could not find a crust anywhere, and had been on the point of waking his mother a dozen times. He felt frightened at last in the darkness: it had long been dusk, but no light was kindled. Touching his mother's face, he was surprised that she did not move at all, and that she was as cold as the wall. "It is very cold here," he thought. He stood a little, unconsciously letting his hands rest on the dead woman's shoulders, then he breathed on his fingers to warm them, and then quietly fumbling for his cap on the bed, he went out of the cellar. He would have gone earlier, but was afraid of the big dog which had been howling all day at the neighbour's door at the top of the stairs. But the dog was not there now, and he went out into the street.

Mercy on us, what a town! He had never seen anything like it before. In the town from which he had come, it was always such black darkness at night. There was one lamp for the whole street, the little, low-pitched, wooden houses were closed up with shutters, there was no one to be seen in the street after dusk, all the people shut themselves up in their houses, and there was nothing but the howling of packs of dogs, hundreds and thousands of them barking and howling all night. But there it was so warm and he was given food, while here—oh, dear, if he only had something to eat! And what a noise and rattle here, what light and what people, horses and carriages, and what a frost! The frozen steam hung in clouds over the horses, over their warmly breathing mouths; their hoofs clanged against the stones through the powdery snow, and everyone pushed so, and—oh, dear, how he longed for some morsel to eat, and how wretched he suddenly felt. A police-man walked by and turned away to avoid seeing the boy.

Here was another street—oh, what a wide one, here he would be run over for certain; how everyone was shouting, racing and driving along, and the light, the light! And what was this? A huge glass window, and through the window a tree reaching up to the ceiling; it was a fir tree, and on it were ever so many lights, gold papers and apples and little dolls and horses; and

309

there were children clean and dressed in their best running
about the room, laughing and playing and eating and drinking
something. And then a little girl began dancing with one of the
boys, what a pretty little girl! And he could hear the music
through the window. The boy looked and wondered and
laughed, though his toes were aching with the cold and his
fingers were red and stiff so that it hurt him to move them.
And all at once the boy remembered how his toes and fingers
hurt him, and began crying, and ran on; and again through
another window-pane he saw another Christmas tree, and on a
table cakes of all sorts—almond cakes, red cakes and yellow
cakes, and three grand young ladies were sitting there, and
they gave the cakes to anyone who went up to them, and the
door kept opening, lots of gentlemen and ladies went in from
the street. The boy crept up, suddenly opened the door and
went in. Oh, how they shouted at him and waved him back!
One lady went up to him hurriedly and slipped a kopeck into
his hand, and with her own hands opened the door into the
street for him! How frightened he was. And the kopeck rolled
away and clinked upon the steps; he could not bend his red
fingers to hold it tight. The boy ran away and went on, where
he did not know. He was ready to cry again but he was afraid,
and ran on and on and blew his fingers. And he was miserable
because he felt suddenly so lonely and terrified, and all at once,
mercy on us! What was this again? People were standing in
a crowd admiring. Behind a glass window there were three
little dolls, dressed in red and green dresses, and exactly,
exactly as though they were alive. One was a little old man
sitting and playing a big violin, the two others were standing
close by and playing little violins and nodding in time, and
looking at one another, and their lips moved, they were speaking, actually speaking, only one couldn't hear through the
glass. And at first the boy thought they were alive, and when
he grasped that they were dolls he laughed. He had never seen

such dolls before, and had no idea there were such dolls! And
he wanted to cry, but he felt amused, amused by the dolls. All
at once he fancied that someone caught at his smock behind:
a wicked big boy was standing beside him and suddenly hit
him on the head, snatched off his cap and tripped him up. The
boy fell down on the ground, at once there was a shout, he was
numb with fright, he jumped up and ran away. He ran and,
not knowing where he was going, ran in at the gate of someone's courtyard, and sat down behind a stack of wood: "They
won't find me here, besides it's dark!"

He sat huddled up and was breathless from fright, and all at
once, quite suddenly, he felt so happy: his hands and feet
suddenly left off aching and grew so warm, as warm as though
he were on a stove; then he shivered all over, then he gave a
start, why, he must have been asleep. How nice to have a
sleep here! "I'll sit here a little and go and look at the dolls
again," said the boy, and smiled thinking of them. "Just as
though they were alive! . . ." And suddenly he heard his
mother singing over him. "Mammy, I am asleep; how nice it
is to sleep here!"

"Come to my Christmas tree, little one," a soft voice
suddenly whispered over his head.

He thought that this was still his mother, but no, it was not
she. Who it was calling him, he could not see, but someone
bent over and embraced him in the darkness; and he stretched
out his hands to him, and . . . and all at once—oh, what a bright
light! Oh, what a Christmas tree! And yet it was not a fir
tree, he had never seen a tree like that! Where was he now?
Everything was bright and shining, and all round him were
dolls; but no, they were not dolls, they were little boys and
girls, only so bright and shining. They all came flying round
him, they all kissed him, took him and carried him along with
them, and he was flying himself, and he saw that his mother
was looking at him and laughing joyfully. "Mammy, Mammy;

oh, how nice it is here, Mammy!" And again he kissed the children and wanted to tell them at once of those dolls in the shop window. "Who are you, boys? Who are you, girls?" he asked, laughing and admiring them.

"This is Christ's Christmas tree," they answered. "Christ always has a Christmas tree on this day, for the little children who have no tree of their own. . . ." And he found out that all these little boys and girls were children just like himself; that some had been frozen in the baskets in which they had as babies been laid on the doorsteps of well-to-do Petersburg people, others had been boarded out with Finnish women by the Foundling and had been suffocated, others had died at their starved mother's breasts (in the Samara famine), others had died in the third-class railway carriages from the foul air; and yet they were all here, they were all like angels about Christ, and He was in the midst of them and held out His hands to them and blessed them and their sinful mothers. . . . And the mothers of these children stood on one side weeping; each one knew her boy or girl, and the children flew up to them and kissed them and wiped away their tears with their little hands, and begged them not to weep because they were so happy.

And down below in the morning the porter found the little dead body of the frozen child on the woodstack; they sought out his mother too. . . . She had died before him. They met before the Lord God in heaven.

Why have I made up such a story, so out of keeping with an ordinary diary, and a writer's above all? And I promised two stories dealing with real events! But that is just it, I keep fancying that all this may have happened really—that is, what took place in the cellar and on the woodstack; but as for Christ's Christmas tree, I cannot tell you whether that could have happened or not.

312

The Peasant Marey

It was the second day in Easter week. The air was warm, the sky was blue, the sun was high, warm, bright, but my soul was very gloomy. I sauntered behind the prison barracks. I stared at the palings of the stout prison fence, counting them over; but I had no inclination to count them, though it was my habit to do so. This was the second day of the 'holidays' in the prison; the convicts were not taken out to work, there were numbers of men drunk, loud abuse and quarrelling was springing up continually in every corner. There were hideous, disgusting songs and card-parties installed beside the platform-beds. Several of the convicts who had been sentenced by their comrades, for special violence, to be beaten till they were half dead, were lying on the platform-bed, covered with sheepskins till they should recover and come to themselves again; knives had already been drawn several times. For these two days of holiday all this had been torturing me till it made me ill. And indeed I could never endure without repulsion the noise and disorder of drunken people, and especially in this place. On these days even the prison officials did not look into the prison, made no searches, did not look for vodka, understanding that they must allow even these outcasts to enjoy themselves once a year, and that things would be even worse if they did not. At last a sudden fury flamed up in my heart. A political prisoner called M. met me; he looked at me gloomily, his eyes flashed and his lips quivered. "*Je haïs ces brigands!*" he hissed to me through his teeth, and walked on. I returned to the prison ward, though only a quarter of an hour before I had rushed out

313

of it, as though I were crazy, when six stalwart fellows had all together flung themselves upon the drunken Tatar Gazin to suppress him and had begun beating him; they beat him stupidly, a camel might have been killed by such blows, but they knew that this Hercules was not easy to kill, and so they beat him without uneasiness. Now on returning I noticed on the bed in the furthest corner of the room Gazin lying unconscious, almost without sign of life. He lay covered with a sheepskin, and everyone walked round him, without speaking; though they confidently hoped that he would come to himself next morning, yet if luck was against him, maybe from a beating like that, the man would die. I made my way to my own place opposite the window with the iron grating, and lay on my back with my hands behind my head and my eyes shut. I liked to lie like that; a sleeping man is not molested, and meanwhile one can dream and think. But I could not dream, my heart was beating uneasily, and M.'s words, "*Je haïs ces brigands!*" were echoing in my ears. But why describe my impressions; I sometimes dream even now of those times at night, and I have no dreams more agonising. Perhaps it will be noticed that even to this day I have scarcely once spoken in print of my life in prison. *The House of the Dead* I wrote fifteen years ago in the character of an imaginary person, a criminal who had killed his wife. I may add by the way that since then, very many persons have supposed, and even now maintain, that I was sent to penal servitude for the murder of my wife.

Gradually I sank into forgetfulness and by degrees was lost in memories. During the whole course of my four years in prison I was continually recalling all my past, and seemed to live over again the whole of my life in recollection. These memories rose up of themselves, it was not often that of my own will I summoned them. It would begin from some point, some little thing, at times unnoticed, and then by degrees there

314

would rise up a complete picture, some vivid and complete impression. I used to analyse these impressions, give new features to what had happened long ago, and best of all, I used to correct it, correct it continually, that was my great amusement. On this occasion, I suddenly for some reason remembered an unnoticed moment in my early childhood when I was only nine years old—a moment which I should have thought I had utterly forgotten; but at that time I was particularly fond of memories of my early childhood. I remembered the month of August in our country house: a dry bright day but rather cold and windy; summer was waning and soon we should have to go to Moscow to be bored all the winter over French lessons, and I was so sorry to leave the country. I walked past the threshing-floor and, going down the ravine, I went up to the dense thicket of bushes that covered the further side of the ravine as far as the copse. And I plunged right into the midst of the bushes, and heard a peasant ploughing alone on the clearing about thirty paces away. I knew that he was ploughing up the steep hill and the horse was moving with effort, and from time to time the peasant's call "come up!" floated upwards to me. I knew almost all our peasants, but I did not know which it was ploughing now, and I did not care who it was, I was absorbed in my own affairs. I was busy, too; I was breaking off switches from the nut trees to whip the frogs with. Nut sticks made such fine whips, but they do not last; while birch twigs are just the opposite. I was interested, too, in beetles and other insects; I used to collect them, some were very ornamental. I was very fond, too, of the little nimble red and yellow lizards with black spots on them, but I was afraid of snakes. Snakes, however, were much more rare than lizards. There were not many mushrooms there. To get mushrooms one had to go to the birch wood, and I was about to set off there. And there was nothing in the world that I loved so much as the wood with its mushrooms and wild berries, with

315

its beetles and its birds, its hedgehogs and squirrels, with its damp smell of dead leaves which I loved so much, and even as I write I smell the fragrance of our birch wood: these impressions will remain for my whole life. Suddenly in the midst of the profound stillness I heard a clear and distinct shout, "Wolf!" I shrieked and, beside myself with terror, calling out at the top of my voice, ran out into the clearing and straight to the peasant who was ploughing.

It was our peasant Marey. I don't know if there is such a name, but everyone called him Marey—a thick-set, rather well-grown peasant of fifty, with a good many grey hairs in his dark brown, spreading beard. I knew him, but had scarcely ever happened to speak to him till then. He stopped his horse on hearing my cry, and when, breathless, I caught with one hand at his plough and with the other at his sleeve, he saw how frightened I was.

"There is a wolf!" I cried, panting.

He flung up his head, and could not help looking round for an instant, almost believing me.

"Where is the wolf?"

"A shout . . . someone shouted: 'wolf' . . ." I faltered out.

"Nonsense, nonsense! A wolf? Why, it was your fancy! How could there be a wolf?" he muttered, reassuring me. But I was trembling all over, and still kept tight hold of his smock frock, and I must have been quite pale. He looked at me with an uneasy smile, evidently anxious and troubled over me.

"Why, you have had a fright, *aïe*, *aïe*!" He shook his head. "There, dear. . . . Come, little one, *aïe*!"

He stretched out his hand, and all at once stroked my cheek.

"Come, come, there; Christ be with you! Cross yourself!"

But I did not cross myself. The corners of my mouth were twitching, and I think that struck him particularly. He put out his thick, black-nailed, earth-stained finger and softly touched my twitching lips.

316

"*Aïe*, there, there," he said to me with a slow, almost motherly smile. "Dear, dear, what is the matter? There; come, come!"

I grasped at last that there was no wolf, and that the shout that I had heard was my fancy. Yet that shout had been so clear and distinct, but such shouts (not only about wolves) I had imagined once or twice before, and I was aware of that. (These hallucinations passed away later as I grew older.)

"Well, I will go then," I said, looking at him timidly and inquiringly.

"Well, do, and I'll keep watch on you as you go. I won't let the wolf get at you," he added, still smiling at me with the same motherly expression. "Well, Christ be with you! Come, run along then," and he made the sign of the cross over me and then over himself. I walked away, looking back almost at every tenth step. Marey stood still with his mare as I walked away, and looked after me and nodded to me every time I looked round. I must own I felt a little ashamed at having let him see me so frightened, but I was still very much afraid of the wolf as I walked away, until I reached the first barn half-way up the slope of the ravine; there my fright vanished completely, and all at once our yard-dog Voltchok flew to meet me. With Voltchok I felt quite safe, and I turned round to Marey for the last time; I could not see his face distinctly, but I felt that he was still nodding and smiling affectionately to me. I waved to him; he waved back to me and started his little mare. "Come up!" I heard his call in the distance again, and the little mare pulled at the plough again.

All this I recalled all at once, I don't know why, but with extraordinary minuteness of detail. I suddenly roused myself and sat up on the platform-bed, and, I remember, found myself still smiling quietly at my memories. I brooded over them for another minute.

When I got home that day I told no one of my 'adventure'

with Marey. And indeed it was hardly an adventure. And in fact I soon forgot Marey. When I met him now and then afterwards, I never even spoke to him about the wolf or anything else; and all at once now, twenty years afterwards in Siberia, I remembered this meeting with such distinctness to the smallest detail. So it must have lain hidden in my soul, though I knew nothing of it, and rose suddenly to my memory when it was wanted; I remembered the soft motherly smile of the poor serf, the way he signed me with the cross and shook his head. "There, there, you have had a fright, little one!" And I remembered particularly the thick earth-stained finger with which he softly and with timid tenderness touched my quivering lips. Of course any one would have reassured a child, but something quite different seemed to have happened in that solitary meeting; and if I had been his own son, he could not have looked at me with eyes shining with greater love. And what made him like that? He was our serf and I was his little master, after all. No one would know that he had been kind to me and reward him for it. Was he, perhaps, very fond of little children? Some people are. It was a solitary meeting in the deserted fields, and only God, perhaps, may have seen from above with what deep and humane civilised feeling, and with what delicate, almost feminine tenderness, the heart of a coarse, brutally ignorant Russian serf, who had as yet no expectation, no idea even of his freedom, may be filled. Was not this, perhaps, what Konstantin Aksakov meant when he spoke of the high degree of culture of our peasantry?

And when I got down off the bed and looked around me, I remember I suddenly felt that I could look at these unhappy creatures with quite different eyes, and that suddenly by some miracle all hatred and anger had vanished utterly from my heart. I walked about, looking into the faces that I met. That shaven peasant, branded on his face as a criminal, bawling his

318

hoarse, drunken song, may be that very Marey; I cannot look into his heart.

I met M. again that evening. Poor fellow! he could have no memories of Russian peasants, and no other view of these people but: "*Je haïs ces brigands!*" Yes, the Polish prisoners had more to bear than I.

The Crocodile

An Extraordinary Incident

A true story of how a gentleman of a certain age and of respectable appearance was swallowed alive by the crocodile in the Arcade, and of the consequences that followed.

Ohé Lambert! Où est Lambert?
As-tu vu Lambert?

I

ON the thirteenth of January of this present year, 1865, at half-past twelve in the day, Elena Ivanovna, the wife of my cultured friend Ivan Matveitch, who is a colleague in the same department, and may be said to be a distant relation of mine, too, expressed the desire to see the crocodile now on view at a fixed charge in the Arcade. As Ivan Matveitch had already in his pocket his ticket for a tour abroad (not so much for the sake of his health as for the improvement of his mind), and was consequently free from his official duties and had nothing whatever to do that morning, he offered no objection to his wife's irresistible fancy, but was positively aflame with curiosity himself.

"A capital idea!" he said, with the utmost satisfaction. "We'll have a look at the crocodile! On the eve of visiting Europe it is as well to acquaint ourselves on the spot with its indigenous inhabitants." And with these words, taking his wife's arm, he set off with her at once for the Arcade. I joined them, as I usually do, being an intimate friend of the family. I have never seen Ivan Matveitch in a more agreeable frame of mind than he was on that memorable morning—how true it is that we know not beforehand the fate that awaits us! On entering the Arcade he was at once full of admiration for the

320

splendours of the building and, when we reached the shop in which the monster lately arrived in Petersburg was being exhibited, he volunteered to pay the quarter-rouble for me to the crocodile owner—a thing which had never happened before. Walking into a little room, we observed that besides the crocodile there were in it parrots of the species known as cockatoo, and also a group of monkeys in a special case in a recess. Near the entrance, along the left wall stood a big tin tank that looked like a bath covered with a thin iron grating, filled with water to the depth of two inches. In this shallow pool was kept a huge crocodile, which lay like a log absolutely motionless and apparently deprived of all its faculties by our damp climate, so inhospitable to foreign visitors. This monster at first aroused no special interest in any one of us.

"So this is the crocodile!" said Elena Ivanovna, with a pathetic cadence of regret. "Why, I thought it was . . . something different."

Most probably she thought it was made of diamonds. The owner of the crocodile, a German, came out and looked at us with an air of extraordinary pride.

"He has a right to be," Ivan Matveitch whispered to me, "he knows he is the only man in Russia exhibiting a crocodile."

This quite nonsensical observation I ascribe also to the extremely good-humoured mood which had overtaken Ivan Matveitch, who was on other occasions of rather envious disposition.

"I fancy your crocodile is not alive," said Elena Ivanovna, piqued by the irresponsive stolidity of the proprietor, and addressing him with a charming smile in order to soften his churlishness—a manœuvre so typically feminine.

"Oh, no, madam," the latter replied in broken Russian; and instantly moving the grating half off the tank, he poked the monster's head with a stick.

Then the treacherous monster, to show that it was alive,

faintly stirred its paws and tail, raised its snout and emitted something like a prolonged snuffle.

"Come, don't be cross, Karlchen," said the German caressingly, gratified in his vanity.

"How horrid that crocodile is! I am really frightened," Elena Ivanovna twittered, still more coquettishly. "I know I shall dream of him now."

"But he won't bite you if you do dream of him," the German retorted gallantly, and was the first to laugh at his own jest, but none of us responded.

"Come, Semyon Semyonitch," said Elena Ivanovna, addressing me exclusively, "let us go and look at the monkeys. I am awfully fond of monkeys; they are such darlings . . . and the crocodile is horrid."

"Oh, don't be afraid, my dear!" Ivan Matveitch called after us, gallantly displaying his manly courage to his wife. "This drowsy denison of the realms of the Pharaohs will do us no harm." And he remained by the tank. What is more, he took his glove and began tickling the crocodile's nose with it, wishing, as he said afterwards, to induce him to snort. The proprietor showed his politeness to a lady by following Elena Ivanovna to the case of monkeys.

So everything was going well, and nothing could have been foreseen. Elena Ivanovna was quite skittish in her raptures over the monkeys, and seemed completely taken up with them. With shrieks of delight she was continually turning to me, as though determined not to notice the proprietor, and kept gushing with laughter at the resemblance she detected between these monkeys and her intimate friends and acquaintances. I, too, was amused, for the resemblance was unmistakable. The German did not know whether to laugh or not, and so at last was reduced to frowning. And it was at that moment that a terrible, I may say unnatural, scream set the room vibrating. Not knowing what to think, for the first moment I stood still, numb with horror, but, noticing that Elena Ivanovna was screaming too, I quickly turned round—and what did I behold! I saw—oh, heavens!—I saw the luckless Ivan Matveitch in the terrible jaws of the crocodile, held by them round the waist, lifted horizontally in the air and desperately kicking. Then— one moment, and no trace remained of him. But I must describe it in detail, for I stood all the while motionless, and had time to watch the whole process taking place before me with an attention and interest such as I never remember to have felt before. "What," I thought at that critical moment, "what if all that had happened to me instead of to Ivan Matveitch—how unpleasant it would have been for me!"

But to return to my story. The crocodile began by turning the unhappy Ivan Matveitch in his terrible jaws so that he could swallow his legs first; then bringing up Ivan Matveitch, who kept trying to jump out and clutching at the sides of the tank, sucked him down again as far as his waist. Then bringing him up again, gulped him down, and so again and again. In this way Ivan Matveitch was visibly disappearing before our eyes. At last, with a final gulp, the crocodile swallowed my cultured friend entirely, this time leaving no trace of him. From the outside of the crocodile we could see the protuberances of Ivan Matveitch's figure as he passed down the inside of the monster. I was on the point of screaming again when destiny played another treacherous trick upon us. The crocodile made a tremendous effort, probably oppressed by the magnitude of the object he had swallowed, once more opened his terrible jaws, and with a final hiccup he suddenly let the head of Ivan Matveitch pop out for a second, with an expression of despair on his face. In that brief instant the spectacles dropped off his nose to the bottom of the tank. It seemed as though that despairing countenance had only popped out to cast one last look on the objects around it, to take its last farewell of all earthly pleasures. But it had not time to carry out its intention;

the crocodile made another effort, gave a gulp and instantly it vanished again—this time for ever. This appearance and disappearance of a still living human head was so horrible, but at the same—either from its rapidity and unexpectedness or from the dropping of the spectacles—there was something so comic about it that I suddenly quite unexpectedly exploded with laughter. But pulling myself together and realising that to laugh at such a moment was not the thing for an old family friend, I turned at once to Elena Ivanovna and said with a sympathetic air:

"Now it's all over with our friend Ivan Matveitch!"

I cannot even attempt to describe how violent was the agitation of Elena Ivanovna during the whole process. After the first scream she seemed rooted to the spot, and stared at the catastrophe with apparent indifference, though her eyes looked as though they were starting out of her head; then she suddenly went off into a heart-rending wail, but I seized her hands. At this instant the proprietor, too, who had at first been also petrified by horror, suddenly clapsed his hands and cried, gazing upwards:

"Oh, my crocodile! *Oh, mein allerliebster Karlchen! Mutter, Mutter, Mutter!*"

A door at the rear of the room opened at this cry, and the *Mutter*, a rosy-cheeked, elderly but dishevelled woman in a cap made her appearance, and rushed with a shriek to her German.

A perfect Bedlam followed. Elena Ivanovna kept shrieking out the same phrase, as though in a frenzy, "Flay him! flay him!" apparently entreating them—probably in a moment of oblivion—to flay somebody for something. The proprietor and *Mutter* took no notice whatever of either of us; they were both bellowing like calves over the crocodile.

"He did for himself! He will burst himself at once, for he did swallow a *ganz* official!" cried the proprietor.

"*Unser Karlchen, unser allerliebster Karlchen wird sterben,*" howled his wife.

"We are bereaved and without bread!" chimed in the proprietor.

"Flay him! flay him! flay him!" clamoured Elena Ivanovna, clutching at the German's coat.

"He did tease the crocodile. For what did your man tease the crocodile?" cried the German, pulling away from her. "You will, if *Karlchen wird* burst, therefore pay, *das war mein Sohn, das war mein einziger Sohn.*"

I must own I was intensely indignant at the sight of such egoism in the German and the cold-heartedness of his dishevelled *Mutter*; at the same time Elena Ivanovna's reiterated shriek of "Flay him! flay him!" troubled me even more and absorbed at last my whole attention, positively alarming me. I may as well say straight off that I entirely misunderstood this strange exclamation: it seemed to me that Elena Ivanovna had for the moment taken leave of her senses, but nevertheless wishing to avenge the loss of her beloved Ivan Matveitch, was demanding by way of compensation that the crocodile should be severely thrashed, while she was meaning something quite different. Looking round at the door, not without embrarassment, I began to entreat Elena Ivanovna to calm herself, and above all not to use the shocking word 'flay'. For such a reactionary desire here, in the midst of the Arcade and of the most cultured society, not two paces from the hall where at this very minute Mr. Lavrov was perhaps delivering a public lecture, was not only impossible but unthinkable, and might at any moment bring upon us the hisses of culture and the caricatures of Mr. Stepanov. To my horror I was immediately proved to be correct in my alarmed suspicions: the curtain that divided the crocodile room from the little entry where the quarter-roubles were taken suddenly parted, and in the opening there appeared a figure with moustaches and beard, carrying

325

a cap, with the upper part of its body bent a long way forward, though the feet were scrupulously held beyond the threshold of the crocodile room in order to avoid the necessity of paying the entrance money.

"Such a reactionary desire, madam," said the stranger, trying to avoid falling over in our direction and to remain standing outside the room, "does no credit to your development, and is conditioned by lack of phosphorus in your brain. You will be promptly held up to shame in the *Chronicle of Progress* and in our satirical prints . . ."

But he could not complete his remarks; the proprietor coming to himself, and seeing with horror that a man was talking in the crocodile room without having paid entrance money, rushed furiously at the progressive stranger and turned him out with a punch from each fist. For a moment both vanished from our sight behind a curtain, and only then I grasped that the whole uproar was about nothing. Elena Ivanovna turned out quite innocent; she had, as I have mentioned already, no idea whatever of subjecting the crocodile to a degrading corporal punishment, and had simply expressed the desire that he should be opened and her husband released from his interior.

"What! You wish that my crocodile be perished!" the proprietor yelled, running in again. "No! let your husband be perished first, before my crocodile! . . . *Mein Vater* showed crocodile, *mein Grossvater* showed crocodile, *mein Sohn* will show crocodile, and I will show crocodile! All will show crocodile! I am known to *ganz Europa*, and you are not known to *ganz Europa*, and you must pay me a *Strafe!*"

"*Ja, ja,*" put in the vindictive German woman, "we shall not let you go. *Strafe,* since Karlchen is burst!"

"And, indeed, it's useless to flay the creature," I added calmly, anxious to get Elena Ivanovna away home as quickly

326

as possible, "as our dear Ivan Matveitch is by now probably soaring somewhere in the empyrean."

"My dear"—we suddenly heard, to our intense amazement, the voice of Ivan Matveitch—"my dear, my advice is to apply direct to the superintendent's office, as without the assistance of the police the German will never be made to see reason."

These words, uttered with firmness and aplomb, and expressing an exceptional presence of mind, for the first minute so astounded us that we could not believe our ears. But, of course, we ran at once to the crocodile's tank, and with equal reverence and incredulity listened to the unhappy captive. His voice was muffled, thin and even squeaky, as though it came from a considerable distance. It reminded one of a jocose person who, covering his mouth with a pillow, shouts from an adjoining room, trying to mimic the sound of two peasants calling to one another in a deserted plain or across a wide ravine—a performance to which I once had the pleasure of listening in a friend's house at Christmas.

"Ivan Matveitch, my dear, and so you are alive!" faltered Elena Ivanovna.

"Alive and well," answered Ivan Matveitch, "and, thanks to the Almighty, swallowed without any damage whatever. I am only uneasy as to the view my superiors may take of the incident; for after getting a permit to go abroad I've got into a crocodile, which seems anything but clever."

"But, my dear, don't trouble your head about being clever; first of all we must somehow excavate you from where you are," Elena Ivanovna interrupted.

"Excavate!" cried the proprietor. "I will not let my crocodile be excavated. Now the *Publicum* will come many more, and I will *fünfzig* kopecks ask and Karlchen will cease to burst."

"*Gott sei Dank!*" put in his wife.

"They are right," Ivan Matveitch observed tranquilly; "the principles of economics before everything."

327

"My dear! I will fly at once to the authorities and lodge a complaint, for I feel that we cannot settle this mess by ourselves."

"I think so too," observed Ivan Matveitch; "but in our age of industrial crisis it is not easy to rip open the belly of a crocodile without economic compensation, and meanwhile the inevitable question presents itself: What will the German take for his crocodile? And with it another: How will it be paid? For, as you know, I have no means . . ."

"Perhaps out of your salary . . ." I observed timidly, but the proprietor interrupted me at once.

"I will not the crocodile sell; I will for three thousand the crocodile sell! I will for four thousand the crocodile sell! Now the *Publicum* will come very many. I will for five thousand the crocodile sell!"

In fact he gave himself insufferable airs. Covetousness and a revolting greed gleamed joyfully in his eyes.

"I am going!" I cried indignantly.

"And I! I too! I shall go to Andrey Osipitch himself. I will soften him with my tears," whined Elena Ivanovna.

"Don't do that, my dear," Ivan Matveitch hastened to interpose. He had long been jealous of Andrey Osipitch on his wife's account, and he knew she would enjoy going to weep before a gentleman of refinement, for tears suited her. "And I don't advise you to do so either, my friend," he added, addressing me. "It's no good plunging headlong in that slap-dash way; there's no knowing what it may lead to. You had much better go to-day to Timofey Semyonitch, as though to pay an ordinary visit; he is an old-fashioned and by no means brilliant man, but he is trustworthy, and what matters most of all, he is straightforward. Give him my greetings and describe the circumstances of the case. And since I owe him seven roubles over our last game of cards, take the opportunity to pay him the money; that will soften the stern old man. In any

328

case his advice may serve as a guide for us. And meanwhile take Elena Ivanovna home. . . . Calm yourself, my dear," he continued, addressing her. "I am weary of these outcries and feminine squabblings, and should like a nap. It's soft and warm in here, though I have hardly had time to look round in this unexpected haven."

"Look round! Why, is it light in there?" cried Elena Ivanovna in a tone of relief.

"I am surrounded by impenetrable night," answered the poor captive, "but I can feel and, so to speak, have a look round with my hands. . . . Good-bye; set your mind at rest and don't deny yourself recreation and diversion. Till to-morrow! And you, Semyon Semyonitch, come to me in the evening, and as you are absent-minded and may forget it, tie a knot in your handkerchief."

I confess I was glad to get away, for I was overtired and somewhat bored. Hastening to offer my arm to the disconsolate Elena Ivanovna, whose charms were only enhanced by her agitation, I hurriedly led her out of the crocodile room.

"The charge will be another quarter-rouble in the evening," the proprietor called after us.

"Oh, dear, how greedy they are!" said Elena Ivanovna, looking at herself in every mirror on the walls of the Arcade, and evidently aware that she was looking prettier than usual.

"The principles of economics," I answered with some emotion, proud that passers-by should see the lady on my arm.

"The principles of economics," she drawled in a touching little voice. "I did not in the least understand what Ivan Matveitch said about those horrid economics just now."

"I will explain to you," I answered, and began at once telling her of the beneficial effects of the introduction of foreign capital into our country, upon which I had read an article in the *Petersburg News* and the *Voice* that morning.

"How strange it is," she interrupted, after listening for some time. "But do leave off, you horrid man. What nonsense you are talking. . . . Tell me, do I look purple?"

"You look perfect, and not purple!" I observed, seizing the opportunity to pay her a compliment.

"Naughty man!" she said complacently. "Poor Ivan Matveitch," she added a minute later, putting her little head on one side coquettishly. "I am really sorry for him. Oh, dear!" she cried suddenly, "how is he going to have his dinner . . . and . . . and . . . what will he do . . . if he wants anything?"

"An unforeseen question," I answered, perplexed in my turn. To tell the truth, it had not entered my head, so much more practical are women than we men in the solution of the problems of daily life!

"Poor dear! how could he have got into such a mess . . . nothing to amuse him, and in the dark. . . . How vexing it is that I have no photograph of him. . . . And so now I am a sort of widow," she added, with a seductive smile, evidently interested in her new position. "Hm! . . . I am sorry for him, though."

It was, in short, the expression of the very natural and intelligible grief of a young and interesting wife for the loss of her husband. I took her home at last, soothed her, and after dining with her and drinking a cup of aromatic coffee, set off at six o'clock to Timofey Semyonitch, calculating that at that hour all married people of settled habits would be sitting or lying down at home.

Having written this first chapter in a style appropriate to the incident recorded, I intended to proceed in a language more natural though less elevated, and I beg to forewarn the reader of the fact.

330

II

THE venerable Timofey Semyonitch met me rather nervously, as though somewhat embarrassed. He led me to his tiny study and shut the door carefully, "that the children may not hinder us," he added with evident uneasiness. There he made me sit down on a chair by the writing-table, sat down himself in an easy chair, wrapped round him the skirts of his old wadded dressing-gown, and assumed an official and even severe air, in readiness for anything, though he was not my chief nor Ivan Matveitch's, and had hitherto been reckoned as a colleague and even a friend.

"First of all," he said, "take note that I am not a person in authority, but just such a subordinate official as you and Ivan Matveitch. . . . I have nothing to do with it, and do not intend to mix myself up in the affair."

I was surprised to find that he apparently knew all about it already. In spite of that I told him the whole story over in detail. I spoke with positive excitement, for I was at that moment fulfilling the obligations of a true friend. He listened without special surprise, but with evident signs of suspicion.

"Only fancy," he said, "I always believed that this would be sure to happen to him."

"Why, Timofey Semyonitch? It is a very unusual incident in itself . . ."

"I admit it. But Ivan Matveitch's whole career in the service was leading up to this end. He was flighty—conceited indeed. It was always 'progress' and ideas of all sorts, and this is what progress brings people to!"

"But this is a most unusual incident and cannot possibly serve as a general rule for all progressives."

"Yes, indeed it can. You see, it's the effect of over-education, I assure you. For over-education leads people to poke their

331

noses into all sorts of places, especially where they are not invited. Though perhaps you know best," he added, as though offended. "I am an old man and not of much education. I began as a soldier's son, and this year has been the jubilee of my service."

"Oh, no, Timofey Semyonitch, not at all. On the contrary, Ivan Matveitch is eager for your advice; he is eager for your guidance. He implores it, so to say, with tears."

"So to say, with tears! Hm! Those are crocodile's tears and one cannot quite believe in them. Tell me, what possessed him to want to go abroad? And how could he afford to go? Why, he has no private means!"

"He had saved the money from his last bonus," I answered plaintively. "He only wanted to go for three months—to Switzerland . . . to the land of William Tell."

"William Tell? Hm!"

"He wanted to meet the spring at Naples, to see the museums, the customs, the animals . . ."

"Hm! The animals! I think it was simply from pride. What animals? Animals, indeed! Haven't we animals enough? We have museums, menageries, camels. There are bears quite close to Petersburg! And here he's got inside a crocodile himself . . ."

"Oh, come, Timofey Semyonitch! The man is in trouble, the man appeals to you as to a friend, as to an older relation, craves for advice—and you reproach him. Have pity at least on the unfortunate Elena Ivanovna!"

"You are speaking of his wife? A charming little lady," said Timofey Semyonitch, visibly softening and taking a pinch of snuff with relish. "Particularly prepossessing. And so plump, and always putting her pretty little head on one side. . . . Very agreeable. Andrey Osipitch was speaking of her only the other day."

"Speaking of her?"

"Yes, and in very flattering terms. Such a bust, he said, such

332

eyes, such hair. . . . A sugar-plum, he said, not a lady—and then he laughed. He is still a young man, of course," Timofey Semyonitch blew his nose with a loud noise. "And yet, young though he is, what a career he is making for himself."

"That's quite a different thing, Timofey Semyonitch."

"Of course, of course."

"Well, what do you say then, Timofey Semyonitch?"

"Why, what can I do?"

"Give advice, guidance, as a man of experience, a relative! What are we to do? What steps are we to take? Go to the authorities and . . ."

"To the authorities? Certainly not," Timofey Semyonitch replied hurriedly. "If you ask my advice, you had better, above all, hush the matter up and act, so to speak, as a private person. It is a suspicious incident, quite unheard of. Unheard of, above all; there is no precedent for it, and it is far from creditable. . . . And so discretion above all. . . . Let him lie there a bit. We must wait and see. . . ."

"But how can we wait and see, Timofey Semyonitch? What if he is stifled there?"

"Why should he be? I think you told me that he made himself fairly comfortable there?"

I told him the whole story over again. Timofey Semyonitch pondered.

"Hm!" he said, twisting his snuff-box in his hands. "To my mind it's really a good thing he should lie there a bit, instead of going abroad. Let him reflect at his leisure. Of course he mustn't be stifled, and so he must take measures to preserve his health, avoiding a cough, for instance, and so on. . . . And as for the German, it's my personal opinion he is within his rights, and even more so than the other side, because it was the other party who got into *his* crocodile without asking permission, and not *he* who got into Ivan Matveitch's crocodile without asking permission, though, so far as I recollect, the latter has

333

no crocodile. And a crocodile is private property, and so it is impossible to slit him open without compensation."

"For the saving of human life, Timofey Semyonitch."

"Oh, well, that's a matter for the police. You must go to them."

"But Ivan Mat eitch may be needed in the department. He may be asked for."

"Ivan Matvcitch needed? Ha-ha! Besides, he is on leave, so that we may ignore him—let him inspect the countries of Europe! It will be a different matter if he doesn't turn up when his leave is over. Then we shall ask for him and make inquiries."

"Three months! Timofey Semyonitch, for pity's sake!"

"It's his own fault. Nobody thrust him there. At this rate we should have to get a nurse to look after him at government expense, and that is not allowed for in the regulations. But the chief point is that the crocodile is private property, so that the principles of economics apply in this question. And the principles of economics are paramount. Only the other evening, at Luke Andreitch's, Ignaty Prokofyitch was saying so. Do you know Ignaty Prokofyitch? A capitalist, in a big way of business, and he speaks so fluently. 'We need industrial development,' he said; 'there is very little development among us. We must create it. We must create capital, so we must create a middle-class, the so-called bourgeoisie. And as we haven't capital we must attract it from abroad. We must, in the first place, give facilities to foreign companies to buy up lands in Russia as is done now abroad. The communal holding of land is poison, is ruin.' And, you know, he spoke with such heat; well, that's all right for him—a wealthy man, and not in the service. 'With the communal system,' he said, 'there will be no improvement in industrial development or agriculture. Foreign companies,' he said, 'must as far as possible buy up the whole of our land in big lots, and then split it up, split it

334

up, split it up, in the smallest parts possible'—and do you know he pronounced the words 'split it up' with such determination —'and then sell it as private property. Or rather, not sell it, but simply let it. When,' he said, 'all the land is in the hands of foreign companies they can fix any rent they like. And so the peasant will work three times as much for his daily bread and he can be turned out at pleasure. So that he will feel it, will be submissive and industrious, and will work three times as much for the same wages. But as it is, with the commune, what does he care? He knows he won't die of hunger, so he is lazy and drunken. And meanwhile money will be attracted into Russia, capital will be created and the bourgeoisie will spring up. The English political and literary paper, *The Times*, in an article the other day on our finances stated that the reason our financial position was so unsatisfactory was that we had no middle-class, no big fortunes, no accommodating proletariat.' Ignaty Prokofyitch speaks well. He is an orator. He wants to lay a report on the subject before the authorities, and then to get it published in the *News*. That's something very different from verses like Ivan Matveitch's . . ."

"But how about Ivan Matveitch?" I put in, after letting the old man babble on.

Timofey Semyonitch was sometimes fond of talking and showing that he was not behind the times, but knew all about things.

"How about Ivan Matveitch? Why, I am coming to that. Here we are, anxious to bring foreign capital into the country —and only consider: as soon as the capital of a foreigner, who has been attracted to Petersburg, has been doubled through Ivan Matveitch, instead of protecting the foreign capitalist, we are proposing to rip open the belly of his original capital—the crocodile. Is it consistent? To my mind, Ivan Matveitch, as the true son of his fatherland, ought to rejoice and to be proud that through him the value of a foreign crocodile has been doubled and possibly even trebled. That's just what is wanted to attract capital. If one man succeeds, mind you, another will come with a crocodile, and a third will bring two or three of them at once, and capital will grow up about them—there you have a bourgeoisie. It must be encouraged."

"Upon my word, Timofey Semyonitch!" I cried, "you are demanding almost supernatural self-sacrifice from poor Ivan Matveitch."

"I demand nothing, and I beg you, before everything—as I have said already—to remember that I am not a person in authority and so cannot demand anything of anyone. I am speaking as a son of the fatherland, that is, not as the *Son of the Fatherland*, but as a son of the fatherland. Again, what possessed him to get into the crocodile? A respectable man, a man of good grade in the service, lawfully married—and then to behave like that! Is it consistent?"

"But it was an accident."

"Who knows? And where is the money to compensate the owner to come from?"

"Perhaps out of his salary, Timofey Semyonitch?"

"Would that be enough?"

"No, it wouldn't, Timofey Semyonitch," I answered sadly. "The proprietor was at first alarmed that the crocodile would burst, but as soon as he was sure that it was all right, he began to bluster and was delighted to think that he could double the charge for entry."

"Treble and quadruple perhaps! The public will simply stampede the place now, and crocodile owners are smart people. Besides, it's not Lent yet, and people are keen on diversions, and so I say again, the great thing is that Ivan Matveitch should preserve his incognito, don't let him be in a hurry. Let everybody know, perhaps, that he is in the crocodile, but don't let them be officially informed of it. Ivan Matveitch is in particularly favourable circumstances for that, for he is reckoned to be abroad. It will be said he is in the crocodile, and we will refuse to believe it. That is how it can be managed. The great thing is that he should wait; and why should he be in a hurry?"

"Well, but if . . ."

"Don't worry, he has a good constitution . . ."

"Well, and afterwards, when he has waited?"

"Well, I won't conceal from you that the case is exceptional in the highest degree. One doesn't know what to think of it, and the worst of it is there is no precedent. If we had a precedent we might have something to go by. But as it is, what is one to say? It will certainly take time to settle it."

A happy thought flashed upon my mind.

"Cannot we arrange," I said, "that, if he is destined to remain in the entrails of the monster and it is the will of Providence that he should remain alive, he should send in a petition to be reckoned as still serving?"

"Hm! . . . Possibly as on leave and without salary . . ."

"But couldn't it be with salary?"

"On what grounds?"

"As sent on a special commission."

"What commission and where?"

"Why, into the entrails, the entrails of the crocodile. . . . So to speak, for exploration, for investigation of the facts on the spot. It would, of course, be a novelty, but that is progressive and would at the same time show zeal for enlightenment."

Timofey Semyonitch thought a little.

"To send a special official," he said at last, "to the inside of a crocodile to conduct a special inquiry is, in my personal opinion, an absurdity. It is not in the regulations. And what sort of special inquiry could there be there?"

"The scientific study of nature on the spot, in the living subject. The natural sciences are all the fashion nowadays, botany. . . . He could live there and report his observations. . . . For instance, concerning digestion or simply habits. For the sake of accumulating facts."

"You mean as statistics. Well, I am no great authority on that subject, indeed I am no philosopher at all. You say 'facts'—we are overwhelmed with facts as it is, and don't know what to do with them. Besides, statistics are a danger."

"In what way?"

"They are a danger. Moreover, you will admit he will report facts, so to speak, lying like a log. And, can one do one's official duties lying like a log? That would be another novelty and a dangerous one; and again, there is no precedent for it. If we had any sort of precedent for it, then, to my thinking, he might have been given the job."

"But no live crocodiles have been brought over hitherto, Timofey Semyonitch."

"Hm . . . yes," he reflected again. "Your objection is a just one, if you like, and might indeed serve as a ground for carrying the matter further; but consider again, that if with the arrival of living crocodiles government clerks begin to disappear, and then on the ground that they are warm and comfortable there, expect to receive the official sanction for their position, and then take their ease there . . . you must admit it would be a bad example. We should have everyone trying to go the same way to get a salary for nothing."

"Do your best for him, Timofey Semyonitch. By the way, Ivan Matveitch asked me to give you seven roubles he had lost to you at cards."

"Ah, he lost that the other day at Nikifor Nikiforitch's. I remember. And how gay and amusing he was—and now!"

The old man was genuinely touched.

"Intercede for him, Timofey Semyonitch!"

"I will do my best. I will speak in my own name, as a private person, as though I were asking for information. And

338

meanwhile, you find out indirectly, unofficially, how much would the proprietor consent to take for his crocodile?"

Timofey Semyonitch was visibly more friendly.

"Certainly," I answered. "And I will come back to you at once to report."

"And his wife . . . is she alone now? Is she depressed?"

"You should call on her, Timofey Semyonitch."

"I will. I thought of doing so before; it's a good opportunity. . . . And what on earth possessed him to go and look at the crocodile. Though, indeed, I should like to see it myself."

"Go and see the poor fellow, Timofey Semyonitch."

"I will. Of course, I don't want to raise his hopes by doing so. I shall go as a private person. . . . Well, good-bye, I am going to Nikifor Nikiforitch's again; shall you be there?"

"No, I am going to see the poor prisoner."

"Yes, now he is a prisoner! . . . Ah, that's what comes of thoughtlessness!"

I said good-bye to the old man. Ideas of all kinds were straying through my mind. A good-natured and most honest man, Timofey Semyonitch, yet, as I left him, I felt pleased at the thought that he had celebrated his fiftieth year of service, and that Timofey Semyonitchs are now a rarity among us. I flew at once, of course, to the Arcade to tell poor Ivan Matveitch all the news. And, indeed, I was moved by curiosity to know how he was getting on in the crocodile and how it was possible to live in a crocodile. And, indeed, was it possible to live in a crocodile at all? At times it really seemed to me as though it were all an outlandish, monstrous dream, especially as an outlandish monster was the chief figure in it.

III

AND yet it was not a dream, but actual, indubitable fact.

Should I be telling the story if it were not? But to continue.

It was late, about nine o'clock, before I reached the Arcade, and I had to go into the crocodile room by the back entrance, for the German had closed the shop earlier than usual that evening. Now in the seclusion of domesticity he was walking about in a greasy old frock-coat, but he seemed three times as pleased as he had been in the morning. It was evidently that he had no apprehensions now, and that the public had been coming "many more". The *Mutter* came out later, evidently to keep an eye on me. The German and the *Mutter* frequently whispered together. Although the shop was closed he charged me a quarter-rouble. What unnecessary exactitude!

"You will every time pay; the public will one rouble, and you one quarter pay; for you are the good friend of your good friend; and I a friend respect . . ."

"Are you alive, are you alive, my cultured friend?" I cried, as I approached the crocodile, expecting my words to reach Ivan Matveitch from a distance and to flatter his vanity.

"Alive and well," he answered, as though from a long way off or from under the bed, though I was standing close beside him. "Alive and well; but of that later. . . . How are things going?"

As though purposely not hearing the question, I was just beginning with sympathetic haste to question him how he was, what it was like in the crocodile, and what, in fact, there was inside a crocodile. Both friendship and common civility demanded this. But with capricious annoyance he interrupted me.

"How are things going?" he shouted, in a shrill and on this occasion particularly revolting voice, addressing me peremptorily as usual.

I described to him my whole conversation with Timofey Semyonitch down to the smallest detail. As I told my story I tried to show my resentment in my voice.

340

"The old man is right," Ivan Matveitch pronounced as abruptly as usual in his conversation with me. "I like practical people, and can't endure sentimental milk-sops. I am ready to admit, however, that your idea about a special commission is not altogether absurd. I certainly have a great deal to report, both from a scientific and from an ethical point of view. But now all this has taken a new and unexpected aspect, and it is not worth while to trouble about mere salary. Listen attentively. Are you sitting down?"

"No, I am standing up."

"Sit down on the floor if there is nothing else, and listen attentively.

Resentfully I took a chair and put it down on the floor with a bang, in my anger.

"Listen," he began dictatorially. "The public came to-day in masses. There was no room left in the evening, and the police came in to keep order. At eight o'clock, that is, earlier than usual, the proprietor thought it necessary to close the shop and end the exhibition to count the money he had taken and prepare for to-morrow more conveniently. So I know there will be a regular fair to-morrow. So we may assume that all the most cultivated people in the capital, the ladies of the best society, the foreign ambassadors, the leading lawyers and so on, will all be present. What's more, people will be flowing here from the remotest provinces of our vast and interesting empire. The upshot of it is that I am the cynosure of all eyes, and though hidden to sight, I am eminent. I shall teach the idle crowd. Taught by experience, I shall be an example of greatness and resignation to fate! I shall be, so to say, a pulpit from which to instruct mankind. The mere biological details I can furnish about the monster I am inhabiting are of priceless value. And so, far from repining at what has happened, I confidently hope for the most brilliant of careers."

"You won't find it wearisome?" I asked sarcastically.

341

What irritated me more than anything was the extreme pomposity of his language. Nevertheless, it all rather disconcerted me. "What on earth, what, can this frivolous blockhead find to be so cocky about?" I muttered to myself. "He ought to be crying instead of being cocky."

"No!" he answered my observation sharply, "for I am full of great ideas, only now can I at leisure ponder over the amelioration of the lot of humanity. Truth and light will come forth now from the crocodile. I shall certainly develop a new economic theory of my own and I shall be proud of it—which I have hitherto been prevented from doing by my official duties and by trivial distractions. I shall refute everything and be a new Fourier. By the way, did you give Timofey Semyonitch the seven roubles?"

"Yes, out of my own pocket," I answered, trying to emphasise that fact in my voice.

"We will settle it," he answered superciliously. "I confidently expect my salary to be raised, for who should get a rise if not I? I am of the utmost service now. But to business. My wife?"

"You are, I suppose, inquiring after Elena Ivanovna?"

"My wife?" he shouted, this time in a positive squeal.

There was no help for it! Meekly, though gnashing my teeth, I told him how I had left Elena Ivanovna. He did not even hear me out.

"I have special plans in regard to her," he began impatiently. "If I am celebrated *here*, I wish her to be celebrated *there*. Savants, poets, philosophers, foreign mineralogists, statesmen, after conversing in the morning with me, will visit her *salon* in the evening. From next week onwards she must have an 'At Home' every evening. With my salary doubled, we shall have the means for entertaining, and as the entertainment must not go beyond tea and hired footmen—that's settled. Both here and there they will talk of me. I have long thirsted for an

342

opportunity for being talked about, but could not attain it, fettered by my humble position and low grade in the service. And now all this has been attained by a simple gulp on the part of the crocodile. Every word of mine will be listened to, every utterance will be thought over, repeated, printed. And I'll teach them what I am worth! They shall understand at last what abilities they have allowed to vanish in the entrails of a monster. 'This man might have been Foreign Minister or might have ruled a kingdom,' some will say. 'And that man did not rule a kingdom,' others will say. In what way am I inferior to a Garnier-Pagesishky or whatever they are called? My wife must be a worthy second—I have brains, she has beauty and charm. 'She is beautiful, and that is why she is his wife,' some will say. 'She is beautiful *because* she is his wife,' others will amend. To be ready for anything let Elena Ivanovna buy to-morrow the Encyclopædia edited by Andrey Kraevsky, that she may be able to converse on any topic. Above all, let her be sure to read the political leader in the *Petersburg News*, comparing it every day with the *Voice*. I imagine that the proprietor will consent to take me sometimes with the crocodile to my wife's brilliant *salon*. I will be in a tank in the middle of the magnificent drawing-room, and I will scintillate with witticisms which I will prepare in the morning. To the statesman I will impart my projects; to the poet I will speak in rhyme; with the ladies I can be amusing and charming without impropriety, since I shall be no danger to their husbands' peace of mind. To all the rest I shall serve as a pattern of resignation to fate and the will of Providence. I shall make my wife a brilliant literary lady; I shall bring her forward and explain her to the public; as my wife she must be full of the most striking virtues; and if they are right in calling Andrey Alexandrovitch our Russian Alfred de Musset, they will be still more right in calling her our Russian Yevgenia Tour."

I must confess that, although this wild nonsense was rather

in Ivan Matveitch's habitual style, it did occur to me that he was in a fever and delirious. It was the same, everyday Ivan Matveitch, but magnified twenty times.

"My friend," I asked him, "are you hoping for a long life? Tell me, in fact, are you well? How do you eat, how do you sleep, how do you breathe? I am your friend, and you must admit that the incident is most unnatural, and consequently my curiosity is most natural."

"Idle curiosity and nothing else," he pronounced sententiously, "but you shall be satisfied. You ask how I am managing in the entrails of the monster? To begin with, the crocodile, to my amusement, turns out to be perfectly empty. His inside consists of a sort of huge empty sack made of gutta-percha, like the elastic goods sold in the Gorohovy Street, in the Morskaya, and, if I am not mistaken, in the Voznesensky Prospect. Otherwise, if you think of it, how could I find room?"

"Is it possible?" I cried, in a surprise that may well be understood. "Can the crocodile be perfectly empty?"

"Perfectly," Ivan Matveitch maintained sternly and impressively. "And in all probability, it is so constructed by the laws of Nature. The crocodile possesses nothing but jaws furnished with sharp teeth, and besides the jaws, a tail of considerable length—that is all, properly speaking. The middle part between these two extremities is an empty space enclosed by something of the nature of gutta-percha, probably really gutta-percha."

"But the ribs, the stomach, the intestines, the liver, the heart?" I interrupted quite angrily.

"There is nothing, absolutely nothing of all that, and probably there never has been. All that is the idle fancy of frivolous travellers. As one inflates an air-cushion, I am now with my person inflating the crocodile. He is incredibly elastic. Indeed, you might, as the friend of the family, get in with me if you were generous and self-sacrificing enough—and even with you

344

here there would be room to spare. I even think that in the last resort I might send for Elena Ivanovna. However, this void, hollow formation of the crocodile is quite in keeping with the teachings of natural science. If, for instance, one had to construct a new crocodile, the question would naturally present itself. What is the fundamental characteristic of the crocodile? The answer is clear: to swallow human beings. How is one, in constructing the crocodile, to secure that he should swallow people? The answer is clearer still: construct him hollow. It was settled by physics long ago that Nature abhors a vacuum. Hence the inside of the crocodile must be hollow so that it may abhor the vacuum, and consequently swallow and so fill itself with anything it can come across. And that is the sole rational cause why every crocodile swallows men. It is not the same in the constitution of man: the emptier a man's head is, for instance, the less he feels the thirst to fill it, and that is the one exception to the general rule. It is all as clear as day to me now. I have deduced it by my own observation and experience, being, so to say, in the very bowels of Nature, in its retort, listening to the throbbing of its pulse. Even etymology supports me, for the very word crocodile means voracity. Crocodile —*crocodillo*—is evidently an Italian word, dating perhaps from the Egyptian Pharaohs, and evidently derived from the French verb *croquer*, which means to eat, to devour, in general to absorb nourishment. All these remarks I intend to deliver as my first lecture in Elena Ivanovna's *salon* when they take me there in the tank."

"My friend, oughtn't you at least to take some purgative?" I cried involuntarily.

"He is in a fever, a fever, he is feverish!" I repeated to myself in alarm.

"Nonsense!" he answered contemptuously. "Besides, in my present position it would be most inconvenient. I knew, though, you would be sure to talk of taking medicine."

"But, my friend, how . . . how do you take food now? Have you dined to-day?"

"No, but I am not hungry, and most likely I shall never take food again. And that, too, is quite natural; filling the whole interior of the crocodile I make him feel always full. Now he need not be fed for some years. On the other hand, nourished by me, he will naturally impart to me all the vital juices of his body; it is the same as with some accomplished coquettes who embed themselves and their whole persons for the night in raw steak, and then, after their morning bath, are fresh, supple, buxom and fascinating. In that way nourishing the crocodile, I myself obtain nourishment from him, consequently we mutually nourish one another. But as it is difficult even for a crocodile to digest a man like me, he must, no doubt, be conscious of a certain weight in his stomach—an organ which he does not, however, possess—and that is why, to avoid causing the creature suffering, I do not often turn over, and although I could turn over I do not do so from humanitarian motives. This is the one drawback of my present position, and in an allegorical sense Timofey Semyonitch was right in saying I was lying like a log. But I will prove that even lying like a log—nay, that only lying like a log—one can revolutionise the lot of mankind. All the great ideas and movements of our newspapers and magazines have evidently been the work of men who were lying like logs; that is why they call them divorced from the realities of life—but what does it matter, their saying that! I am constructing now a complete system of my own, and you wouldn't believe how easy it is! You have only to creep into a secluded corner or into a crocodile, to shut your eyes, and you immediately devise a perfect millennium for mankind. When you went away this afternoon I set to work at once and have already invented three systems, now I am preparing the fourth. It is true that at first one must refute everything that has gone before, but from the crocodile it is so

346

easy to refute it; besides, it all becomes clearer, seen from the inside of the crocodile. . . . There are some drawbacks, though small ones, in my position, however; it is somewhat damp here and covered with a sort of slime; moreover, there is rather a smell of india-rubber exactly like the smell of my old goloshes. That is all, there are no other drawbacks."

"Ivan Matveitch," I interrupted, "all this is a miracle in which I can scarcely believe. And can you, can you intend never to dine again?"

"What trivial nonsense you are troubling about, you thought-less, frivolous creature! I talk to you about great ideas, and you . . . Understand that I am sufficiently nourished by the great ideas which light up the darkness in which I am enveloped. The good-natured proprietor has, however, after consulting the kindly *Mutter*, decided with her that they will every morning insert into the monster's jaws a bent metal tube, something like a whistle pipe, by means of which I can absorb coffee or broth with bread soaked in it. The pipe has already been bespoken in the neighbourhood, but I think this is superfluous luxury. I hope to live at least a thousand years, if it is true that crocodiles live so long, which, by the way—good thing I thought of it—you had better look up in some natural history to-morrow and tell me, for I may have been mistaken and have mixed it up with some excavated monster. There is only one reflection rather troubles me: as I am dressed in cloth and have boots on, the crocodile can obviously not digest me. Besides, I am alive, and so am opposing the process of digestion with my whole will power; for you can understand that I do not wish to be turned into what all nourishment turns into, for that would be too humiliating for me. But there is one thing I am afraid of: in a thousand years the cloth of my coat, unfortunately of Russian make, may decay, and then, left without clothing, I might perhaps, in spite of my indignation, begin to be digested; and though by day nothing would induce me to allow it, at night,

347

in my sleep, when a man's will deserts him, I may be overtaken by the humiliating destiny of a potato, a pancake, or veal. Such an idea reduces me to fury. This alone is an argument for the revision of the tariff and the encouragement of the importation of English cloth, which is stronger and so will withstand Nature longer when one is swallowed by a crocodile. At the first opportunity I will impart this idea to some statesman and at the same time to the political writers on our Petersburg dailies. Let them publish it abroad. I trust this will not be the only idea they will borrow from me. I foresee that every morning a regular crowd of them, provided with quarter-roubles from the editorial office, will be flocking round me to seize my ideas on the telegrams of the previous day. In brief, the future presents itself to me in the rosiest light."

"Fever, fever!" I whispered to myself.

"My friend, and freedom?" I asked, wishing to learn his views thoroughly. "You are, so to speak, in prison, while every man has a right to the enjoyment of freedom."

"You are a fool," he answered. "Savages love independence, wise men love order; and if there is no order . . ."

"Ivan Matveitch, spare me, please!"

"Hold your tongue and listen!" he squealed, vexed at my interrupting him. "Never has my spirit soared as now. In my narrow refuge there is only one thing that I dread—the literary criticisms of the monthlies and the hiss of our satirical papers. I am afraid that thoughtless visitors, stupid and envious people and nihilists in general, may turn me into ridicule. But I will take measures. I am impatiently awaiting the response of the public to-morrow, and especially the opinion of the newspapers. You must tell me about the papers to-morrow."

"Very good; to-morrow I will bring a perfect pile of papers with me."

"To-morrow it is too soon to expect reports in the news-

348

papers, for it will take four days for it to be advertised. But from to-day come to me every evening by the back way through the yard. I am intending to employ you as my secretary. You shall read the newspapers and magazines to me, and I will dictate to you my ideas and give you commissions. Be particularly careful not to forget the foreign telegrams. Let all the European telegrams be here every day. But enough; most likely you are sleepy by now. Go home, and do not think of what I said just now about criticisms: I am not afraid of it, for the critics themselves are in a critical position. One has only to be wise and virtuous and one will certainly get on to a pedestal. If not Socrates, then Diogenes, or perhaps both of them together—that is my future rôle among mankind."

So frivolously and boastfully did Ivan Matveitch hasten to express himself before me, like feverish weak-willed women who, as we are told by the proverb, cannot keep a secret. All that he told me about the crocodile struck me as most suspicious. How was it possible that the crocodile was absolutely hollow? I don't mind betting that he was bragging from vanity and partly to humiliate me. It is true that he was an invalid and one must make allowances for invalids; but I must frankly confess, I never could endure Ivan Matveitch. I have been trying all my life, from a child up, to escape from his tutelage and have not been able to! A thousand times over I have been tempted to break with him altogether, and every time I have been drawn to him again, as though I were still hoping to prove something to him or to revenge myself on him. A strange thing, this friendship! I can positively assert that nine-tenths of my friendship for him was made up of malice. On this occasion, however, we parted with genuine feeling.

"Your friend a very clever man!" the German said to me in an undertone as he moved to see me out; he had been listening all the time attentively to our conversation.

"À *propos*," I said, "while I think of it: how much would

you ask for your crocodile in case anyone wanted to buy it?"

Ivan Matveitch, who heard the question, was waiting with curiosity for the answer; it was evident that he did not want the German to ask too little; anyway, he cleared his throat in a peculiar way on hearing my question.

At first the German would not listen—was positively angry.

"No one will dare my own crocodile to buy!" he cried furiously, and turned as red as a boiled lobster. "Me not want to sell the crocodile! I would not for the crocodile a million thalers take. I took a hundred and thirty thalers from the public to-day, and I shall to-morrow ten thousand take, and then a hundred thousand every day I shall take. I will not him sell."

Ivan Matveitch positively chuckled with satisfaction. Controlling myself—for I felt it was a duty to my friend—I hinted coolly and reasonably to the crazy German that his calculations were not quite correct, that if he makes a hundred thousand every day, all Petersburg will have visited him in four days, and then there will be no one left to bring him roubles, that life and death are in God's hands, that the crocodile may burst or Ivan Matveitch may fall ill and die, and so on and so on.

The German grew pensive.

"I will him drops from the chemist's get," he said, after pondering, "and will save your friend that he die not."

"Drops are all very well," I answered, "but consider, too, that the thing may get into the law courts. Ivan Matveitch's wife may demand the restitution of her lawful spouse. You are intending to get rich, but do you intend to give Elena Ivanovna a pension?"

"No, me not intend," said the German in stern decision.

"No, we not intend," said the *Mutter*, with positive malignancy.

"And so would it not be better for you to accept something now, at once, a secure and solid though moderate sum, than to

350

leave things to chance? I ought to tell you that I am inquiring simply from curiosity."

The German drew the *Mutter* aside to consult with her in a corner where there stood a case with the largest and ugliest monkey of his collection.

"Well, you will see!" said Ivan Matveitch.

As for me, I was at that moment burning with the desire, first, to give the German a thrashing, next, to give the *Mutter* an even sounder one, and, thirdly, to give Ivan Matveitch the soundest thrashing of all for his boundless vanity. But all this paled beside the answer of the rapacious German.

After consultation with the *Mutter* he demanded for his crocodile fifty thousand roubles in bonds of the last Russian loan with lottery voucher attached, a brick house in Gorohovy Street with a chemist's shop attached, and in addition the rank of Russian colonel.

"You see!" Ivan Matveitch cried triumphantly. "I told you so! Apart from this last senseless desire for the rank of a colonel, he is perfectly right, for he fully understands the present value of the monster he is exhibiting. The economic principle before everything!"

"Upon my word!" I cried furiously to the German. "But what should you be made a colonel for? What exploit have you performed? What service have you done? In what way have you gained military glory? You are really crazy!"

"Crazy!" cried the German, offended. "No, a person very sensible, but you very stupid! I have a colonel deserved for that I have a crocodile shown and in him a live *Hofrath* sitting! And a Russian can a crocodile not show and a live *Hofrath* in him sitting! Me extremely clever man and much wish colonel to be!"

"Well, good-bye, then, Ivan Matveitch!" I cried, shaking with fury, and I went out of the crocodile room almost at a run.

I felt that in another minute I could not have answered for myself. The unnatural expectations of these two blockheads were insupportable. The cold air refreshed me and somewhat moderated my indignation. At last, after spitting vigorously fifteen times on each side, I took a cab, got home, undressed and flung myself into bed. What vexed me more than anything was my having become his secretary. Now I was to die of boredom there every evening, doing the duty of a true friend! I was ready to beat myself for it, and I did, in fact, after putting out the candle and pulling up the bedclothes, punch myself several times on the head and various parts of my body. That somewhat relieved me, and at last I fell asleep fairly soundly, in fact, for I was very tired. All night long I could dream of nothing but monkeys, but towards morning I dreamt of Elena Ivanovna.

IV

THE monkeys I dreamed about, I surmise, because they were shut up in the case at the German's; but Elena Ivanovna was a different story.

I may as well say at once, I loved the lady, but I make haste —post-haste—to make a qualification. I loved her as a father, neither more nor less. I judge that because I often felt an irresistible desire to kiss her little head or her rosy cheek. And though I never carried out this inclination, I would not have refused even to kiss her lips. And not merely her lips, but her teeth, which always gleamed so charmingly like two rows of pretty, well-matched pearls when she laughed. She laughed extraordinarily often. Ivan Matveitch in demonstrative moments used to call her his "darling absurdity"—a name extremely happy and appropriate. She was a perfect sugar-plum, and that was all one could say of her. Therefore I am utterly at a loss to understand what possessed Ivan Matveitch to imagine his wife as a Russian Yevgenia Tour? Anyway, my dream, with the exception of the monkeys, left a most pleasant impression upon me, and going over all the incidents of the previous day as I drank my morning cup of tea, I resolved to go and see Elena Ivanovna at once on my way to the office—which, indeed, I was bound to do as the friend of the family.

In a tiny little room out of the bedroom—the so-called little drawing-room, though their big drawing-room was little too—Elena Ivanovna was sitting, in some half-transparent morning wrapper, on a smart little sofa before a little tea-table, drinking coffee out of a little cup in which she was dipping a minute biscuit. She was ravishingly pretty, but struck me as being at the same time rather pensive.

"Ah, that's you, naughty man!" she said, greeting me with an absent-minded smile. "Sit down, feather-head, have some coffee. Well, what were you doing yesterday? Were you at the masquerade?"

"Why, were you? I don't go, you know. Besides, yesterday I was visiting our captive. . . ." I sighed and assumed a pious expression as I took the coffee.

"Whom? . . . What captive? . . . Oh, yes! Poor fellow! Well, how is he—bored? Do you know . . . I wanted to ask you . . . I suppose I can ask for a divorce now?"

"A divorce!" I cried in indignation and almost spilled the coffee. "It's that swarthy fellow," I thought to myself bitterly.

There was a certain swarthy gentleman with little moustaches who was something in the architectural line, and who came far too often to see them, and was extremely skilful in amusing Elena Ivanovna. I must confess I hated him and there was no doubt that he had succeeded in seeing Elena Ivanovna yesterday either at the masquerade or even here, and putting all sorts of nonsense into her head.

"Why," Elena Ivanovna rattled off hurriedly, as though it were a lesson she had learnt, "if he is going to stay on in the crocodile, perhaps not come back all his life, while I sit waiting for him here! A husband ought to live at home, and not in a crocodile. . . ."

"But this was an unforeseen occurrence," I was beginning, in very comprehensible agitation.

"Oh, no, don't talk to me, I won't listen, I won't listen," she cried, suddenly getting quite cross. "You are always against me, you wretch! There's no doing anything with you, you will never give me any advice! Other people tell me that I can get a divorce because Ivan Matveitch will not get his salary now."

"Elena Ivanovna! is it you I hear!" I exclaimed pathetically. "What villain could have put such an idea into your head? And divorce on such a trivial ground as a salary is quite impossible. And poor Ivan Matveitch, poor Ivan Matveitch is, so to speak, burning with love for you even in the bowels of the monster. What's more, he is melting away with love like a lump of sugar. Yesterday while you were enjoying yourself at the masquerade, he was saying that he might in the last resort send for you as his lawful spouse to join him in the entrails of the monster, especially as it appears the crocodile is exceedingly roomy, not only able to accommodate two but even three persons. . . ."

And then I told her all that interesting part of my conversation the night before with Ivan Matveitch.

"What, what!" she cried, in surprise. "You want me to get into the monster too, to be with Ivan Matveitch? What an idea! And how am I to get in there, in my hat and crinoline? Heavens, what foolishness! And what should I look like while I was getting into it, and very likely there would be someone there to see me! It's absurd! And what should I have to eat there? And . . . and . . . and what should I do there when . . . Oh, my goodness, what will they think of next? . . . And

354

what should I have to amuse me there? . . . You say there's a smell of gutta-percha? And what should I do if we quarrelled —should we have to go on staying there side by side? Foo, how horrid!"

"I agree, I agree with all those arguments, my sweet Elena Ivanovna," I interrupted, striving to express myself with that natural enthusiasm which always overtakes a man when he feels the truth is on his side. "But one thing you have not appreciated in all this, you have not realised that he cannot live without you if he is inviting you there; that is a proof of love, passionate, faithful, ardent love. . . . You have thought too little of his love, dear Elena Ivanovna!"

"I won't, I won't, I won't hear anything about it!" waving me off with her pretty little hand with glistening pink nails that had just been washed and polished. "Horrid man! You will reduce me to tears! Get into it yourself, if you like the prospect. You are his friend, get in and keep him company, and spend your life discussing some tedious science. . . ."

"You are wrong to laugh at this suggestion"—I checked the frivolous woman with dignity—"Ivan Matveitch has invited me as it is. You, of course, are summoned there by duty; for me, it would be an act of generosity. But when Ivan Matveitch described to me last night the elasticity of the crocodile, he hinted very plainly that there would be room not only for you two, but for me also as a friend of the family, especially if I wished to join you, and therefore . . ."

"How so, the three of us?" cried Elena Ivanovna, looking at me in surprise. "Why, how should we . . . are we going to be all three there together? Ha-ha-ha! How silly you both are! Ha-ha-ha! I shall certainly pinch you all the time, you wretch! Ha-ha-ha! Ha-ha-ha!"

And falling back on the sofa, she laughed till she cried. All this—the tears and the laughter—were so fascinating that I could not resist rushing eagerly to kiss her hand, which she did not oppose, though she did pinch my ears lightly as a sign of reconciliation.

Then we both grew very cheerful, and I described to her in detail all Ivan Matveitch's plans. The thought of her evening receptions and her *salon* pleased her very much.

"Only I should need a great many new dresses," she observed, "and so Ivan Matveitch must send me as much of his salary as possible and as soon as possible. Only . . . only I don't know about that," she added thoughtfully. "How can he be brought here in the tank? That's very absurd. I don't want my husband to be carried about in a tank. I should feel quite ashamed for my visitors to see it. . . . I don't want that, no, I don't."

"By the way, while I think of it, was Timofey Semyonitch here yesterday?"

"Oh, yes, he was; he came to comfort me, and do you know, we played cards all the time. He played for sweetmeats, and if I lost he was to kiss my hands. What a wretch he is! And only fancy, he almost came to the masquerade with me, really!"

"He was carried away by his feelings!" I observed. "And who would not be with you, you charmer?"

"Oh, get along with your compliments! Stay, I'll give you a pinch as a parting present. I've learnt to pinch awfully well lately. Well, what do you say to that? By the way, you say Ivan Matveitch spoke several times of me yesterday?"

"N-no, not exactly. . . . I must say he is thinking more now of the fate of humanity, and wants . . ."

"Oh, let him! You needn't go on! I am sure it's fearfully boring. I'll go and see him some time. I shall certainly go to-morrow. Only not to-day; I've got a headache, and besides, there will be such a lot of people there to-day. . . . They'll say, 'That's his wife,' and I shall feel ashamed. . . . Good-bye. You will be . . . there this evening, won't you?"

"To see him, yes. He asked me to go and take him the papers."

356

"That's capital. Go and read to him. But don't come and see me to-day. I am not well, and perhaps I may go and see someone. Good-bye, you naughty man."

"It's that swarthy fellow is going to see her this evening," I thought.

At the office, of course, I gave no sign of being consumed by these cares and anxieties. But soon I noticed some of the most progressive papers seemed to be passing particularly rapidly from hand to hand among my colleagues, and were being read with an extremely serious expression of face. The first one that reached me was the *News-sheet*, a paper of no particular party but humanitarian in general, for which it was regarded with contempt among us, though it was read. Not without surprise I read in it the following paragraph:

"Yesterday strange rumours were circulating among the spacious ways and sumptuous buildings of our vast metropolis. A certain well-known *bon-vivant* of the highest society, probably weary of the *cuisine* at Borel's and at the X. Club, went into the Arcade, into the place where an immense crocodile recently brought to the metropolis is being exhibited, and insisted on its being prepared for his dinner. After bargaining with the proprietor he at once set to work to devour him (that is, not the proprietor, a very meek and punctilious German, but his crocodile), cutting juicy morsels with his penknife from the living animal, and swallowing them with extraordinary rapidity. By degrees the whole crocodile disappeared into the vast recesses of his stomach, so that he was even on the point of attacking an ichneumon, a constant companion of the crocodile, probably imagining that the latter would be as savoury. We are by no means opposed to that new article of diet with which foreign *gourmands* have long been familiar. We have, indeed, predicted that it would come. English lords and travellers make up regular parties for catching crocodiles in Egypt, and consume the back of the monster cooked like

357

beef-steak, with mustard, onions and potatoes. The French who followed in the train of Lesseps prefer the paws baked in hot ashes, which they do, however, in opposition to the English, who laugh at them. Probably both ways would be appreciated among us. For our part, we are delighted at a new branch of industry, of which our great and varied fatherland stands pre-eminently in need. Probably before a year is out crocodiles will be brought in hundreds to replace this first one, lost in the stomach of a Petersburg *gourmand*. And why should not the crocodile be acclimatised among us in Russia? If the water of the Neva is too cold for these interesting strangers, there are ponds in the capital and rivers and lakes outside it. Why not breed crocodiles at Pargolovo, for instance, or at Pavlovsk, in the Presnensky Ponds and in Samoteka in Moscow? While providing agreeable, wholesome nourishment for our fastidious *gourmands*, they might at the same time entertain the ladies who walk about these ponds and instruct the children in natural history. The crocodile skin might be used for making jewel-cases, boxes, cigar-cases, pocket-books, and possibly more than one thousand saved up in the greasy notes that are peculiarly beloved of merchants might be laid by in crocodile skin. We hope to return more than once to this interesting topic."

Though I had foreseen something of the sort, yet the reckless inaccuracy of the paragraph overwhelmed me. Finding no one with whom to share my impression, I turned to Prohor Savvitch who was sitting opposite to me, and noticed that the latter had been watching me for some time, while in his hand he held the *Voice* as though he were on the point of passing it to me. Without a word he took the *News-sheet* from me, and as he handed me the *Voice* he drew a line with his nail against an article to which he probably wished to call my attention. This Prohor Savvitch was a very queer man: a taciturn old bachelor, he was not on intimate terms with any of us, scarcely spoke to

358

anyone in the office, always had an opinion of his own about everything, but could not bear to impart it to anyone. He lived alone. Hardly anyone among us had ever been in his lodging.

This was what I read in the *Voice*.

"Everyone knows that we are progressive and humanitarian and want to be on a level with Europe in this respect. But in spite of all our exertions and the efforts of our paper we are still far from maturity, as may be judged from the shocking incident which took place yesterday in the Arcade and which we predicted long ago. A foreigner arrives in the capital bringing with him a crocodile which he begins exhibiting in the Arcade. We immediately hasten to welcome a new branch of useful industry such as our powerful and varied fatherland stands in great need of. Suddenly yesterday at four o'clock in the afternoon a gentleman of exceptional stoutness enters the foreigner's shop in an intoxicated condition, pays his entrance money, and immediately without any warning leaps into the jaws of the crocodile, who was forced, of course, to swallow him, if only from an instinct of self-preservation, to avoid being crushed. Tumbling into the inside of the crocodile, the stranger at once dropped asleep. Neither the shouts of the foreign proprietor, nor the lamentations of his terrified family, nor threats to send for the police made the slightest impression. Within the crocodile was heard nothing but laughter and a promise to flay him (*sic*), though the poor mammal, compelled to swallow such a mass, was vainly shedding tears. An uninvited guest is worse than a Tartar. But in spite of the proverb the insolent visitor would not leave. We do not know how to explain such barbarous incidents which prove our lack of culture and disgrace us in the eyes of foreigners. The recklessness of the Russian temperament has found a fresh outlet. It may be asked what was the object of the uninvited visitor? A warm and comfortable abode? But there are many excellent

359

houses in the capital with very cheap and comfortable lodgings, with the Neva water laid on, and a staircase lighted by gas, frequently with a hall-porter maintained by the proprietor. We would call our readers' attention to the barbarous treatment of domestic animals: it is difficult, of course, for the crocodile to digest such a mass all at once, and now he lies swollen out to the size of a mountain, awaiting death in insufferable agonies. In Europe persons guilty of inhumanity towards domestic animals have long been punished by law. But in spite of our European enlightenment, in spite of our European pavements, in spite of the European architecture of our houses, we are still far from shaking off our time-honoured traditions.

"Though the houses are new, the conventions are old."

And, indeed, the houses are not new, at least the staircases in them are not. We have more than once in our paper alluded to the fact that in the Petersburg Side in the house of the merchant Lukyanov the steps of the wooden staircase have decayed, fallen away, and have long been a danger for Afimya Skapidarov, a soldier's wife who works in the house, and is often obliged to go up the stairs with water or armfuls of wood. At last our predictions have come true: yesterday evening at half-past eight Afimya Skapidarov fell down with a basin of soup and broke her leg. We do not know whether Lukyanov will mend his staircase now, Russians are often wise after the event, but the victim of Russian carelessness has by now been taken to the hospital. In the same way we shall never cease to maintain that the house-porters who clear away the mud from the wooden pavement in the Viborgsky Side ought not to spatter the legs of passers-by, but should throw the mud up into heaps as is done in Europe," and so on, and so on.

"What's this?" I asked in some perplexity, looking at Prohor Savvitch. "What's the meaning of it?"

"How do you mean?"

"Why, upon my word! Instead of pitying Ivan Matveitch, they pity the crocodile!"

"What of it? They have pity even for a beast, a *mammal*. We must be up to Europe, mustn't we? They have a very warm feeling for crocodiles there too. He-he-he!"

Saying this, queer old Prohor Savvitch dived into his papers and would not utter another word.

I stuffed the *Voice* and the *News-sheet* into my pocket and collected as many old copies of the newspapers as I could find for Ivan Matveitch's diversion in the evening, and though the evening was far off, yet on this occasion I slipped away from the office early to go to the Arcade and look, if only from a distance, at what was going on there, and to listen to the various remarks and currents of opinion. I foresaw that there would be a regular crush there, and turned up the collar of my coat to meet it. I somehow felt rather shy—so unaccustomed are we to publicity. But I feel that I have no right to report my own prosaic feelings when faced with this remarkable and original incident.

Bobok

From Somebody's Diary

SEMYON ARDALYONOVITCH said to me all of a sudden the day before yesterday: "Why, will you ever be sober, Ivan Ivanovitch? Tell me that, pray."

A strange requirement. I did not resent it, I am a timid man; but here they have actually made me out mad. An artist painted my portrait as it happened: "After all, you are a literary man," he said. I submitted, he exhibited it. I read: "Go and look at that morbid face suggesting insanity."

It may be so, but think of putting it ᴊ bluntly into print. In print everything ought to be decorous; there ought to be ideals, while instead of that . . .

Say it indirectly, at least; that's what you have style for. But no, he doesn't care to do it indirectly. Nowadays humour and a fine style have disappeared, and abuse is accepted as wit. I do not resent it: but God knows I am not enough of a literary man to go out of my mind. I have written a novel, it has not been published. I have written articles—they have been refused. Those articles I took about from one editor to another; everywhere they refused them: you have no salt they told me. "What sort of salt do you want?" I asked with a jeer. "Attic salt?"

They did not even understand. For the most part I translate from the French for the booksellers. I write advertisements for shopkeepers too: "Unique opportunity! Fine tea, from our own plantations . . ." I made a nice little sum over a panegyric on his deceased excellency Pyotr Matveyitch. I compiled the "Art of pleasing the ladies", a commission from a bookseller.

362

I have brought out some six little works of this kind in the course of my life. I am thinking of making a collection of the *bons mots* of Voltaire, but am afraid it may seem a little flat to our people. Voltaire's no good now; nowadays we want a cudgel, not Voltaire. We knock each other's last teeth out nowadays. Well, so that's the whole extent of my literary activity. Though indeed I do send round letters to the editors gratis and fully signed. I give them all sorts of counsels and admonitions, criticise and point out the true path. The letter I sent last week to an editor's office was the fortieth I had sent in the last two years. I have wasted four roubles over stamps alone for them. My temper is at the bottom of it all.

I believe that the artist who painted me did so not for the sake of literature, but for the sake of two symmetrical warts on my forehead, a natural phenomenon, he would say. They have no ideas, so now they are out for phenomena. And didn't he succeed in getting my warts in his portrait—to the life. That is what they call realism.

And as to madness, a great many people were put down as mad among us last year. And in such language! "With such original talent" . . . "and yet, after all, it appears" . . . "however, one ought to have foreseen it long ago." That is rather artful; so that from the point of view of pure art one may really commend it. Well, but after all, these so-called madmen have turned out cleverer than ever. So it seems the critics can call them mad, but they cannot produce anyone better.

The wisest of all, in my opinion, is he who can, if only once a month, call himself a fool—a faculty unheard of nowadays. In old days, once a year at any rate a fool would recognise that he was a fool, but nowadays not a bit of it. And they have so muddled things up that there is no telling a fool from a wise man. They have done that on purpose.

I remember a witty Spaniard saying when, two hundred and fifty years ago, the French built their first madhouses: "They have shut up all their fools in a house apart, to make sure that they are wise men themselves." Just so: you don't show your own wisdom by shutting someone else in a madhouse. "K. has gone out of his mind, means that we are sane now." No, it doesn't mean that yet.

Hang it though, why am I maundering on? I go on grumbling and grumbling. Even my maidservant is sick of me. Yesterday a friend came to see me. "Your style is changing," he said; "it is choppy: you chop and chop—and then a parenthesis, then a parenthesis in the parenthesis, then you stick in something else in brackets, then you begin chopping and chopping again."

The friend is right. Something strange is happening to me. My character is changing and my head aches. I am beginning to see and hear strange things, not voices exactly, but as though someone beside me were muttering, "*bobok, bobok, bobok!*"

What's the meaning of this *bobok*? I must divert my mind.

I went out in search of diversion, I hit upon a funeral. A distant relation—a collegiate counsellor, however. A widow and five daughters, all marriageable young ladies. What must it come to even to keep them in slippers. Their father managed it, but now there is only a little pension. They will have to eat humble pie. They have always received me ungraciously. And indeed I should not have gone to the funeral now had it not been for a peculiar circumstance. I followed the procession to the cemetery with the rest; they were stuck-up and held aloof from me. My uniform was certainly rather shabby. It's five-and-twenty years, I believe, since I was at the cemetery; what a wretched place!

To begin with the smell. There were fifteen hearses, with palls varying in expensiveness; there were actually two catafalques. One was a general's and one some lady's. There were many mourners, a great deal of feigned mourning and a great

364

deal of open gaiety. The clergy have nothing to complain of; it brings them a good income. But the smell, the smell. I should not like to be one of the clergy here.

I kept glancing at the faces of the dead cautiously, distrusting my impressionability. Some had a mild expression, some looked unpleasant. As a rule the smiles were disagreeable, and in some cases very much so. I don't like them; they haunt one's dreams.

During the service I went out of the church into the air: it was a grey day, but dry. It was cold too, but then it was October. I walked about among the tombs. They are of different grades. The third grade cost thirty roubles; it's decent and not so very dear. The first two grades are tombs in the church and under the porch; they cost a pretty penny. On this occasion they were burying in tombs of the third grade six persons, among them the general and the lady.

I looked into the graves—and it was horrible: water and such water! Absolutely green, and . . . but there, why talk of it! The gravedigger was baling it out every minute. I went out while the service was going on and strolled outside the gates. Close by was an almshouse, and a little further off there was a restaurant. It was not a bad little restaurant: there was lunch and everything. There were lots of the mourners here. I noticed a great deal of gaiety and genuine heartiness. I had something to eat and drink.

Then I took part in the bearing of the coffin from the church to the grave. Why is it that corpses in their coffins are so heavy? They say it is due to some sort of inertia, that the body is no longer directed by its owner . . . or some nonsense of that sort, in opposition to the laws of mechanics and common sense. I don't like to hear people who have nothing but a general education venture to solve the problems that require special knowledge; and with us that's done continually. Civilians love to pass opinions about subjects that are the

365

province of the soldier and even of the field-marshal; while men who have been educated as engineers prefer discussing philosophy and political economy.

I did not go to the requiem service. I have some pride, and if I am only received owing to some special necessity, why force myself on their dinners, even if it be a funeral dinner. The only thing I don't understand is why I stayed at the cemetery; I sat on a tombstone and sank into appropriate reflections.

I began with the Moscow exhibition and ended with reflecting upon astonishment in the abstract. My deductions about astonishment were these:

"To be surprised at everything is stupid of course, and to be astonished at nothing is a great deal more becoming and for some reason accepted as good form. But that is not really true. To my mind to be astonished at nothing is much more stupid than to be astonished at everything. And, moreover, to be astonished at nothing is almost the same as feeling respect for nothing. And indeed a stupid man is incapable of feeling respect."

"But what I desire most of all is to feel respect. I *thirst* to feel respect," one of my acquaintances said to me the other day.

He thirsts to feel respect! Goodness, I thought, what would happen to you if you dared to print that nowadays?

At that point I sank into forgetfulness. I don't like reading the epitaphs of tombstones: they are everlastingly the same. An unfinished sandwich was lying on the tombstone near me; stupid and inappropriate. I threw it on the ground, as it was not bread but only a sandwich. Though I believe it is not a sin to throw bread on the earth, but only on the floor. I must look it up in Suvorin's calendar.

I suppose I sat there a long time—too long a time, in fact; I must have lain down on a long stone which was of the shape of a marble coffin. And how it happened I don't know, but I began to hear things of all sorts being said. At first I did not pay attention to it, but treated it with contempt. But the conversation went on. I heard muffled sounds as though the speakers' mouths were covered with a pillow, and at the same time they were distinct and very near. I came to myself, sat up and began listening attentively.

"Your Excellency, it's utterly impossible. You led hearts, I return your lead, and here you play the seven of diamonds. You ought to have given me a hint about diamonds."

"What, play by hard and fast rules? Where is the charm of that?"

"You must, your Excellency. One can't do anything without something to go upon. We must play with dummy, let one hand not be turned up."

"Well, you won't find a dummy here."

What conceited words! And it was queer and unexpected. One was such a ponderous, dignified voice, the other softly suave; I should not have believed it if I had not heard it myself. I had not been to the requiem dinner, I believe. And yet how could they be playing preference here and what general was this? That the sounds came from under the tombstones of that there could be no doubt. I bent down and read on the tomb:

"Here lies the body of Major-General Pervoyedov . . . a cavalier of such and such orders." Hm! "Passed away in August of this year . . . fifty-seven. . . . Rest, beloved ashes, till the joyful dawn!"

Hm, dash it, it really is a general! There was no monument on the grave from which the obsequious voice came, there was only a tombstone. He must have been a fresh arrival. From his voice he was a lower court councillor.

"Oh-ho-ho-ho!" I heard in a new voice a dozen yards from the general's resting-place, coming from quite a fresh grave.

The voice belonged to a man and a plebeian, mawkish with its affectation of religious fervour. "Oh-ho-ho-ho!"

"Oh, here he is hiccupping again!" cried the haughty and disdainful voice of an irritated lady, apparently of the highest society. "It is an affliction to be by this shopkeeper!"

"I didn't hiccup; why, I've had nothing to eat. It's simply my nature. Really, madam, you don't seem able to get rid of your caprices here."

"Then why did you come and lie down here?"

"They put me here, my wife and little children put me here, I did not lie down here of myself. The mystery of death! And I would not have lain down beside you not for any money; I lie here as befitting my fortune, judging by the price. For we can always do that—pay for a tomb of the third grade."

"You made money, I suppose? You fleeced people?"

"Fleece you, indeed! We haven't seen the colour of your money since January. There's a little bill against you at the shop."

"Well, that's really stupid; to try and recover debts here is too stupid, to my thinking! Go to the surface. Ask my niece —she is my heiress."

"There's no asking anyone now, and no going anywhere. We have both reached our limit and, before the judgment-seat of God, are equal in our sins."

"In our sins," the lady mimicked him contemptuously. "Don't dare to speak to me."

"Oh-ho-ho-ho!"

"You see, the shopkeeper obeys the lady, your Excellency."

"Why shouldn't he?"

"Why, your Excellency, because, as we all know, things are different here."

"Different? How?"

"We are dead, so to speak, your Excellency."

"Oh, yes! But still . . ."

Well, this is an entertainment, it is a fine show, I must say! If it has come to this down here, what can one expect on the surface? But what a queer business! I went on listening, however, though with extreme indignation.

"Yes, I should like a taste of life! Yes, you know . . . I should like a taste of life." I heard a new voice suddenly somewhere in the space between the general and the irritable lady.

"Do you hear, your Excellency, our friend is at the same game again. For three days at a time he says nothing, and then he bursts out with 'I should like a taste of life, yes, a taste of life!' And with such appetite, he-he!"

"And such frivolity."

"It gets hold of him, your Excellency, and do you know, he is growing sleepy, quite sleepy—he has been here since April; and then all of a sudden 'I should like a taste of life!' "

"It is rather dull, though," observed his Excellency.

"It is, your Excellency. Shall we tease Avdotya Ignatyevna again, he-he?"

"No, spare me, please. I can't endure that quarrelsome virago."

"And I can't endure either of you," cried the virago disdainfully. "You are both of you bores and can't tell me anything ideal. I know one little story about you, your Excellency— don't turn up your nose, please—how a manservant swept you out from under a married couple's bed one morning."

"Nasty woman," the general muttered through his teeth.

"Avdotya Ignatyevna, ma'am," the shopkeeper wailed suddenly again, "my dear lady, don't be angry, but tell me, am I going through the ordeal by torment now, or is it something else?"

"Ah, he is at it again, as I expected! For there's a smell from him which means he is turning round!"

"I am not turning round, ma'am, and there's no particular smell from me, for I've kept my body whole as it should be, while you're regularly high. For the smell is really horrible even for a place like this. I don't speak of it, merely from politeness."

"Ah, you horrid, insulting wretch. He positively stinks and talks about me."

"Oh-ho-ho-ho! If only the time for my requiem would come quickly: I should hear their tearful voices over my head, my wife's lament and my children's soft weeping! . . ."

"Well, that's a thing to fret for! They'll stuff themselves with funeral rice and go home. . . . Oh, I wish somebody would wake up!"

"Avdotya Ignatyevna," said the insinuating government clerk, "wait a bit, the new arrivals will speak."

"And are there any young people among them?"

"Yes, there are, Avdotya Ignatyevna. There are some not more than lads."

"Oh, how welcome that would be!"

"Haven't they begun yet?" inquired his Excellency.

"Even those who came the day before yesterday haven't awakened yet, your Excellency. As you know, they sometimes don't speak for a week. It's a good job that to-day and yesterday and the day before they brought a whole lot. As it is, they are all last year's for seventy feet round."

"Yes, it will be interesting."

"Yes, your Excellency, they buried Tarasevitch, the privy councillor, to-day. I knew it from the voices. I know his nephew, he helped to lower the coffin just now."

"Hm, where is he, then?"

"Five steps from you, your Excellency, on the left. . . . Almost at your feet. You should make his acquaintance, your Excellency."

"Hm, no—it's not for me to make advances."

"Oh, he will begin of himself, your Excellency. He will be flattered. Leave it to me, your Excellency, and I . . ."

"Oh, oh! . . . What is happening to me?" croaked the frightened voice of a new arrival.

"A new arrival, your Excellency, a new arrival, thank God! And how quick he's been! Sometimes they don't say a word for a week."

"Oh, I believe it's a young man!" Avdotya Ignatyevna cried shrilly.

"I . . . I . . . it was a complication, and so sudden!" faltered the young man again. "Only the evening before, Schultz said to me, 'There's a complication,' and I died suddenly before morning. Oh! oh!"

"Well, there's no help for it, young man," the general observed graciously, evidently pleased at a new arrival. "You must be comforted. You are kindly welcome to our Vale of Jehoshaphat, so to call it. We are kind-hearted people, you will come to know us and appreciate us. Major-General Vassili Vassilitch Pervoyedov, at your service."

"Oh, no, no! Certainly not! I was at Schultz's; I had a complication, you know, at first it was my chest and a cough, and then I caught a cold: my lungs and influenza . . . and all of a sudden, quite unexpectedly . . . the worst of all was its being so unexpected."

"You say it began with the chest," the government clerk put in suavely, as though he wished to reassure the new arrival.

"Yes, my chest and catarrh and then no catarrh, but still the chest, and I couldn't breathe . . . and you know . . ."

"I know, I know. But if it was the chest you ought to have gone to Ecke and not to Schultz."

"You know, I kept meaning to go to Botkin's, and all at once . . ."

"Botkin is quite prohibitive," observed the general.

371

"Oh, no, he is not forbidding at all; I've heard he is so attentive and foretells everything beforehand."

"His Excellency was referring to his fees," the government clerk corrected him.

"Oh, not at all, he only asks three roubles, and he makes such an examination, and gives you a prescription . . . and I was very anxious to see him, for I have been told . . . Well, gentlemen, had I better go to Ecke or to Botkin?"

"What? To whom?" The general's corpse shook with agreeable laughter. The government clerk echoed it in falsetto.

"Dear boy, dear, delightful boy, how I love you!" Avdotya Ignatyevna squealed ecstatically. "I wish they had put some-one like you next to me."

No, that was too much! And these were the dead of our times! Still, I ought to listen to more and not be in too great a hurry to draw conclusions. That snivelling new arrival—I remember him just now in his coffin—had the expression of a frightened chicken, the most revolting expression in the world! However, let us wait and see.

But what happened next was such a Bedlam that I could not keep it all in my memory. For a great many woke up at once; an official—a civil councillor—woke up, and began discussing at once the project of a new sub-committee in a government department and of the probable transfer of various func-tionaries in connection with the sub-committee—which very greatly interested the general. I must confess I learnt a great deal that was new myself, so much so that I marvelled at the channels by which one may sometimes in the metropolis learn government news. Then an engineer half woke up, but for a long time muttered absolute nonsense, so that our friends left off worrying him and let him lie till he was ready. At last the distinguished lady who had been buried in the morning under the catafalque showed symptoms of the reanimation of the tomb. Lebeziatnikov (for the obsequious lower court councillor whom I detested and who lay beside General Pervoyedov was called, it appears, Lebeziatnikov) became much excited, and surprised that they were all waking up so soon this time. I must own I was surprised too; though some of those who woke had been buried for three days, as, for instance, a very young girl of sixteen who kept giggling . . . giggling in a horrible and predatory way.

"Your Excellency, privy councillor Tarasevitch is waking!" Lebeziatnikov announced with extreme fussiness.

"Eh? What?" the privy councillor, waking up suddenly mumbled, with a lisp of disgust. There was a note of ill-humoured peremptoriness in the sound of his voice.

I listened with curiosity—for during the last few days I had heard something about Tarasevitch—shocking and upsetting in the extreme.

"It's I, your Excellency, so far only I."

"What is your petition? What do you want?"

"Merely to inquire after your Excellency's health; in these unaccustomed surroundings everyone feels at first, as it were, oppressed. . . . General Pervoyedov wishes to have the honour of making your Excellency's acquaintance, and hopes . . ."

"I've never heard of him."

"Surely, your Excellency! General Pervoyedov, Vassili Vassilitch . . ."

"Are you General Pervoyedov?"

"No, your Excellency, I am only the lower court councillor Lebeziatnikov, at your service, but General Pervoyedov . . ."

"Nonsense! And I beg you to leave me alone."

"Let him be." General Pervoyedov at last himself checked with dignity the disgusting officiousness of his sycophant in the grave.

"He is not fully awake, your Excellency, you must consider

373

that; it's the novelty of it all. When he is fully awake he will take it differently."

"Let him be," repeated the general.

"Vassili Vassilitch! Hey, your Excellency!" a perfectly new voice shouted loudly and aggressively from close beside Avdotya Ignatyevna. It was a voice of gentlemanly insolence, with the languid pronunciation now fashionable and an arrogant drawl. "I've been watching you all for the last two hours. Do you remember me, Vassili Vassilitch? My name is Klinevitch, we met at the Volokonskys' where you, too, were received as a guest, I am sure I don't know why."

"What, Count Pyotr Petrovitch? . . . Can it be really you . . . and at such an early age? How sorry I am to hear it."

"Oh, I am sorry myself, though I really don't mind, and I want to amuse myself as far as I can everywhere. And I am not a count but a baron, only a baron. We are only a set of scurvy barons, risen from being flunkeys, but why I don't know and I don't care. I am only a scoundrel of the pseudo-aristocratic society, and I am regarded as 'a charming *polisson*'. My father is a wretched little general, and my mother was at one time received *en haut lieu*. With the help of the Jew Zifel I forged fifty thousand rouble notes last year and then I informed against him, while Julie Charpentier de Lusignan carried off the money to Bordeaux. And only fancy, I was engaged to be married—to a girl still at school, three months under sixteen, with a dowry of ninety thousand. Avdotya Ignatyevna, do you remember how you seduced me fifteen years ago when I was a boy of fourteen in the Corps des Pages?"

"Ah, that's you, you rascal! Well, you are a godsend, anyway, for here. . . ."

"You were mistaken in suspecting your neighbour, the business gentleman, of unpleasant fragrance. . . . I said nothing,

374

but I laughed. The stench came from me: they had to bury me in a nailed-up coffin."

"Ugh, you horrid creature! Still, I am glad you are here; you can't imagine the lack of life and wit here."

"Quite so, quite so, and I intend to start here something original. Your Excellency—I don't mean you, Pervoyedov— your Excellency the other one, Tarasevitch, the privy councillor! Answer! I am Klinevitch, who took you to Mlle. Furie in Lent, do you hear?"

"I do, Klinevitch, and I am delighted, and trust me . . ."

"I wouldn't trust you with a halfpenny, and I don't care. I simply want to kiss you, dear old man, but luckily I can't. Do you know, gentlemen, what this *grand-père's* little game was? He died three or four days ago, and would you believe it, he left a deficit of four hundred thousand government money from the fund for widows and orphans. He was the sole person in control of it for some reason, so that his accounts were not audited for the last eight years. I can fancy what long faces they all have now, and what they call him. It's a delectable thought, isn't it? I have been wondering for the last year how a wretched old man of seventy, gouty and rheumatic, succeeded in preserving the physical energy for his debaucheries—and now the riddle is solved! Those widows and orphans—the very thought of them must have egged him on! I knew about it long ago, I was the only one who did know; it was Julie told me, and as soon as I discovered it, I attacked him in a friendly way at once in Easter week: 'Give me twenty-five thousand, if you don't they'll look into your accounts to-morrow.' And just fancy, he had only thirteen thousand left then, so it seems it was very apropos his dying now. *Grand-père, grand-père;* do you hear?"

"*Cher* Klinevitch, I quite agree with you, and there was no need for you . . . to go into such details. Life is so full of suffering and torment and so little to make up for it . . . that

I wanted at last to be at rest, and so far as I can see I hope to get all I can from here too."

"I bet that he has already sniffed Katiche Berestov!"

"Who? What Katiche?" There was a rapacious quiver in the old man's voice.

"A-ah, what Katiche? Why, here on the left, five paces from me and ten from you. She has been here for five days, and if only you knew, *grand-père*, what a little wretch she is! Of good family and breeding and a monster, a regular monster! I did not introduce her to anyone there, I was the only one who knew her. . . . Katiche, answer!"

"He-he-he!" the girl responded with a jangling laugh, in which there was a note of something as sharp as the prick of a needle. "He-he-he!"

"And a little blonde?" the *grand-père* faltered, drawling out the syllables.

"He-he-he!"

"I . . . have long . . . I have long," the old man faltered breathlessly, "cherished the dream of a little fair thing of fifteen and just in such surroundings."

"Ach, the monster!" cried Avdotya Ignatyevna.

"Enough!" Klinevitch decided. "I see there is excellent material. We shall soon arrange things better. The great thing is to spend the rest of our time cheerfully; but what time? Hey, you, government clerk, Lebeziatnikov or whatever it is, I hear that's your name!"

"Semyon Yevseitch Lebeziatnikov, lower court councillor, at your service, very, very, very much delighted to meet you."

"I don't care whether you are delighted or not, but you seem to know everything here. Tell me first of all how it is we can talk? I've been wondering ever since yesterday. We are dead and yet we are talking and seem to be moving—and yet we are not talking and not moving. What jugglery is this?"

376

"If you want an explanation, baron, Platon Nikolaevitch could give you one better than I."

"What Platon Nikolaevitch is that? To the point. Don't beat about the bush."

"Platon Nikolaevitch is our home-grown philosopher, scientist and Master of Arts. He has brought out several philosophical works, but for the last three months he has been getting quite drowsy, and there is no stirring him up now. Once a week he mutters something utterly irrelevant."

"To the point, to the point!"

"He explains all this by the simplest fact, namely, that when we were living on the surface we mistakenly thought that death there was death. The body revives, as it were, here, the remains of life are concentrated, but only in consciousness. I don't know how to express it, but life goes on, as it were, by inertia. In his opinion everything is concentrated somewhere in consciousness and goes on for two or three months . . . sometimes even for half a year. . . . There is one here, for instance, who is almost completely decomposed, but once every six weeks he suddenly utters one word, quite senseless of course, about some *bobok*,[1] 'Bobok, bobok,' but you see that an imperceptible speck of life is still warm within him."

"It's rather stupid. Well, and how is it I have no sense of smell and yet I feel there's a stench?"

"That . . . he-he . . . Well, on that point our philosopher is a bit foggy. It's apropos of smell, he said, that the stench one perceives here is, so to speak, moral—he-he! It's the stench of the soul, he says, that in these two or three months it may have time to recover itself . . . and this is, so to speak, the last mercy. . . . Only, I think, baron, that these are mystic ravings very excusable in his position. . . ."

"Enough; all the rest of it, I am sure, is nonsense. The great thing is that we have two or three months more of life and then

[1] *i. e.* small bean.

—bobok! I propose to spend these two months as agreeably as possible, and so to arrange everything on a new basis. Gentlemen! I propose to cast aside all shame."

"Ah, let us cast aside all shame, let us!" many voices could be heard saying; and strange to say, several new voices were audible, which must have belonged to others newly awakened. The engineer, now fully awake, boomed out his agreement with peculiar delight. The girl Katiche giggled gleefully.

"Oh, how I long to cast off all shame!" Avdotya Ignatyevna exclaimed rapturously.

"I say, if Avdotya Ignatyevna wants to cast off all shame . . ."

"No, no, no, Klinevitch, I was ashamed up there all the same, but here I should like to cast off shame, I should like it awfully."

"I understand, Klinevitch," boomed the engineer, "that you want to rearrange life here on new and rational principles."

"Oh, I don't care a hang about that! For that we'll wait for Kudeyarov who was brought here yesterday. When he wakes he'll tell you all about it. He is such a personality, such a titanic personality! To-morrow they'll bring along another natural scientist, I believe, an officer for certain, and three or four days later a journalist, and, I believe, his editor with him. But deuce take them all, there will be a little group of us anyway, and things will arrange themselves. Though meanwhile I don't want us to be telling lies. That's all I care about, for that is one thing that matters. One cannot exist on the surface without lying, for life and lying are synonymous, but here we will amuse ourselves by not lying. Hang it all, the grave has some value after all! We'll all tell our stories aloud, and we won't be ashamed of anything. First of all I'll tell you about myself. I am one of the predatory kind, you know. All that was bound and held in check by rotten cords up there on the surface. Away with cords and let us spend these two months in shameless truthfulness! Let us strip and be naked!"

"Let us be naked, let us be naked!" cried all the voices.

"I long to be naked, I long to be," Avdotya Ignatyevna shrilled.

"Ah . . . ah, I see we shall have fun here; I don't want Ecke after all."

"No, I tell you. Give me a taste of life!"

"He-he-he!" giggled Katiche.

"The great thing is that no one can interfere with us, and though I see Pervoyedov is in a temper, he can't reach me with his hand. *Grand-père*, do you agree?"

"I fully agree, fully, and with the utmost satisfaction, but on condition that Katiche is the first to give us her biography."

"I protest! I protest with all my heart!" General Pervoyedov brought out firmly.

"Your Excellency!" the scoundrel Lebeziatnikov persuaded him in a murmur of fussy excitement, "your Excellency, it will be to our advantage to agree. Here, you see, there's this girl's . . . and all their little affairs."

"There's the girl, it's true, but . . ."

"It's to our advantage, your Excellency, upon my word it is! If only as an experiment, let us try it. . . ."

"Even in the grave they won't let us rest in peace."

"In the first place, General, you were playing preference in the grave, and in the second we don't care a hang about you," drawled Klinevitch.

"Sir, I beg you not to forget yourself."

"What? Why, you can't get at me, and I can tease you from here as though you were Julie's lapdog. And another thing, gentlemen, how is he a general here? He was a general there, but here is mere refuse."

"No, not mere refuse. . . . Even here . . ."

"Here you will rot in the grave and six brass buttons will be all that will be left of you."

"Bravo, Klinevitch, ha-ha-ha!" roared voices.

"I have served my sovereign. . . . I have the sword . . ."

"Your sword is only fit to prick mice, and you never drew it even for that."

"That makes no difference; I formed a part of the whole."

"There are all sorts of parts in a whole."

"Bravo, Klinevitch, bravo! Ha-ha-ha!"

"I don't understand what the sword stands for," boomed the engineer.

"We shall run away from the Prussians like mice, they'll crush us to powder!" cried a voice in the distance that was unfamiliar to me, that was positively spluttering with glee.

"The sword, sir, is an honour," the general cried, but only I heard him. There arose a prolonged and furious roar, clamour, and hubbub, and only the hysterically impatient squeals of Avdotya Ignatyevna were audible.

"But do let us make haste! Ah, when are we going to begin to cast off all shame!"

"Oh-ho-ho! . . . The soul does in truth pass through torments!" exclaimed the voice of the plebeian, "and . . ."

And here I suddenly sneezed. It happened suddenly and unintentionally, but the effect was striking: all became as silent as one expects it to be in a churchyard, it all vanished like a dream. A real silence of the tomb set in. I don't believe they were ashamed on account of my presence: they had made up their minds to cast off all shame! I waited five minutes—not a word, not a sound. It cannot be supposed that they were afraid of my informing the police; for what could the police do to them? I must conclude that they had some secret unknown to the living, which they carefully concealed from every mortal.

"Well, my dears," I thought, "I shall visit you again." And with those words, I left the cemetery.

No, that I cannot admit; no, I really cannot! The *bobok*

380

case does not trouble me (so that is what the bobok signified!)

Depravity in such a place, depravity of the last aspirations, depravity of sodden and rotten corpses—and not even sparing the last moments of consciousness! Those moments have been granted, vouchsafed to them, and . . . and, worst of all, in such a place! No, that I cannot admit.

I shall go to other tombs, I shall listen everywhere. Certainly one ought to listen everywhere and not merely at one spot in order to form an idea. Perhaps one may come across something reassuring.

But I shall certainly go back to those. They promised their biographies and anecdotes of all sorts. Tfoo! But I shall go, I shall certainly go; it is a question of conscience!

I shall take it to the *Citizen*; the editor there has had his portrait exhibited too. Maybe he will print it.

The Dream of a Ridiculous Man

I

I AM a ridiculous person. Now they call me a madman. That would be a promotion if it were not that I remain as ridiculous in their eyes as before. But now I do not resent it, they are all dear to me now, even when they laugh at me—and, indeed, it is just then that they are particularly dear to me. I could join in their laughter—not exactly at myself, but through affection for them, if I did not feel so sad as I look at them. Sad because they do not know the truth and I do know it. Oh, how hard it is to be the only one who knows the truth! But they won't understand that. No, they won't understand it.

In old days I used to be miserable at seeming ridiculous. Not seeming, but being. I have always been ridiculous, and I have known it, perhaps, from the hour I was born. Perhaps from the time I was seven years old I knew I was ridiculous. Afterwards I went to school, studied at the university, and, do you know, the more I learned, the more thoroughly I understood that I was ridiculous. So that it seemed in the end as though all the sciences I studied at the university existed only to prove and make evident to me as I went more deeply into them that I was ridiculous. It was the same with life as it was with science. With every year the same consciousness of the ridiculous figure I cut in every relation grew and strengthened. Everyone always laughed at me. But not one of them knew or guessed that if there were one man on earth who knew better than anybody else that I was absurd, it was myself, and what I resented most of all was that they did not know that. But that was my own fault; I was so proud that nothing would have ever induced me to tell it to anyone. This pride grew in me with the years; and if it had happened that I allowed myself to confess to anyone that I was ridiculous, I believe that I should have blown out my brains the same evening. Oh, how I suffered in my early youth from the fear that I might give way and confess it to my schoolfellows. But since I grew to manhood, I have for some unknown reason become calmer, though I realised my awful characteristic more fully every year. I say 'unknown', for to this day I cannot tell why it was. Perhaps it was owing to the terrible misery that was growing in my soul through something which was of more consequence than anything else about me: that something was the conviction that had come upon me that *nothing in the world mattered*. I had long had an inkling of it, but the full realisation came last year almost suddenly. I suddenly felt that it was all the same to me whether the world existed or whether there had never been anything at all: I began to feel with all my being that there was *nothing existing*. At first I fancied that many things had existed in the past, but afterwards I guessed that there never had been anything in the past either, but that it had only seemed so for some reason. Little by little I guessed that there would be nothing in the future either. Then I left off being angry with people and almost ceased to notice them. Indeed this showed itself even in the pettiest trifles: I used, for instance, to knock against people in the street. And not so much from being lost in thought: what had I to think about? I had almost given up thinking by that time; nothing mattered to me. If at least I had solved my problems! Oh, I had not settled one of them, and how many they were! But I gave up caring about anything, and all the problems disappeared.

And it was after that that I found out the truth. I learnt the truth last November—on the third of November, to be precise —and I remember every instant since. It was a gloomy evening, one of the gloomiest possible evenings. I was going home at about eleven o'clock, and I remember that I thought that the evening could not be gloomier. Even physically. Rain had been falling all day, and it had been a cold, gloomy, almost menacing rain, with, I remember, an unmistakable spite against mankind. Suddenly between ten and eleven it had stopped, and was followed by a horrible dampness, colder and damper than the rain, and a sort of steam was rising from everything, from every stone in the street, and from every by-lane if one looked down it as far as one could. A thought suddenly occurred to me, that if all the street lamps had been put out it would have been less cheerless, that the gas made one's heart sadder because it lighted it all up. I had had scarcely any dinner that day, and had been spending the evening with an engineer, and two other friends had been there also. I sat silent—I fancy I bored them. They talked of something rousing and suddenly they got excited over it. But they did not really care, I could see that, and only made a show of being excited. I suddenly said as much to them. "My friends," I said, "you really do not care one way or the other." They were not offended, but they all laughed at me. That was because I spoke without any note of reproach, simply because it did not matter to me. They saw it did not, and it amused them.

As I was thinking about the gas lamps in the street I looked up at the sky. The sky was horribly dark, but one could distinctly see tattered clouds, and between them fathomless black patches. Suddenly I noticed in one of these patches a star, and began watching it intently. That was because that star gave me an idea: I decided to kill myself that night. I had firmly determined to do so two months before, and poor as I was, I bought a splendid revolver that very day, and loaded it. But two months had passed and it was still lying in my drawer; I was so utterly indifferent that I wanted to seize a moment when I would not be so indifferent—why, I don't know. And so for two months every night that I came home I thought I would shoot myself. I kept waiting for the right moment. And so now this star gave me a thought. I made up my mind that it should certainly be that night. And why the star gave me the thought I don't know.

And just as I was looking at the sky, this little girl took me by the elbow. The street was empty, and there was scarcely anyone to be seen. A cabman was sleeping in the distance in his cab. It was a child of eight with a kerchief on her head, wearing nothing but a wretched little dress all soaked with rain, but I noticed particularly her wet broken shoes and I recall them now. They caught my eye particularly. She suddenly pulled me by the elbow and called me. She was not weeping, but was spasmodically crying out some words which she could not utter properly, because she was shivering and shuddering all over. She was in terror about something, and kept crying, "Mammy, mammy!" I turned facing her, I did not say a word and went on; but she ran, pulling at me, and there was that note in her voice which in frightened children means despair. I know that sound. Though she did not articulate the words, I understood that her mother was dying, or that something of the sort was happening to them, and that she had run out to call someone, to find something to help her mother. I did not go with her; on the contrary, I had an impulse to drive her away. I told her first to go to a policeman. But clasping her hands, she ran beside me sobbing and gasping, and would not leave me. Then I stamped my foot, and shouted at her. She called out "Sir! sir! . . ." but suddenly abandoned me and rushed headlong across the road. Some other passer-by appeared there, and she evidently flew from me to him.

I mounted up to my fifth storey. I have a room in a flat where there are other lodgers. My room is small and poor, with a garret window in the shape of a semicircle. I have a sofa covered with American leather, a table with books on it, two chairs and a comfortable arm-chair, as old as old can be, but of the good old-fashioned shape. I sat down, lighted the candle, and began thinking. In the room next to mine, through the partition wall, a perfect Bedlam was going on. It had been going on for the last three days. A retired captain lived there, and he had half a dozen visitors, gentlemen of doubtful reputation, drinking vodka and playing *stoss* with old cards. The night before there had been a fight, and I know that two of them had been for a long time engaged in dragging each other about by the hair. The landlady wanted to complain, but she was in abject terror of the captain. There was only one other lodger in the flat, a thin little regimental lady, on a visit to Petersburg, with three little children who had been taken ill since they came into the lodgings. Both she and her children were in mortal fear of the captain, and lay trembling and crossing themselves all night, and the youngest child had a sort of fit from fright. That captain, I know for a fact, sometimes stops people in the Nevsky Prospect and begs. They won't take him into the service, but strange to say (that's why I am telling this), all this month that the captain has been here his behaviour has caused me no annoyance. I have, of course, tried to avoid his acquaintance from the very beginning, and he, too, was bored with me from the first; but I never care how much they shout the other side of the partition nor how many of them there are in there: I sit up all night and forget them so completely that I do not even hear them. I stay awake till daybreak, and have been going on like that for the last year. I sit up all night in my arm-chair at the table, doing nothing. I only read by day. I sit—don't even think; ideas of a sort wander through my mind and I let them come and go as they will. A whole candle is burnt every night. I sat down quietly at the table, took out the revolver and put it down before me. When I had put it down I asked myself, I remember, "Is that so?" and answered with complete conviction, "It is." That is, I shall shoot myself. I knew that I should shoot myself that night for certain, but how much longer I should go on sitting at the table I did not know. And no doubt I should have shot myself if it had not been for that little girl.

II

You see, though nothing mattered to me, I could feel pain, for instance. If anyone had struck me it would have hurt me. It was the same morally: if anything very pathetic happened, I should have felt pity just as I used to do in old days when there were things in life that did matter to me. I had felt pity that evening. I should have certainly helped a child. Why, then, had I not helped the little girl? Because of an idea that occurred to me at the time: when she was calling and pulling at me, a question suddenly arose before me and I could not settle it. The question was an idle one, but I was vexed. I was vexed at the reflection that if I were going to make an end of myself that night, nothing in life ought to have mattered to me. Why was it that all at once I did not feel that nothing mattered and was sorry for the little girl? I remember that I was very sorry for her, so much so that I felt a strange pang, quite incongruous in my position. Really I do not know better how to convey my fleeting sensation at the moment, but the sensation persisted at home when I was sitting at the table, and I was very much irritated as I had not been for a long time past. One reflection followed another. I saw clearly that so long as I was still a human being and not nothingness, I was alive and so could suffer, be angry and feel shame at my actions. So be it. But if I am going to kill myself, in two hours, say, what is the little girl to me and what have I to do with shame or with anything else in the world? I shall turn into nothing, absolutely nothing. And can it really be true that the consciousness that I shall *completely* cease to exist immediately

387

and so everything else will cease to exist, does not in the least affect my feeling of pity for the child nor the feeling of shame after a contemptible action? I stamped and shouted at the unhappy child as though to say—not only I feel no pity, but even if I behave inhumanly and contemptibly, I am free to, for in another two hours everything will be extinguished. Do you believe that that was why I shouted that? I am almost convinced of it now. It seemed clear to me that life and the world somehow depended upon me now. I may almost say that the world now seemed created for me alone: if I shot myself the world would cease to be at least for me. I say nothing of its being likely that nothing will exist for anyone when I am gone, and that as soon as my consciousness is extinguished the whole world will vanish too and become void like a phantom, as a mere appurtenance of my consciousness, for possibly all this world and all these people are only me myself. I remember that as I sat and reflected, I turned all these new questions that swarmed one after another quite the other way, and thought of something quite new. For instance, a strange reflection suddenly occurred to me, that if I had lived before on the moon or on Mars and there had committed the most disgraceful and dishonourable action and had there been put to such shame and ignominy as one can only conceive and realise in dreams, in nightmares, and if, finding myself afterwards on earth, I were able to retain the memory of what I had done on the other planet and at the same time knew that I should never, under any circumstances, return there, then looking from the earth to the moon—*should I care or not?* Should I feel shame for that action or not? These were idle and superfluous questions for the revolver was already lying before me, and I knew in every fibre of my being that *it* would happen for certain, but they excited me and I raged. I could not die now without having first settled something. In short, the child had saved me, for I put off my pistol shot for the sake

I lay still, strange to say I expected nothing, accepting without dispute that a dead man had nothing to expect. But it was damp. I don't know how long a time passed—whether an hour, or several days, or many days. But all at once a drop of water fell on my closed left eye, making its way through a coffin lid; it was followed a minute later by a second, then a minute later by a third—and so on, regularly every minute. There was a sudden glow of profound indignation in my heart, and I suddenly felt in it a pang of physical pain. "That's my wound," I thought; "that's the bullet. . . ." And drop after drop every minute kept falling on my closed eyelid. And all at once, not with my voice, but with my whole being, I called upon the power that was responsible for all that was happening to me:

"Whoever you may be, if you exist, and if anything more rational than what is happening here is possible, suffer it to be here now. But if you are revenging yourself upon me for my senseless suicide by the hideousness and absurdity of this subsequent existence, then let me tell you that no torture could ever equal the contempt which I shall go on dumbly feeling, though my martyrdom may last a million years!"

I made this appeal and held my peace. There was a full minute of unbroken silence and again another drop fell, but I knew with infinite unshakable certainty that everything [would] change immediately. And behold my grave sudden[ly] asunder, that is, I don't know whether it was but I was caught up by some dark and found ourselves in space. I suddenly was the dead of night, and never, never darkness. We were flying through space earth. I did not question the being who w proud and waited. I assured myself that I w was thrilled with ecstasy at the thought that I do not know how long we were flying, I can happened as it always does in dreams when you

of these questions. Meanwhile the clamour had begun to subside in the captain's room: they had finished their game, were settling down to sleep, and meanwhile were grumbling and languidly winding up their quarrels. At that point I suddenly fell asleep in my chair at the table—a thing which had never happened to me before. I dropped asleep quite unawares.

Dreams, as we all know, are very queer things: some parts are presented with appalling vividness, with details worked up with the elaborate finish of jewellery, while others one gallops through, as it were, without noticing them at all, as, for instance, through space and time. Dreams seem to be spurred on not by reason but by desire, not by the head but by the heart, and yet what complicated tricks my reason has played sometimes in dreams, what utterly incomprehensible things happen to it! My brother died five years ago, for instance. I sometimes dream of him; he takes part in my affairs, we are very much interested, and yet all through my dream I quite know and remember that my brother is dead and buried. How is it that I am not surprised that, though he is dead, he is here beside me and working with me? Why is it that my reason fully accepts it? But enough. I will begin about my dream.

Yes, I dreamed a dream, my dream of the third of November. They tease me now, telling me it was only a dream. But does it matter whether it was a dream or reality, if the dream made known to me the truth? If once one has recognised the truth and seen it, you know that it is the truth and that there is no other and there cannot be, whether you are asleep or awake. Let it be a dream, so be it, but that real life of which you make so much I had meant to extinguish by suicide, and my dream, my dream—oh, it revealed to me a different life, renewed, grand and full of power!

Listen.

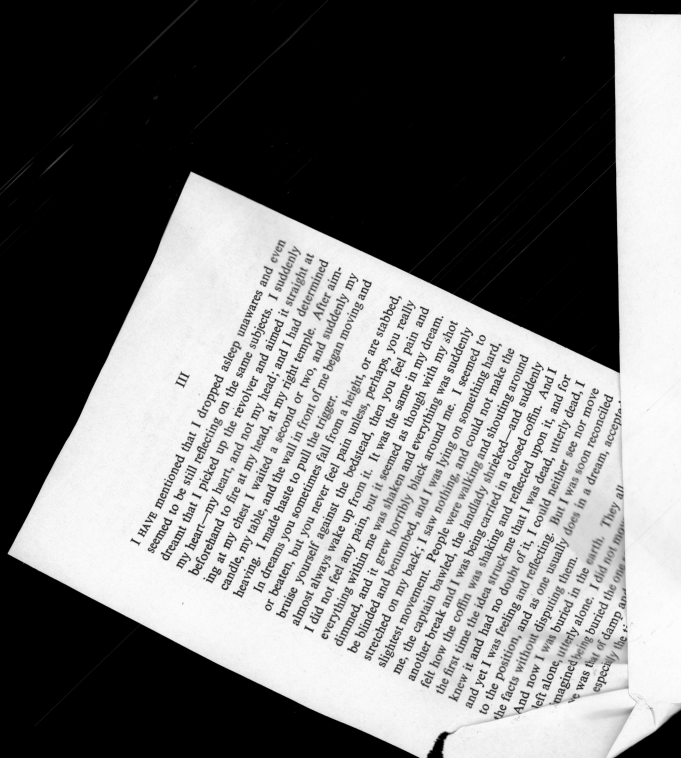

III

I HAVE mentioned that I dropped asleep unawares and even seemed to be still reflecting on the same subjects. I suddenly dreamt that I picked up the revolver and aimed it straight at my heart—my heart, and not my head; and I had determined beforehand to fire at my head, at my right temple. After aiming at my chest I waited a second or two, and suddenly my candle, my table, and the wall in front of me began moving and heaving. I made haste to pull the trigger.

In dreams you sometimes fall from a height, or are stabbed, or beaten, but you never feel any pain unless, perhaps, you really bruise yourself against the bedstead, then you feel pain and almost always wake up from it. It was the same in my dream. I did not feel any pain, but it seemed as though with my shot everything within me was shaken and everything was suddenly dimmed, and it grew horribly black around me. I seemed to be blinded and benumbed, and I was lying on something hard, stretched on my back; I saw nothing, and could not make the slightest movement. People were walking and shouting hard, me, the captain bawled, the landlady shrieked—and suddenly another break and I was being carried in a closed coffin. And I felt how the coffin was shaking and reflected upon it, and for the first time the idea struck me that I was dead, utterly dead, I knew it and had no doubt of it, I could neither see nor move and yet I was feeling and reflecting. But I was soon reconciled to the position, and as one usually does in a dream, accepted the facts without disputing them.

And now I was buried in the earth. They all left alone, utterly alone. I did not move...

and time, and the laws of thought and existence, and only pause upon the points for which the heart yearns. I remember that I suddenly saw in the darkness a star. "Is that Sirius?" I asked impulsively, though I had not meant to ask any questions.

"No, that is the star you saw between the clouds when you were coming home," the being who was carrying me replied.

I knew that it had something like a human face. Strange to say, I did not like that being, in fact I felt an intense aversion for it. I had expected complete non-existence, and that was why I had put a bullet through my heart. And here I was in the hands of a creature not human, of course, but yet living, existing. "And so there is life beyond the grave," I thought with the strange frivolity one has in dreams. But in its inmost depth my heart remained unchanged. "And if I have got to exist again," I thought, "and live once more under the control of some irresistible power, I won't be vanquished and humiliated."

"You know that I am afraid of you and despise me for that," I said suddenly to my companion, unable to refrain from the humiliating question which implied a confession, and feeling my humiliation stab my heart as with a pin. He did not answer my question, but all at once I felt that he was not even despising me, but was laughing at me and had no compassion for me, and that our journey had an unknown and mysterious object that concerned me only. Fear was growing in my heart. Something was mutely and painfully communicated to me from my silent companion, and permeated my whole being. We were flying through dark, unknown space. I had for some time lost sight of the constellations familiar to my eyes. I knew that there were stars in the heavenly spaces the light of which took thousands or millions of years to reach the earth. Perhaps we were already flying through those spaces. I expected something with a terrible anguish that tortured my heart. And suddenly I was thrilled by a familiar feeling that stirred me to of these questions. Meanwhile the clamour had begun to subside in the captain's room: they had finished their game, were settling down to sleep, and meanwhile were grumbling and languidly winding up their quarrels. At that point I suddenly fell asleep in my chair at the table—a thing which had never happened to me before. I dropped asleep quite unawares.

Dreams, as we all know, are very queer things: some parts are presented with appalling vividness, with details worked up with the elaborate finish of jewellery, while others one gallops through, as it were, without noticing them at all, as, for instance, through space and time. Dreams seem to be spurred on not by reason but by desire, not by the head but by the heart, and yet what complicated tricks my reason has played sometimes in dreams, what utterly incomprehensible things happen to it! My brother died five years ago, for instance. I sometimes dream of him; he takes part in my affairs, we are very much interested, and yet all through my dream I quite know and remember that my brother is dead and buried. How is it that I am not surprised that, though he is dead, he is here beside me and working with me? Why is it that my reason fully accepts it? But enough. I will begin about my dream. Yes, I dreamed a dream, my dream of the third of November. They tease me now, telling me it was only a dream. But does it matter whether it was a dream or reality, if the dream made known to me the truth? If once one has recognised the truth and seen it, you know that is is the truth and that there is no other and there cannot be, whether you are asleep or awake. Let it be a dream, so be it, but that real life of which you make so much I had meant to extinguish by suicide, and my dream, my dream—oh, it revealed to me a different life, renewed, grand and full of power!

Listen.

I HAVE mentioned that I dropped asleep unawares and even seemed to be still reflecting on the same subjects. I suddenly dreamt that I picked up the revolver and aimed it straight at my heart—my heart, and not my head; and I had determined beforehand to fire at my head, at my right temple. After aiming at my chest I waited a second or two, and suddenly my candle, my table, and the wall in front of me began moving and heaving. I made haste to pull the trigger.

In dreams you sometimes fall from a height, or are stabbed, or beaten, but you never feel pain unless, perhaps, you really bruise yourself against the bedstead, then you feel pain and almost always wake up from it. It was the same in my dream. I did not feel any pain, but it seemed as though with my shot everything within me was shaken and everything was suddenly dimmed, and it grew horribly black around me. I seemed to be blinded and benumbed, and I was lying on something hard, stretched on my back; I saw nothing, and could not make the slightest movement. People were walking and shouting around me, the captain bawled, the landlady shrieked—and suddenly another break and I was being carried in a closed coffin. And I felt how the coffin was shaking and reflected upon it, and for the first time the idea struck me that I was dead, utterly dead, I knew it and had no doubt of it, I could neither see nor move and yet I was feeling and reflecting. But I was soon reconciled to the position, and as one usually does in a dream, accepted the facts without disputing them.

And now I was buried in the earth. They all went away, I was left alone, utterly alone. I did not move. Whenever before I had imagined being buried the one sensation I associated with the grave was that of damp and cold. So now I felt that I was very cold, especially the tips of my toes, but I felt nothing else.

I lay still, strange to say I expected nothing, accepting without dispute that a dead man had nothing to expect. But it was damp. I don't know how long a time passed—whether an hour, or several days, or many days. But all at once a drop of water fell on my closed left eye, making its way through a coffin lid; it was followed a minute later by a second, then a minute later by a third—and so on, regularly every minute. There was a sudden glow of profound indignation in my heart, and I suddenly felt in it a pang of physical pain. "That's my wound," I thought; "that's the bullet. . . ." And drop after drop every minute kept falling on my closed eyelid. And all at once, not with my voice, but with my whole being, I called upon the power that was responsible for all that was happening to me:

"Whoever you may be, if you exist, and if anything more rational than what is happening here is possible, suffer it to be here now. But if you are revenging yourself upon me for my senseless suicide by the hideousness and absurdity of this subsequent existence, then let me tell you that no torture could ever equal the contempt which I shall go on dumbly feeling, though my martyrdom may last a million years!"

I made this appeal and held my peace. There was a full minute of unbroken silence and again another drop fell, but I knew with infinite unshakable certainty that everything would change immediately. And behold my grave suddenly was rent asunder, that is, I don't know whether it was opened or dug up, but I was caught up by some dark and unknown being and we found ourselves in space. I suddenly regained my sight. It was the dead of night, and never, never had there been such darkness. We were flying through space far away from the earth. I did not question the being who was taking me; I was proud and waited. I assured myself that I was not afraid, and was thrilled with ecstasy at the thought that I was not afraid. I do not know how long we were flying, I cannot imagine; it happened as it always does in dreams when you skip over space and time, and the laws of thought and existence, and only pause upon the points for which the heart yearns. I remember that I suddenly saw in the darkness a star. "Is that Sirius?" I asked impulsively, though I had not meant to ask any questions.

"No, that is the star you saw between the clouds when you were coming home," the being who was carrying me replied.

I knew that it had something like a human face. Strange to say, I did not like that being, in fact I felt an intense aversion for it. I had expected complete non-existence, and that was why I had put a bullet through my heart. And here I was in the hands of a creature not human, of course, but yet living, existing. "And so there is life beyond the grave," I thought with the strange frivolity one has in dreams. But in its inmost depth my heart remained unchanged. "And if I have got to exist again," I thought, "and live once more under the control of some irresistible power, I won't be vanquished and humiliated."

"You know that I am afraid of you and despise me for that," I said suddenly to my companion, unable to refrain from the humiliating question which implied a confession, and feeling my humiliation stab my heart as with a pin. He did not answer my question, but all at once I felt that he was not even despising me, but was laughing at me and had no compassion for me, and that our journey had an unknown and mysterious object that concerned me only. Fear was growing in my heart. Something was mutely and painfully communicated to me from my silent companion, and permeated my whole being. We were flying through dark, unknown space. I had for some time lost sight of the constellations familiar to my eyes. I knew that there were stars in the heavenly spaces the light of which took thousands or millions of years to reach the earth. Perhaps we were already flying through those spaces. I expected something with a terrible anguish that tortured my heart. And suddenly I was thrilled by a familiar feeling that stirred me to the depths: I suddenly caught sight of our sun! I knew that it could not be *our* sun, that gave life to *our* earth, and that we were an infinite distance from our sun, but for some reason I knew in my whole being that it was a sun exactly like ours, a duplicate of it. A sweet, thrilling feeling resounded with ecstasy in my heart: the kindred power of the same light which had given me light stirred an echo in my heart and awakened it, and I had a sensation of life, the old life of the past for the first time since I had been in the grave.

"But if that is the sun, if that is exactly the same as our sun," I cried, "where is the earth?"

And my companion pointed to a star twinkling in the distance with an emerald light. We were flying straight towards it.

"And are such repetitions possible in the universe? Can that be the law of Nature? ... And if that is an earth there, can it be just the same earth as ours ... just the same, as poor, as unhappy, but precious and beloved for ever, arousing in the most ungrateful of her children the same poignant love for her that we feel for our earth?" I cried out, shaken by irresistible, ecstatic love for the old familiar earth which I had left. The image of the poor child whom I had repulsed flashed through my mind.

"You shall see it all," answered my companion, and there was a note of sorrow in his voice.

But we were rapidly approaching the planet. It was growing before my eyes; I could already distinguish the ocean, the outline of Europe; and suddenly a feeling of a great and holy jealousy glowed in my heart.

"How can it be repeated and what for? I love and can love only that earth which I have left, stained with my blood, when, in my ingratitude, I quenched my life with a bullet in my heart. But I have never, never ceased to love that earth, and perhaps on the very night I parted from it I loved it more than

393

ever. Is there suffering upon this new earth? On our earth we can only love with suffering and through suffering. We cannot love otherwise, and we know of no other sort of love. I want suffering in order to love. I long, I thirst, this very instant, to kiss with tears the earth that I have left, and I don't want, I won't accept life on any other!"

But my companion had already left me. I suddenly, quite without noticing how, found myself on this other earth, in the bright light of a sunny day, fair as paradise. I believe I was standing on one of the islands that make up on our globe the Greek archipelago, or on the coast of the mainland facing that archipelago. Oh, everything was exactly as it is with us, only everything seemed to have a festive radiance, the splendour of some great, holy triumph attained at last. The caressing sea, green as emerald, splashed softly upon the shore and kissed it with manifest, almost conscious love. The tall, lovely trees stood in all the glory of their blossom, and their innumerable leaves greeted me, I am certain, with their soft, caressing rustle and seemed to articulate words of love. The grass glowed with bright and fragrant flowers. Birds were flying in flocks in the air, and perched fearlessly on my shoulders and arms and joyfully struck me with their darling, fluttering wings. And at last I saw and knew the people of this happy land. They came to me of themselves, they surrounded me, kissed me. The children of the sun, the children of their sun—oh, how beautiful they were! Never had I seen on our own earth such beauty in mankind. Only perhaps in our children, in their earliest years, one might find, some remote faint reflection of this beauty. The eyes of these happy people shone with a clear brightness. Their faces were radiant with the light of reason and fullness of a serenity that comes of perfect understanding, but those faces were gay; in their words and voices there was a note of childlike joy. Oh, from the first moment, from the first glance at them, I understood it all! It was the earth untarnished by

394

the Fall; on it lived people who had not sinned. They lived just in such a paradise as that in which, according to all the legends of mankind, our first parents lived before they sinned; the only difference was that all this earth was the same paradise. These people, laughing joyfully, thronged round me and caressed me; they took me home with them, and each of them tried to reassure me. Oh, they asked me no questions, but they seemed, I fancied, to know everything without asking, and they wanted to make haste and smoothe away the signs of suffering from my face.

<h2 style="text-align:center">IV</h2>

AND do you know what? Well, granted that it was only a dream, yet the sensation of the love of those innocent and beautiful people has remained with me for ever, and I feel as though their love is still flowing out to me from over there. I have seen them myself, have known them and been convinced; I loved them, I suffered for them afterwards. Oh, I understood at once even at the time that in many things I could not understand them at all; as an up-to-date Russian progressive and contemptible Petersburger, it struck me as inexplicable that, knowing so much, they had, for instance, no science like ours. But I soon realised that their knowledge was gained and fostered by intuitions different from those of us on earth, and that their aspirations, too, were quite different. They desired nothing and were at peace; they did not aspire to knowledge of life as we aspire to understand it, because their lives were full. But their knowledge was higher and deeper than ours; for our science seeks to explain what life is, aspires to understand it in order to teach others how to live, while they without science knew how to live; and that I understood, but I could not understand their knowledge. They showed me their trees, and I could not understand the intense love with which they looked at them; it was as though they were talking with creatures like themselves. And perhaps I shall not be mistaken if I say that they conversed with them. Yes, they had found their language, and I am convinced that the trees understood them. They looked at all Nature like that—at the animals who lived in peace with them and did not attack them, but loved them, conquered by their love. They pointed to the stars and told me something about them which I could not understand, but I am convinced that they were somehow in touch with the stars, not only in thought, but by some living channel. Oh, these people did not persist in trying to make me understand them, they loved me without that, but I knew that they would never understand me, and so I hardly spoke to them about our earth. I only kissed in their presence the earth on which they lived and mutely worshipped them themselves. And they saw that and let me worship them without being abashed at my adoration, for they themselves loved much. They were not unhappy on my account when at times I kissed their feet with tears, joyfully conscious of the love with which they would respond to mine. At times I asked myself with wonder how it was they were able never to offend a creature like me, and never once to arouse a feeling of jealousy or envy in me? Often I wondered how it could be that, boastful and untruthful as I was, I never talked to them of what I knew—of which, of course, they had no notion—that I was never tempted to do so by a desire to astonish or even to benefit them.

They were as gay and sportive as children. They wandered about their lovely woods and copses, they sang their lovely songs; their fare was light—the fruits of their trees, the honey from their woods, and the milk of the animals who loved them. The work they did for food and raiment was brief and not laborious. They loved and begot children, but I never noticed in them the impulse of that *cruel* sensuality which overcomes almost every man on this earth, all and each, and is the source of almost every sin of mankind on earth. They rejoiced at the arrival of children as new beings to share their happiness. There was no quarrelling, no jealousy among them, and they did not even know what the words meant. Their children were the children of all, for they all made up one family. There was scarcely any illness among them, though there was death; but their old people died peacefully, as though falling asleep, giving blessings and smiles to those who surrounded them to take their last farewell with bright and lovely smiles. I never saw grief or tears on those occasions, but only love, which reached the point of ecstasy, but a calm ecstasy, made perfect and contemplative. One might think that they were still in contact with the departed after death, and that their earthly union was not cut short by death. They scarcely understood me when I questioned them about immortality, but evidently they were so convinced of it without reasoning that it was not for them a question at all. They had no temples, but they had a real living and uninterrupted sense of oneness with the whole of the universe; they had no creed, but they had a certain knowledge that when their earthly joy had reached the limits of earthly nature, then there would come for them, for the living and for the dead, a still greater fullness of contact with the whole of the universe. They looked forward to that moment with joy, but without haste, not pining for it, but seeming to have a foretaste of it in their hearts, of which they talked to one another.

In the evening before going to sleep they liked singing in musical and harmonious chorus. In those songs they expressed all the sensations that the parting day had given them, sang its glories and took leave of it. They sang the praises of nature, of the sea, of the woods. They liked making songs about one another, and praised each other like children; they were the simplest songs, but they sprang from their hearts and went to one's heart. And not only in their songs but in all their lives they seemed to do nothing but admire one another. It was like being in love with each other, but an all-embracing, universal feeling.

Some of their songs, solemn and rapturous, I scarcely understood at all. Though I understood the words I could never fathom their full significance. It remained, as it were, beyond the grasp of my mind, yet my heart unconsciously absorbed it more and more. I often told them that I had had a presentiment of it long before, that this joy and glory had come to me on our earth in the form of a yearning melancholy that at times approached insufferable sorrow; that I had had a foreknowledge of them all and of their glory in the dreams of my heart and the visions of my mind; that often on our earth I could not look at the setting sun without tears . . . that in my hatred for the men of our earth there was always a yearning anguish: why could I not hate them without loving them? why could I not help forgiving them? and in my love for them there was a yearning grief: why could I not love them without hating them? They listened to me, and I saw they could not conceive what I was saying, but I did not regret that I had spoken to them of it: I knew that they understood the intensity of my yearning anguish over those whom I had left. But when they looked at me with their sweet eyes full of love, when I felt that in their presence my heart, too, became as innocent and just as theirs, the feeling of the fullness of life took my breath away, and I worshipped them in silence.

Oh, everyone laughs in my face now, and assures me that one cannot dream of such details as I am telling now, that I only dreamed or felt one sensation that arose in my heart in delirium and made up the details myself when I woke up. And when I told them that perhaps it really was so, my God, how they shouted with laughter in my face, and what mirth I caused! Oh, yes, of course I was overcome by the mere sensation of my dream, and that was all that was preserved in my

398

cruelly wounded heart; but the actual forms and images of my dream, that is, the very ones I really saw at the very time of my dream, were filled with such harmony, were so lovely and enchanting and were so actual, that on awakening I was, of course, incapable of clothing them in our poor language, so that they were bound to become blurred in my mind; and so perhaps I really was forced afterwards to make up the details, and so of course to distort them in my passionate desire to convey some at least of them as quickly as I could. But on the other hand, how can I help believing that it was all true? It was perhaps a thousand times brighter, happier and more joyful than I describe it. Granted that I dreamed it, yet it must have been real. You know, I will tell you a secret: perhaps it was not a dream at all! For then something happened so awful, something so horribly true, that it could not have been imagined in a dream. My heart may have originated the dream, but would my heart alone have been capable of originating the awful event which happened to me afterwards? How could I alone have invented it or imagined it in my dream? Could my petty heart and my fickle, trivial mind have risen to such a revelation of truth? Oh, judge for yourselves: hitherto I have concealed it, but now I will tell the truth. The fact is that I . . . corrupted them all!

V

YES, yes, it ended in my corrupting them all! How it could come to pass I do not know, but I remember it clearly. The dream embraced thousands of years and left in me only a sense of the whole. I only know that I was the cause of their sin and downfall. Like a vile trichina, like a germ of the plague infecting whole kingdoms, so I contaminated all this earth, so happy and sinless before my coming. They learnt to lie, grew fond of lying, and discovered the charm of falsehood. Oh, at first perhaps it began innocently, with a jest, coquetry, with amorous play, perhaps indeed with a germ, but that germ of falsity made its way into their hearts and pleased them. Then sensuality was soon begotten, sensuality begot jealousy, jealousy—cruelty. . . . Oh, I don't know, I don't remember; but soon, very soon the first blood was shed. They marvelled and were horrified, and began to be split up and divided. They formed into unions, but it was against one another. Reproaches, upbraidings followed. They came to know shame, and shame brought them to virtue. The conception of honour sprang up, and every union began waving its flags. They began torturing animals, and the animals withdrew from them into the forests and became hostile to them. They began to struggle for separation, for isolation, for individuality, for mine and thine. They began to talk in different languages. They became acquainted with sorrow and loved sorrow; they thirsted for suffering, and said that truth could only be attained through suffering. Then science appeared. As they became wicked they began talking of brotherhood and humanitarianism, and understood those ideas. As they became criminal, they invented justice and drew up whole legal codes in order to observe it, and to ensure their being kept, set up a guillotine. They hardly remembered what they had lost, in fact refused to believe that they had ever been happy and innocent. They even laughed at the possibility of this happiness in the past, and called it a dream. They could not even imagine it in definite form and shape, but, strange and wonderful to relate, though they lost all faith in their past happiness and called it a legend, they so longed to be happy and innocent once more that they succumbed to this desire like children, made an idol of it, set up temples and worshipped their own idea, their own desire; though at the same time they fully believed that it was unattainable and could not be realised, yet they bowed down to it and adored it with tears! Nevertheless, if it could have happened that they had returned to the innocent and happy condition which they had lost, and if someone had shown it to them again and had asked them whether they wanted to go back to it, they would certainly have refused. They answered me:

"We may be deceitful, wicked and unjust, we *know* it and weep over it, we grieve over it; we torment and punish ourselves more perhaps than that merciful Judge Who will judge us and whose Name we know not. But we have science, and by means of it we shall find the truth and we shall arrive at it consciously. Knowledge is higher than feeling, the consciousness of life is higher than life. Science will give us wisdom, wisdom will reveal the laws, and the knowledge of the laws of happiness is higher than happiness."

That is what they said, and after saying such things everyone began to love himself better than anyone else, and indeed they could not do otherwise. All became so jealous of the rights of their own personality that they did their very utmost to curtail and destroy them in others, and made that the chief thing in their lives. Slavery followed, even voluntary slavery; the weak eagerly submitted to the strong, on condition that the latter aided them to subdue the still weaker. Then there were saints who came to these people, weeping, and talked to them of their pride, of their loss of harmony and due proportion, of their loss of shame. They were laughed at or pelted with stones. Holy blood was shed on the threshold of the temples. Then there arose men who began to think how to bring all people together again, so that everybody, while still loving himself best of all, might not interfere with others, and all might live together in something like a harmonious society. Regular wars sprang up over this idea. All the combatants at the same time firmly believed that science, wisdom and the instinct of self-preservation would force men at last to unite into a harmonious and rational society; and so, meanwhile, to hasten matters, 'the wise' endeavoured to exterminate as rapidly as possible all who were 'not wise' and did not understand their idea, that the latter might not hinder its triumph. But the instinct of self-preservation grew rapidly weaker; there arose men, haughty and sensual, who demanded all or nothing. In order to obtain everything they resorted to crime, and if they did not succeed—to suicide. There arose religions with a cult of non-existence and self-destruction for the sake of the everlasting peace of annihilation. At last these people grew weary of their meaningless toil, and signs of suffering came into their faces, and then they proclaimed that suffering was a beauty, for in suffering alone was there meaning. They glorified suffering in their songs. I moved about among them, wringing my hands and weeping over them, but I loved them perhaps more than in old days when there was no suffering in their faces and when they were innocent and so lovely. I loved the earth they had polluted even more than when it had been a paradise, if only because sorrow had come to it. Alas! I always loved sorrow and tribulation, but only for myself, for myself; but I wept over them, pitying them. I stretched out my hands to them in despair, blaming, cursing and despising myself. I told them that all this was my doing, mine alone; that it was I had brought them corruption, contamination and falsity. I besought them to crucify me, I taught them how to make a cross. I could not kill myself, I had not the strength, but I wanted to suffer at their hands. I yearned for suffering, I longed that my blood should be drained to the last drop in these agonies. But they only laughed at me, and began at last to look upon me as crazy. They justified me, they declared that they had only got what they wanted themselves, and that all that now was could not have been otherwise. At last they declared to me that I was becoming dangerous and that they should lock me up in a madhouse if I did not hold my tongue. Then such grief took possession of my soul that my heart was wrung, and I felt as though I were dying; and then . . . then I awoke.

It was morning, that is, it was not yet daylight, but about six o'clock. I woke up in the same arm-chair; my candle had burnt out; everyone was asleep in the captain's room, and there was a stillness all round, rare in our flat. First of all I leapt up in great amazement: nothing like this had ever happened to me before, not even in the most trivial detail; I had never, for instance, fallen asleep like this in my arm-chair. While I was standing and coming to myself I suddenly caught sight of my revolver lying loaded, ready—but instantly I thrust it away! Oh, now, life, life! I lifted up my hands and called upon eternal truth, not with words, but with tears; ecstasy, immeasurable ecstasy flooded my soul. Yes, life and spreading the good tidings! Oh, I at that moment resolved to spread the tidings, and resolved it, of course, for my whole life. I go to spread the tidings, I want to spread the tidings—of what? Of the truth, for I have seen it, have seen it with my own eyes, have seen it in all its glory.

And since then I have been preaching! Moreover I love all those who laugh at me more than any of the rest. Why that is so I do not know and cannot explain, but so be it. I am told that I am vague and confused, and if I am vague and confused now, what shall I be later on? It is true indeed: I am vague and confused, and perhaps as time goes on I shall be more so. And of course I shall make many blunders before I find out how to preach, that is, find out what words to say, what things to do, for it is a very difficult task. I see all that as clear as daylight, but, listen, who does not make mistakes? And yet, you know, all are making for the same goal, all are striving in the same direction anyway, from the sage to the lowest robber, only by different roads. It is an old truth, but this is what is new: I cannot go far wrong. For I have seen the truth; I have

seen and I know that people can be beautiful and happy without losing the power of living on earth. I will not and cannot
believe that evil is the normal condition of mankind. And it is
just this faith of mine that they laugh at. But how can I help
believing it? I have seen the truth—it is not as though I had
invented it with my mind, I have seen it, seen it, and *the living
image* of it has filled my soul for ever. I have seen it in such
full perfection that I cannot believe that it is impossible for
people to have it. And so how can I go wrong? I shall make
some slips no doubt, and shall perhaps talk in second-hand
language, but not for long: the living image of what I saw will
always be with me and will always correct and guide me. Oh,
I am full of courage and freshness, and I will go on and on if it
were for a thousand years! Do you know, at first I meant to
conceal the fact that I corrupted them, but that was a mistake
—that was my first mistake! But truth whispered to me that I
was *lying*, and preserved me and corrected me. But how
establish paradise—I don't know, because I do not know how
to put it into words. After my dream I lost command of words.
All the chief words, anyway, the most necessary ones. But
never mind, I shall go and I shall keep talking, I won't leave
off, for anyway I have seen it with my own eyes, though I
cannot describe what I saw. But the scoffers do not understand that. It was a dream, they say, delirium, hallucination.
Oh! As though that meant so much! And they are so proud!
A dream! What is a dream? And is not our life a dream? I
will say more. Suppose that this paradise will never come to
pass (that I understand), yet I shall go on preaching it. And
yet how simple it is: in one day, *in one hour* everything could be
arranged at once! The chief thing is to love others like yourself, that's the great thing, and that's everything; nothing else
is wanted—you will find out at once how to arrange it all. And
yet it's an old truth which has been told and retold a billion
times—but it has not formed part of our lives! The conscious-

ness of life is higher than life, the knowledge of the laws of happiness is higher than happiness—that is what one must contend against. And I shall. If only everyone wants it, it can all be arranged at once.

And I tracked out that little girl . . . and I shall go on and on!

FYODOR DOSTOEVSKY

THE COLLECTED EDITION

The Brothers Karamazov
Crime and Punishment
The Eternal Husband *and other stories*
The Friend of the Family *and another story*
The Gambler *and other stories*
An Honest Thief *and other stories*
The House of the Dead
The Idiot
The Insulted and Injured
The Possessed
A Raw Youth
White Nights *and other stories*

TRANSLATED FROM THE RUSSIAN BY CONSTANCE GARNETT

LEO TOLSTOY

Anna Karenin
War and Peace

IVAN TURGENEV

A House of Gentlefolk
On the Eve
Rudin
The Torrents of Spring, *with* First Love *and* Mumu

TRANSLATED FROM THE RUSSIAN BY CONSTANCE GARNETT